A. S. Packard, Jr.

Outlines of comparative embryology

A. S. Packard, Jr.

Outlines of comparative embryology

ISBN/EAN: 9783742819246

Manufactured in Europe, USA, Canada, Australia, Japa

Cover: Foto ©Andreas Hilbeck / pixelio.de

Manufactured and distributed by brebook publishing software
(www.brebook.com)

A. S. Packard, Jr.

Outlines of comparative embryology

ERRATA.

P. 24 and 25, *for* Urella *read* Uvella.

P. 78, for line 13 *substitute* have no connection after embryonic life with the complicated.

P. 117, line 3, *for* 125¹ *read* 126 ; line 4, *for* 126 *read* 125¹.

P. 120, line 3 from the bottom, *for* young *read* adult.

P. 120, line 2 from the bottom, *for* disappear in ·the adult, *read* are not present in the young.

P. 154, line 29, *after* developed *insert* the former.

P. 157, line 14 from bottom, *for* none *read* most.

P. 157, line 13 from bottom, *after* there *insert* are no ; *and after* bristles *insert* (*Echiurus* and others excepted.)

P. 165, line 8, *dele* ? *and for* (not observed) *insert* (observed in Fabricia.)

P. 187, line 10, *dele* with the two claws alike.

P. 187, line 13, *for* one or more *insert* several.

P. 216, line 18, *for* not yet *read* partially, *and after* formed *insert* at birth ; line 21, *for* canal is *read* canal becoming after birth.

P. 225, in explanation of Fig. 252, *for* (Fowl) *read* (Mammal.)

P. 236, line 7, *for* Didelphia *read* Monodelphia.

OUTLINES

OF

COMPARATIVE EMBRYOLOGY

BY

A. S. PACKARD, Jr.

AUTHOR OF "A GUIDE TO THE STUDY OF INSECTS," ETC.

NEW YORK

HENRY HOLT AND COMPANY

1878

TO THE

MEMORY OF

LOUIS AGASSIZ

IN RECOGNITION

OF

THE IMPULSE HE GAVE TO THE STUDY OF

COMPARATIVE EMBRYOLOGY

THIS LITTLE WORK

IS GRATEFULLY DEDICATED

BY

THE AUTHOR.

PREFACE.

THESE condensed biographies of animals have grown out of a series of notes made originally for the writer's own information. It then occurred that what had been found useful to him might prove of service to others, and accordingly they were printed from time to time in the "American Naturalist" for 1875.

These papers are now offered to the public after undergoing careful revision, and with the addition of the chapters on Mammals and Man.

It is hoped that in their present form, they will be useful as containing the outlines of Comparative Embryology, forming a book of reference for teachers and advanced students, designed to supplement text books of zoölogy and comparative anatomy, in which little or nothing is said of the modes of growth of animals, especially of the surprising changes undergone before birth.

The embryology of the leading groups of the animal kingdom is treated of without reference to a rigid classification, which it was not the intention of the author to present in this connection.

A large number of the illustrations engraved especially for the work have been drawn as a labor of love by Mr. S. E. Cassino, of Salem. Due acknowledgments of the sources from which they are copied are made in the text.

PEABODY ACADEMY OF SCIENCE,
Salem, Mass., Dec. 24, 1875.

LIFE HISTORIES

OF

ANIMALS, INCLUDING MAN.

I. THE MONERA.

Structure and Habits. Hæckel, in 1868, applied to this group of organisms, which are doubtfully referred to the animal kingdom, the term *Monera* (from μονήρης, simple) in allusion to the extreme simplicity of their structure. "Their whole body," he remarks, "in a fully developed and freely moving condition, consists of an entirely homogeneous and structureless substance, a living particle of albumen, capable of nourishment and reproduction." They differ from the Amœbæ, hitherto supposed to be as simple as any organism, in the want of a nucleus and of contractile vesicles. Moreover, they (as in Protamœba) differ from the Rhizopodous Amœba in being entirely homogeneous in structure, there being, as Hæckel observes, "no apparent difference between a more tenacious outer and a softer inner sarcode mass," as is "perceptible in most, perhaps in all, true Amœbæ."

The motions of these Moners are effected by contraction of the homogeneous substance of the body, and by the irregular protrusion of portions of the body, forming either simple processes (pseudopodia) or a net-work of gelatinous threads. The food is taken in after the manner of the Amœba, the diatom, desmid or some protozoan being surrounded by the pseudopodia and gradually enfolded by the extremely extensible body mass.

The Monera are divided into two groups:

1. *Gymnomonera*, comprising the genera *Bathybius, Protobathybius, Protamœba, Protogenes* and *Myxodictyum*, which do not become encysted and consequently protected by a case.

2. *Lepomonera*, which become encysted and protected by a case, as in the genera *Protomonas*, *Protomyxa*, *Vampyrella* and *Myxastrum*.

The simplest form of all is Protamœba, which is a simple mass

Fig 1.

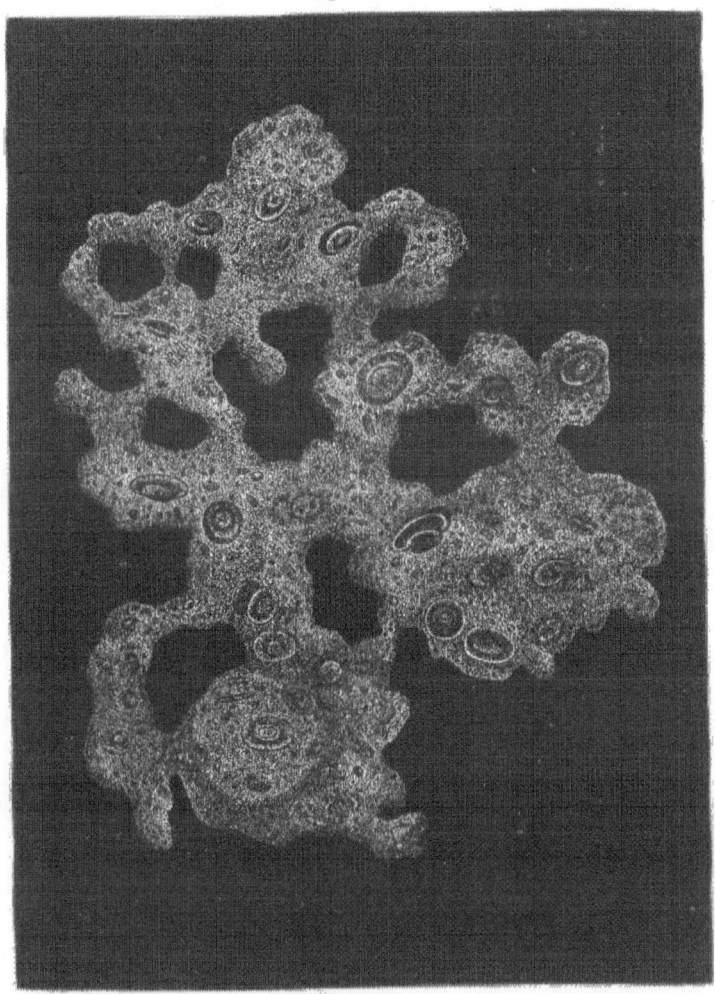

Bathybius.

of protoplasm without vacuoles (little cavities), which protrudes simple processes (pseudopodia) not ramifying or forming a network. Protogenes differs in protruding ramifying and anastomosing gelatinous threads, while Myxodictyum, the most complicated form, is made up of several simple Actinophrys-like bodies, whose pseudopodia branch out and interlace, forming a net.

Bathybius was first discovered by Prof. Wyville Thompson in 1869 in dredging at a depth of 2435 fathoms at the mouth of the Bay of Biscay. He describes it as a "soft, gelatinous, organic matter, enough to give a slight viscosity to the mud of the surface layer." Thompson also adds that if a "little of the mud in which this viscid condition is most marked be placed in a drop of sea water under the microscope, we can usually see, after a time, an irregular net-work of matter resembling white of eggs, distinguishable by its maintaining its outline and not mixing with the water. This net-work may gradually alter in form, and entangled granules and foreign bodies change their relative positions." To this low Moner, Huxley has given the name of *Bathybius Hæckelii* (Fig. 1, with coccoliths embedded in the protoplasm, from Thompson's "Depths of the Sea"). This Moner, adds Thompson, "whether it be continuous in one vast sheet, or broken up into circumscribed individual particles, appears to extend over a large part of the bed of the ocean." It should be stated that Thompson and others do not believe that Bathybius is really an organic being. Bathybius has been discovered at a depth of from fifty fathoms downwards in the Adriatic Sea, by Oscar Schmidt. The

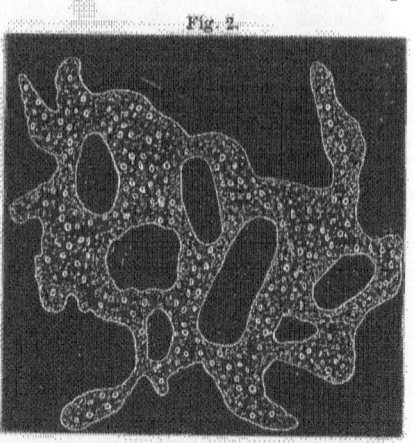

Fig. 2.

Protobathybius Robesonii.

Bathybius mud was detected by its yellowish gray color and its characteristic greasy nature.

Under the name of *Protobathybius Robesonii* Dr. Bessels mentions a Moner allied to Bathybius. I am indebted to Dr. Bessels for the following account and figure of it (Fig. 2, × 500 diameters): "It is mainly distinguished from Bathybius by the absence of both the Discolithes and Cyatholithes. For this reason I take it to be an older form than Bathybius, whence the name given to it. It consists of nearly pure protoplasm, tinged most intensely by a solution of carmine in ammonia. It contains fine gray granules of considerable refracting power, and besides the latter a great number of oleaginous drops, soluble in ether. It manifests very marked amœboid motions and takes up particles of carmine or other foreign substances suspended in the water in which it is kept. It hardly contained any foreign matter, except a fine sediment of limestone constituting the bottom of the sea. It was taken by means of a water bottle at a depth of ninety fathoms in Smith's Sound, lat. 79° 30′ N."

The *Protogenes primordialis* of Hæckel is a simple, shapeless mass of protoplasm, without vacuoles, but with over 1000 very fine pseudopodia, with numerous ramifications and anastomoses. The largest specimens are ·04 inch in diameter. It is a marine form, found at Nice. It reproduces by fission.

Myxodictyum is made up of several individuals, each one of which is like Protogenes, but with fewer pseudopods. *M. sociale* Hæckel, in the single specimen observed, formed a mass nearly an inch and a half in diameter, and was discovered in the Straits of Gibraltar.

Protomonas amyli (Ckski) is a fresh-water, monad-like form, found by Cienkowski in Germany and Russia, and is from ·08 to ·20 inch in diameter. *Protomyxa aurantiaca* Hæckel has vacuoles in its simple, shapeless, orange-red body, and in the encysted condition is a globular jelly-like mass over half an inch in diameter. It occurred on empty shells of *Spirula* Peronii, floating about on the open sea, and driven in on the coast of one of the Canary Islands. *Vampyrella*, as its name implies, is a jelly-like mass, which according to Cienkowski bores into the cells of confervæ and other fresh-water algæ, and sucks out their contents. Another species, *V. vorax*, engulfs diatoms, desmids and infusoria, drawing them into the interior of its body.

The highest form among the Moners is *Myxastrum radians* of Hæckel, which forms a radiating ball of jelly of tough consistence from ·12 to ·20 inch in diameter. It has very tough, stiff pseudopods. In the encysted condition it is nearly half an inch in diameter, and occurred on the beach of one of the Canary Islands.

Development. In Protamœba and Protogenes, Hæckel tells us we find the simplest possible mode of reproduction. They multiply by merely dividing into two portions, each part becoming an individual.

The distinguished Russian microscopist Cienkowski has given an account of the mode of development of *Protomonas amyli*, which corresponds to that of the lowest algæ, such as Protococcus (see Clark's Mind in Nature, p. 136, Figs. 73–79); both reproduce by spores; those of the animal Protomonas may be called "zoospores." Fig. 3 (copied from Cienkowski) represents at A this moner during the formation of the zoospores; B, a zoospore hatched out; C, D (A — D X 350 diameters), the Amœba-like form it afterwards assumes. From these stages Cienkowski traced it to the encysted, or resting stage, E (*y*, food; *s*, a projection inwards of the cell-wall; *x*, moner-cyst X 450). This form lives in putrefying Nitellæ. It should be observed that the

Fig. 3.

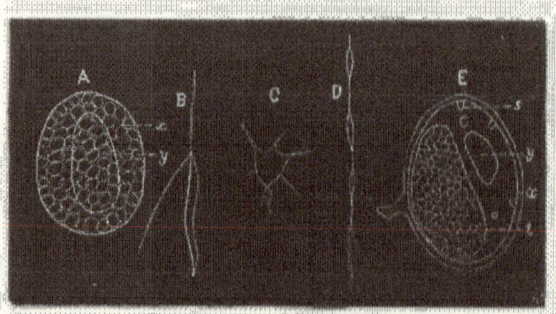

Development of Protomonas.

cyst of this Protomonas, as in the true Monads studied by Cienkowski, is composed of cellulose, while the granular contents become colored with chlorophyll. In these respects they are *plants*, but it should be remembered that cellulose is said to occur in the mantle of the Tunicates and various parts of Articulates and Vertebrates, while chlorophyll occurs in the Infusoria and Hydra.

The course of development of Protomyxa has been observed by Hæckel. The orange-red contents of the ball or cyst (Fig. 4, A) of this moner, divided, after it had retracted itself from the hyaline capsular wall, into several hundred small, round, thoroughly structureless, naked balls (Fig. 4, B). This process Hæckel regards rather as a "germ formation," than a process of division or gemmation. These small globular masses of protoplasm (*a*) are each drawn out into a long tail (*d*), and issue from the cyst as "swarm-spores" (zoospores, Fig. 4, C a, d, c). These zoospores then assume an amœba-form. These unite by twos or threes, or more, and form a new individual as at D, where two amœba-like germs unite themselves by their anastomosing pseudopods and draw themselves over a Diatom (a), meet in the middle, and unite into one individual moner. Fig. 4, E, represents a fully grown *P. aurantiaca* after having had a liberal diet of shelled Infusoria (E, a). From the central sarcode body the very strong, branching, tree-like pseudopods radiate, their outer

Fig. 4.

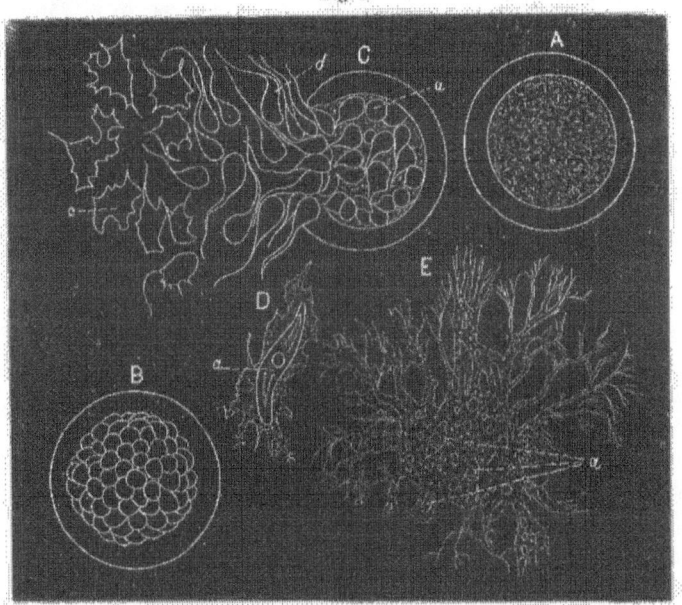

Development of Protomyxa.

anastomoses forming numerous crescent-shaped meshes. The vacuoles extend into the larger pseudopods; they first appear in the Amœba stage after they begin to take food.

This adult, Amœba-like form becomes encysted in the manner thus described by Hæckel. "To complete the natural history of the Protomyxa, it still remained only to observe the encysting of the adult form, the transition from the free moving plasmodia to the stationary red balls which had attached themselves to the Spirula shells near the latter. I succeeded in establishing this also. Two of the largest of the best fed plasmodia, which contained very numerous vacuoli, and which had formed a very extended sarcode net, with many branches and anastomoses, after some time began to slacken their extremely rapid currents, and to simplify their pseudopods. The silicious shells of the many diatoms which had been absorbed were rejected, and the branches and twigs of the pseudopods were successively retracted. At last they drew back the main stems, which had everywhere become simple, into the central plasma-body, and the entirely homogeneous sarcode body took the form of an irregular lump, and finally rounded itself into a regular ball.

"Now commenced the separation of the covering of the cyst, in which the sharply defined single outline of the orange-red plasma-balls passed into a perceptible, though certainly fine, double outline. A second, and then a third, concentric boundary line soon followed this, and then the proper concentric hyaline cyst-covering appeared somewhat quickly (in the course of a day) ; its layers corresponded with the above stated breaks of the separated gelatinous skin. At first a quantity of vacuoli were still perceptible in the plasma during the encysting process, which appeared and disappeared here and there, but visibly decreased in numbers ; and after the complete development of the cyst covering, no vacuoli could be any longer perceived in the orange-red plasma, now interspersed with numerous granules. The encysted plasma-ball was now no longer to be distinguished from those red balls whose transition to the mass of sporules I have above described. Thus was the cycle of the generation of the Protomyxa completed, and the course of its simple and remarkable life history established."

The phases may be thus summed up :—

1. The free swimming flagellate state (sporule or zoospore).
2. The creeping Amœba state.
3. The reticulated Rhizopod state.
4. The encysted state.

Somewhat similar is the development of *Vampyrella spirogyræ*, which penetrates into the cells of the fresh-water plant Spirogyra, and absorbs its protoplasm. Fig. 5, A, represents the adult, with its radiating pseudopods, and a large one in the act of boring into the walls of the plant. It then withdraws its pseudopodia, and assumes what Cienkowski calls the cell-state. During this period it is surrounded by a delicate membrane. The granular

contents divide into three portions, each of which becomes an
Amœba-like being (Fig. 5, B, showing one creeping out of the
cell, *x*. C, D, E, the Amœba-like stage). Finally one of these

Fig. 5.

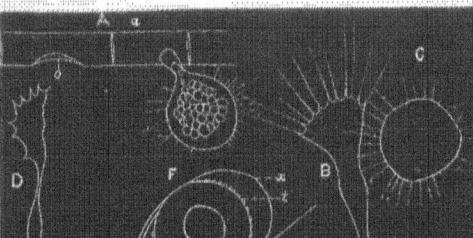

Development of Vampyrella.

Amœba-like forms becomes encysted (Fig. 5, F, *y*, the food-
granules; *t*, cell-wall of the cyst). To sum up the life-history of
Vampyrella as observed by Cienkowski, we have:—

    1. An Amœba-stage.
    2. A cell-stage.
    3. A second Amœba-stage.
    4. An encysted stage.

So exactly does this mode of development parallel that of *Colpodella pugnax* described by Cienkowski, who regards it as a flagellate infusorian allied to Monas, that we doubt the naturalness
of Hæckel's division of Monera. Colpodella and in fact Protomonas differ from the Monads (Flagellata) simply in having no
nucleus. Whether this may not be found on further observation,
or whether its absence or presence is so important as Hæckel
thinks, future observation will show. We are now inclined to regard the Monera as a somewhat artificial group. It should be
noticed that none of the other Moners have a "cell-state," but the
Amœba-like organism becomes encysted at once after becoming
fully fed.

The development of *Myxastrum radians* of Hæckel is much like that of Protomyxa, but differs in some important respects. The cyst becomes filled with numerous conical portions, whose points rest towards the centre of the ball, while

Fig. 6.

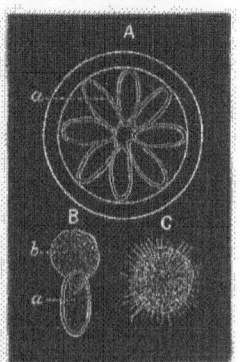

their rounded bases produce a mulberry-shaped outline externally. In the next stage these cone-shaped divisions have assumed a spindle shape, and each separate spore has developed a silicious covering (Fig. 6, A, a). When the spindle-shaped spore has been set free the protoplasmic contents (b) slip out of the silicious shell (Fig. 6, B, a), and assume an Amœba form, with numerous radial pseudopods (Fig. 6, C), which in the fully formed Moner become as long as the diameter of the body.

Development of Myxastrum.

With the facts that have been presented, the question arises whether these moners are animals or vegetables. Structurally, and in their mode of development, the Monera would seem not to differ essentially from the lowest plants, such as the Myxomycetes and lowest Algæ; but physiologically, or *in what they do*, they differ, as H. J. Clark (Mind in Nature, pp. 151, 156) says of Amœba, in taking in living organisms entire, digesting their protoplasm and rejecting the silicious coverings of the diatoms or infusoria they have swallowed. The plants of correspondingly low organization on the contrary absorb only the elements in an unorganized state.

LITERATURE.

Hæckel. Ueber den Sarcodekörper der Rhizopoden. (Siebold und Kölliker's Zeitschrift für naturwissenchaftliche Zoologie, xv. 1865.)

—— Monographie der Moneren. (Jenaische Zeitschrift für Medicin und Naturwissenschaft, iv. 1868. Translated in Quart. Journ. Microscopical Science, 1869.)

Cienkowski. Beiträge zur Kenntniss der Monaden. Schultze's Archiv für Microskopische Anatomie. Bd. 1. 1865.

Huxley. On some Organisms living at great Depths in the North Atlantic Ocean (Bathybius. (Quart. Journ. Micr. Sc.. viii. 1868.)

II. THE GREGARINIDA.

Structure and Habits. First discovered by Dufour, these parasitic protozoans, with an organ, *i. e.*, a nucleus, were considered as the lowest animals until the discovery by Hæckel of the still simpler Monera. It is now known that they pass through the Moner-state and attain a true Amœba condition, having an outer, clear-

muscular, and an inner, medullary or granular, layer, which are
more distinct than in the Amœbæ, and also a nucleus. In form
they are more or less worm-like. They are parasitic, living in
many types of animals, especially the insects and worms, and vary
greatly in form. The largest species known is *Gregarina gigantea*
(Fig. 7, after E. Van Beneden), which lives in the intestinal canal
of the European lobster. It is worm-like, remarkably slender, being ·64 inch in length. It is, in fact, the largest one-celled animal
known, and in size may be compared with the cells of some vegetables ; in the animal kingdom it is only surpassed by the eggs of
birds, which are really cells. In this organism an external, structureless, perfectly transparent membrane, with a double contour,
can be very clearly distinguished. It represents the cell wall of
other cells. Beneath this outer wall is a continuous layer of contractile substance, by which these animals retain their form, not
changing as in the Amœba ; it was first discovered in 1852, by
Prof. J. Leidy. He showed that there existed under the cuticular,
structureless membrane. a so-called muscular layer, which in contracting becomes longitudinally folded, so as to produce a marked
striation. Van Beneden adds that in " the immense Gregarina of
the lobster I have assured myself of the presence of, under the
cuticle, a true system of muscular fibrillæ, comparable to those of
the Infusoria." From this fact he places these animals above the
Amœbæ, which move by the simple contractility of their sarcode
or protoplasm, a property of all animal and vegetable protoplasm
generally. He therefore opposes the opinion of Hæckel that the
Gregarina is an Amœba, degraded by its parasitic life.

The internal granular matter of the Gregarina is extremely
mobile, like protoplasm generally. "The whole cavity of the
body is filled," says Van Beneden, "with a granular matter formed
by a viscid liquid, which is perfectly transparent. This holds in
suspension fine granulations of a rounded form, which are formed
by a highly refractive and slightly yellow matter." In this granular matter the nucleus is suspended. The nucleus is surrounded
by a membrane, and the cavity of the vesicle is filled by a homogeneous, colorless and transparent liquid. This nucleus contains
an inner vesicle, or nucleolus, which has the singular feature of
spontaneously appearing and disappearing in a very short space
of time. "If one of these Gregarinæ of moderate size is observed, the nucleus is seen at first provided with a single nucle-

olus, presenting some seconds later a great number of little refracting corpuscles, of very variable dimensions, which are also nucleoli. Some of these enlarge considerably, whilst the primitive nucleolus diminishes in volume little by little, finally disappearing. The number of nucleoli varies at every instant." These novel observations are considered of great importance by Van Beneden as showing that the nucleolus of the Gregarina, and consequently the nucleoli of cells generally are sometimes, if not always, devoid of a membrane. And he draws the inference "that the nucleus of a cell is not necessarily a vesicle, and that

Fig. 7.

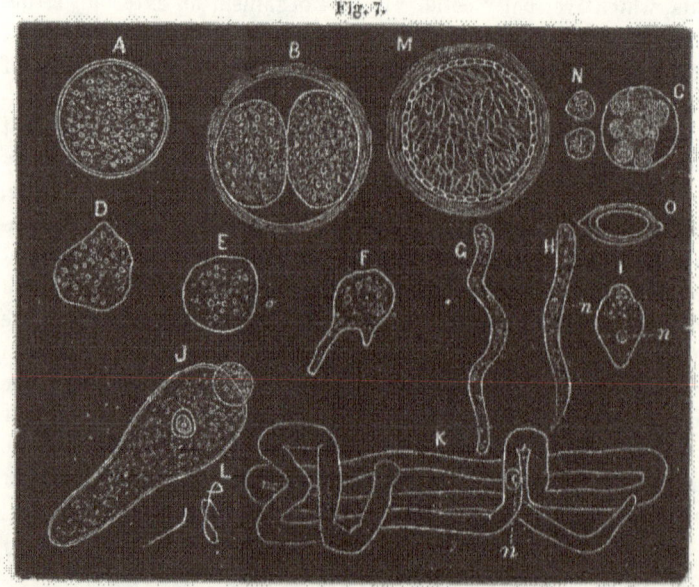

Development of Gregarina.

contrary to the generally received opinion, a nucleus of a cell may be equally devoid of membrane," though we may add that he saw it in the Gregarina of the lobster. Van Beneden distinguishes three kinds of motions in the Gregarinæ. 1. They present a very slow movement of translation, in a straight line and without the possibility of distinguishing any contraction of the walls of the body which could be considered as the cause of the movement. It seems impossible to account for this kind of motion. 2. The next kind of movement consists in the lateral displacement of every part, taking place suddenly and often very violently, from a

more or less considerable part of its body. Then the posterior
part of the body may be often seen to throw itself out laterally by
a brusque and instantaneous movement, forming an angle with the
anterior part. 3. Owing to the contractions of the body the granules within the body move about.

Development. The history of Gregarina has been worked out
by Siebold, Stein, Lieberkuhn, and more recently by E. Van Beneden. The course of development is as follows : the worm-like
adult, *G. gigantea* (Fig. 7, K, *n* nucleus ; L, two individuals of
natural size), which is common in lobsters on the European coast
in May, June and August, becomes encysted in September in the
walls of the rectum of the lobster, the cysts (Fig. 7, A) appearing like "little white grains of the size of the head of a small
pin." When thus encysted the animal loses its nucleus, and the
granular contents of the cyst divide into two masses (B), like the
beginning of the segmentation of the yolk of the higher animals.
The next step is not figured by Van Beneden, and we therefore
introduce some figures from Lieberkuhn which show how the granular mass breaks up into zoospores (called by authors "pseudonavicellæ," and by Lieberkuhn "psorosperms") with hard shells.
After the disappearance of the nucleus and vesicle, and when
the encysted portion has become a homogeneous granular mass,
this mass divides into a number of rounded balls (Fig. 7, C).
These balls consist of fine granules, which are the zoospores in
their first stage (Fig. 7, N). They then become spindle-shaped
(O), and fill the cyst (Fig. 7, M), the balls having meanwhile disappeared. From these zoospores are expelled Amœba-like masses
of albumen (D, E) which, as Van Beneden remarks, exactly resemble the Protamœba already described. This moner-like being,
without a nucleus, is the young Gregarina.

But soon the Amœba characters arise. The moner-like young
(Fig. 7, D, E) now undergoes a further change. Its outer portion becomes a thick layer of a brilliant, perfectly homogeneous
protoplasm, entirely free from granules, which surrounds the central granular contents of the cytode (Hæckel) or non-nucleated
cell. This is the Amœba stage of the young Gregarina, the body,
as in the Amœba, consisting of a clear cortical and granular medullary or central portion.

The next step is the appearance of two arm-like projections
(Fig. 7, F), comparable to the pseudopods of an Amœba. One

of these arms elongates, and separating forms a perfect Gregarina. Soon afterwards the other arm elongates, absorbs the moner-like mass and also becomes a perfect Gregarina. This elongated stage is called a Pseudofilaria (Fig. 7, G). No nucleus has yet appeared. In the next stage (Fig. 7, H, n, nucleus) the body is shorter and broader, and the nucleus appears, while a number of granules collect at one end, indicating a head. After this the body shortens a little more (I, J), and then attains the elongated, worm-like form of the adult Gregarina (K). Van Beneden thus sums up the phases of growth :—

1. The Moner phase.
2. The generating Cytode phase.
3. The Pseudo-filaria phase.
4. The Protoplast[1] (adult Gregarina).
5. The encysted Gregarina.
6. The sporogony phase (producing zoospores).

It seems evident that the mode of development of the Gregarina in part corresponds quite closely with the mode of growth of the Moners; for example, it becomes encysted, *i. e.*, sexually mature, produces zoospores (pseudonavicellæ), and from these zoospores issues the young or larval form of the Gregarina. These zoospores abound in damp places and are devoured by insects and worms. After they are swallowed the shells burst and the Amœba-like young are set free in the body of their host.

It will be seen that there is here a total absence of sexual reproduction. The Moner-stage arises by self-division of the contents of the cyst, a process analogous to the segmentation of the yolk of eggs; and the Pseudofilariæ arise by self-division of the young in the Moner-stage, *i. e.*, by a budding process.

LITERATURE.

Dufour. Note sur la Grégarine. (Annales des Sciences Naturelles, xiii. 1828.)

Siebold. Beiträge zur Geschichte wirbelloser Thiere. 1839.

Stein. Ueber die Natur der Gregarinen. (Müller's Archiv für Anatomie. 1848.)

Kölliker. Beiträge zur Kenntniss niederes Thiere. (Siebold und Kölliker's Zeitschrift 1, 1849.)

Lieberkühn. Evolution des Grégarines. (Mémoires couronnés de l'Académie Royale de Bruxelles, xxvi. 1855.)

E. Van Beneden. On a New Species of Gregarina to be called *Gregarina gigantea.* (Quart. Journ. Microscopical Science, x. 1870.)

———— ———— Recherches sur l'Evolution des Grégarines. (Bulletins de l'Académie Royale de Belgique, xxxi. 1871.)

---

[1] The Gregarinæ and Amœbæ constitute Hæckel's group of *Protoplasta.*

III. THE RHIZOPODA.

Structure and Habits. We have almost anticipated a definition of the Rhizopoda, of which the Amœba, or Protean animalcule, is the simplest form, by our frequent references to the "Amœba-form" or "Amœba-like" stages in the Moners and Gregarinas. The Amœba is the starting point, the unit of the nucleated Protozoa, the primitive, ancestral form to which the members of the subkingdom may be reduced. Until the Monera were discovered the Amœba was regarded as the lowest possible animal.

With the form of the Monera, a shapeless mass of protoplasm, changing each instant, throwing out threads or larger protrusions

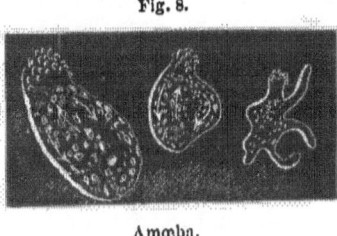

Fig. 8.

Amœba.

of the body, the Amœba possesses a distinct organ, the nucleus, and its body mass is divided into a clear cortical and a medullary granular mass; the outer highly contractile, the inner granular portion acting virtually as a stock of food. These granules, like the grains of chlorophyll in vegetable cells and Diatoms and Desmids, circulate in regular fixed currents, according to II. J. Clark. (See Fig. 8, after Clark; the usual form of *Amœba diffluens* Ehrenberg, magnified 100 diameters; the arrows indicate the course of the circulating food. The head end is knobbed, and within free from granules.) We have then in Amœba:—

1. A nucleus, probably representing the nucleus and ovary of the Infusoria.

2. A head and posterior end.

3. A circulation analogous to that of the Infusoria.

This animal, as we may justly call it, since it takes in living protozoans and rejects their shells, has the power of moving in a particular direction, one end of the body always advancing first; which indicates the rudiments of a nervous and muscular power; and can swallow, digest and circulate its food. Whether it gives out nitrogen and absorbs oxygen or not is unknown. It reproduces by self-division, and some allied forms by the production of monad-like, flagellate spores.

The Amœba is a fresh-water form, living on the stems and

leaves of fresh-water plants. The late H. J. Clark, our most eminent microscopist, thus describes its habits in his "Mind in Nature." "The three figures [8] represent the various forms which I have seen the same individual assume, whilst I had it under the microscope, as it crept over the water-plants upon which it is accustomed to dwell. The most usual form which it assumed is that of an elongated oval (A), but from time to time the sides of its body would project either in the form of simple bulgings (B), or suddenly it would spread out from several parts of the body (C), as if it were falling apart; just as you must have seen a drop of water do on a dusty floor, or a drop of oil on the surface of water; and then again it retracted these transparent arms and became perfectly smooth and rounded, resembling a drop of slimy, mucous matter, such as is oftentimes seen about the stems of aquatic plants."

Pelomyxa (Fig. 10) is a fresh-water Amœba-like form, but provided with spicules. Under the name of *Amœba sabulosa* Prof. Leidy describes[2] a form which he thinks "is probably a member of the genus Pelomyxa," and which is characterized by the comparatively enormous quantity of quartzose sand which it swallows with its food. "The animal might be viewed as a bag of sand!" It is from one-eighth to three-eighths of a line in diameter, and was found on the muddy bottom of ponds in Pennsylvania and New Jersey. It is possibly *Pamphagus mutabilis*, figured by Professor Bailey in the "American Journal of Science and Arts," 1853. Another form resembling Greef's Pelomyxa, and found by Professor Leidy in a pond in New Jersey, is *Deinamœba mirabilis;*[3] its body bristles with minute spicules. He has also described in the same Proceedings (p. 88) *Gromia terricola*, which lives in the earth about the roots of mosses growing in the crevices of the bricks of the pavements of the streets of Philadelphia. He thus graphically describes this singular form. "Imagine an animal, like one of our autumnal spiders, stationed at the centre of its well spread net; imagine every thread of this net to be a living extension of the animal, elongating, branching, and becoming confluent so as to form a most intricate net; and imagine every thread to exhibit actively moving currents of a viscid liquid both outward and inward, carrying along particles of food and

[2] Proceedings of the Academy of Natural Sciences, Philadelphia, 1874. p. 86.
[3] l. c. p. 142.

dirt, and you have some idea of the general character of a Gromia."

A convenient division of the Rhizopods is into two groups, Foraminifera and Radiolaria. Schultze divides the former into :—

1. *Nuda*, or naked forms, such as Amœba and Actinophrys.

2. *Monothalamia*, forming a one-chambered shell, but with the animal undivided, living in the simple hollow of the shell. Fresh-water forms are Arcella, Difflugia and Gromia, while Cornuspira is a marine form.

3. *Polythalamia*, with many-chambered shells ; all marine. The three divisions are represented by (1) Acervulina, (2) Nodosaria and (3) Miliola, Rotalina, Globigerina, Textularia, Nummulina, Polystomella, etc.

The Rhizopods are divided by Hæckel into 1. *Acyttaria*, or the one and many chambered Foraminifera; 2. The *Heliozoa*, repre-sented by *Actinosphærium* (*Actinophrys*) *Eichhornii*, or sun-animal-cule ; and 3. The *Radiolaria*. These last two groups he divides (*a*) into the *Monocyttaria* (represented by Cyrtidosphæra, Thalassi-colla and Acanthometra, etc.) and (*b*) the *Polycyttaria*, represented by Collozoum, Sphærozoum and Collosphæra. Hæckel, who has studied these Radiolaria more than any one else, though Johannes Müller gave us the first definite information about them, says that "in the lower forms they are allied to the sun-animalcules and Foraminifera, but the higher forms are much more highly devel-oped. They differ from both the Actinophrys and Foraminifera, in that the central part of the body is made up of many cells, and is surrounded by a strong membrane. This closed, more or less spherical "central capsule" is surrounded by a slimy layer of protoplasm, from which thousands of very fine threads radi-ate, and often branch out and anastomose. Among them are scattered numerous yellow cells, which contain starch granules." (Whether these yellow cells are parasitic organisms, or belong to the animal, is not yet known.) Most Radiolaria are provided with a highly developed silicious frame-work, like the outer shell of a nest of Chinese carved balls, the outer surface of which is studded with spines ; but both the form of the silicious box and the spines varies greatly, as may be seen by a glance at the accompanying plate, I.[4] (after J. Müller), illustrating the Polycystina. Some

---

[4] Explanation of the plate. **Fig. 1**, *Tetrapyle octacantha*; **Fig. 2**, *Haliomma amphidis-cus*; **Fig. 3**, *Haliomma longispinum*; **Fig. 4**, *Haliomma hexacanthum*; **Fig. 5**, *Haliomma?*

Radiolaria have a many chambered shell like those of the Poly-thalamia.

While the Foraminifera live mostly at the bottom of the sea (some, however, occurring between tide marks) on stones and sea-weeds, creeping over sand and mud by means of their pseudopods, the marine Radiolaria for the most part float with outstretched pseudopods on the surface of the sea. They occur in countless numbers, but are usually so small that until 1858 they had been almost entirely overlooked by naturalists. The compound, or so-cial forms, such as Collosphæra, are nearly an inch in diameter, while most of the simple species cannot be seen with the naked eye. The Polycystina occur fossil in abundance at Barbadoes, Richmond, Va., and the Nicobar islands.

Development. So far as is known Amœba multiplies its kind only by the simplest mode of reproduction known, that of self-divis-ion. The following figure (9), copied from Hæckel, represents,

Fig. 9.

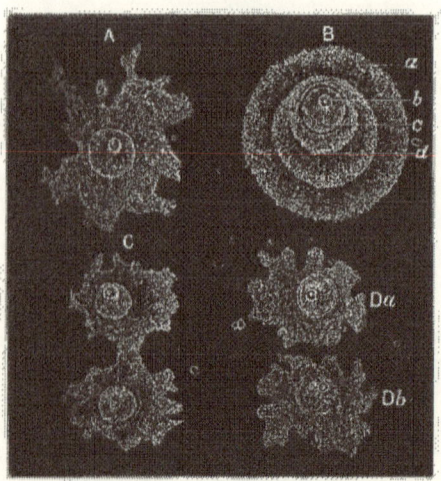

Amœba sphærococcus.

highly magnified, *Amœba sphœrococcus*, a fresh-water species with-out a contractile vesicle, in the process of fission; at B is the encysted Amœba in its "resting stage." It now consists of a spherical lump of protoplasm (*d*), in which is a nucleus (*c*) with its nucleolus (*b*) and the whole surrounded by a cyst or cell-membrane (*a*). It breaks the cell-wall and becomes free as at

A.   Self-division then begins as at C, the nucleus doubling itself, until at *Da* and *Db*, we have as a result two individuals.

In Pelomyxa, a higher form than Amœba, we have according to Greef a production of ciliated zoospores. This form, described

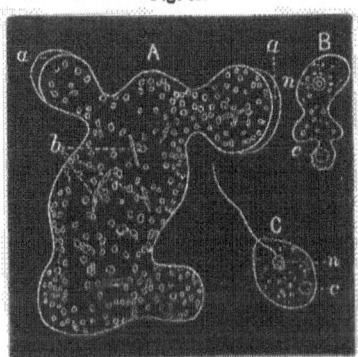

Pelomyxa palustris.

by Prof. Greef under the name of *Pelomyxa palustris* (Fig. 10, A, a, clear portion ; b, diatoms enclosed in the body mass), lives in the mud at the bottom of pools, and when first seen resembles little dark balls of mud ·04–·05 inch in diameter. The body mass contains numerous vacuoles filled with water, and numbers of nuclei and spicules. These nuclei and spicules have a dancing motion, like the ordinary Brownian movements of molecules. There are also numerous hyaline, oval or rounded bodies which Greef calls " shining bodies," and which originate from the nuclei. They increase by division within the body-mass of the Pelomyxa, becoming Amœba-like bodies (Fig. 10, B, *n* nucleus, *c* contractile vesicle) which issue in great numbers from the parent-mass. These Amœboid forms gradually pass into flagellate zoospores (Fig. 10, C) with a nucleus and contractile vesicle. It thus seems that the zoospores of this Rhizopod are produced without the animal becoming encysted.

As regards the development of Actinophrys and the allied spiny forms, Greef thinks that besides being formed by direct self-division, there is a resting or encysted stage. " The latter consists in the withdrawal of the sarcode body-mass from the inner boundary formed by the union of the bases of the radial spines, leaving a rather wide empty border, and its becoming invested by a double coat, viz., a firm inner one, when empty, dotted, as if perforated, and an outer hyaline one."

According to Schneider, *Actinophrys Eichhornii* undergoes division ; the central mass divides twice or thrice. Then the alveolar cortical layer disappears, and each mass resulting from the self-division becomes encysted. This process is undergone in two days. It remains encysted through the winter until the beginning of May, when the cyst drops off and a small Actinophrys with a number of nuclei appears.

As an example of the reproduction of these forms by fission, we may cite the case of *Gromia socialis*, figured by Archer. He represents the body of a Gromia after having undergone a transverse self-fission, having in each portion a nucleus with its nucleolus, the upper segment giving off branched pseudopodia as usual.

Of the mode of development of the shelled Amœbæ or Foraminifera (Polythalamia), numerous and often accessible as these animals are, we know but little. In fact, we have only the fragmentary observations of Max Schultze, made in 1856, on a species of Miliola sent him from Trieste. He says that this Foraminifer, after remaining from eight to fourteen days in the same place on the side of the jar, became surrounded with a thin layer of brownish mud, so that the shell was lost to view. On the 15th of May he noticed that small, round, sharply defined bodies escaped from the brownish slimy mass, and after some hours as many as forty such bodies surrounded the Miliola. These round bodies were young Foraminifera in calcareous shells with one turn, but no inner walls, somewhat resembling Cornuspira, and with pseudopodia already like those of the adult. It is probable, therefore, that the shell of the young is formed within the parent. Schultze adds that the almost complete want of organic contents in the shell of the parent at this time, rendered it probable that the whole or greater part of its body had passed into those of the young.

Of the mode of development of the Radiolaria, Prof. Cienkowski afforded, in 1871, the first definite information. He states that "J. Müller saw in the interior of an Acanthometra a swarming of small monad-like vesicles, which moved about for a time, and then changed themselves into Actinophrys-like structures. Afterwards," Hæckel saw, first, in Sphærozoids, "the contents of the capsules break up into many vesicles, and secondly, in Sphærozoum, he observed masses of vesicles which exhibited a vibratory movement." Lastly, Schneider had noticed in Thalassicolla groups of amœboid vesicles with movable flagellum-like processes. These facts rendered it probable, what Cienkowski has proved, that the Radiolaria reproduce by motile germs, *i.e.*, zoospores.

He studied the compound forms, such as Collosphæra and Collozoum, which are composed of aggregations of capsules (Fig. 11, A, a capsule of a young Collosphæra without the latticed shell), held together by a common mass of protoplasm. These capsules are separated by a certain interval from one another, while the protoplasm binding them together consists of alveoli (vesicles) of various sizes, between and on to which sarcodic threads and networks are disposed. "I always found," he adds, "the capsules supported on the surface of the alveoli, often lenticular, compressed, and enclosed by a radiating layer of protoplasm, which also spreads itself over the alveoli, and passed over continuously into the sarcodic envelope of neighboring capsules. Besides those alveoli which carry capsules, there are many smaller, which are free from capsules."

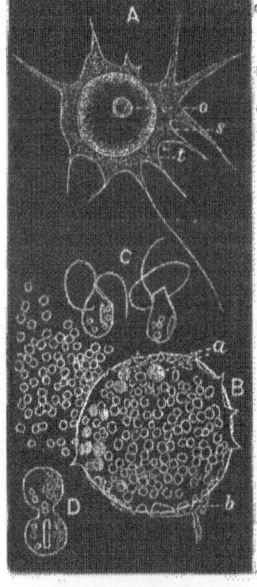

Fig. 11.

Collosphæra spinosa (Fig. 11, B) possesses a fenestrated shell beset with small spines, which encloses a capsule with a protoplasmic investment. Fig. 11, B, a, indicates the problematical yellow cells. Fig. 11, A, indicates a young capsule of another spineless species, *C. Huxleyi* Müll. The young capsule of this species is naked, embedded, without any shell, in a radiated protoplasmic sheath, not emarginated by any sharply marked envelope. "In this stage they often divide themselves by fission into two halves. Not until maturer age does the capsule obtain a resisting membrane, and become enclosed in a fenestrated shell.

The next change which takes place in the capsule is its division into a number

Collosphæra.

of little spheroids. This process is accomplished in a single day in *C. Huxleyi*. These spheroids become monad-like bodies, filling the capsule with a mass of corpuscles having a tremulous movement, and which finally swarm out in all directions (Fig. 11, B) from the capsule as true zoospores (C). The capsules now die and break up. These zoospores are provided with two long cilia. In the interior are a few oil drops, and a little crystalline rod, which sometimes projects out of the body.

"Among the swarms of swimming zoospores lay many motionless ones dispersed," continues Cienkowski. "They were round or angular, with drawn-out points," and one or more constrictions could be seen in them (Fig. 11, D). "Apparently they were developmental stages of the zoospores, obtained as they were in course of formation from the contents of the capsule." Cienkowski observed the same process in *Collozoum inerme*, thus substantiating his observations on Collosphæra.

In the Rhizopods, then, we know certainly two modes of reproduction :—

A. By self-division, as in Amœba.

B. By the production of zoospores, as in Pelomyxa and the Radiolaria.

In the Radiolaria the following phenomena take place :—

1. The capsule is filled with spheroids by a probable division of the contents of the capsule, as in the encysted stage of Monera and Gregarinida.

2. The "out-swarming" of zoospores.

LITERATURE.

A. Naked Rhizopods.

Auerbach. Ueber die Einzelligkeit der Amœben. (Siebold and Kölliker's Zeitschrift, 1855.)

Kölliker. Das Sonnenthierchen, *Actinophrys sol*. (Siebold and Kölliker's Zeitschrift, 1849. Translated in Quart. Journ. Micr. Science, 1853.)

Clark. Mind in Nature. 1865.

Archer. On some fresh-water Rhizopoda, new or little known. (Quart. Journ. Micr. Sc., 1869-71.)

B. Foraminifera.

Schultze. Ueber den Organismus der Polythalamien nebst Bemerkungen über die Rhizopoden in Allgemeinen. 1854.

———— Beobachtungen ueber die Fortpflanzung der Polythalamien. (Müller's Archiv für Anatomie, etc. 1856.)

Carpenter. Researches on the Foraminifera. (Philosophical Transactions of the Royal Society. London, 1856-7.)

C. Radiolaria.

Müller. Ueber die Thalassicollen, Polycystinen und Acanthometren des Mittelmeeres. (Abhandlungen der K. Akad. Berlin, 1858.)

Hæckel. Die Radiolarien. Eine Monographie, folio, 1862.

Cienkowski. Ueber Schwärmerbildung bei Radiolarien. (Schultze's Archiv für Mikros. Anatomie, VII. 1871. Translated in Quart. Journ. Micr. Sc., 1871.)

Schneider. Zur Kenntniss der Radiolarien. (Siebold and Kölliker's Zeitschrift, xxi, 1871.)

IV. THE LABYRINTHULÆ.

WE would not pass over certain forms doubtfully referred to the Protozoa, by Cienkowski, the only one who has studied them, and placed by Hæckel near the Diatoms and Desmids, in his

Fig. 12.

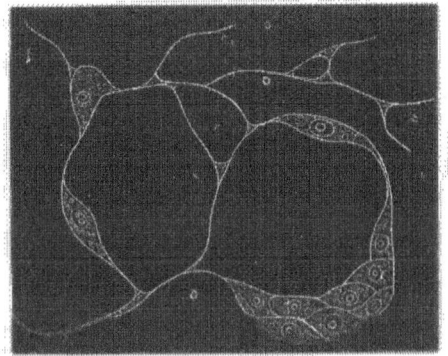

Labyrinthula.

kingdom "Protista," but which may be provisionally located near the Rhizopods. These organisms were found by Cienkowski at Odessa beneath the seaweeds growing on the piles in the harbor. They are minute, orange-colored organisms, forming reticulated threads which enclose spindle-shaped nucleated bodies. Fig. 12, represents *Labyrinthula macrocystis*, highly magnified, with the single spindle-shaped bodies starting out from the mass on the left, and gliding over the "rope walk," or framework of threads. This framework of cells, as Cienkowski, who studied its development, says, is to be "considered as an exudation of cells, — as a peculiar fibrous jelly-like formation." In this respect it resembles, he adds, the Palmellaceæ, Conjugatæ, and Flagellate Algæ in which a jelly-like substance is exuded to which the cells adhere. Cienkowski gives the following results of his investigations on the nature of these singular organisms, which we hope may be discovered in this country :

1. They present masses of cells which enclose a nucleus, and which increase in number by division; they possess a certain degree of contractility, and now and then are covered with a cortical substance.

2. These cells exude a fibrous substance, which makes a stiff, tree-like network, forming a branching framework.

3. The cells leave the mass and glide in different directions along the framework to the periphery of the mass. The Labyrinthula cells can only continue their peregrinations when supported by this line of threads.

Development. The moving cells unite in a new mass and become cysts, in which each cell is surrounded by a hard covering, the whole being held together by a rind-like substance.

After some time four small granules are formed from each cyst, which most likely become young Labyrinthula cells.

He concludes that "these peculiar organisms bear no relation to any known group of beings of either of the organic kingdoms. They cannot be classed with the sponges, Rhizopoda, Gregarinæ, or ciliated Infusoria, or with the algæ or fungi."

LITERATURE.

Cienkowski. Ueber die Bau und Entwicklung der Labyrinthuleen. (Schultze's Archiv, 1867. Abstract in Quart. Journ. Micr. Science, 1867.)

V. THE FLAGELLATA.

As with the Amœba-stage of the lower Protozoa, so we have had anticipations of the Monads, as the Flagellata may be popularly styled, in the zoospores of the lower Protozoa and Monera. The monads in point of structure are scarcely more highly organized in their lowest forms than the spores of the algæ and the zoospores of the other Protozoa, for which they are often mistaken. They are exceedingly minute, oval bodies, with a nucleus and contractile vesicle and one or two long whip-like cilia, whence the term *Flagellata.*

The true monads have been studied by the late Professor H. J. Clark with more success than by any one else. *Monas termo* Ehr.? is much like single individuals of *Urella glauconia* Ehr.? (Fig. 13), though the body is shorter and more regularly oval. It is faint olive in color. The monads are provided with one or more flagella, or bristle-like cilia, situated in *M. termo* on the front near the beaklike prolongation of the body. In swimming the monad stretches out the flagellum, which "vibrates with an undulating, whirling motion, which is most especially observable at its tip, and produces by this mode of propulsion the peculiar rolling of the body, which at times lends so much grace to its movements as it glides from place to place" (Clark). When the monad is fixed the flagellum is used to convey food to the mouth, which lies between the base of the flagellum and beak, or "lip," as Clark calls it. The food is thrown by a sudden jerk and with precision, directly against the mouth. "If acceptable for food, the flagellum presses its base down upon the morsel, and at the same time the lip is thrown back so as to disclose the mouth, and then bent over the particle as it sinks into the latter. When the lip has obtained a fair hold upon the food, the flagellum withdraws from its incumbent position and returns to its former rigid, watchful condition. The process of deglutition is then carried on by the help of the lip alone, which expands latterly until it completely overlies the particle. All this is done quite rapidly, in a few seconds, and then the food glides quickly into the depths of the body, and is enveloped in a digestive vacuole, whilst the lip assumes its usual conical shape and proportions."

All the monads have a contractile vesicle. In *Monas termo*, Clark observes that it is "so large and conspicuous that its globular form may be readily seen, even through the greatest diameter of the body; and contracts so vigorously and abruptly, at the rate of six times a minute, that there seems to be a quite sensible shock over that side of the body in which it is embedded." The contractile vesicle is thought to represent the heart of the higher animals. The reproductive organ may possibly, says Clark, be represented in *Monas termo*, by a "very conspicuous, bright, highly refracting, colorless oil-like globule which is enclosed in a clear vesicle" called the nucleus. This and other monads live either free, or attached by a slender stalk. As an example of the compound or aggregated monads may be cited *Urella*

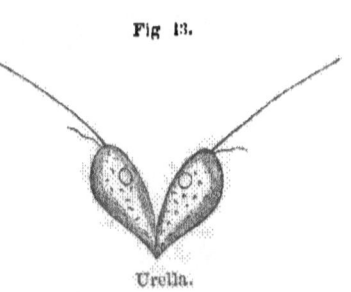

Fig 13.

Urella.

(Fig. 13), probably *glauconia* of Ehrenberg, of which an account, with accompanying figures, here reproduced, was published by Prof. A. H. Tuttle in the "American Naturalist," vi, 286. Figs. 13, 14 and 15 represent two, five, and about forty monads of this species, magnified 1000 diameters. Fig. 16 is an ideal section through a colony of this monad. Urella, as Tuttle observes, "probably

Fig. 14.

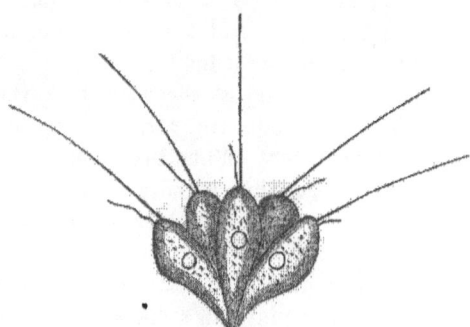

A group of five Monads (Urella).

Fig. 15.

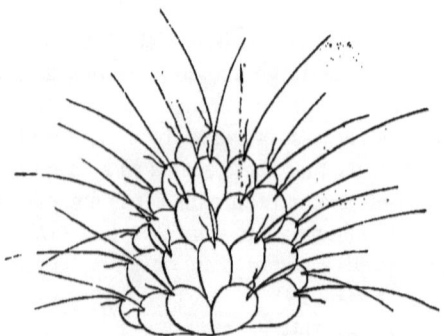

A colony of about forty Monads (Urella).

Fig. 16.

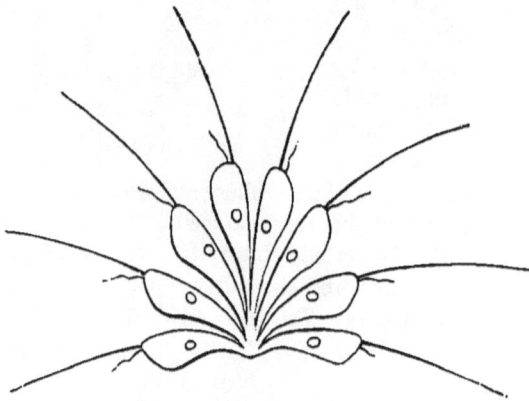

Ideal section through a colony of Urellæ.

finds its nearest ally in Anthophysa, differing from that genus principally in being free swimming instead of fixed upon a stalk." The genera Chlamydomonas and Colpodella are represented at Fig. 20, B. A higher form than Monas is Codosiga (Fig. 17) in which the oval body is stalked and continued in front into a very high membranous bell-shaped collar. Other monads are certain human parasites, *i.e.*, *Cercomonas urinarius*, *C. intestinalis* and *Trichomonas vaginalis*.

The second family of monads are the *Astasiœa*. Here belong Astasia and Euglena (Fig. 18). The former genus is somewhat amœba-like in the changes which it undergoes, its body, according to Clark, during its amœboid retroversions becoming "contorted into a shapeless, writhing mass." They have a conspicuous, red so-called "eye-spot." A similar organ occurs in the zoospores of some algæ.

The third family of Flagellata, the *Peridinea*, is represented by Heteromastix, Dysteria, Pleuronema, Peridinium and Ceratium. Clark observes that Heteromastix is a transitional form connecting the Flagellata with the Ciliata or true Infusoria. Dysteria is still nearer to the Infusoria. Clark describes it as a two-shelled infusorian, with the open space between the shells provided with "a row of closely set, large vibratile cilia," with one larger than the others, the true flagellum. After a careful description of this organism he concludes that "in all the organization of this animal there is nothing which is not strictly infusorian in character. The jaw-like bodies are not confined to this alone, for there are quite a number of others which possess a similar apparatus at or near the mouth. Chilodon has a complete circle of straight rods around the mouth. As for the pivot it is nothing but a kind of stem, such as exists on a larger scale in Stentor, or is more particularly specialized in the pedestals of Epistylis, Zoothamnium, or Podophrya; and as counter to what we see in these last, I would state that there are certain of the Vorticellians closely related to Epistylis, which have no stem whatever, and swim about as freely as Dysteria."

The Monads are divided into three families, thus characterized by Claus in his "Grundzüge der Zoologie:"

1. *Monadina.* Body small, rounded, naked or with a tough membrane; resembling the zoospores of algæ, etc.

2. *Astasiœa.* Body naked and changeable like the monads, only bearing flagella.

3. *Peridinea.* Body having, besides the flagellum, a row of cilia.

Development. The common form of reproduction is by simple self-division. Clark describes this as he observed it in *Codosiga pulcherrimus* (Fig. 17, A). The act requires forty minutes. The first sign of fission is a bulging out of the collar, which becomes still more bell-shaped. The flagellum next disappears. Then marks of self-division appear in a narrow, slight furrow (Fig. 17, B, *e*), extending from the front half-way back along the middle of the body. Meanwhile the collar, which had become conical, expands, and, most striking change of all, two new flagella appear. Then the collar splits into two (Fig. 17), and soon the two new Codosigæ become perfected, when they split asunder, and become like the original Codosiga. Such is the usual mode of multiplication of the species in the monads.

A second mode, that of becoming encysted, has been rarely observed. Carter, so far as we are aware, was the first to attempt to trace the life history of a monad. We copy the following figures from his memoir. Fig. A represents two *Euglena viridis* in conjunction; *n*, the nucleus, *c*, contractile vesicle, and *r*, the red body; B and C the same after the breaking up of the contents into the embryonic zoospores. The two Euglenæ finally

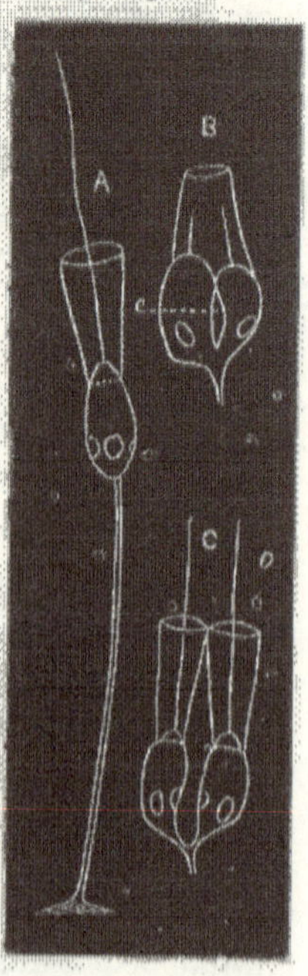

Fig. 17.

Fission of Codosiga.

Fig. 18.

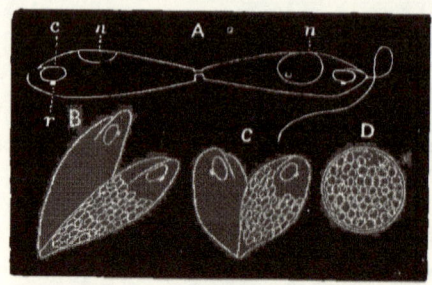

Development of Euglena viridis.

separate and each becomes spherical, encysted as at D. Fig. 18 illustrates the mode of development in *Euglena agilis*. A represents the adult Euglena, taken from the brackish water of marshes at Bombay; B, the resting stage, transverse division having taken place, and showing that the red body is not developed in the lower

Fig. 19.

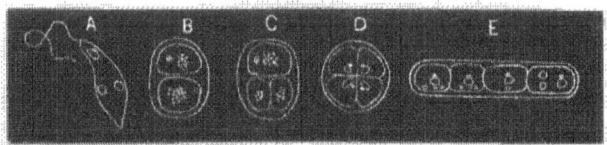

Development of Euglena agilis.

half; D, the same, with a quadruple longitudinal division, showing that the red body is equally multiplied; E, linear development, probably by longitudinal division, as the red body is present in each cell.

We copy a portion of the figures and account of the development of *Colpodella pugnax* as given by Cienkowski. Figure

Fig. 20.

Development of Colpodella.

20, A, represents this monad before taking food; B represents three Colpodellæ in the act of absorbing the nucleus of a Chlamydomonas; at C is a single Colpodella, without the nucleus, and much swollen anteriorly. Finally the Chlamydomonas is, as it were, eviscerated, nothing but the body walls being left. After this wholesale plundering of the contents of the Chlamydomonas, it then passes into a "cell" or encysted state, as at D (*a*, the mass of food, colored red). The contents of the cell then break up into a number of masses, as at E, which finally, as at F (the masses destined to change into zoospores), issue from the cyst in a mass surrounded by a thin membrane, which gradually disappears, when the free zoospores make off in every direction. G represents the encysted body of the monad, without the ball of food. He also shows that another unknown monad, a species of Bodo, and three species of Pseudospora also develop by becoming encysted.

Messrs. Dallinger and Drysdale describe in two unknown monads the process of encysting and the development of zoospores, the sarcode mass passing through a process resembling the segmentation of the egg into four, eight and many spheres, each sphere ultimately becoming a monad. The changes were noticed with greater fulness of detail in another unknown monad, Fig. 21, A. When about to pass into the encysted stage it became amœboid in its form, but still very active; at the stage B, however, it became spherical and quiet, and finally lost the flagellum,

Fig. 21.

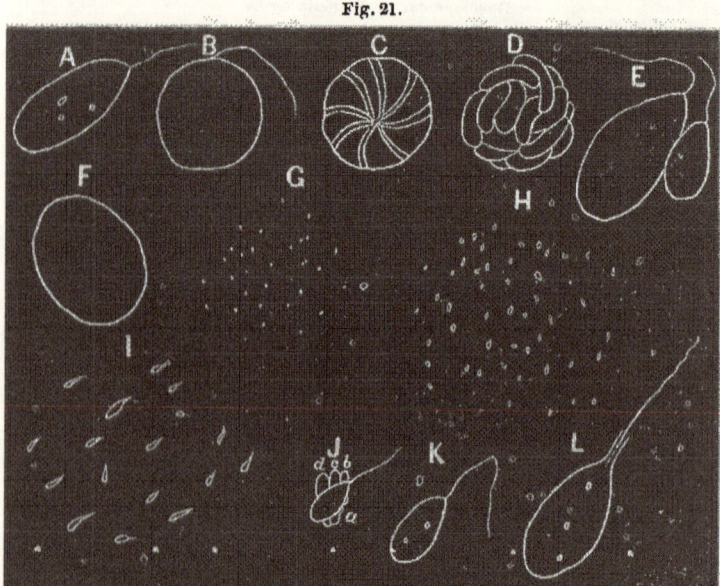

Development of a Monad.

and the contents suddenly divided into four portions, separated by a white cruciform mark or furrow. Then an intense activity pervaded the sarcode mass, "a sort of interior whirling motion" like the rushing of water "round the interior of a hollow glass sphere on its way to the jet of a fountain," as indicated at C. This action lasted from ten to seventy minutes, when it stopped and the mass broke up into small embryonic zoospores, as at D, which began a "quick writhing motion upon each other, like a knot of eels." After remaining in this state from seven to thirty minutes, they separated and swam away. Thus far they had passed through the ordinary mode of formation of young monads, but the authors noticed among the swarm of monads some much larger, and differing from the others in being very granular towards the flagellate end. These fastened themselves upon one of the smaller common forms, Fig. 21, E, and finally absorbed it, a process certainly analogous to, if not identical with, conjugation. It then assumed a resting condition, as at F. The sphere then opened slowly and a glairy looking fluid poured out. On careful examination of this fluid, with powers of 2500 to 5000 diameters, seven hours after emission tiny dots, semitransparent and yellowish, appeared as at G. In an hour and ten minutes the dots appeared as at H; after two hours more as at I. The sharp-pointed bodies at I became rounder, and from the pointed end a flagellum developed as at J, when they were ninety minutes older than at I. At this time "motion first showed itself; this, however, was not the motion usual to the monad, but a motion of horizontal vibration from *a* through *b* and *c*, to *d*, and then back again." It then swam away, became plump as in K and then was followed into the stages from A to E, the last figure (L) representing the complete monad, thus passing through two cycles of existence.

Three modes of development in the Flagellata seem therefore established, as follows:—

1. Simple fission.

2. The production of monads by encysting.

3. The production of monads by encysting and conjugation, with a resting stage and the production of excessively minute zoospores which grow, finally becoming normal monads.

It will be seen that these methods of increase are paralleled by those observed in the Monera, the Gregarinida and the Rhizopoda. It appears that there is here nothing like a sexual development, unless we have something analogous to it in the conjugation (?) of the monads described by Dallinger and Drysdale, but which they themselves do not call conjugation, merely confining themselves to a statement of the facts observed by them.

LITERATURE.

Carter. Notes on the Fresh Water Infusoria of the Island of Bombay. (Annals and Magazine of Natural History, Aug. and Sept., 1856.)

Cienskowski. Beitrage zur Kenntniss der Monaden. (Schultze's Archiv, 1, 1865.)

Clark. Spongiæ Ciliatæ as Infusoria Flagellata. (Memoirs Boston Society of Nat. Hist., 1867.)

Dallinger and Drysdale. Researches into the Life History of the Monads. (Monthly Microscopical Journal, 1871.)

VI. THE NOCTILUCÆ.

Tossed from one place to another among the Protozoa, we have now, thanks to the researches of Cienkowski, certain grounds for placing the Noctilucæ near, if not among the Flagellata, from the resemblance of the zoospores to the monads; while they seem to form a more highly developed type. It thus appears that by a study of the mode of growth of the Protozoa, as in the rest of the animal world, we can alone obtain correct ideas as to the affinities of the respective groups.

The Noctiluca (Fig. 22) is a highly phosphorescent organism, so small as scarcely to be seen with the naked eye, being from ·01

Fig. 22.

to ·04 inch in diameter. It occurs in great numbers on the surface of the sea. It has a nearly spherical jelly-like body, with a groove on one side from which issues a curved filament, used in locomotion. Near the base of this filament is the mouth, having on one side a tooth-like projection. Connecting with the mouth is an œsophagus which passes into the digestive cavity, in front of which lies an oval nucleus. Beneath the outer skin or firm membrane sur-

Noctiluca miliaris.

rounding the body is a gelatinous layer, containing numerous granules. A network of granular fibres arises from the granular layer; these fibres pass into the middle of the body to the nucleus and digestive cavity.

Development. Baddely had noticed a multiplication by division and reproduction by internal buds, and Busch had observed round, transparent disks, of the same size, consistence and optical properties as the Noctilucæ occurring among them, but could not determine what relations they bore to the former. It was, however, reserved for Cienkowski to trace the development of monad-like zoospores in these reproductive bodies. Fig. 23 represents these zoospores. They move about by a long flagellum. The tooth-like process (*s*) is thought by Cienkowski to be a rudimentary condition of the "whip" near the mouth of the adult Noctiluca. By keeping specimens in a drop of water on a thin glass which was placed over a moist chamber so as to ex-

Fig. 23.

Zoospores of Noctiluca.

elude all access of dry air to the water in which the animals were living, he was enabled to observe them for twelve hours. The stages he observed were—

" 1st. Noctiluca-like bodies, but without mouth or lash, and having a doubly spherical or so-called biscuit form, each partial sphere having a granular protoplasmic mass with fine branching rays, the two masses being connected more or less. 2d. The protoplasm connects so as to form a disk on one pole of the irregular double spheroid, which gradually becomes spherical, exhibiting three or four depressions at one pole. 3d. The formation of the disk is preceded by a segmentation of the entire mass of the protoplasm of the Noctilucæ into two, four, eight, sixteen, etc. parts, after which the disk begins to grow up on the surface of the Noctiluca. 4th. The protoplasmic disk sends out stumpy processes which project from the surface of the spheroid and exhibit peculiar wriggling movements. 5th. The mass commences to divide into smaller pieces, the vesicle being now quite spherical. The commencement of this division was not directly observed, but later stages, in which clumps of protoplasmic matter were seen arranged at first in groups of eight; these, then, were followed carefully through their division into groups of sixteen irregular, oblong particles. These products of division appear like denser, sharply-defined masses or nuclei, lying in a less dense surrounding granular plasma. 6th. The next stage was one of the first and most commonly observed, in which the protoplasmic disk, formed as above described, has become entirely split up into small oval bodies, each ·016 millimetre long. The aggregated mass of these oval spores sometimes appears as a disk at one pole of a Noctilucæa-like vesicle, or as a girdle passing round it. 7th. By high powers each oval particle is seen to have a terminal cilium, and whilst under observation many were seen to separate from the disk and swim about as free swarm-spores " (Fig. 23).

Cienkowski also observed the fusion of two Noctilucæ. " The two animals place themselves with the two so-called 'oral apertures' close to one another, and through these a protoplasmic bridge is formed, which unites the nuclei of the two individuals. Later, at the points of contact, the outlines of the two Noctiluca-vesicles fuse, and thus the double-spheroid or biscuit-shaped bladders are formed. By further fusion the pinching in of the vesicle disappears from one side, so that the vesicle becomes more nearly spherical. Meanwhile the two nuclei become completely fused into one, retaining, however, their radiating threads and network, as in normal individuals. The cross-striped 'lashes' and the 'teeth' of the two fused Noctilucæ also disappear. All trace of the double origin of these 'copulated Noctilucæ' may pass away by the disappearance of the fold on the surface, near to which the nucleus lies, and thus a Noctiluca vesicle is formed, which is always larger than the normal Noctiluca, and seems identical with the bodies noticed by Busch, and also very probably identical with the biscuit-shaped and spherical Noctiluca vesicles in which Cienkowski has traced the formation of the swarm-spores. A direct observation of the formation of swarm-spores in the copulated forms Cienkowski was not able to obtain."

This fusion of two Noctilucæ is not, however, essential for the production of zoospores, as they appear whether conjugation has occurred or not. When it does occur, however, it seems to be of a sexual nature. Conjugation, though by no means necessary, does frequently take place, and "as in the fusion of the zoospores of Myxomycetæ, and the copulation of Actinophrys, and others, leads to an augmentation of the mass of the protoplasm." "Zoospores," he adds, "occur in quite small Noctilucæ, which certainly could not be the product of the fusion of two individuals. Sometimes the zoospores develop very rapidly whilst still in the disk, and their protoplasm becomes differentiated into a nucleus and radiating threads." Cienkowski considers that the zoospores of Noctiluca decide the systematic position which must be assigned to this organism. It seems to him that they are animals of large dimensions belonging to the division of the Flagellata.

A single mode of growth, therefore, occurs in Noctiluca, *i.e.* development from zoospores.

LITERATURE.

Busch. Das Meerleuchten und die Noctiluca (in Beobachtungen über Anatomie und Entwicklung einiger wirbellosen Seethiere. 1851).

Huxley. On the Structure of Noctiluca miliaris. (Quart. Journal Mic. Sci., 1855.)

Quatrefages. Observations sur les Noctiluques. (Annales des Science Nat., 1850, and Annals Nat. Hist., 1853.)

Cienkowski. Schwärmerbildung bei Noctiluca miliaris. (Schultze's Archiv, 1871. Translation in Annals and Magazine Natural History, 1871. See also 1872, p. 414.)

VII. THE INFUSORIA (CILIATA).

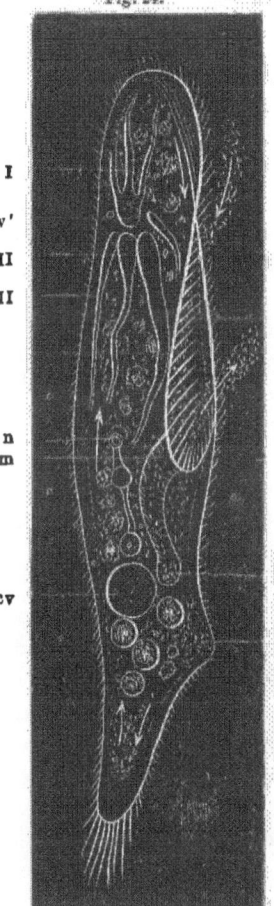

Fig. 24.

Paramecium.

THOUGH the term Infusoria has usually been applied to nearly all the Protozoa provided with cilia or flagella, it is now restricted to the highest division of the Protozoa. Instead of an attempt to define the group, the following brief description of some of the well-known forms will perhaps best show how they differ from the Flagellata, with which they are most apt to be confounded.

One of the simplest and most abundant forms is Paramecium. The accompanying figure (24), copied from Clark's "Mind in Nature," represents *Paramecium caudatum*, of Ehrenberg.[5] This animalcule is a mass of protoplasm, representing, perhaps, a cell. In the body-mass are excavated a mouth and a throat leading to a so-called stomach or digestive cavity. Two hollows in the body form the contractile vesicles, and another cavity forms the reproductive organ. Prolongations of the body-mass form the cilia, which characterize the Infusoria and give their name, Ciliata. No specialized tissues composed of cells exist in these organisms, and they are regarded as on the whole representing a single cell. Some authors, as Claparède, regard them as composed of several cells, but the whole animal, though performing functions nearly

[5] Fig. 24. A view from the dorsal side, magnified 340 diameters. H, the head: T, the tail; *m*, the mouth; *m* to *g*, the throat; *a*, the posterior opening of the digestive cavity; cv^1, the anterior and *cv*, posterior contractile vesicles; I, II, III, the radiating canals of cv^1; *n*, the reproductive organ; *v*, the large vibrating cilia at the edge of the vestibule. —After H. J. Clark.

as complicated as those of sponges, low worms and radiates which have bodies composed of many cells, should be regarded as made up of indifferent or unorganized sarcode or protoplasm, somewhat like that of the bodies of the embryos of the higher animals in their earliest stages.

Paramecium has an elongated, oval body "with one end (H) flattened out broader than the other, and twisted about one-third way round, so that the flattened part resembles a very long figure 8." In this form, as in Stentor (Fig. 25), as Clark remarks, "we have the mouth at the bottom of a broad notch or incurvation, and the contractile vesicle on the opposite side, next the convex back, whilst the general cavity of the body lies between these two." The arrows in the figure represent the course of the particles of indigo with which Clark fed his specimens, "as they are whirled along, by the large vibrating cilia (v) of the edge of the disk, against the vestibule of the mouth." During the circuit the food is digested, a mass of *rejectamenta* is formed near the protuberance, a, which has appeared a short time before. This finally opens, allows the rejected matter to pass out and then closes over, leaving no trace of an outlet. This and other Infusoria seem, then, to have a definite digestive tract, hollowed out of the parenchyma of the body.

"The system," says Clark, "which is analogous to the blood circulation of the higher animals, is represented in Paramecium by two contractile vesicles (cv, cv^1, I, II, III), both of which have a degree of complication which, perhaps, exceeds that of any other similar organ" in these animals. When fully expanded they appear round, as at cv; but when contracted they appear, observes Clark, as "fine radiating streaks, and as the main portion lessens they gradually broaden and swell until the former is emptied and nearly invisible, and they are extended over half the length of the body. In this condition they might be compared to the arterial vessels of the more elevated classes of animals, but they would at the same time represent the veins, since they serve at the next moment to return the fluid to the main reservoir again, which is effected in this very remarkable way." The contents of these vesicles is a clear fluid.

The reproductive organ in Paramecium is a small tube (n), only seen at the reproductive period when the eggs (n) are fully grown. Clark says that the eggs are arranged in it "in a single line, one after the other, at varying distances." It usually lies in the midst of the body, and extends from one-half to two-thirds of the length

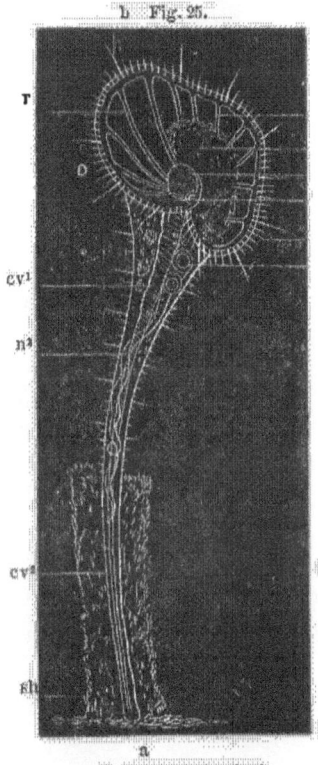

Trumpet Animalcule.

of the animal. "According to Balbiani's observations upon a closely allied species, when the eggs are laid they pass out from the ovary through an aperture near the mouth" (Clark).

In the Trumpet animalcule (Fig. 25, *Stentor polymorphus* of Ehrenberg, after Clark[6]) we have a higher grade of development than in Paramecium, the animalcule attaching itself at one end, and building up a slight tube in which it contracts when disturbed; an anticipation in nature of the worm in its tube. Prof. Clark has studied in this animalcule certain circular bands within the edge of the disk, from which arise twelve very thin stripes (*rr*) which converge towards the mouth (*m*). These bands are evidently, he says, in close relation with the mouth and cilia, the most active organs of the animal, and he concludes that it is a nervous system.

The most complicated form of all among the Infusoria is the Vorticella, or bell-shaped animalcule. These animals are very common on submerged plants and leaves, appearing to the naked eye like mould. Their motions, as they suddenly contract and then

[6] "*Stentor polymorphus*, magnified 130 diameters, expanded and bent slightly over towards the observer; the mouth, *m*, next the eye, and the dorsal edge in the distance. *a*, posterior end; *sh*, the tube enclosing a; *c*, the ciliated border of the disk (*s*); *b*, the larger, rigid cilia; *cv*, the contractile vesicle in the extreme distance, seen through the whole thickness of the body; *cv¹*, *cv²*, the posterior prolongation of *cv*, in the distance; *r*, *r¹*, the circular and radiating branches of the nervous system; *n*, *n¹*, the reproductive system, extending from the right side, at *n*, posteriorly, but towards the eye at *n¹* (Clark).

shoot out their bell, mounted on a long stalk, are very interesting.
They form the most available and
attractive infusoria for study and
amusement. The throat is quite distinct, while the nucleus is the most
conspicuous organ of the body. The
digestive cavity is "one vast hollow," in which the whole mass of food
revolves in a determinate channel
(Clark). In fact, so highly developed are these Infusoria that they
seem to anticipate certain low worms
to which they bear a certain resemblance, and indicate that the worms
may have sprung either from the Infusoria or early organisms like them.

Bütschli claims to have discovered
that lasso cells like those in the
Hydra and jelly fishes are developed
in a certain infusorium named by him
Polykrikos.

The Infusoria may be divided into
three groups; 1, represented by Paramecium; 2, by Vaginicola and
Vorticella, and 3, by Acineta (Fig. 28,
H). This latter form is not ciliated,
the body is stalked and in front prolonged into slender suckers,
each terminating in a mouth. At one time Stein supposed that
the Vaginicola or Vorticella passed into an "Acineta-form," but
Claparède disproved this and Stein retracted his opinion.

Development. The different modes of development among the
Infusoria are still involved in doubt. The best observers have
advanced theories that have appeared sound, and then revoked
them. All agree, however, that the simplest and commonest mode
of development is fission, a process analogous to the ordinary

Fig. 26.

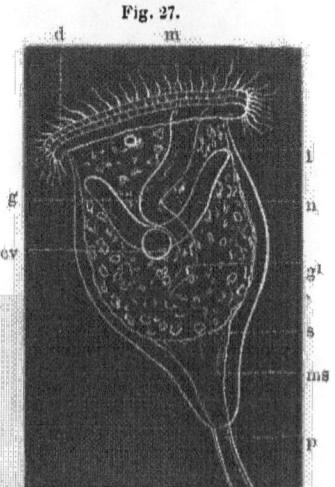
Fig. 27.

Bell-shaped Animalcule,
natural size; and one enlarged.

[7] Fig. 26 "*Epistylis flavicans* Ehr., a single, many-forked colony of bell animalcules, slightly magnified. Fig. 27, one of the animalcules magnified 250 diameters. *p*, the stem; *d*. the flat spiral of vibrating cilia at the edge of the disk; *ms*, the muscle; *m* to *s*, the depth of the digestive cavity; *m*, the mouth, *g*, *g¹*, the throat; *l*, the single vibratory lash, which projects from the depths of the throat; *cv*, the contractile vesicle; *n*, the reproductive organ" (Clark).

self-division of the nucleus of eggs, and the primary mode of
growth in both animals and plants, not involving the idea of sex.

As a good example of *fission*, by which all Infusoria are supposed to multiply their kind, though some may at certain times
reproduce from eggs, we may cite a case observed by Clark, the
full account of which is given in his admirable "Mind in Nature."
He observed a *Stentor polymorphus* divide in two.   The first
change taking place is in the contractile vesicle, which divides into
two distinct vesicles.   The mouth of the new Stentor is formed in
the middle of the under side, first appearing as a shallow pit,
around which arises a semicircle of vibratile cilia.   The new
mouth deepens, the throat is hollowed out; all this taking place
before any external sign of division appears.   But in the course
of two hours the body splits asunder, and two new individuals
appear, each exactly like the other.

In Vaginicola there is a modification of this simple process,

Fig. 28.

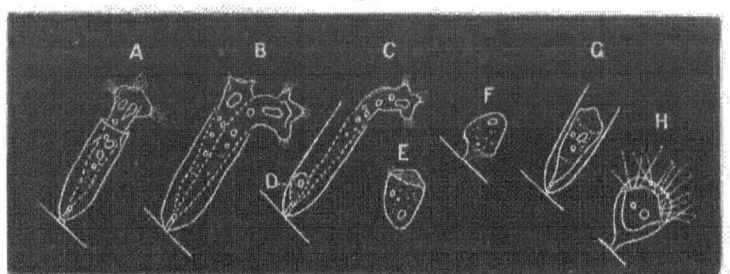

Development of Vaginicola.

which is more like true gemmation or budding, and is accompanied
by a process of encysting. Our figures of the mode of development
are taken from a short paper by C. J. Müller. He first traced
the fission of this infusorium (Fig. 28, A), which takes place in
the following manner. After the animal has withdrawn within
its case, and assumed a pear-shaped form, its cilia, meanwhile,
apparently lost, a conical fissure appears at the base, and soon
after "a wavy line of division shows itself at the upper extremity
of the animalcule;" the two fissures enlarge and meet; pulsating
vesicles become active on both sides of the line of fission, and
cilia begin to grow out, until at the end of an hour, two separate
animals are formed, which soon afterwards appear as in Fig. 28, B.

Now begins a new process; the production of a free swimming embryo. On one of the two Vaginicolas is developed "a delicate ring or band at about one-third its length from the lower extremity." Then it contracts in its cell, becomes quiet (as in Fig. 28, C, D) and from the ring or band develops a new circle of cilia, the former ones having disappeared. It then swims off as at Fig. 28, E, darting about rapidly until it attaches itself to a piece of Conferva, as at Fig. 28, F. After some hours, perhaps twenty, a fringe of cilia begins to appear on the upper end, the old ones begin to be absorbed, and the tube arises, as at Fig. 28, G, and a new Vaginicola appears. Stein had some years previous made similar observations on *Vaginicola crystallina* Ehr., and thought he had traced their further development into a form resembling Acineta (Fig. 28, H), but this proved afterwards to be a young parasitic Acineta, a suctorial Infusorian.

We have seen that Vaginicola passes through a resting stage, withdrawing into the case in which it lives, and being for a time inactive. Stein has shown that all the Vorticellinæ " at an earlier or later stage of their development become encysted, by drawing in their ciliated disk and contracting their bodies into a ball; at the same time secreting around themselves a gelatinous mass which solidifies into a firmer elastic covering." Fig. 29, G, after Stein, shows a Vorticella thus encysted. After becoming thus encysted the interior becomes homogeneous, as in Fig. 29, H. From this cyst the Vorticellæ arise directly.

Now a second mode of development, and the simplest, has been observed by Stein, *i. e.*, that of monad-like young which result from the breaking up of the cyst. While examining a cyst Stein observed that it burst, and the free contents " remained as a round, transparent limpid drop of jelly, of about the same diameter as the cyst, in which some thirty embryos, of the form of *Monas colpoda* or *Monas scintillans*, sailed about with varied and active motion, as if in a little ocean." These embryos resulted from the breaking up of the band-like nucleus. This breaking up did not take place " by successive acts of division, but in the nucleus, round disks become marked off contemporaneously, at the most distant points; whilst the intermediate substance of the nucleus becomes re-absorbed."

It thus seems that the Ciliata pass through a flagellate or monad condition. Stein regards the above described propagation by the change of the whole inner encysted body of a Vorticella into numerous embryos, as the equivalent of the sexual propagation of the higher animals. We also quote Stein's summary of the cycle of changes undergone by the Vorticella: "We may thus ideally arrange the different stages of development through which the *Vorticellæ* pass; the largest end their lives by becoming encysted; the whole of the contents of their bodies then passes into embryos, to which the dividing germ-nucleus first gives origin.

"The embryos become fixed, develop from their posterior extremity a stalk, which is at first not contractile, and gradually change their monad-like bodies into that of a common Vorticella.

"As soon as this has taken place, their very much smaller size only distinguishes them from the perfect Vorticellæ. Even in this imperfect condition they frequently multiply by continual division and in a subordinate degree by external gemmation. This power of multiplication in the imperfect state, however, is one of the most certain criteria that we have to do with an alternation of generations. * * * * Finally, the last generation become encysted, not to re-awake to an independent existence, but to break up into a swarm of embryos."

Let us now look at the development of *Epistylis plicatilis* as studied by Claparède. Fig. 29, A, represents an individual con-

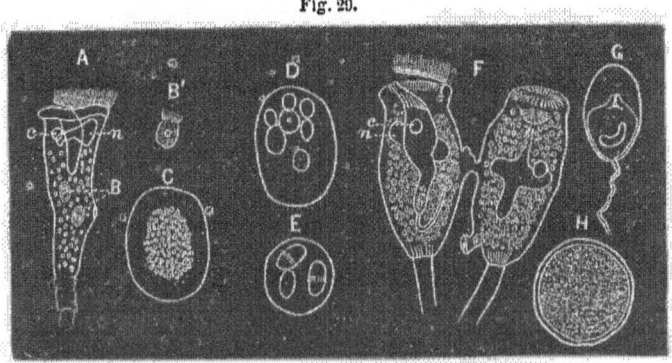

Development of Epistylis.

taining several embryos (B) and opposite the lower one on the right side is a projection, through which the embryo at B' has passed out. The specimen figured at B' is a fair example of the embryos of species belonging to six families of Infusoria, and may, perhaps, serve as a typical example of most Infusoria at the time of birth. This young stage may, then, be contrasted with the embryos of the Flagellata, which are of a much simpler form, resembling the zoospores of the algæ and lower Protozoa.

The embryos of the Infusoria arise from the nucleus, which corresponds to the ovary of the higher animals. The nucleus is a curved, oblong, oval body, represented in Figs. 29, A, n; 30, E. When the Epistylis is about to reproduce its young, the nucleus sends off a portion which enlarges until it assumes the appearance indicated by Fig. 29, C. It has become round, and contains a central, granular mass, from which the embryos arise. At Fig. 29, D, is a globular mass, detached from the nucleus, and containing several embryos in the first state of development. Fig. 29, E, represents the embryos provided with a circle of cilia, and nearly ready to swim about freely. Claparède did not watch their further development, but thought it probable that they grew directly into the Epistylis form.

What is the meaning of conjugation in the Infusoria is not clearly understood. Whether it is analogous to sexual union is not certainly known, but it is now thought by Balbiani that the smaller individuals found conjugating with the larger are males, and he even thinks that some Infusoria contain spermatozoa. Fig. 29 represents an Epistylis conjugating, each one provided with two buds; the bud of the individual on the left is conjugated with that of the individual on the right hand. Epistylis also passes through encysted stages as indicated at Fig. 29, G and H.

The same mode of development was observed by Claparède in

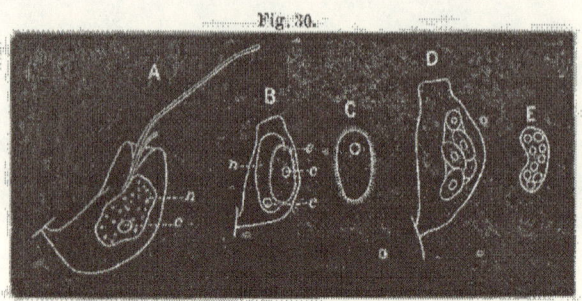

Fig. 30.

Development of Urnula.

a parasite of the Epistylis, $i.\ e.$, *Urnula epistylidis* (Fig. 30), which, besides reproducing by fission, also produces ciliated young. Fig. 30, B, *e*, represents the ciliated young within the body of the parent, B; Fig. 30, C, the free swimming ciliated young. In another specimen Claparède observed the interior of the body subdivide into several masses, as at Fig. 30, D. These masses increase in size and become filled with a number of small corpuscles, with active movements, which finally press through the walls of the Urnula. These are probably spermatozoa, as Stein considers Urnula as the male of Epistylis, contrary to the opinion of Claparède, who regarded it as a Rhizopod, though its ciliated young is, in the light of later studies, sufficient to prove that it is a ciliate infusorian.

As to the sexuality of the Infusoria, Balbiani has advanced the idea that they are in reality hermaphrodite, the nucleus representing the ovary, and the nucleolus the testis, the latter producing bodies which he regards as spermatozoa. Claparède regards this view as well founded, as it had already been suggested by himself, Lieberkühn, J. Müller and Stein that certain Infusoria contained spermatic particles, found not only in the nucleolus, but also in the nucleus, into which they had penetrated from the nucleolus. This has been observed in Paramecium, where, as Claparède quotes as Stein's opinion, "Fecundation having been accomplished, these zoosperms disappear, and the nucleus then divides in a manner comparable to the segmentation of the egg into a certain number of segments, or reproductive bodies, destined each to give rise to an embryo. The Infusoria, then," adds Claparède, " are androgynous."

It appears, also from the observations of Balbiani, that the Infusoria, as Stentor, Paramecium, Vorticella, etc., have true eggs, each egg consisting of "two hollow membranous spheres, the smaller being enclosed within the other, and separated from it by a considerable interval." The smaller vesicle he regards as the germinal vesicle, and the larger as the vitelline membrane. After the fecundation, "at the end of four or five days, the development of the eggs is complete, and each, with the aid of reagents, displays in a very distinct manner its characteristic elements, namely, vitelline membrane, vitellus, germ-vesicle and germ-spot." Bütschli, however, it should be stated, denies that Infusoria produce spermatozoids which fertilize the nucleus. As to the development of the Acinetæ, self-fission is in them very rare, while conjugation is very frequent.

There are, then, two modes of development among the Infusoria (Ciliata) :—

1. By fission.

2. By production of internal ciliated embryos arising from eggs.

We have, then, for the first time among the Protozoa, if the observations of Balbiani be correct (though this is denied by good observers), truly sexual animals, producing true eggs and spermatic particles. The same animal reproduces both by fission and by the production of ciliated embryos. Most of them before producing embryos undergo fission. This is comparable to the alternation of generations among the Hydroids, Aphides, etc.

LITERATURE.

Ehrenberg. Die Infusionsthiere als vollkommene Organismen, 1838.

Dujardin. Infusoires, 1841.

Stein. Infusionsthiere auf ihre Entwicklungsgeschichte untersucht. 1854.

—— Untersuchungen über die Entwickelung der Infusorien. (Wiegmann's Archiv. 1849.)

—— Der Organismus des Infusorien. 1867.

Claparède und *Lachmann.* Études sur les Infusoires et les Rhizopodes (Memoires de l'Institut National Genevois, 1858–61).

Balbiani. Recherches sur les Phénomènes sexuels des Infusoires. (Brown-Séqnard's Journal de la Physiologie. 1861. Translated in Quart. Journ. Mier. Science. 1862.)

Clark. Mind in Nature. 1865.

Everts. Untersuchungen an Vorticella nebulifera. (Siebold and Kölliker's Zeitschrift, 1873.)

VIII. THE SPONGIÆ (PORIFERA)

We now come to animals whose bodies are composed of numerous cells, and which produce true eggs, sometimes even with a thin calcareous shell, and genuine sperm cells. The embryo sponge arises from eggs which undergo a total segmentation of the yolk. The free swimming larva later in its life becomes fixed, loses its external cilia, but retains its cellular walls, now composed of two layers, which are supported by silicious or calcareous needles or spicules developed in the inner layer.

To regard such an organism as a Protozoan, or even to compare it with a compound Radiolarian such as Sphærozoum, with its silicious spicules and aggregations of one-celled organisms, would not seem warranted. We have, in fact, in the light of the anatomical investigations of Lieberkühn, Carter and Clark, and the combined anatomical and embryological studies of Hæckel, Metschnikoff and Carter, no grounds for leaving them among the Protozoa. Indeed, one of the most striking illustrations of the value

of a knowledge of the early history of an organism is afforded
by the embryology of the sponge. Hæckel's discovery that the
larval sponge is a planula, though not homologous with the embryo polype or jelly-fish, enables the naturalist to at once decide
that the sponge is not a Protozoan, but belongs to a type only less
highly organized than the lower polypes, and with more analogy
to the Radiates than the Protozoa.

If, under the guidance of the results of the studies of Lieberkühn, Carter, Clark, and particularly of Hæckel and Metschnikoff,

Fig. 31.

Fig. 32.

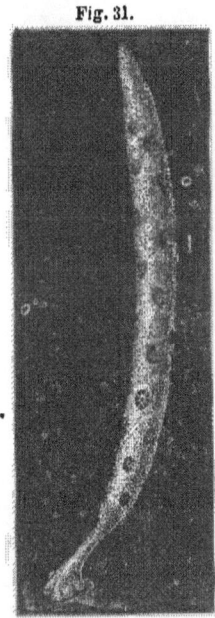

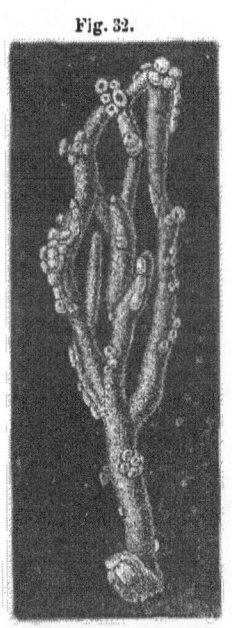

Axinella polypoides.

Axinella, with a parasitic
polype, 2-3 natural size. After Schmidt.

we examine the structure of a sponge, we shall find that in its
simplest form it is a hollow, vertical cylinder, fastened by its base,
with the mouth opening upwards from a central gastro-vascular
cavity, with ciliated epithelial cells lining the cavity, and possessing a surprising degree of individuality. There are usually several mouths, and the cavity usually opens into a labyrinth of
chambers connected by passages through the cellular tissue; these
round chambers being lined with ciliated epithelial cells. This

body is supported by a basket-work of interlaced needles of silica or lime, developed in the inner layer of cells of the larva.

Such, in brief, is the sponge. Does the fact that in the simplest, immature forms, we have quite a regular body-wall and a single cavity, compel us to range the sponges side by side and in the same natural division with the polypes and jelly-fishes, in the

Fig. 33.

Fig. 35.

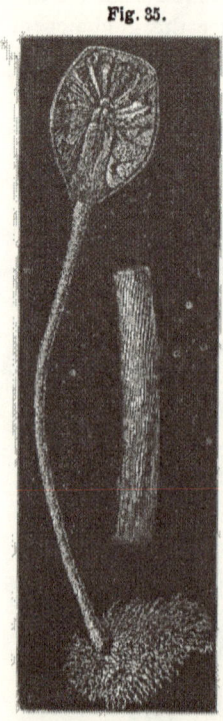

Tethilla polyura. After Schmidt.

Hyalonema boreale. Nat. size; with part of stem enlarged. After Lovén.

typical forms of which the central cavity acts as a true stomach and the outlet surrounded with tentacles acts as a mouth? Metschnikoff has shown that it would seem to be a violation of the existing principles of classification to place together animals so unlike. The sponges apparently represent a class lower than, but possibly equivalent, systematically, to the polypes and jelly-fishes.

Currents of water, created by the cilia and bearing along particles of food, enter through the system of mouths, and when the food is absorbed by the cells of the inner lining, they pass out through the larger openings. Both the larger and smaller "mouths" are capable of opening and closing.

The eggs and sperm cells are scattered at irregular intervals among the cells composing the body-walls; the spermatozoa are

Fig. 34.

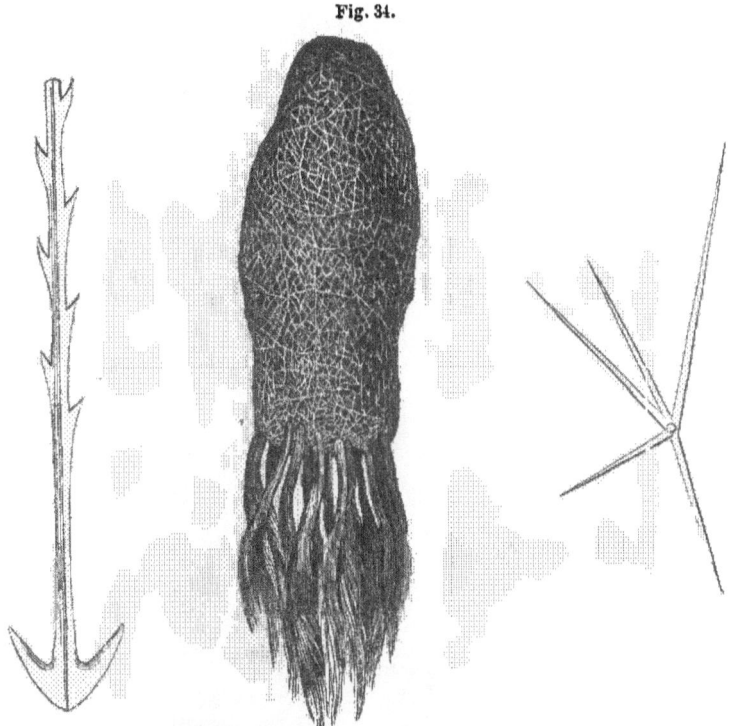

Pheronema Annæ and spicules. After Leidy.

in some species developed in "mother" cells, as in many of the higher animals.

The sponges are by Hæckel regarded as closely allied to the Hydroid polypes, members of the Cœlenterates, a division formed by Leuckart, including the polypes and acalephs. His reasons are based on the fact that the sponges are made up of two layers of cells (ectoderm and entoderm, or outer and inner layer) surrounding a central cavity, and that both reproduce by eggs and spermatozoa, and pass through a Gastrula ("planula") stage.

Fig. 37.

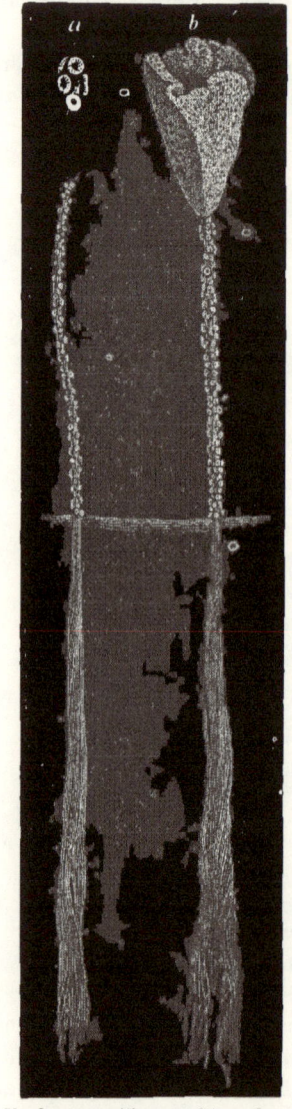

Hyalonema with parasitic polypes, embedded half its length in the mud. After Gray.

Gegenbaur and some English naturalists have endorsed this view. Hæckel goes so far as to state that the only character ex-

Fig. 38.

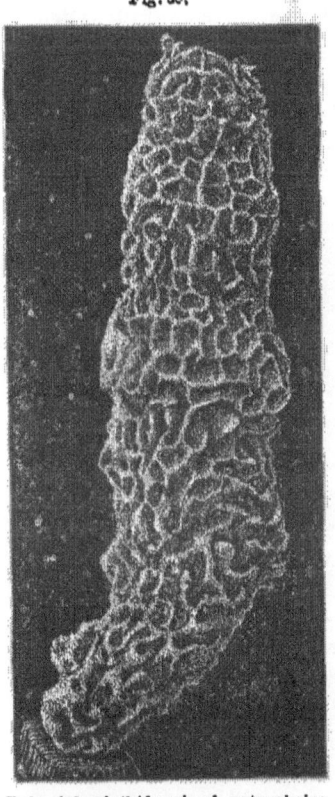

Tuba labyrinthiformis, ⅓ natural size.
After Lütken.

Fig. 39.

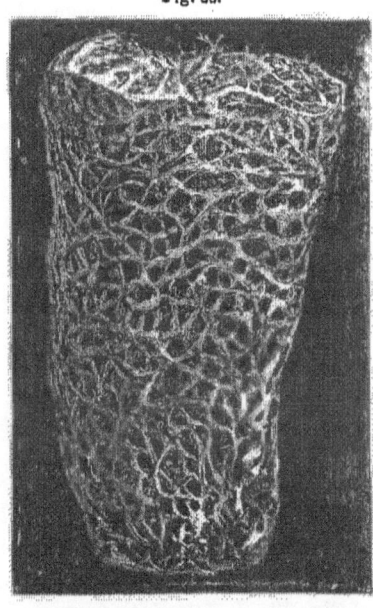

Corbitella, ⅔ natural size. After Lütken.

cluding the sponges from the Cœlenterates is the want of lasso cells,[8] but we have seen that the true Infusoria possess them.

---

[8] Eimer claims to have found true lasso cells in Reniera, a sponge observed by him at Capri; but Carter attributes their presence to a parasitic polype which he detected in this sponge. Eimer on other grounds claims that he has discovered a sponge which affords a passage into the Hydroids. "In an Esperia,'in another silicious sponge allied to Myxilla, and in a horny sponge, the surface is studded with small chitinous tubes, which are external prolongations of a similar investment of the whole channel-system, becoming, however, more delicate below, and finally passing into a sarcode-like condition; each of these tubes is inhabited by a retractile, sac-like body, provided with ectoderm, a muscular layer, and entoderm, with thread cells, and with 6-12 long, unbranched tentacles, with cilia and thread cells; below, they pass successively into the common sponge-substance, and generally lie four in each channel, each, however, with

Metschnikoff has, however, shown that there is no true homology between the sponges and Radiates.

The sponges are divided into (1) the *Myxospongiæ*, represented by Halisarea; (2) the *Fibrospongiæ*, or the silicious sponges, represented by Axinella (Fig. 31, *A. polypoides;* 32, another species of Axinella), the fresh water Spongilla; Thethya; Tethilla (Fig. 33, *T. polyura*); Pheronema (Fig. 34, *P. Annæ* and spines); the glass sponges, such as Hyalonema (*H. boreale*, Fig. 35, from the

Fig. 40.

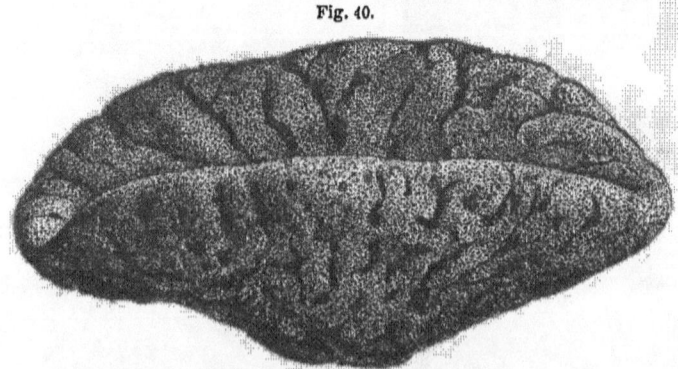

Dactyocalyx pumicea. After Lütken.

Arctic Ocean; Fig. 36, *H. Sieboldii;* Fig. 37, another Hyalonema, anchored in the mud by its silicious threads) the Venus flower basket, or *Euplectella aspergillum* from the Philippines; the Tuba (Fig. 38, *T. labyrinthiformis*) from the West Indies; the Corbitella from the Moluccas (Fig. 39); and Dactyocalyx (Fig. 40, *D. pumicea*[9]) from the West Indies. The third division of sponges comprises the calcareous sponges (*Calcispongiæ*), represented by the Sycon (*Sycandra ciliata*, Fig. 41), a common little white sponge found on our shores, and in the North Atlantic generally.

its own special chitinous tube. In other sponges (Renierœ) these polypoids were found in a lower stage of evolution, with short or absent tentacles, thread-cells present or wanting, no muscular layer, chitinous investment sometimes strongly developed, annular and projecting—in other instances reduced to a delicate, almost sarcode-like membrane, or almost totally wanting. The idea of parasitism is, according to the author, quite out of the question; the 'polypoids' he constantly regards as the true nutritive zooids of the sponge, and the sponges in which they occur in a more rudimentary shape as intermediate forms, leading to the great majority of sponges without nutritive zooids of any kind." Lütken in Zoological Record for 1872. London, 1874.

[9] This and Figs. 31-33, 35-41 were kindly loaned me by Dr. C. F. Lütken, of the Royal Zoological Museum at Copenhagen. They are from the Tidsskrift for Populære Fremstillinger af Naturvidenskaben. 1871.

Development. Lieberkühn made the astonishing discovery, confirmed by Hæckel, that sponges were really hermaphrodite animals

Fig. 41.

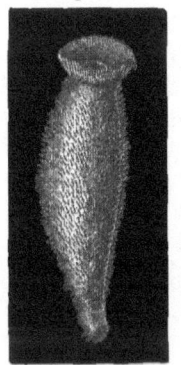

reproducing by eggs and sperm cells developed in the same individual sponge. Hæckel showed that they were probably developed from the inner (endodermal) layer of cells forming the body, being simply modifications of these endodermal cells, much as the eggs of the higher animals are modified epithelial cells. Fig. 42, from Hæckel, shows one of these cells (of *Sycortes quadrangulata*) with several spermatozoa mingling their protoplasmic contents with the protoplasm of the egg itself.

Sycandra ciliata, a calcareous sponge enlarged. After Schmidt.

The endodermal cell transforms into an egg, according to Hæckel, in the following manner. At first provided with a "collar" and flagellum much as in the Codosiga figured on page 27, it begins to draw these in until they disappear; then a nucleus (nucleolinus) appears within the nucleolus of the cell. The egg soon becomes detached from the body wall, and moves about, sometimes penetrating into the exoderm, or "emigrating, in the oviparous species, from the ' stomach' to be fecundated abroad."

Fig. 42.

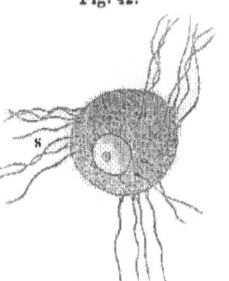

"The spermatozoa are apparently developed through repeated divisions of modified endodermal cells; the 'head' is formed by the 'nucleus,' the tail by the protoplasm of the minute sperm-cells."

After fecundation of the egg, it begins to undergo self-division, splitting into two, four, eight, sixteen, etc., nucleolinated cells (Fig 43, total seg-

Fusion of spermatic particles with egg of sponge. After Hæckel.

Fig. 43.

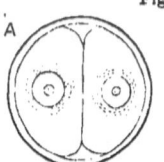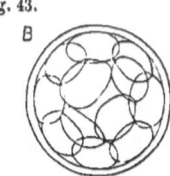

mentation of eggs of Halisarca), the process being exactly as in the eggs of nearly all the higher animals including man. This stage of segmentation, like the mulberry mass of the egg after segmentation in the higher ani-

Segmentation of egg of sponge.

mals, Hæckel terms the Morula stage (from its likeness to the mulberry, Morus; see Fig. 43, after Carter). The cells of the

Morula afterwards become separated into two kinds, a few remaining round, the majority becoming long and prismatic, and provided each with a cilium (flagellum), by means of which it swims about and looks like a "planula" or larval jelly-fish. This stage Hæckel consequently calls the "Planula" stage. The next step is the formation of a "stomach" or internal cavity in the body of the ciliated larva. This stage Hæckel calls Gastrula. Fig. 44, from Hæckel, represents the gastrula of *Leuculmis echinus*, as seen in optical section, the outer layer (ec-

Fig. 44.

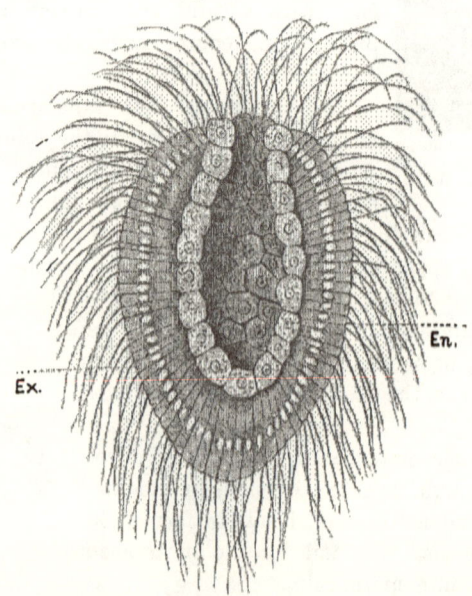

Larva of a Sponge (gastrula).

toderm) being composed of long prismatic, nucleated cells (*ex*) provided with a lash, while the cells (*en*) of the lining (endoderm) of the cavity are much larger and rounder.[10] After swimming about for a time it becomes fixed by the end of the body to some object, the cavity finally opening out by a mouth. The external cilia now disappear, and others become developed in the cells lining the interior of the cavity.[11] Afterwards the true sponge char-

---

[10] Metschnikoff shows that this "entoderm" is really an invaginated portion of Hæckel's "ectoderm."

[11] Metschnikoff observed on the contrary that the ciliated external cells are withdrawn in the process of growth and line the cavity.

acter of the organism is revealed. The body-wall becomes perforated with pores, which open into the general cavity of the body, while currents of water are maintained by means of the cilia, and flow out through the so-called mouth. This is the "Protospongia" state, and when spicules of silex or lime are developed to strengthen the walls of the body, the young sponge is termed by Hæckel, the " Olynthus."

Thus, following the course of development as Hæckel supposed to be the case with the calcareous sponges, for he, as Metschnikoff remarks, did not actually observe the stages after the formation of the ciliated larva, we obtain a very clear idea of the typical structure of the sponge. I cannot do better than employ the condensed account of the discoveries of Hæckel given by Dr. Lütken in the "Zoological Record" for 1872, with a few corrections taken from Metschnikoff's paper. The Olynthus, the simplest type of the sponge, is a " cylindrical, clavate or pyriform, etc., tube, closed at the extremity by which it is affixed, commonly open by a ' mouth' at the other ; the body-wall, enclosing the 'gastric' cavity, is a thin membrane composed of the two layers named above—the 'syncytium' or exoderm [Metschnikoff's inner layer] a mass of sarcodine with nuclei, the cells of which are so completely fused together that the original cellular structure cannot be made visible through any chemical reaction ; if torn mechanically, the fragments will, whether containing one or more or no nuclei, take the shape of Amœbæ and walk about. In this layer[12] the spicula are developed, chiefly of three types — simple, 3-radiate and 4-radiate, anchor-shaped spicula are rare (*Syculmis synapta*, anchoring the animal in the mud bottom) ; the stellate spicula sometimes occurring are foreign bodies, belonging originally to Didemnia (Ascidiæ). The spicula are invested with a delicate sheath of condensed sarcodine ; they contain an axial filament, and are composed of concentric layers, like the silicious spicula ; chemically they are composed partly of CO_2, CaO, partly of an organic substance ('spiculin'). The endodermal cells are, like certain flagellate Infusoria, provided with a collar and flagellum ; they contain a 'nucleus' (with 'nucleolus'), and often one or two contractile 'vacuola' (water drops) ; though without 'mouth,' they both 'drink' and 'eat,' or receive

---

[12] Metschnikoff shows that the spicules really arise from the inner layer.

into their interior, not only fluid, but also minutely diffused solid matter (*e. g.*, carmine), probably through the soft exoplasm between the collar and flagellum. Liberated artificially, they also assume amœboid shapes and motions. On the endodermal cells devolve the whole of the nutritive (digestive, respiratory and secretory) functions; and there can be little doubt that both eggs and spermatozoa are modified endodermal cells."

Hæckel did not observe the development of the larva, his gastrula, into the young sponge. This gap has been filled by Metschnikoff. He observed the course of development in *Sycon ciliatum* (Fig. 45) from the segmentation of the yolk, through the larval state, up to the time when the sponge is fixed and the spicules are

Fig. 45.

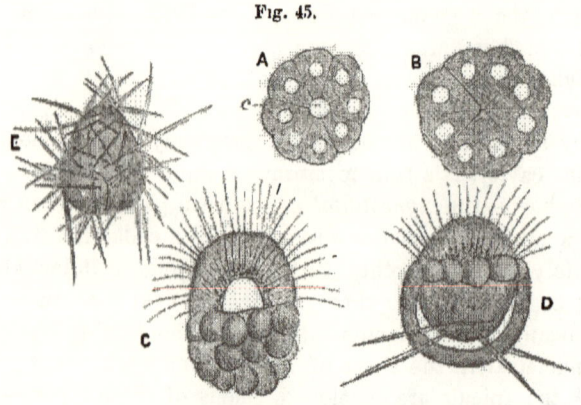

Development of a Sponge (Sycon ciliatum).

well developed; in fact, through nearly every important stage in its life. By making a section through the sponge he found eggs and embryos in different stages of development in springtime. The total segmentation occurred as Hæckel describes. Metschnikoff, however, observed that a small "segmentation-cavity" appeared in the egg (Fig. 45, A, c) which soon disappeared (Fig. 45, B). As a result of the process of division, a roundish embryo appears, which is made up of a large number of small cells. He was unable to study the mode of origin of the germ-layers. The freeswimming larva (Fig. 45, C) is an oval body, made up of two sorts of cells: those which are small, long and ciliated, and certain large round ones, much fewer in number. The first form a sort of arch, with a hollow in the middle, around which a large number of very fine brown pigment corpuscles are collected. The next change of importance is the disappearance of the cavity, the upper or ciliated half of the body being much reduced in size. Then the large round cells of the hinder part are united into a compact mass, leaving only a single row. The ciliated cells are gradually withdrawn into the body cavity. Fig. 45, D, shows this process going on. At this period also the larva becomes sessile, and now begins the formation of the sponge spicules, which develop from the non-ciliated round cells. Metschnikoff calls attention to the fact that at this early stage the Sycon passes through a phase which is persistent in the genus Sycyssa. The layer of ciliated cells are gradually withdrawn into the body cavity, until a small opening is left, surrounded with a circle of cilia. These cilia finally disappear, and a few more spicules grow out, and meanwhile the opening disappears. In the next stage (represented at D) a considerable (gastrovascular) cavity appears, which may be seen through the body-walls. At this time, by soaking the specimen in acetic acid, the body of the sponge was seen to consist of two layers, the inner layer of ciliated cells forming a closed sac, enveloped in the spicule-generating layer (representing the entoderm). At this time no mouth-opening was formed, though three-pointed spicules had appeared.

It results from Metschnikoff's observations that the body of the larval sponge is composed of two primary germ-layers, an "entoderm" and "ectoderm," the two germ layers about which we shall hear much more hereafter.

The observations of Carter, made on several additional species both of silicious and calcareous sponges, confirm the results of Metschnikoff as to the later history of the larval sponge, and those of Hæckel as to the mode of segmentation of the egg. Our Fig. 43, A (copied from Carter), shows the total segmentation of the yolk in *Halisarca lobularis* into two portions; these portions farther subdivide, as at Fig. 43, B, until an immense number of small embryonic cells are produced.

Carter observes that the embryos may be found at all seasons, from March through the summer. These observations are not difficult to follow out. We have, by tearing apart a species of Sycandra (or Sycon) perhaps *S. ciliata*, which grows on a Ptilota, found the planula much as figured by Hæckel, Metschnikoff and

Carter, and any one can with patience and care observe the life history of the marine sponges.

It seems, then, that the life history of the sponges consists of the following stages :—

1. Fertilization of a true egg by genuine spermatozoa ; both eggs and sperm cells arising from the inner germ-layer.

2. Total segmentation of the yolk, or protoplasmic contents of the egg.

3. A ciliated embryo.

4. A free swimming "planula "-like larva, with two germ-layers. The planula becomes sessile, spicules are developed in the hinder end of the body, afterwards a gastro-vascular cavity appears, constituting the

5. Gastrula stage.

6. A mouth and side openings appear and the true sponge characters are assumed.

LITERATURE.

Lieberkühn. Zur Entwickelungsgeschichte der Spongillen (Muller's Archiv, 1856.)

O. Schmidt. Die Spongien des Adriatisches Meeres. Leipsig. 1862–66.

Clark. Spongiæ Ciliatæ as Infusoria Flagellata. 1867.

Hæckel. Die Kalkschwämme. Eine Monograph. 2 vols. and atlas. Berlin, 1872.

Metschnikoff. Zur Entwickelungsgeschichte der Kalkschwämme. (Siebold and Kölliker's Zeitschrift. (Feb., 1874.)

Carter. Development of the Marine Sponges, etc. (Annals & Mag. Nat. Hist., Nov and Dec.. 1874.)

IX. THE HYDROIDA.

THE animal next higher in structure than the sponge is the curious Protohydra discovered by Greef among diatoms and seaweeds in the oyster park at Ostend. It is regarded by Greef as the marine ancestral form of the Cœlenterates (Hydroids, Jelly fishes and Actiniæ). It is the simplest possible radiate form yet discovered. As the form of the fresh-water Hydra is familiar, Protohydra may be best described as similar to that, except that it is entirely wanting in tentacles. Like Hydra it is made up of two layers (an ectoderm and endoderm), with a mouth and stomach (gastro-vascular cavity). Nothing is known of its history, though Greef is positive that it is not a young Actinia. His interesting and detailed account was published with excellent illustrations in Siebold and Kolliker's "Journal of Scientific Zoology" in 1869.

The next higher form is the fresh-water Hydra, which is commonly found on the under side of the leaves of aquatic plants. There are two varieties of *Hydra vulgaris* apparently common to the fresh waters of the old and new world. They are *viridis* and *fusca*. This well known animal is the simplest form of the division of radiates known as Hydroids. The somewhat club-shaped body consists of two layers, the inner (endoderm) lining the general cavity of the body, which serves both as mouth and stomach and for the circulation of the nutritive fluid, and is called the gastrovascular cavity. The mouth is surrounded with eight tentacles, which are prolongations of the body-wall and are hollow, communicating with the body cavity.

Such is the general structure of the Hydra. In the ectoderm are situated the lasso-cells or nettling organs, being minute barbed filaments coiled up in a cell-wall. From Kleinenberg's recent researches on the Hydra it appears that there are scattered irregularly through the endodermal lining of the body-cavity isolated ciliated cells. They do not form a continuous lining membrane, and thus bear an interesting analogy to the ciliated cells of the sponge. While the endoderm forms a simple cell-layer, the outer layer (ectoderm) is more complex, as just within an external simple layer of large cells is a multitude of smaller cells, some of them being thread or lasso cells, while still within are fine muscular fibrillæ which form a continuous layer. The large cells first named end in fibre-like processes, which alone possess contractility and are thought by Kleinenberg to be motor-nerve endings. These large cells, from combining the functions of muscle and nerve, are termed "nervo-muscle cells." The little cavities between the large endodermal cells and the muscular layer which lies next to the endoderm is filled with small cells and lasso-cells, forming what Kleinenberg calls the interstitial tissue. From this tissue are developed the eggs and spermatozoa.

The organization of all the hydroids and even Lucernaria and the larger jelly-fishes (Discophora) is based on the plan of the Hydra. They all have a simple body-cavity, but no true alimentary canal surrounded by a perivisceral cavity. This is the distinguishing character of the Cœlenterates. In the jelly-fishes, the often complicated water vascular system of canals are simply passages leading out from the axial gastro-vascular cavity. If we place a jelly fish in the same position as the Hydra, i.e., with the tentacles directed upwards, the general homology between the parts can be clearly traced. In the Hydroids, such as Sertularia, etc., the ectoderm is surrounded by a chitinous sheath, secreted from this layer. While in Hydra the young bud out from the side of the body, in the Hydroids the young are developed on a separate stalk from the barren or nutritive stalk or "zooid." The individual Hydroid is thus subdivided into a reproductive and a nutritive zooid. The reproductive zooids seldom or never take in food, but are nourished by the nutritive zooids, the two zooids being connected by a common creeping stem called the "cœnosarc."

The Anthozoa or sea anemones and coral polypes differ from the Hydroids and Medusæ in having the stomach open at the bottom into a second and larger cavity communicating with the radiating chambers. In the Ctenophoræ there is a decided approach in the complication of the body to the Echinoderms. The radiated structure so clearly shown in the lower forms is here in part subordinated to the bilateral arrangement of parts; they have a right side and a left side. They also differ in the mouth opening into a wide digestive cavity, enclosed between two vertical tubes, uniting at the end of the body, where the stomach forms a reservoir for the gastro-vascular tubes ramifying throughout the body. They move by a peculiar apparatus consisting of bands of comb-like flappers. Not detaining the reader with a definition of the subdivisions of the Cœlenterates we shall be content with giving the following tabular view of the lowest subdivision of Radiates :—

CŒLENTERATA.

ACALEPHS OR HYDROZOA.

1. *Hydroida.*   *a.* Hydriform (Hydra, Hydractinia, Tubularia, Sertularia)
           b. Siphonophora (Velella, Agalma, Physalia).
2. *Calycozoa* (Lucernaria).
3. *Medusæ* or *Discophoræ* (Aurelia.)

ANTHOZOA (Actinia, Cerianthus, Astræa, Alcyonium, Gorgonia and Renilla).
CTENOPHORÆ (Beroë, Cydippe, Cestum).

Development of Hydra and the Hydroids. Ehrenberg first showed that the Hydra reproduced by eggs which become fertilized by spermatic particles. Kleinenberg describes the testis, which is lodged in the ectoderm and which develops tailed spermatozoa like those of the higher animals. They arise, as in other higher animals, from a self-division of the nuclei of the testis-cells. There is a true ovary formed in the same interstitial tissue of the ectoderm, consisting of a group of cells, which differ entirely in their mode of formation from the ovaries (gonophores) of the marine Hydroids, which are genuine buds.

It thus seems that Hydra is monœcious or hermaphrodite, *i. e.*, the sexes are not distinct. The egg of Hydra originates from the central cell of the ovary; thus confirming the opinion now generally held that all animals as a rule arise from a simple cell. After the egg-cell has escaped from the ovary through the ectoderm, it still holds on by a narrow point to the sides of the Hydra, where it is fecundated by the spermatic particles discharged into the surrounding water from the testis.

Fecundation is succeeded by a true segmentation of the egg. The young Hydra thus passes through a true "Morula" stage.[13] There is an outer layer of prismatic cells, forming the surface of the germs, and surrounding the inner mass of polygonal cells. At first none of these cells are nucleated, but afterwards nuclei appear, and it is an important fact that these nuclei do not arise from any preëxistent egg-nucleus.

The next step is the formation of a true chitinous shell, enveloping the germ or embryo. After this Kleinenberg asserts that the cells of the germ become fused together, and that the germ is like an unsegmented egg, being a single continuous mass of protoplasm. Allman remarks that "as this phenomenon does not occur

---

[13] Hereafter we shall often use Hæckel's convenient term "Morula," instead of "stage of segmentation of the egg," for the sake of brevity.

in other Hydroids it can have no general significance for the development of the order."

The remaining history of Hydra is soon told. In this protoplasmic germ-mass there is formed a small excentric cavity; this is the beginning of the body cavity, which finally forms a closed sac. Allman remarks on this discovery of Kleinenberg's that " it is clear that the formation of a body cavity by invagination of the walls [*i. e.*, ectoderm] with the significance which Kowalevsky has assigned to it in other animals, does not exist in Hydra, and just as little will it be found in any other hydroid." It will be seen farther on that in certain medusæ, Kowalevsky has discovered that the digestive cavity is formed by the invagination of the ectoderm, and we have seen (p. 54) that Metznikoff declares that the ciliated cells lining the gastro-vascular cavity in the embryo of the sponge are the originally external ciliated cells of the planula withdrawn into and lining the body cavity.

After several weeks the germ bursts the hard shell and escapes into the surrounding water, but is still surrounded by a thin inner shell. After this a clear superficial zone appears, and a darker one beneath, which is the first indication of the splitting of the germ into the two definitive germ-lamellæ, common to all animals except the one-celled Protozoa.

The embryo soon stretches itself out, a star-shaped cleft appears, which forms the mouth. The tentacles next appear. The animal now bursts open the thin inner shell, and the young Hydra appears much like its parent form.

There is, then, no metamorphosis in the Hydra; no ciliated planula. The adult form is thus reached by a continuous growth.

It will be seen, to anticipate somewhat, that the Hydra, exactly as in the vertebrates, including man, arises from an egg developed from a true ovary, which is fertilized by a true tailed spermatic particle; that the egg passes through a morula stage; that the germ consists of two germinal layers, while from the outer layer, as probably in the vertebrates, an intermediate or nervo-muscular layer is formed, which Allman thinks is the homologue of the middle germ-lamella of the vertebrates, supposed to have originally split off from the ectoderm. Allman even regards the chitinous shell of the germ of Hydra as the equivalent of the epidermis of vertebrates, being a provisional embryonic organ in Hydra, but permanent in vertebrates.

In all the marine Hydroids, which are more complex in their individualism than Hydra, the sexes being separate, the eggs and spermatic particles are thought by Allman to be developed from the endoderm. But E. Van Beneden has on the other hand shown that the eggs in Hydractinia are exclusively developed from the endoderm, while the spermatic cells arise from the ectoderm.

The simplest form next to Hydra is Hydractinia, in which the individual is differentiated into three sets of zooids; i.e., a, hydra-like, sterile or nutritive zooids; b and c, the reproductive zooids, one male and the other female, both being much alike externally, having below the short rudimentary tentacles several spherical sacs, which produce either male or female medusæ. These medusa buds or closed generative sacs are fundamentally like the free medusæ in structure. The marine Hydroids, then, are universally diœcious, and usually each colony is either male or female.

A rather more complicated form is the common *Coryne mirabilis*. Fig. 46 shows the hydrarium with its long tentacles (*t*) and *a* the medusa buds, Fig. 47 its free medusa. Tubularia is a higher form, and allied to the latter is still another form, *Corymorpha pendula* (Fig. 48. After Agassiz).

Figs. 49–53 (after A. Agassiz) represent quite fully the life history of another Tubularian, *Bougainvillia superciliaris*. Fig. 49 represents the hydrarium, with the sterile zooids provided with long tentacles, and the medusa buds of different ages. Fig. 50 shows a bud still more enlarged, with the proboscis (manubrium) just formed, and knob-like, rudimentary tentacles. In an older stage (Fig. 51) the proboscis is enlarged and the tentacles lengthened, while the depression at the upper end indicates the future opening. In Fig. 52 the appendages of the proboscis are plainly indicated, the tentacles are turned outwards. Shortly after this the jelly-fish breaks loose from its attachment and swims around as at Fig. 58.

How do the zooids first arise? This leads us to speak of the simplest mode of reproduction in the Hydroids, which is by budding. The object of sexual reproduction, i. e., by eggs and spermatozoa, throughout the animal and plant world, is by bringing the germ or portion of protoplasm of one individual, which is an epitome potentially of its physical and psychical nature, to mingle with that of another of the same species, so that the offspring may combine the qualities of both parents, and not deteriorate. The species can be reproduced simply by budding, but the result would, if maintained for a number of generations, in the end prove disastrous to its integrity. **Nature** abhors self-fertilization. So that while, as in these Hydroids, the zooid form may be produced by budding, yet the time comes when the individuals of one colony must mingle their reproductive elements with those of a remote colony, through the medium of the water. By this mode of repro-

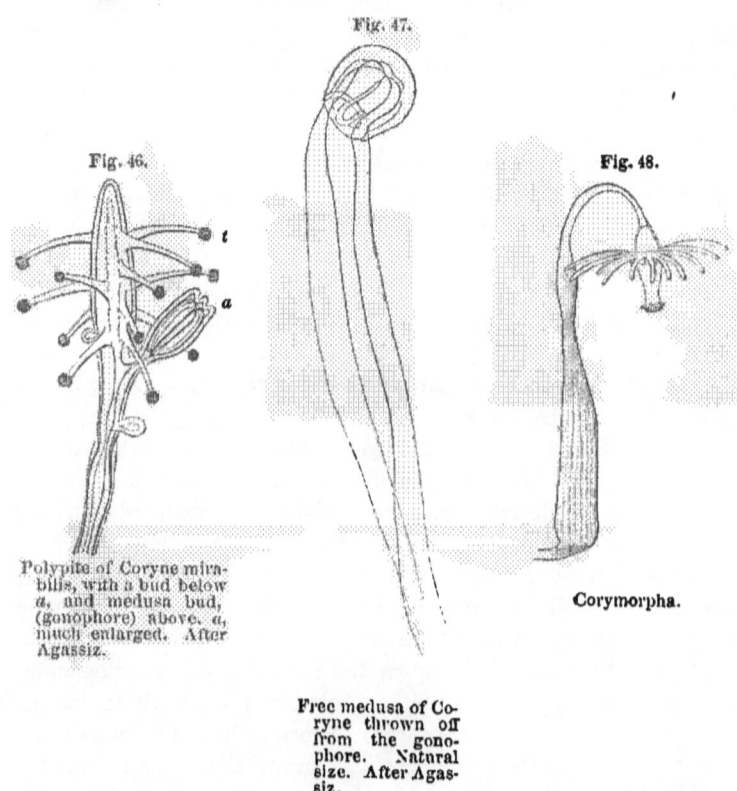

Fig. 47.

Fig. 46.

Fig. 48.

Polypite of Coryne mirabilis, with a bud below a, and medusa bud, (gonophore) above. a, much enlarged. After Agassiz.

Corymorpha.

Free medusa of Coryne thrown off from the gonophore. Natural size. After Agassiz.

duction new colonies are also set up. On the other hand budding or gemmation has for its object the extension of the colony of nutritive and reproductive zooids. This alternation of budding with sexual generation or "alternation of generations," or "parthenogenesis," is first met with in the Hydroids, and we shall find it often recurring in the higher animals when needed to meet some special exigency of the species.

Fig. 49.

Fig. 51.

Fig. 52.

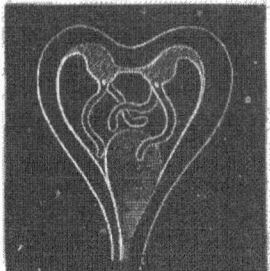

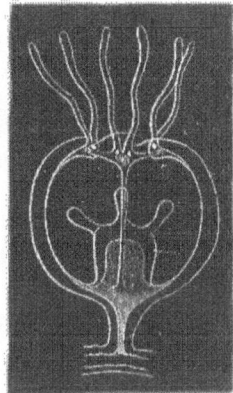

Medusa bud of 49, farther advanced.

Fig. 50.

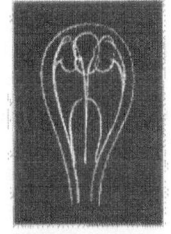

Medusa bud with the tentacles turned out. Magnified.

Hydrarium of Bougainvillia, magnified.

Medusa bud of 49.

Fig. 53.

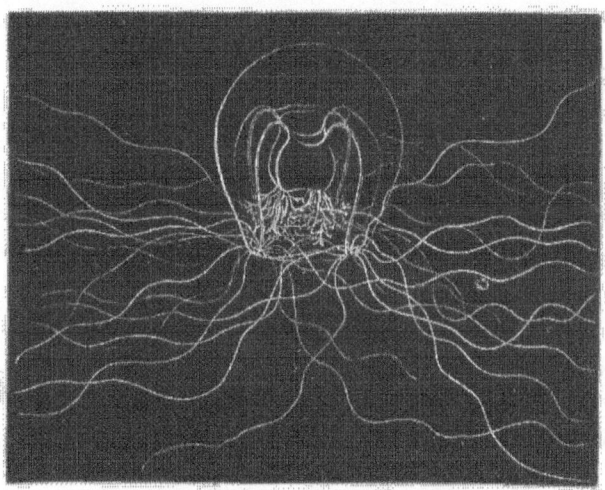

Medusa of Bougainvillia. Magnified. After A. Agassiz.

Budding begins as a slight protrusion of the basal portion (cœnosarc) of the colony, which then becomes spherical and finally club-shaped, as in Fig. 46, until it assumes the form of a zooid. It remains permanently attached in all the Hydroids except in Hydra, where it breaks off and bears a free individual. In some species of Tubularia the heads of the zooids successively drop off, and are renewed.

Multiplication by fission has only been observed in one case, in the medusa of Stomobrachium, observed by Kölliker at Messina. In this the pendent stomach divided in two, becoming doubled, which was followed by a vertical division of the umbrella, separating the animal into two independent halves. These again subdivided, and Kölliker thinks this process went on still farther.

The second mode of generation, i. e., by eggs and spermatic particles, have been observed in many marine Hydroids. As in the Hydra, the eggs, after being fertilized, pass through a morula stage, and finally the germ becomes surrounded by a blastoderm, as in Hydra, formed of long prismatic cells directly comparable with the zone of blastodermic cells of insects, and many other animals, including the mammals. The germ elongates and finally escapes from the ovisac (gonophore) of the parent as a ciliated "planula," a term first applied to it by Dalyell.

Now how do these planulas become converted into hydras, and through them into medusæ? A glance at the accompanying figures will give the main points in the life history of a not uncommon Hydroid found on our shores, a Melicertum allied to Campanularia (Fig. 57). We are indebted to Mr. A. Agassiz (Seaside Studies in Natural History) for the following facts and illustrations regarding its history. After keeping a number of the Melicertum in a large glass jar for a couple of days at the time of spawning, he found that the ovaries, at first filled with eggs, became emptied, and that the planulæ, at first spherical and afterwards pear-shaped (Fig. 54) swam near the bottom of the jar, and soon attached themselves by the larger end to the bottom of the jar (Fig. 55). "Thus their Hydroid life begins; they elongate gradually, the horny sheath is formed around them, tentacles arise on the upper end, short and stunted at first, but tapering rapidly out into fine, flexible feelers; the stem branches, and we have a little Hydroid community (Fig. 56), upon which, in the course of the following spring, the reproductive calycles containing the medusæ buds will be developed."

Fig. 54.

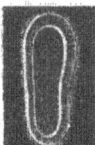

Planula of
Melicertum.

Fig. 55.

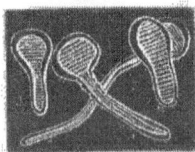

Cluster of Planulæ
just attached to the
ground.

Fig. 56.

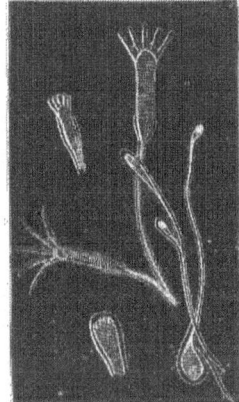

Polypites of Melicertum
developed from the plan-
ulæ; greatly magnified.

Fig. 57.

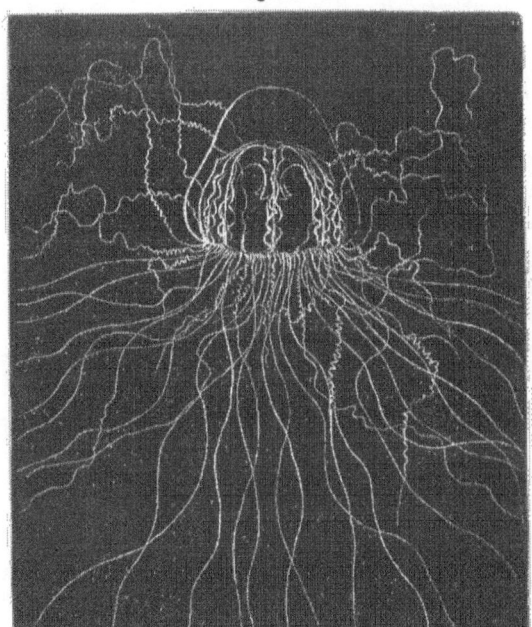

Melicertum campanula, seen in profile.   Natural size.   After
Agassiz.

Coming now to the Portuguese man-of-war (Physalia, Fig. 58), which have so much occupied the attention of the best naturalists, it would seem at first well nigh impossible to trace their relationship with the ordinary Hydroids. A Physalia may, however, be compared to a fixed colony of Hydractinia or Coryne, for example. Each Physalia is either male or female, and consists of four kinds of zooids; viz., nutritive and reproductive, with medusa buds, which, by their contractions and dilatations propel the colony onward; and the "feeders," a set of digestive tubes which nourish the entire colony.

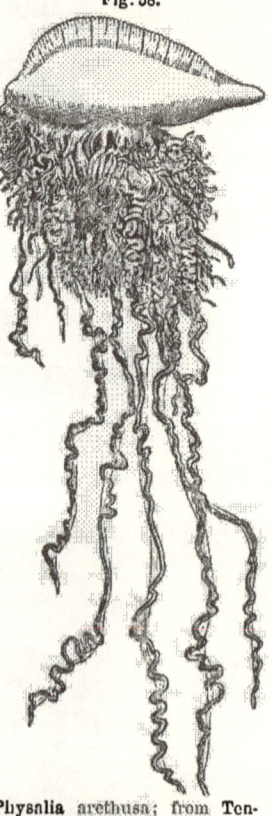

Fig. 58.

Physalia arethusa; from Tenney's Zoology.

The Siphonophores (as observed by Gegenbaur, Kowalevsky, Hæckel and Metschnikoff, in Agalma and several other genera) arise from eggs which pass through a morula stage, into a ciliated planula, whose body consists of an ectoderm and endoderm. The gastro-vascular cavity in the Siphonophores, as in the lower Hydroids so far as observed, is formed by a fold of the endoderm, while, as we shall see farther on, in the Discophorous jelly fishes it is formed by an infolding of the ectoderm.

The further development of Nanomia, a Siphonophore native to our northern shores, from the larval state, has been described and figured by Mr. A. Agassiz. To use nearly his own words, the Nanomia consists, when first formed, of an oblong oil bubble, with but one organ, a simple digestive cavity. Soon between the oil bubble and the cavity arise a number of medusa buds, though without any "proboscis" (manubrium), as these medusa buds, called "swimming bells," are destined to "serve the purpose of locomotion only, having no share in the function of feeding the community." After these swimming buds, three kinds of Hydra-like zooids arise. In one set the Hydra is open-mouthed, and is in fact a digestive tube, its gastro-vascular cavity connecting with that of the stem, and thus the food taken in is circulated through-out the community. These are the so-called "feeders." The second set of Hydras differ only from the "feeders" in having shorter tentacles twisted like a corkscrew. In the third and last set of Hydras the mouth is closed, and they differ from the others in having a single tentacle instead of a cluster. Their function has not yet been clearly explained. Gradually new individuals are added, until a long chain of Hydroids is formed, which move gracefully through the water, with the oil globule uppermost, which serves as a float and is identical with the large-crested "float" of the Physalia.

Finally, the higher Hydroids, such as Æginopsis, Ægineta, Cunina and Lyriope have been found by Müller, Agassiz, McCrady, Leuckart, Gegenbaur, Fritz Muller and others, to develop directly from eggs and pass through a metamorphosis as medusæ. During the past year (1874) Metschnikoff has published, with many fig-ures, an account of the development of Geryonia, Polyxenia (Ægineta) and Æginopsis.

In these animals the egg passes through a morula stage; an outer layer of cells (blastoderm) splits off from the morula, form-ing the ectoderm and entoderm. The embryo, then, as in Polyx-enia, passes through a ciliated planula stage. The embryo may remain spherical, as in Geryonia, or as in Polyxenia and Ægin-opsis, the body of the planula becomes greatly elongated and boomerang-shaped, and from each end are developed the first two tentacles, then others, and after a slight metamorphosis the adult form is attained.

The life history of the Hydroids comprises, then, the following phases in development :—

1, a. Origin of young Hydra by budding.

     b. Origin of embryo from egg fertilized by spermatozoa.

2. Morula stage.

3. Planula (? Gastrula) stage.

4. Hydra-like form, attached.

5. Medusa, free and discharging eggs.

LITERATURE.

Gegenbaur. Versuch eines Systemes der Medusen (Siebold and Kölliker's Zeitschrift. 1857).

McCrady. Gymnophthalmata of Charleston harbor (Proc. Elliott Soc. N. H., i, 1859).

L. Agassiz. Contributions to the Natural History of the United States, vols. 3 and 4, 1860 and 1862.

Allman. Report on the Present State of our Knowledge of the Reproductive System in the Hydroida. (Rep. Brit. Assoc. Adv. Sc., 1863.)

Clark. Mind in Nature, 1865.

A. Agassiz. Catalogue of the Acalephæ of North America. Mus. Comp. Zool., 1865.

E. C. and A. Agassiz. Seaside Studies in Natural History. Radiates. Boston, 1871.

Kleinenberg. Hydra, ein Anatomisch-entwicklungsgeschichtliche Untersuchung. Leipzig, 1872. (Abstract, with notes by Allman in Quatr. Journ. Micr. Science, 1874.)

Metschnikoff. Studien ueber die Entwickelung der Medusen und Siphonophoren (Siebold und Kölliker Zeitschrift, 1874).

X. THE MEDUSÆ (Discophoræ).

PASSING by the Lucernaria, beautiful and interesting, but of whose early development we know nothing, we come to the common larger jelly-fishes of our shores, which differ from the bell-shaped hydroid medusæ in their usually larger size and solid disk, as well as in the larger number and greater complication of the water tubes, which ramify and interbranch along the under side of the disk; and in carrying their eggs in pouches. In our common *Aurelia flavidula* there are four of these large pouches occupying the centre of the disk.

The life history of the Aurelia, which we will select as an example of the mode of development of this group, since it is best known, is far less complicated than that of the Hydroids. The ciliated planulæ may be found in the egg pouches of the female Aurelia during the last of summer. Soon after the ectoderm and entoderm are formed, a mouth is developed, and a gastro-vascular cavity is formed by the invagination of the ectoderm, as stated by Metschnikoff, and they then pass into a gastrula (planula) stage (Fig. 59, Gastrula of a form allied to Aurelia ; *a*, mouth ; *b*, gastro-vascular cavity ; *c*, ectoderm ; *d*, entoderm ; after Metschnikoff), with a mouth and large digestive cavity. After swimming about for a while they fix

Fig. 59.

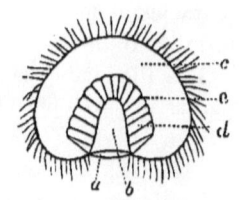

Gastrula of an Aurelia-like Medusa.

themselves to some object at the bottom of the sea and soon a pair of tentacles begin to develop, and then two more, until not more than sixteen are developed. When of this hydra-like form (Fig. 60 *a*, young ; *b*, older, after A. Agassiz) it is called a "Scyphistoma," having originally, as well as the Strobila and Ephyra,

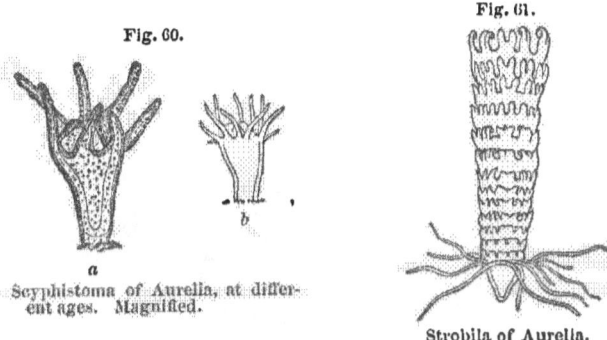

Fig. 60.

Fig. 61.

Scyphistoma of Aurelia, at different ages. Magnified.

Strobila of Aurelia.

been mistaken for and described as an adult animal under that name.

After assuming this scyphistoma condition, transverse constrictions appear at regular intervals, dividing the column, as it were, into a pile of saucers ; the edges rise, tentacles bud out, and the animal assumes the form seen in Fig. 61 (after Agassiz). The

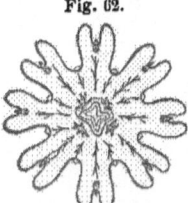

Fig. 62.

Ephyra of Aurelia.

uppermost disk becomes detached, the rest separate one after the other and float away in the form of an "Ephyra" (Fig. 62, after A. Agassiz) and after some weeks assume the aurelia or adult condition (Fig. 63). The gigantic *Cyanea arctica*, which attains a diameter of from three to five feet across the disk, as Agassiz remarks, is produced from "a hydroid measuring not more than half an inch when full-grown."

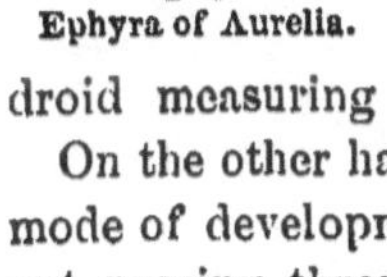

On the other hand there are several exceptions known to this mode of development, a few growing directly from the egg, without passing through a hydra, or scyphistoma stage. Such is the large Pelagia, as observed by Krohn. Mr. A. Agassiz has observed the same fact in *Campanella pachyderma*, a minute jelly fish.

The Discophores, then, develop in two ways :—

A. Directly from the egg (Pelagia and Campanella).

Fig. 63.

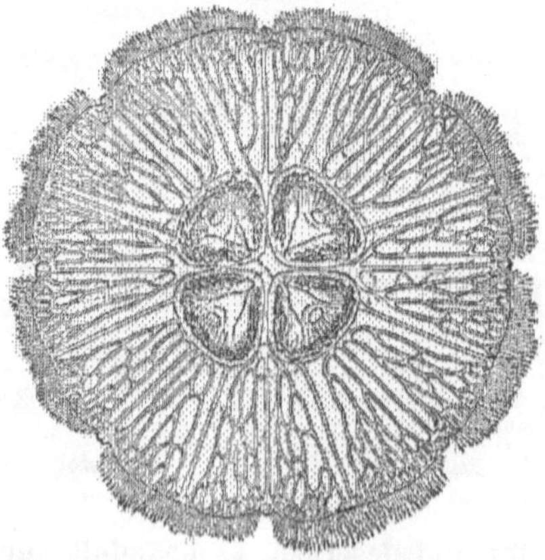

Aurelia flavidula. After Agassiz.

B. From hydra-like young arising from eggs (Aurelia and Cyanea) and presenting the following phases of growth :—

1. Egg.
2. Morula (?)
3. Planula (Gastrula).
4. Scyphistoma.
5. Strobila.
6. Ephyra.
7. Aurelia (adult).

LITERATURE.

Nearly the same as for the Hydroids.

XI. THE ACTINOZOA.

THE sea anemones and coral polypes are more highly developed than the Hydroids, since the mouth opens into a double digestive cavity, which is supported for its whole length by the six primary curtains or septa. The second and lower half of the cavity enlarges greatly, and communicates with the general cavity of the body, the upper portion being entire, tubular, and forming a sort of throat opening into the proper digestive cavity. In the Hydroids, the digestive cavity, it may be remembered, is simply hollowed out of the body cavity and is a more primitive affair than that of the Actinozoa.

While in the Hydroids also the ovaries hang outside the body cavity, in the true polypes they are attached to the septa or walls of the radiating chambers, so that the eggs, when ripe, drop down into the body cavity, whence they pass out through the mouth, or, as observed by Lacaze-Duthiers in the coral polypes, through the tentacles. The chambers between the septa correspond to the water canals, or chymiferous tubes of the Hydroids. The so-called mesenterial filaments attached to the septa are excretory glands supposed to be renal in their nature.

In the coral polypes the coral is secreted in the chambers, so that there are soft partitions alternating with the limestone ones. The tentacles which surround the mouth vary greatly in number. They are hollow, each communicating with a chamber.

The polypes are divided into (1), the Actinoids (Zoantharia) which either secrete no limestone, as in the sea anemones, or form a coral stock, as in the coral polypes, and have an indefinite number of tentacles, and (2), the Halcyonoids, in which the tentacles are eight in number. Such are the sea fans (Gorgonia) and Halcyonium, which does not secrete a coral stock.

Development. Nearly all the Actinozoa increase by budding, new individuals arising at the base of the large ones. In Zoanthus the young grow out in stolons branching from the parent polype. The life history of a polype from the egg is soon told. Naturalists are indebted to the magnificent memoirs of Lacaze-Duthiers for a full biography of not only several genera of sea anemones (*Actinia mesembryanthemum,* Bunodes and Sagartia) but also of the Gorgonia, Halcyonium, red coral, and the Astroides, a Mediterranean form (Fig. 65).

The young sea anemone develops without any metamorphosis, directly into the adult condition. Lacaze-Duthiers could not determine by actual sight how fecundation of the egg takes place, or whether the egg passes through a morula stage or not, though he infers, with every reason, that this stage, *i. e.*, the segmentation of the egg contents, takes place in the ovary. The ovaries and spermaries are in the Actiniæ situated in the same individual; the eggs are oval, while the spermatic cells are of the usual tailed form. The fecundated egg in the state in which it was first seen

by Lacaze-Duthiers was oval, and surrounded by a dense coat of transparent conical spinules. He was soon able to detect the presence of the two primitive germinal layers, the ectoderm and endoderm. Fig. 64 (from Metschnikoff) illustrates the relation of the embryonal layers in the larva of another polype which he calls "kaliphobenartige Polypen larve;" *a*, primitive opening into the gastro-vascular cavity, *b; c*, ectoderm; *d*, entoderm; *e*, body cavity), show-

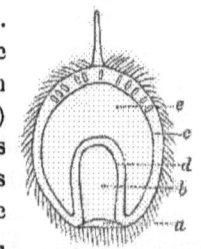

Fig. 64.

Ciliated larva (gastrula) of a Polype.

ing that the walls of the digestive cavity are formed by the entoderm; and Metschnikoff's figure shows that the embryo polype has a greater resemblance to the embryo starfish of the same age than the acalephs.

Two lobes next appear within the body, these subdivide into four, eight and finally twelve primitive lobes. This stage is represented by the corresponding stage of the coral (Fig. 66, B). Not until after the twelve primitive lobes are fully formed do the tentacles begin to make their appearance. When the first twelve tentacles have grown out, twenty-four more arise, and so on, until with its increasing size the actinia is provided with the full number peculiar to each species. The preceding remarks apply to *Actinia mesembryanthemum*, but Lacaze-Duthiers observed the same changes in two species of Sagartia and in *Bunodes gemmacea*.

Turning now to the stony corals we will give more fully the sequence of events in the life of a coral builder of the Mediterranean, the *Astroides calycularis*, so faithfully narrated by Lacaze-Duthiers. Fig. 65 taken from Tenney's "Manual of Zoology" illustrates this coral in various stages of expansion.

He studied this coral on the coast of Algiers, and found that reproduction took place between the end of May and July, the young developing most actively at the end of June. Unlike Actinia, which is always hermaphrodite, this coral is rarely so, but the polypes of different branches belong to different sexes.

As in the other polypes, including Actinia, the eggs and spermatic particles rupture the walls of their respective glands situated in the fleshy partitions. As in Actinia, Lacaze-Duthiers thinks the fecundation of the egg occurs before it leaves the ovary, when also the segmentation of the yolk must take place. Unlike the embryo Actinia, the ciliated young of the coral, after remaining in the digestive cavity for three or four weeks, make their way out into the world through the tentacles. "Many times," says Lacaze-Duthiers "have I seen the end of the tentacle break and let out

Fig. 65.

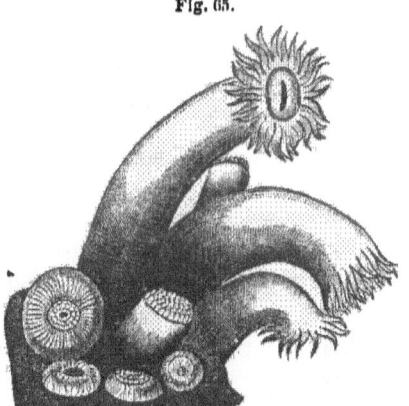

Coral polype (Astroides calycularis) expanded.

the embryo." The appearance of the embryo, when first observed, was like that in Fig. 66, A, an oval, ciliated body with a small mouth and a digestive cavity. This may be called the gastrula, adopting Hæckel's phraseology.

The gastrula changes into an actinoid polype in from thirty to forty days in confinement, after exclusion from the parent, but in nature in a less time, and it probably does not usually leave the mother until ready to fix itself to the bottom.

Before the embryo becomes fixed and the tentacles arise, the lime destined to form the partitions begins to be deposited in the endoderm. Fig. 66, C, shows the twelve rudimentary septa. These after the young polype, or "actinula" (Allman), has become stationary, finally enlarge and become joined to the external walls of the coral now in course of formation (Fig. 66, C, c) forming a groundwork or pedestal on which the actinula rests. D represents the young polype resting on the limestone pedestal.

Fig. 66.

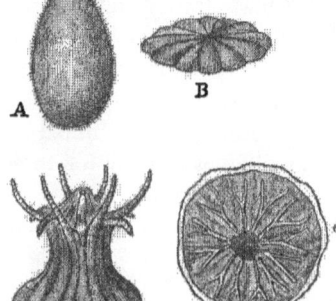

In the experience of Lacaze-Duthiers it happened that the embryo polype which had been swimming

Fig. 67.

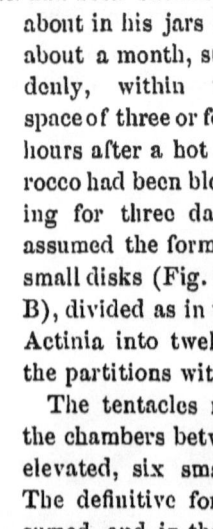

about in his jars for about a month, suddenly, within the space of three or four hours after a hot sirocco had been blowing for three days, assumed the form of small disks (Fig. 66, B), divided as in the

Development of a coral polype, Astroides calycularis. After L.-Duthiers.

Actinia into twelve small folds forming the bases of the partitions within.

The tentacles next arise, being the elongation of the chambers between the partitions, six larger and elevated, six smaller and depressed (Fig. 66, D). The definitive form of the coral polype is now assumed, and in the Astroides it becomes a compound polypary.

The singular floating young Edwardsia, originally described under the name *Arachnactis*, has been found by Mr. A. Agassiz to be the early swimming stage of Edwardsia, a worm-like Actinian, which, like *Halcampa albida* (Fig. 67), lives in the sand or mud, unattached to any fixed object.

Halcampa albida.

Kowalevsky has lately found that the Cerianthus, a gigantic Actinia which lives in a tube in the mud at great depths, has a free swimming early stage like Edwardsia.

The following is a summary of the changes undergone by the polypes so far as known :—

1. Egg fertilized by true spermatozoa.

2 ? Morula.

3. Gastrula.

4. Actinula, with twelve primitive tentacles (in the Actinoids).

5. Adult actinia or polype.

LITERATURE.

Lacaze-Duthiers. Développment des Coralliaires (Lacaze-Duthiers' Archives de Zoologie Experimentale, etc. 1872, 1873).

XII. THE CTENOPHORÆ.

These beautiful animals derive their name Ctenophorœ, or "comb-bearers," from the vertical rows of comb-like paddles, situated on horizontal bands of muscles, which serve as locomotive organs, the body not contracting and dilating as in the true jelly fishes. In their organization they are much more complicated than any animals of which we have yet spoken, as it has been shown by the two Agassizs that they have a true digestive cavity, passing through the body cavity, with a posterior outlet, and originating in the same manner as in the Echinoderms. From this alimentary canal are sent off chymiferous tubes which "correspond in every respect with the water tubes of the Echinoderms" (A. Agassiz). The rows of paddles are intimately connected with the chymiferous tubes, so that the movements of the body are in direct relation with the act of breathing. Moreover these animals, while in the disposition of the organs following the radiate plan of structure, are also more truly bilateral than any of the lower classes of radiates. The sexes are united in the same individual; the ovaries in Idyia are on one side of the main chymiferous tube, and the spermaries on the other, both being brilliantly colored.

Referring the reader for farther details to Mr. A. Agassiz's "Sea Side Studies," where these animals are described and illustrated with sufficient detail for the general reader, we will now turn to their mode of growth, under the guidance of the same author, whose recent richly illustrated memoir, with others by Kowalevsky and Fol leave but few gaps to be filled by future observers.

Development. Agassiz states that the Ctenophorœ are readily kept in confinement, and from twelve to twenty-four hours after they are captured lay their eggs, either singly or in strings, or, as in Idyia, in a thick slimy mass. The Ctenophorœ of our eastern coast spawn from late in July through August and September. "The young brood developed during the fall, comes to

the surface again the following spring as nearly full-grown Ctenophoræ, to lay their eggs late in the summer." Fortunately the
eggs are so transparent that in some forms (Pleurobrachia and
Bolina) the embryology can be studied, not only in the egg but
also through nearly all the earlier stages of the larva.

Selecting Pleurobrachia as an example of the mode of growth,
we find that as in Idyia the egg consists of two layers, *i. e.*, an
inner yolk mass and an outer, thin, finely granular layer surrounded
by a transparent envelope. The inner mass acts merely as a nutritive mass, while the outer is the true embryonic layer, which
builds up the body at the expense of the central nutritive mass.
No nucleus nor nucleolus has been observed by Agassiz in the
eggs of any Ctenophoræ, after they are once laid, until late in the
stage of segmentation. The egg divides into four and again eight
spheres of segmentation, each of which has, like the egg, originally an outer and inner mass. In a second stage of segmentation
small cells arise which surround the original eight large cells.
From these small cells (the blastoderm) the external organs are
destined to arise, while the larger cells form a yolk mass out of
which the internal organs arise.

The embryonal layer is next formed, then the outer wall by "the
gradual encroachment of the actinal cells over the whole of the
yolk mass." Finally, the mouth (actinos-
tome) of the germ is formed, and afterwards the digestive cavity, which results
from an invagination of the outer embryonic layer (ectoderm). Fig. 68 (after
Metschnikoff) represents the larva of a
Cydippe; *a*, primitive opening; *b*, gastro-
vascular cavity; *c*, ectoderm; *d*, endoderm; *e*, interspace corresponding to the
body cavity of the larva of the polype. The development of the
chymiferous tubes is succeeded by that of the locomotive flappers,
eight or nine pairs in each row appearing before the young leave
the egg, and of the fringed tentacle, which attains a great length
after the young is hatched.

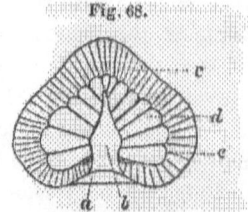

Fig. 68.

Gastrula of Cydippe.

Finally the definitive form of the Pleurobrachia is attained
before it leaves the egg, as seen in Fig. 69 (*t*, tentacles; *e*, eye-
speck; *c, c*, rows of locomotive flappers; *d*, digestive cavity;
greatly magnified after A. Agassiz).

Fig. 70 shows the young Pleurobrachia swimming about in the egg just before hatching, and in Fig. 71 (after A. Agassiz),

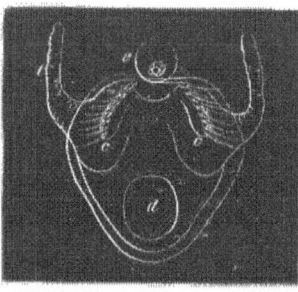

Fig. 69.

we see the young after hatching (magnified) with nearly the same form as the adult; *f* indicates the funnel leading to the anal opening, *l*, the lateral tubes, and *c c c' c'* the rows of locomotive flappers. The remaining changes are slight, and there is not even a slight metamorphosis, the body simply becoming spherical and the tentacles increasing enormously in length. In Bolina and its allies,

Young Pleurobrachia still in the egg.

as A. Agassiz states, "the morphological changes are very great, and it would indeed puzzle the most accurate systematist to recognize in the early stages of some of the Mnemidæ the young of well known genera. We cannot say that there is a metamorphosis in the ordinary sense of the word, as supposed by Gegenbaur, but there certainly are remark-

Fig. 71.

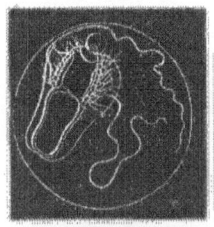

Fig. 70.

Young Pleurobrachia swimming in egg ready to hatch.

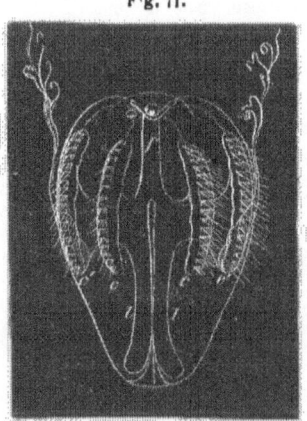

The same after hatching.

able changes, such as the almost total suppression of the tentacular apparatus, the development of auricles, of lobes, with their complicated winding chymiferous tubes, which alter radically the appearance of the Ctenophoræ at successive periods of growth, and present between the younger and the older stages differences usually considered as of great systematic value."

The summary of stages is very brief, the Ctenophore passing through three phases :—

1. Egg stage.
2. Morula state.
3. Gastrula state.
4. Adult form, assumed before hatching.

LITERATURE.

A. Agassiz. Catalogue of North American Acalephæ. 1865.

Kowalevsky. Entwickelungsgeschichte der Rippenquallen. (Mémoires Acad., St. Petersbourg, x, No 4.)

Fol. Ein Beitrag zur Anatomie und Entwickelung einiger Rippenquallen. (Siebold and Kölliker's Zeitschrift, 1869.)

A. Agassiz. Embryology of the Ctenophoræ. (Memoirs Amer. Acad. Arts and Sciences. x, No. 3, 1874.)

XIII. THE ECHINODERMS.

THE Echinoderms (starfishes, sea urchins and sea cucumbers) are far more complicated than the Cœlenterates, having a true alimentary canal passing through the general cavity of the body. In them for the first time among the Radiates appears a well developed nervous system. Not only do the young exhibit a bilateral symmetry, but in the higher forms, as the spantangoid sea urchins,

Fig. 72.

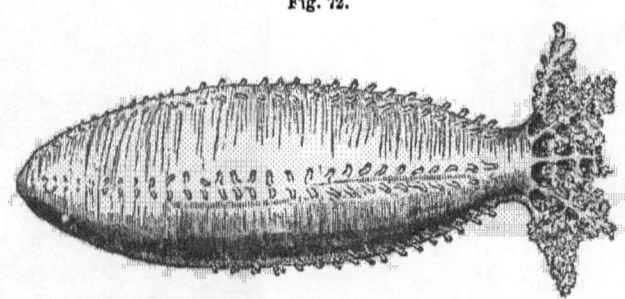

Pendacta frondosa. (From Tenney's Zoology.)

this is quite well marked ; and there is a dorsal and ventral side. Still, in the generality of the forms, the radiated plan of structure is remarkably adhered to, the body as distinctly made up of sphæromeres, or wedge-shaped sections of the body, as the worms are of segments (arthromeres). In this and other respects, as well as the form of the larvæ, there is a remarkable parallelism between the worms and echinoderms.

We will briefly review some of the anatomical features of the Echinoderms, in order to understand their complicated mode of growth.

The stomach and intestinal canal either pass straight or in a spiral course through the body, as in the sea urchins (Fig. 92) and Holothurians (Fig. 72), and open out at the opposite end ; or, as in the Antedon (Comatula), the anal opening is situated near the mouth, while in the Ophiurans (Fig. 74) and Luidia and Astropecten, low starfishes, the undigested food is rejected from the mouth. In the starfishes and Holothurians, the alimentary canal opens into five voluminous cæcal appendages. These are wanting in the Ophiurans, and there are but two in Astropecten. They

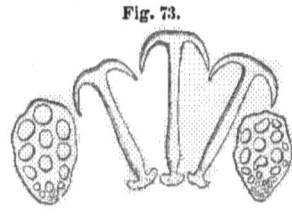

Fig. 73.

Hooks and Plates of Synapta.

are in connection with the complicated water tubes, which consist of a canal surrounding the mouth and sending branches out into the rays of the starfishes in communication with the locomotive organs or suckers, called ambulacra. The water fills the tubes through a duct leading from the sievelike plate, situated in the dorsal (abactinal) portion of the body. Near this duct is the pulsating tube, the so-called heart.

The Echinoderms are further distinguished by the body walls secreting calcareous plates, often forming a solid limestone shell, as in the sea urchins ; or the plates are smaller and movable as in the starfishes, or as in the sea cucumbers they are microscopic, buried in the skin ; sometimes, as in the Synapta forming anchor-like hooks and small plates (Fig. 73).

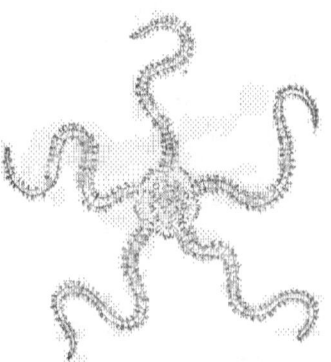

Fig. 74.

Sand star (Ophiopholis aculeata).

The sexes are as a rule distinct. In *Ophiura squamata* and Synapta they are united in the same individual. The ovaries and testes are gland-like masses situated at the base of the arms in the starfishes, or between the ambulacra in the sea urchins. The ovaries are red or yellow, the male glands whitish. In the Ophiurans the eggs and spermatozoa pass out of the body through little holes between the plates on the under side of the body. In those starfishes in which the alimentary canal is a blind sac, the eggs are emptied into the body cavity; but how they pass out is unknown. In some starfishes they escape through certain (interradial) plates on the back. In the Echinoids they make their exit from between the ambulacra. In the Holothurians, however, there is a duct leading from the generative gland opening out near the mouth, between the tentacles. The eggs are usually round, and minute; the spermatozoa of the usual tailed form. Fertilization takes place in the water.

Remembering that there are five well-marked divisions of Echinoderms, i.e., *Crinoidea*, *Ophiuroidea*, *Asteroidea*, *Echinoidea*, and *Holothuroidea*, we will now review some of the main points in the mode of development of the respective orders.

Development of the Crinoids. While we know nothing of the mode of development of the true Pentacrinus and Rhizocrinus, the lineal descendants of the Crinoids of the earlier geological ages, we have quite full information regarding the life-history of the Antedon, which is for a part of its life stalked, and is in fact a true crinoid.

The following account is taken (sometimes word for word) from Professor Wyville Thompson's researches on the *Antedon rosaceus* of the British coast. The ovaries open externally on the pinnules of the arms, while there is no special opening for the spermatic particles, and Prof. Thompson thinks they are "discharged by the thinning away and dehiscence of the integument." The ripe eggs hang for three or four days from the opening like a bunch of grapes, and it is during this period that they are impregnated. The egg then undergoes total segmentation. Fig. 75, A, represents the egg with four nucleated cells, an early phase of the mulberry or morula stage. After the segmentation of the yolk is finished, the cells become fused together into a mass of indifferent protoplasm, with no trace of organization, but with a few fat cells in the centre. This protoplasmic layer becomes converted into an oval embryo, whose surface is uniformly ciliated. The mouth is formed, with the large cilia around it, before the embryo leaves the egg. When hatched, the larva is long, oval, and girded with four zones of cilia, with a tuft of cilia at the end, a mouth and anal opening, and is about ·8 millimetre in length. The body cavity is formed by an inversion of the primitive sarcode layer which seems to correspond to the ectoderm.

Within a few hours or sometimes days, there are indications of the calcareous areolated plates forming the cup of the future crinoid. Soon others appear forming a sort of trellis work of plates and gradually build up the stalk, and lastly appears the cribriform basal plate. Fig. 75, B, c, represents the young crinoid in the middle of the larva, whose body is somewhat compressed under the covering glass. Next appears a hollow sheath of parallel calcareous rods, bound, as it were, in the centre by the calcareous plates. This stalk (B, c) arises on one side of the digestive

Fig. 75.

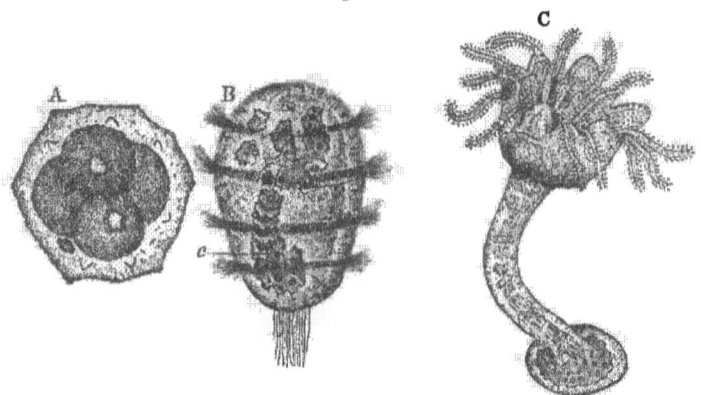

Development of a Crinoid (Antedon).

cavity of the larva, and there is no connection between the body cavity of the larva and that of the embryo crinoid.

Two or three days after the appearance of the plates of the crinoid, the larva begins to change its form. The mouth and digestive cavity disappear, not being converted into those of the crinoid. The larva sinks to the bottom resting on a seaweed or stone to which it finally adheres. The Pentacrinus is embedded in the former larval body (the cilia having disappeared), now constituting a layer of sarcode conforming to the outline of the Antedon.

Meanwhile the cup of the crinoid has been forming. It then assumes the shape of an open bell; the mouth is formed, and five lobes arise from the edges of the calyx. Afterwards five or more, usually fifteen tentacles, grow out, and the young Antedon appears

as in Fig. 75, C (after Thompson). The walls of the stomach then
separate from the body-wall. The animal now represents the primary stage of the crinoids, that which is the permanent stage in
the Pentacrinus and its fossil allies. The Antedon, however, in
after life separates from the stalk and moves about freely.

Development of the Starfish. We will select as a type of the
mode of development of the starfishes, that of the common five
finger, Asterias (Fig. 76), as worked out with great thoroughness

Fig. 76.

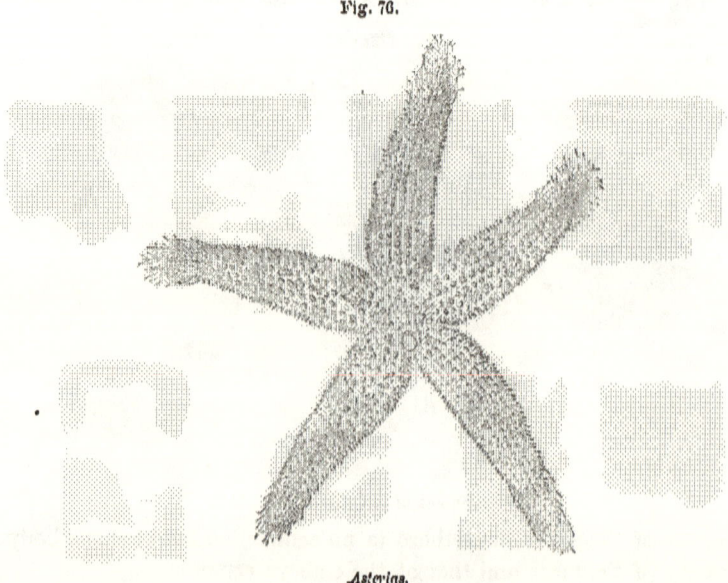

Asterias.

by Mr. A. Agassiz, and given in the "Seaside Studies." The
accompanying illustrations are taken from this work and the original memoir, through the kindness of the author, whose description is here freely used.

Fig. 77 shows the transparent spherical egg, enclosing the germinative vesicle and dot, and Figs. 78, 79, illustrate the segmentation of the yolk into two and eight and more cells, enclosing a
central cavity. After this the embryo hatches and swims about as
a transparent sphere (Fig. 80). A depression (Fig. 81, *ma*) then
begins to appear, the body elongates, and this depression forms
an inversion of the outer wall of the body (ectoderm), constituting the body cavity (*d*, Fig. 82 ; *a*, being the provisional mouth-

opening, afterwards becoming the anal opening; at this time, however, serving both for taking in and rejecting the food). From the upper extremity of the digestive cavity next project two lobes (*w*, *w′*, Fig. 83; *m*, mouth). These separate from their attachment and form two distinct hollow cavities (*w*, *w′*, Fig. 84; *a*, *d*, *c*, digestive system; *v*, vibratile chord; *m*, mouth). Here begins the true history of the young starfish, for these two cavities will develop into two water-tubes, on one of which the back of the starfish, that is, its upper surface, covered with spines, will be developed, while on the other, the lower surface, with the suckers and

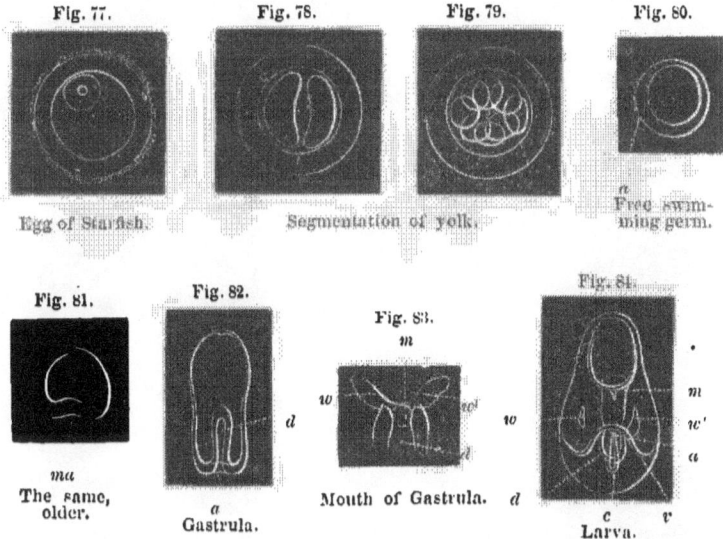

Fig. 77.   Fig. 78.   Fig. 79.   Fig. 80.

Egg of Starfish.   Segmentation of yolk.   *a* Free swimming germ.

Fig. 81.   Fig. 82.   Fig. 83.   Fig. 84.

ma The same, older.   *a* Gastrula.   Mouth of Gastrula.   Larva.

tentacles, will arise. At a very early stage one of these water tubes (*w′*, Fig. 85) connects with a smaller tube opening outwards, which is hereafter to be the madreporic body (*b*, Fig. 85). Almost until the end of its growth, these two surfaces, as we shall see, remain separate and form an open angle with one another; it is only toward the end of their development that they unite, enclosing between them the internal organs, which have been built up in the meanwhile.

"At about the same time with the development of these two pouches, so important in the animal's future history, the digestive cavity becomes slightly curved, bending its upper end sideways till it meets the outer wall, and forms a junction with it (*m*, Fig. 86 ; *o*, digestive cavity). At this point, where the juncture takes place, an aperture is presently formed, which is the true mouth. The digestive sac, which has thus far served as the only internal cavity, now contracts at certain distances, and forms three distinct, though connected cavities as in Fig. 85, viz., the œsophagus leading directly from the mouth (*m*) to the second cavity or stomach (*d*), which opens in its turn into the third cavity, the alimentary canal. Meanwhile the water-tubes have been elongating till they now surround the digestive cavity, extending on the other side of it beyond the mouth, where they unite, thus forming a

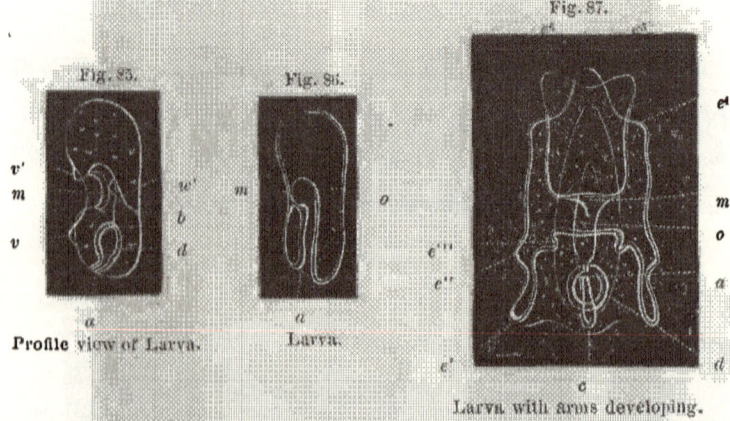

Fig. 87.

Fig. 85.

Fig. 86.

Profile view of Larva.   Larva.

Larva with arms developing.

Y-shaped tube, narrowing at one extremity, and dividing into two branches toward the other end, Fig. 87.[14]

"On the surface where the mouth is formed, and very near it on either side, two small ones arise, as *v* in Fig. 84 ; these are cords consisting entirely of vibratile cilia. They are the locomotive organs of the young embryo, and they gradually extend until they respectively enclose nearly the whole of the upper and lower half of the body, forming two large shields or plastrons (Figs. 87, 88). The corners of these shields project, slightly at first (Fig. 87), but elongating more and more until a number of arms are formed, stretching in various directions (Figs. 88, 89)[15] and, by their con-

[14] Fig. 87 *a*, anus; *c*, intestine; *c' c'' c''' e⁴ e⁵ c⁶*, arms; *o*, œsophagus.
[15] Figs. 88, 89, side view of 88. Adult larva, so-called Brachiolaria, lettering the same in all the figures; *t*, tentacles of young starfish; *ff*, brachiolar appendages; *r*, back of young starfish. Fig. 90, *t'*, odd tentacle.

stant upward and downward play, moving the embryo about in the water" (A. Agassiz).

Having reached the Brachiolaria stage, the body of the future starfish begins to develop. On one of the water-tubes (w') the tentacles of the future starfish arise as a series of lobes (t); while

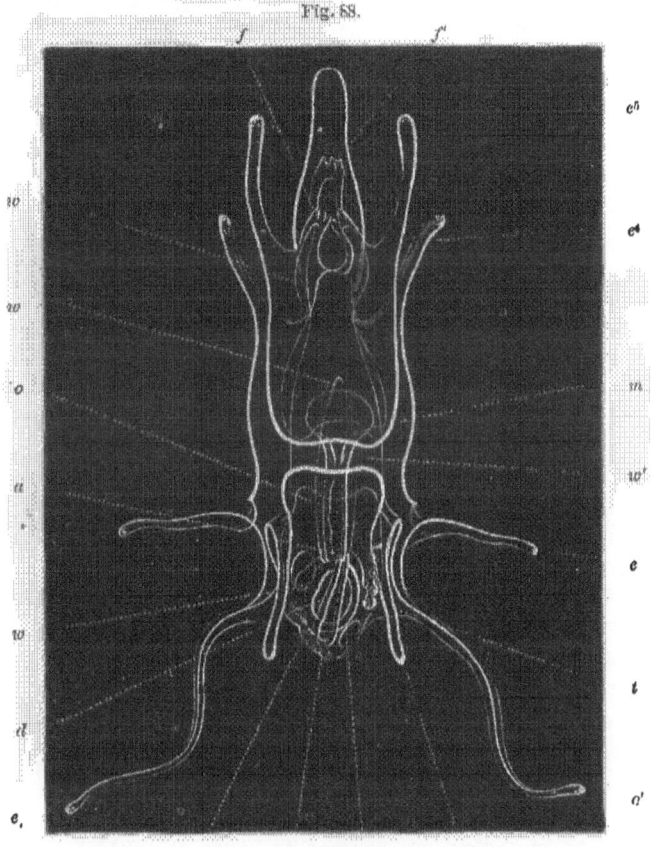

Fig. 88.

Full grown larva of Starfish, or Brachiolaria.

on the opposite water-tube (w), arise a number of little calcareous rods, which afterwards form a continuous net-work; r indicates the back of the young starfish. The larva now shrinks and drops to the bottom and attaches itself there by means of the short arms (ff', Fig. 88). The starfish now absorbs the larva, and

appears of an oval form with a crenulated edge, and soon reaches a
stage indicated by Fig. 90. (Fig. 91, the same seen in profile).

In this stage it remains probably two or three years before the
arms lengthen and the
adult form is assumed.

The development of the
Ophiurans is much like that
of the starfish, with some
characters of the embryo
sea urchin. The larva of
the sand star (Ophiura)
is called a Pluteus, and is
remarkable for the great
length of two of the arms.

*Development of the Echi-
noids.* The researches of
Mr. A. Agassiz, who has
given us a very complete
history of the common sea
urchin of the northern
shores of the United States
in his "Revision of the
Echini," will be our guide
in these studies. The
earlier stages of development were obtained by
artificial fecundation of
the egg during February.
The early embryonic
stages are much as des-
cribed in the starfishes, the
process requiring but a few

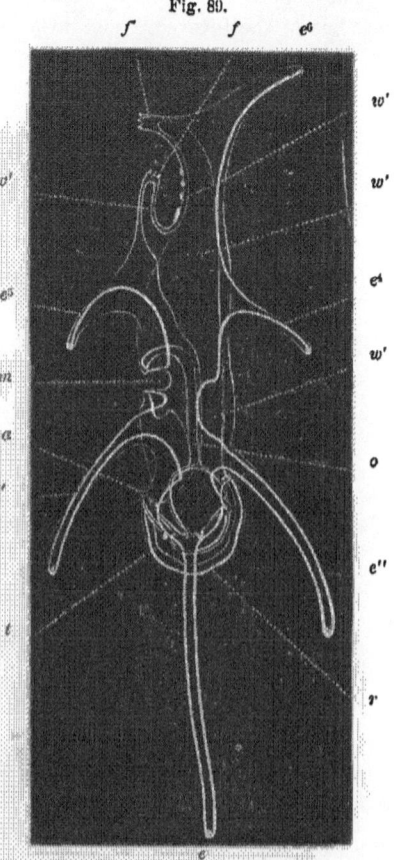

Fig. 80.

Fig. 88 seen in profile.

hours. The embryo when hatched is like that of the starfish at
the same period (Fig. 80) and then it passes into the gastrula
stage (Fig. 93, lettering the same in all the figures as in those of
the starfish) the digestive cavity being formed by an inversion of
the ectoderm. "The embryo, in escaping from the egg, resembles
a starfish embryo, and it would greatly puzzle any one to perceive
any difference between them. The formation of the stomach, of
the œsophagus, of the intestine, and of the water tubes takes

place in exactly the same manner as in the starfish, the time only at which these different organs are differentiated not being the same. In figure 94 we see the begin-

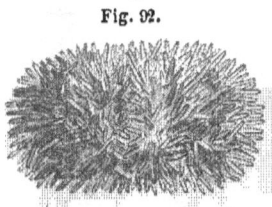

Fig. 92.

ning at *w* and *w'* of the water tubes arising as pouches sent off from the digestive cavity, and T-shaped rudiments of the limestone rods (*r*), so characteristic of the larva of the sea urchin are now visible."

Common Sea Urchin (Echinus).

Fig. 95 represents the larva well advanced towards the pluteus stage. It is now in the tenth day after fecundation.[16] The arms are now well marked, and the "vibratile epaulettes" appear. When the larva is twenty-three days

Fig. 90.

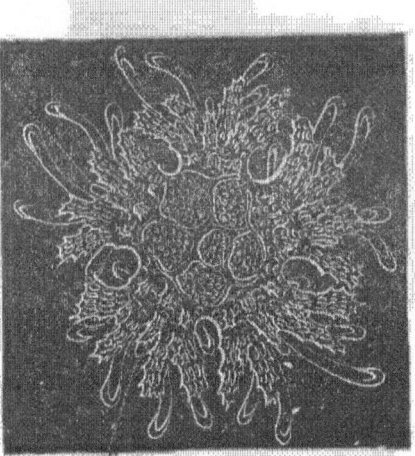

Fig. 91.

Young Starfish seen in profile.

Young Starfish seen from the back.

old, the rudiments of the five tentacles of the sea urchin appear, the first one on the left water tube. The arms have increased in length, until in the full-grown larva, now called the pluteus (Figs. 96, 97, the same seen sidewise), the arms with the calcareous rods supporting them are of great length, opening and shutting like the rods of an umbrella; while the sea urchin growing within has concealed the shape of the digestive cavity of the larva, and the spines are so large as to conceal the tentacles.

---

[16] Fig. 95, *e–e'* arms; *v–v'*, vibratile chord, *w w*, earlets, water tubes; *a o d e*, digestive system; *r–r'''* solid rods of the arms; *m*, mouth; *b*, madreporic opening. Fig. 96, *f*, brachilar appendages.

The pluteus, a nomadic stage of the echinus, is as Mr. A. Agassiz states "a scaffolding in which the future sea urchin plays but a secondary part, and is composed of two open spirals, the one to form eventually the complicated abactinal system (the interambulacral and ambulacral plates), the other to form the water system, and holding between them the digestive cavity and other organs of the pluteus, which as yet appear to have no connection whatever with the spines of the future Echinus. Yet towards the end of the nomadic pluteus life a few hours are sufficient to resorb the whole of the complicated scaffolding, which has been the most striking feature of the Echinoderm, and it passes into

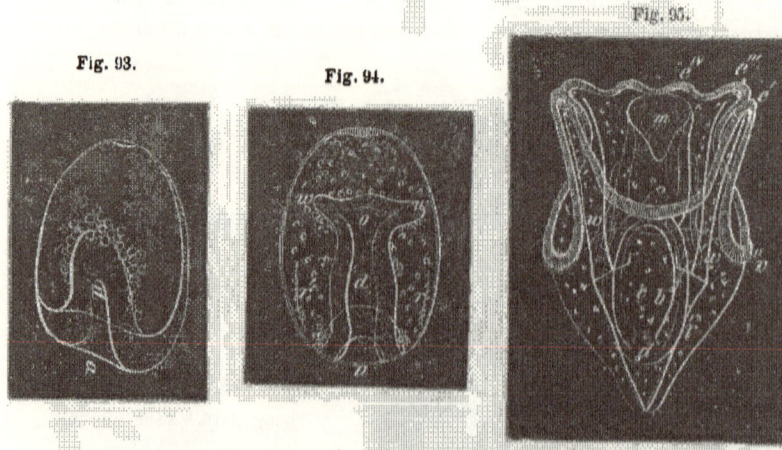

Fig. 93. Fig. 94. Fig. 95.

Development of the Pluteus of the Sea Urchin.

something which, it is true, we could hardly recognize as an Echinus, yet has apparently nothing in common with its former condition."

From this time the body of the pluteus is absorbed by the growing sea-urchin; the spines and suckers of the latter increasing in size and number with age, and by the time the larval body has disappeared the young Echinus is more like the adult than the starfish at the same period in life. Fig. 98 (tt, tentacles; $s''s'''$, spines) represents the sea urchin very soon after the resorption of the pluteus.

In after life the young sea urchin with its few and large spines resembles Cidaris and a number of allied forms, showing that these genera, which appeared earlier geologically than our common Echinus (Fig. 92, *Strongylocentrotus Dröbachiensis*), are lower in development.

Development of the Holothuroids. Of the development of our

Fig. 96.

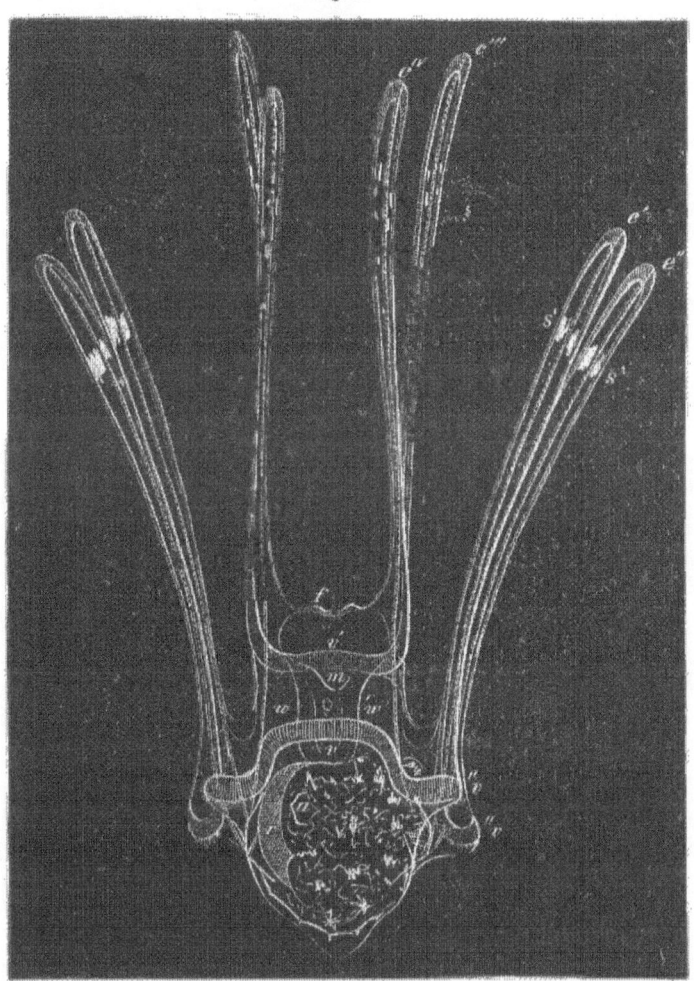

Pluteus of the Sea Urchin.

native sea cucumbers our knowledge is exceedingly fragmentary, and for nearly all that we do know of the mode of growth of these animals in general, we are indebted to the elabo-

rate researches of the distinguished J. Müller. He figures the
earliest stage of the larval Holothurian, which he calls an "Auricularia." The course of de-
velopment is much as in
the starfishes. The earliest
stage known resembles
that of the starfish represented by Fig. 82. It then
passes through a stage represented by Fig. 85, when
the mouth and digestive
tract is formed, and again
a stage analogous with Fig.
87. The Auricularia when
fully grown, is cylindrical,
annulated, with four or
five bands of cilia, usually
with ear-like projections,
whence its name Auricu-
laria. Before it becomes
fully formed the young
Holothurian begins to
grow near the side of the
larval stomach, the cal-
careous crosses appear
and the tentacles of the
future Holothurian bud
out. The ear-like projec-
tions disappear, the Auricularia becomes cylindri-
cal, and is now called the
"pupa." The Auricularia

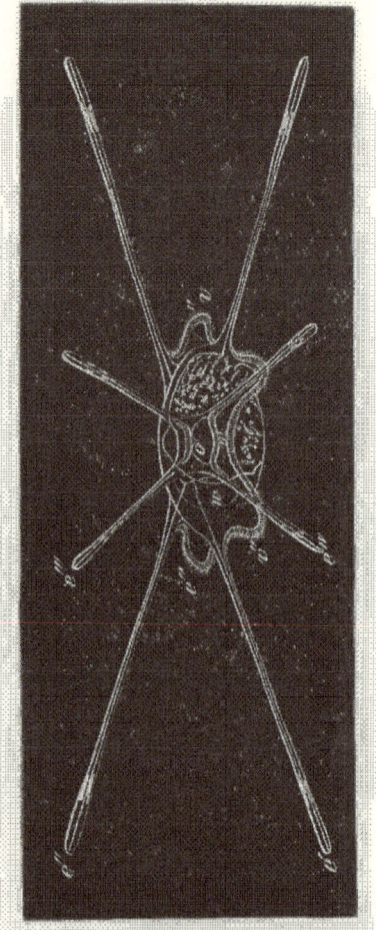

Fig. 9.

Profile view of 96.

is gradually absorbed and the young Holothurian strikingly resembles a worm. In this pupa stage, in certain transparent
forms observed by Müller, the intestine of the embryo Holothurian
could be observed twisted on itself, with the mouth surrounded by
tentacles. The only observations published on our native Holothurians are those of Mr. A. Agassiz, on Cuvieria, our large red,
heavily plated sea-cucumber, which inhabits stony bottoms in deep
water. The young are of a brilliant vermilion. In the earliest
stage observed by Mr. Agassiz (Fig. 99 *l*, "pupa;" *g*, tentacles);

the "pupa" or second form of the Auricularia is very large and
the tentacles do not project beyond the body, as they afterwards
do (Fig. 100) when the Auricularia is nearly absorbed by the growing Holothurian. In a succeeding stage the tentacles begin to
branch, where before they were simple and knobbed. At this time
the œsophagus, stomach, intestine and anus are developed, and
there is a ring of limestone rods and crosses around the mouth.
The madreporic body (*b*) has not yet been drawn within the body.

Fig. 98.

The young Echinus.

Finally, the Auricularia becomes wholly absorbed, the tentacles
are much branched and capable of retraction within the body; the
tegument secretes limestone plates, the suckers are developed in
the ambulacral rows and the adult form is attained without important changes. Fig. 72 represents a common sea-cucumber of our
coast.

Some holothurians, as well as starfishes and ophiurans, as observed by Mr. A. Agassiz, undergo their larval (*i. e.*, Plutens,
Brachiolaria and Auricularia) phases of development above
described without leaving the parent, in pouches held over the
mouth of the parent, making their escape in a form approaching
that of the adult.

Metschnikoff has made some valuable comparisons between the ciliated embryos of the Cœlenterates and Echinoderms, and shows that the primitive body-cavity of the former is not homologous with the peritoneal cavity (*i. e.*, the space in which the digestive canal hangs) of the Echinoderms. He also shows that while the primitive body cavity of the Cœlenterates remains permanently as the digestive tract, in the Echinoderms it is temporary and embryonic. Metschnikoff, on embryological grounds (a view which the structure of the adult animals confirms), thinks that there is the same similarity between the Cœlenterates (Acalephs and Ctenophoræ) and Echinoderms, as between the higher worms (Hirudineæ, Gephyrea and Annelides), and the Crustacea and Insects.

Fig. 101.

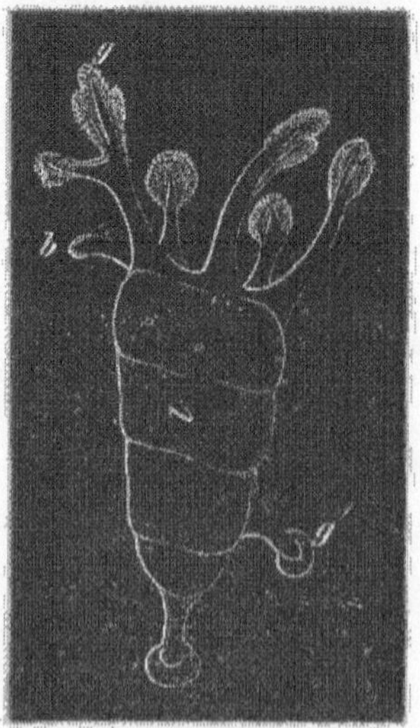

Larva of Cuvieria.

Reproduction by fission as in the Actiniæ and jelly fishes very rarely occurs in the Echinoderms. An Ophiuran deprived of all

Fig. 99.

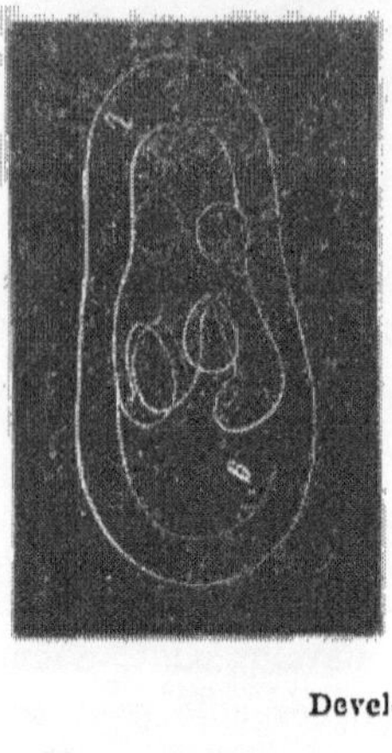

Fig. 100.

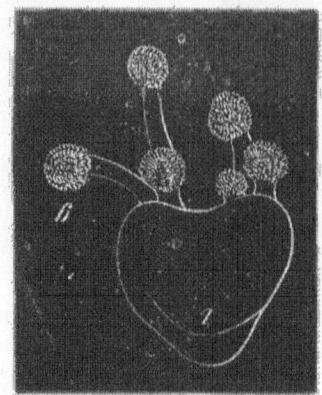

Development of a Holothurian (Cuvieria).

its arms will reproduce them by budding, and Lütken shows that certain starfishes divide in two spontaneously, having three arms on one side and three on the other, while the disk looks as if it had been cut in two by a knife, and three new arms had then grown out from the cut side.

Echinoderms as a rule, then, are reproduced alone by eggs and sperm cells. After fertilization of the egg they pass through :

1. Morula stage.

2. Gastrula stage.

3. A larval, temporary stage (Pluteus, Brachiolaria, Auricularia), the earliest phase of these larvæ being a Cephalula.

4. The Echinoderm grows from a water tube of the larva, finally absorbing the latter, whose form is often materially changed during the process. It thus undergoes a true metamorphosis, in a degree comparable with that of some insects.

LITERATURE.

J. *Müller.* Abhandlungen über die Metamorphose der Echinodermen. (K. Akademie der Wissenschaften. Berlin, 1848-1855).

A. *Agassiz.* On the Embryology of Echinoderms. (Memoirs Amer. Acad. Arts and Sci. ix, 1864.) Revision of the Echini, Part iv. (Ill. Cat. Mus. Comp. Zool. vii, 1874.)

Wyville Thompson. On the Embryology of Antedon rosaceus. (Philosophical Transactions, London, clv, 1865).

XIV. THE LAMELLIBRANCHIATA.

HAVING gone thus far along the track leading from the moners to man, we come to where the road branches in several directions. The path from the Protozoa to the sponges, from the sponges to the polypes, and from the polypes to the Ctenophoræ, and through them to the Echinoderms, though at times devious and readily lost, yet in the retrospect is more easily followed than those lying before us. In fact there is no single track leading directly from the lowest to the highest animals. We have to follow distinct lines of development, and, after toiling up one ascent, find that it ends abruptly, without bringing us very near the goal. We then have to retrace our steps, return to the old fork in the road and essay a new path. For example, following up the line of mollusca, we come to the cuttlefishes with their well developed eyes and circulatory apparatus, nearly as complicated as those of fishes. If we follow the ascidian line of development, we trace immediately in their larval condition a *chorda dorsalis* and a relation of rudimentary organs which bear a striking analogy to those of Amphioxus, the lowest vertebrate. Again, in studying the Brachiopods, we follow a line of life which leads us to forms such as the Lingula, which combines Annelid characters with remarkable features of its own. If after traversing these paths we take up the long and devious route which leads from the non-segmented worms through the Rotifers up to the leeches' and Annelides, to the Crustacea and Insects, we shall then reach animals which in many respects are only inferior to the vertebrates, and in complexity of organization, in their morphology and in their psychological endowments, are on the whole, superior to any other invertebrates.

What is this initial point from which these lines diverge? It is a larval form having a bilateral, cylindrical body, sometimes annulated, divided into a preoral and postoral region, *i. e.*, a head and hind body, with a ciliated crown, often a whip-lash or tuft of bristles, with a mouth, a usually curved alimentary cavity, and anus opening often near the mouth. This stage is seen in the young Echinoderm, such as the earliest stage of the Auricularia or Bipinnaria condition, as represented by Fig. 85 on page 83; or in the Veliger state of the young mollusk; in the young worm, whether the "Actinotrocha" of the Sipunculus, or "Tornaria" of

Balanoglossus, or "Mesotrocha" of a higher annelid, or even in the young Rotifers. For such a form the term *Cephalula* may be proposed in allusion to the fact that a cephalic region is indicated in this state, the Gastrula being a simple sac with the head end not differentiated from the opposite extremity. Let the reader compare the gastrula of the sponge (Fig. 44) with the Cephalula of the Trochus (Fig. 121, B) and he will detect the difference between the two stages. This stage is thus named simply to give emphasis to the fact that it is a form common at one stage in their life-history to several entirely different classes of animals, radiate, articulate and molluscan, independently of any theoretical considerations. I will only say that the Cephalula bears an analogous relation to these classes, as the Planula to the Radiates, the Nauplius to the Crustaceans, or the Leptus to the Insects.

We shall see in our future studies of the life-histories of the different classes of invertebrate animals, how often this Cephalula, with its ciliated crown, recurs.

No one has ever given a thoroughly satisfactory definition of the type of Mollusca, and we shall certainly not attempt one here. It may be said, however, that they are in their early stages, and in nearly all (except the Gastropoda, in which the visceral or abdominal end is asymmetrical), in adult life bisymmetrical animals bearing usually an external or internal shell (sometimes the shell is larval and deciduous), with the under lip converted into an organ of locomotion, the large fleshy foot. The nervous system consists of three pairs of ganglia usually surrounding the œsophagus, sending nerve-threads in irregular directions to the different organs.

The Mollusca usually have a well developed heart, more so than in the Crustacea and Insects, situated dorsally and consisting usually of a ventricle and two auricles. The respiratory organs depend or project from the mantle or tegument, and are permeated by a net-work of blood-vessels. A large number have an "odontophore" or "lingual ribbon, a band of teeth rolled up in the mouth. The mollusks are neither radiate nor segmented as in the Articulates or Vertebrates, though certain larvæ are indistinctly annulate as in that of Chiton.

The Tunicates, Polyzoa and Brachiopoda are not regarded as Mollusks, both on anatomical and developmental grounds, the reasons being given in the chapters treating of them.

For a further discussion of the characters of the mollusks as compared with the worms the reader is referred to Prof. Morse's memoir "On the Systematic Position of the Brachiopoda."[17]

The following tabular view of the mollusks is copied from Gegenbaur's "Principles of Comparative Anatomy." For further information the reader is referred to Woodward's "Manual of the Mollusca."

MOLLUSCA.

I. LAMELLIBRANCHIATA.
  1. *Astphonia* (Ostræa, Anomia, Pecten, Mytilus, Arca, Unio).
  2. *Siphoniata* (Chama, Cardium, Cyclas, Venus, Tellina, Mactra, Solen, Pholas, Teredo).
II. CEPHALOPHORA.
  1. *Scaphopoda* (Dentalium).
  2. *Pteropoda.*
      Thecosomata (Hyalea, Cleodora, Chreseis, Cymbulea, Tiedemannia).
      Gymnosomata (Pneumodermon, Clio).
  3. *Gastropoda.*
      Heteropoda (Atlanta, Carinaria).
      Opisthobranchiata (Bulla, Aplysia, Doris, Glaucus, Æolis).
      Prosobranchiata.
        Cyclobranchiata (Patella, Chiton).
        Ctenobranchiata (Paludina, Neritina, Buccinum, Purpura, Murex, Fusus, Conus, Oliva, Strombus, Haliotis).
  4. *Pulmonata* (Lymnæus, Physa, Planorbis, Helix, Bulimus, Limax).
III. CEPHALOPODA.
  1. *Tetrabranchiata* (Nautilus).
  2. *Dibranchiata.*
      Decapoda (Spirula, Sepia, Loligo).
      Octopoda (Octopus, Argonauta).

Development of the Lamellibranchs. It is only within a comparatively few years that we have learned anything of the mode of growth of our commonest bivalve mollusks. To this day the life history of the common clam or quahaug is a mystery. The early stages of the oyster are only partially known. We know much less about the early stages of the common sea mussel; while the history of the fresh-water mussel (Unio) sketched roughly in 1831 by Carus, is still fragmentary. For the first definite knowledge of the metamorphoses of the Lamellibranchs, we are indebted to the distinguished Swedish observer Lovén, who gave between the years 1844 and 1849, a series of sketches more or less complete of

---

[17] Proceedings of the Boston Society of Natural History, Vol. XV, 1873, 8vo. pp. 60.

a number of marine forms. To him and to Sars, the famous Nor-
wegian zoologist, who made the first sketch of the metamorphoses
of the Gastropods, we are indebted for our earliest and most valuable facts in the life-history of the mollusks. Before this, some
larval mollusks were regarded as infusoria by Ehrenberg.

Of the mode of development of the oyster, the lowest lamellibranch, the first information was supplied by Lacaze-Duthiers
(1854–5), supplemented by the recent (1874) observations of
Salensky. While some lamellibranchs, such as the Unio, are bisexual, the oyster is hermaphroditic. The eggs, which are yellow,
after leaving the ovary are retained among the gills. A single
oyster may lay 2,000,000 eggs. The spawning time of the oyster
in Europe is from June to September. During their development
the eggs are enclosed in a creamy slime, growing darker as the
"sprat" (the term applied to the young oysters) develops.

The course of development is thus: after the segmentation of
the yolk (morula stage), the embryo divides into a clear peripheral
layer (ectoderm), and an opaque inner layer containing the yolk
and representing the inner germinal layer (endoderm). A few filaments or large cilia arise on what is to form the velum or the
future head. The shell then begins to appear at what is destined to be the posterior end of the germ, and before the digestive cavity arises. At this stage the two-layered germ is said
by Salensky to represent the planula of the sponge. The digestive cavity is next formed (gastrula stage), and the anus appears
just behind the mouth, the alimentary canal being bent at right
angles. Meanwhile the shell has grown enough to cover half the
embryo, which is now in the "Veliger" stage, the "velum" being
composed of two ciliated lobes in front of the mouth-opening, and
comparable with that of the gastropod larvæ. The young oyster,
as figured by Salensky, is directly comparable with the Veliger of
the Cardium (Fig. 102).

We have, then, three stages of growth in the oyster, (1) the
morula, (2) the gastrula (with the digestive cavity as yet undeveloped and, (3) the veliger with an alimentary canal and a head
and hind body (cephalula). This is an epitome of the mode of
development of most of the lamellibranchiate mollusks whose embryology is known. Soon the shell covers the entire larva, only
the ciliated velum projecting out of an anterior end from between
the shells. In this stage the larval oyster leaves the mother and

swims around in the water, the cilia of the velum keeping up a lively rotary motion. In this state Lacaze-Duthiers observed it for forty-three days, without any striking change in form, except that the velum increased in size, and the auditory vesicle appeared, containing several otoliths, which kept up a rapid motion. But still the gills and heart were wanting. Of its further history we know but little, except that it becomes fastened to some rock and is incapable of motion. The oyster is said by the appearance of its shell, to be three years in attaining its full growth, but this statement needs confirmation.

The most complete life history of a bivalve mollusk is that of Cardium (*C. pygmæum*), the cockle shell, as described by Lovén. The egg of this shell is spherical, the yolk being surrounded by a layer of white protoplasm, much as in the eggs of vertebrates. The process of fertilization was observed by Lovén, who saw the spermatic particles of the usual form, *i.e.* with a head and long tail, to the number of a dozen penetrating through the envelopes of the egg out toward the yolk. Following the morula condition the embryo consists of two layers, an outer peripheral clear mass like the "white" of an egg (ectoderm), and a central dark mass, regarded by later observers as equivalent to the inner germinal layer. The embryo now becomes ciliated on its upper surface and already rotates in the shell. On one side of the oval embryo is an opening or fissure,[18] on the edges of which arise two tubercles which eventually become the two "sails" of the velum. This probably represents the gastrula stage, and the embryo already shows a tendency to become bilateral. The next step is the differentiation of the body into head and hind body, *i.e.* an oral (cephalic) and postoral region. Out of the middle of the head grows a single very large cilium, like the whip-lash of the Flagellata, the so-called flagellum (Fig. 102 A, *fl; v,* velum). The shell (Fig. 102 B, *sh*) and mantle (*mt; ml,* muscle) now begin to form. From the inner yolk-mass are developed the stomach, the two liver lobes (*li*) on each side of the stomach (*t*), and the intes-

---

[18] This primitive opening, the mouth, appears both in Cardium and Crenella, according to Lovén's figures and descriptions, long before the shell begins to form. It is thus not a secondary formation, as Salensky insists, but a primary invagination of the ectoderm. The embryo is therefore properly a gastrula. It will be remembered that in the oyster on the contrary the shell begins to form before the mouth-opening appears. The young oyster at the stage immediately succeeding the morula is, then, a planula; the Cardium and Crenella, a gastrula. This exception does not warrant us in denying a gastrula state to the Lamellibranchs as a class, as Salensky does.

tine (*i*). The mouth (*m*), which is richly ciliated, lies behind the velum, the alimentary canal is bent nearly at right angles and the anus opens behind and near the mouth. The velum (Fig. 102, *v*) really constitutes the upper lip, while a tongue-like projection (Fig. 102, B *f*) behind the mouth is the under lip, and is destined to form the large unpaired "foot," so characteristic of the mollusks.

In a stage previous to this, when the shell only partially covers the animal, the veliger may be compared with the veliger of Trochus (Fig. 121, B) and a remarkable resemblance be traced, the velum, the bent alimentary canal and the foot being almost identical. The shell arises as a cup-shaped organ in both bivalves and univalves, but the hinge and separate valves are indicated very early in the lamellibranchs. The earliest phase of the veliger stage

Fig. 102.

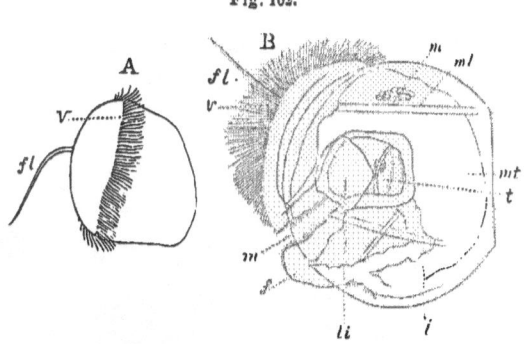

Development of Cardium.   After Lovén.

(trochosphere) indicated at Fig. 102 A, in which a cephalic and abdominal region is demarked, may be compared with profit by the reader with the embryo Infusorian with its cup-shaped body and its crown of cilia, or with the larval Polyzoan or even the larval Brachiopod to be hereafter figured. At the stage represented by Fig. 102, B, the stomach is divided into an anterior and posterior (pyloric) portion. The liver forms on each side of the stomach an oval fold, and communicates by a large opening with its cavity; while the intestine elongates and makes more of a bend. The organ of hearing then arises, and behind it the provisional eyes, each appearing as a vesicle with dark pigment corpuscles arranged around a refractive body. The nerve ganglion (*m*) appears above the stomach. The two ciliated gill-lobes now appear, and the number of lobes increases gradually to three or four. The foot grows larger, and the organ of Bojanus, or kidney, becomes visible. The shell now hardens; the mouth advances, the velum is withdrawn from the under side to the anterior end of the shell. In this condition the veliger remains for a long time, its long flagellum still attached, and used in swimming even after the foot has become a creeping organ. Latest of all appears the heart, with the blood-vessels.

Upon throwing off the veliger condition, the velum contracts, splits up and Lovén thinks it becomes reduced to the two pairs of palpi, which are situated on each side of the mouth of the mature lamellibranch. The provisional eyes disappear, and the eyes of the adult arise on the edge of the mantle.

The mode of development of *Crenella marmorata* is nearly identical with that of Cardium. The Crenella is diœcious, the females being known by their reddish ovaries, the males by their white sexual glands. In this genus, however, there is no egg-capsule, and no "white" enveloping the yolk.

All that we know of the development of the common muscle (*Mytilus edulis*, Fig. 103, after Morse) is from studies made by Lacaze-Duthiers on the shores of the Mediterranean. The larval forms were not discovered. The young about $\frac{1}{5}^{mm}$ in length were found swimming at ebb tide on the surface of the water. The shell at this stage is like a Crenella, and there are four long gill lobes, which arise from the outer lamella of the inner gill.

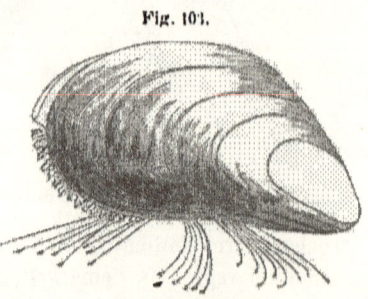

Fig. 103.

Common Mussel.

The fresh water bivalves pass through entirely different phases of development from the marine forms. The eggs of Cyclas have no shell, no "white" and no yolk skin; they are few in number, from one to six existing in unequal degrees of development in broad cavities filled with a nutritive fluid, and hanging free from the base of the inner gill. The velum is either absent or very slightly developed, and the shell begins to develop at two widely separated initial points on the mantle, according to Leydig.

The fresh water mussels (Unio, Fig. 104, after Morse, and Anodonta) represent another mode of development. In their embryo the velum is wanting or exists in a very rudimentary state. The mantle and shell are developed very early. They live within the parent fastened to each other by their byssus. The shell (Fig.

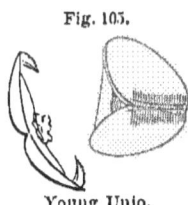

Fig. 105.

Young Unio.

105) differs remarkably from that of the adult, being broader than long, triangular, the apex or outer edge of the shell hooked, while from different points within project a few large, long spines. So different are these young from the parent that they were supposed to be parasites and were described under the name of *Glochidium parasiticum*. They are found in the parent mussel during July and August. The eggs have a shell, "white," and yolk skin and a micropyle. The embryo rotates,

Fig. 104.

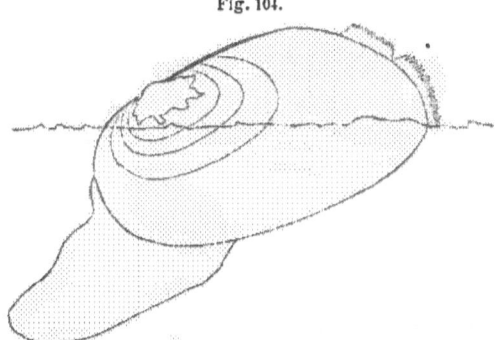

Unio moving through the sand with the siphons expanded.

and remains a month in the egg. When hatched, great numbers still remain among the gills in a mass of slime, and during this time the shell thickens, grows rounder and somewhat longer.

The history of the ship worm (Fig. 106, *Teredo navalis* Linn.) is one of great interest both from a practical and scientific point of view. To the eminent French naturalist, Quatrefages, we are indebted for its life history. Its general development up to the time of the larval stage is much like that of the oyster. The egg has no shell. After fertilization it undergoes total segmentation (Fig. 107, A). The two germinal layers appear as usual, the velum arises much as in the embryo oyster, there being no lash, as in the Cardium, but scattered cilia. Swimming about in this state the embryo would be mistaken for an infusorian. In forty-eight hours after life begins, the cilia begin to disappear and the germ sinks to the bottom. A deep fissure now separates the germ into halves; meanwhile the mantle and shell have grown, and when

Fig. 106.

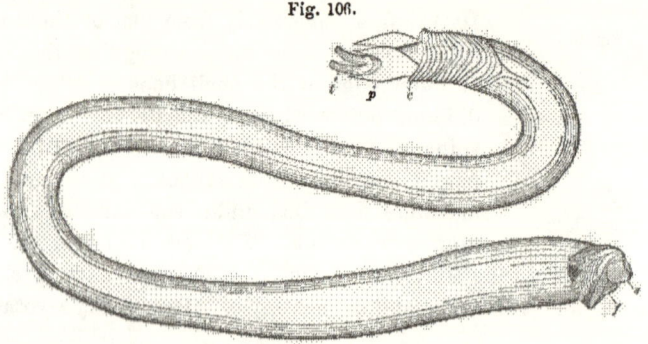

The Ship Worm.[10] After Verrill.

five days and a half old the germ appears as in Fig. 107, B, the shell almost covering the larva. Soon after this the velum becomes larger, and then decreases, the gills arise, the auditory sacs develop, the foot grows, though not reaching to the edge of the shell, and the larva can still swim about free in the water. When of the size of a grain of millet, it becomes spherical, as in Fig. 107, C, brown and opaque. The long and slender foot projects far out of the shell, and the velum assumes the form of a swollen ring on which is a double crown of cilia.

Fig. 107.

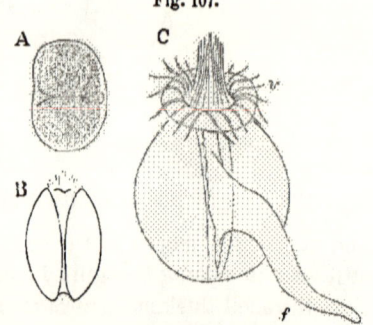

Development of the Ship Worm.

The ears and eyes develop more, and the animal alternately swims with its velum, or walks by means of the foot. At this stage Quatrefages thinks it seeks the piles of wharves and floating wood in which it bores and completes its metamorphosis. The further changes must be very great before it assumes the adult form of the ship worm with its long body, but these stages have not been observed. Keferstein, however, says that Vrolik saw in July the

---

[10] Fig. 106, c, collar; p, pallets; t, siphonal tubes; s. shell; f, foot. After Verrill. Report U. S. Fish Commissioner. Fig. 107, v, velum; f, foot. After Quatrefages.

larvæ swimming about on the coast of Holland, and some by the middle of the month had bored into the wood and attained the adult Teredo form, though still very small, while others in September still retained their larval, veliger shape. It requires about three weeks for them to complete their metamorphosis. Verrill states that the *Teredo navalis* on the coast of New England "produces its young in May, and probably through the greater part or all of the summer." Quatrefages says that the Teredos die during the winter succeeding their birth.

Keferstein tells us that some lamellibranchs attain their growth in one year. The fresh water mussels (Unio and Anodonta) are thought to live from ten to twelve years, while *Tridacna gigantea* probably lives from sixty years to a century.

The time of spawning usually takes place in summer. The edible mussel (*Mytilus edulis*) and different species of Venus are found with eggs and embryos among the gills from March till May, on the coast of Holland and France, while Pholas and Pandora and most other genera breed from July until September. On the Sicilian coast, according to Poli, Mya and Solen breed early in spring; Pholas, Chama, Venus, Donax, Anomia, Tellina and Mactra in summer; Mytilus edulis from October to December.

We have seen that the Lamellibranchs pass through a true veliger stage, and we shall soon see that their larval forms are directly comparable with the veliger state of most Cephalophora. In after life the "head" of the bivalve, *i.e.* the oral and preoral part of the body, which was fully half as large as the body in the veliger, diminishes greatly in size and importance, becoming finally merged with the postoral region and represented simply by the palpi and foot, the mouth-opening being situated at or near the extremity of the body, so that the old term Acephala well indicates the want of a cephalic region as compared with the large and well developed head of the snails (Cephalophora) and cuttle-fishes (Cephalopoda).

The summary of changes is usually as follows:

1. Egg fertilized by tailed spermatic particles.
2. Morula.
3. Gastrula. (Observed in a very few cases.)
4. Veliger (Cephalula). In Unio and Cyclas wholly or mostly suppressed.
5. Adult Lamellibranch.

LITERATURE.

J. E. Carus. Entwicklung von Unio und Anodonta. (Nova Acta Phys. Med. Leopold. 1831).

S. Lovén. Development of Marine Lamellibranchs. (Ofversigt af Kong. Vetensk. Akad. 1844–1849. Wiegmann's Archiv. 1849. See also Keferstein's abstract in Bronn's Classen und Ordnungen der Thierreichs, vol. iii.)

A. de Quatrefages. Anatomie et Embryologie de la Teredo. (Annales des Sciences Nat. 1848–50.)

Lacaze-Duthiers. Development of various Lamellibranchs. (Annales des Sc. Nat. 1854, 1855).

O. Schmidt. Entwickelung von Cyclas. (Müller's Archiv, 1854).

F. Leydig. Cyclas; Anatomie und Entwickelung. (Müller's Archiv, 1855).

W. Salensky. Bemerkungen über Hæckel's Gastræa-Theorie, with three drawings of the embryo oyster and very brief description. (Wiegmann's Archiv, 1874).

XV. THE CEPHALOPHORA.

The Cephalophora include not only the Gastropods (snails and whelks) but more aberrant forms such as the swimming Pteropods

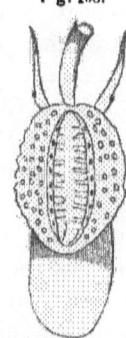

Fig. 108.

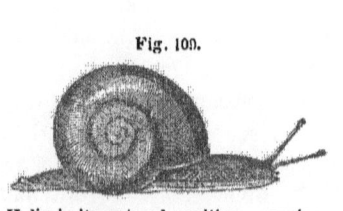

Fig. 109.

Helix in its natural position, creeping.

Trivia, a Gastropod. After Stearns.

and the Dentalium, etc. The term indicates the presence in the adult of a well formed head, as distinguished from the acephalous clams. Not only is there a head, but the eyes are restricted to the most anterior part of the preoral region, being, as in the snail, borne on extensile tentacles, whereas in the bivalves, such as the pecten, the eyes are scattered on the edge of the mantle along the entire body. The adult animal is not symmetrical, the mantle containing the viscera being thrown on one side. The foot is greatly enlarged, forming the entire under side of the animal, as in the snail (Fig. 109). The shell is usually external, spiral and asymmetrical, or cup-shaped.

The tooth shell, or Dentalium, is the lowest of its class, and its life history is one of much interest. For the following facts we are indebted to the memoir of Lacaze-Duthiers. The sexes are distinct. It breeds from the beginning of August until the middle of September. After fertilization by the spermatic particles, which Lacaze-Duthiers saw penetrating into the egg, the yolk undergoes complete segmentation (A). At the end of this time the embryo swims about by means of tufts of fine cilia (Fig. 110, B), and a pencil of large cilia in front. It then lengthens and is provided with seven bands of cilia, and the larva is remarkably worm-like

Fig. 110.

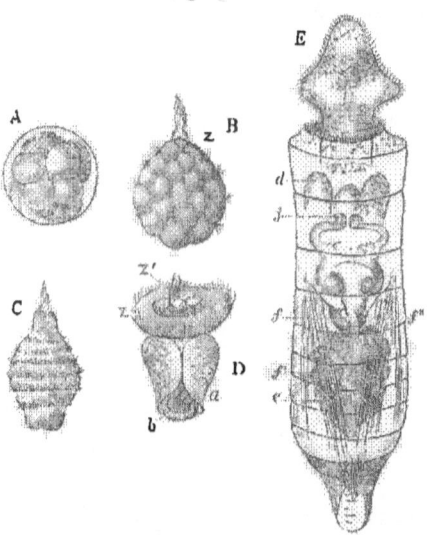

Development of Dentalium.

(C). When two days old the mantle secretes a small shell (a) at the end of the body. The ciliated bands now approach and form a swollen ring, or ciliated crown, the velum, as in fig. 110, D, z. At this time the shell is median, unpaired and situated on the back of the larva. The lobes of the foot next arise. Fig. 110, E, represents the young Dentalium, after leaving the larval state, and when thirty-five days old. The three-lobed foot protrudes from the shell now enclosing the animal, the rudimentary tentacles (E, d) are visible, as well as the suboesophageal nerve-ganglia (E, j) and the digestive canal (E, f, f') and liver (f'). After this, the change into the mature form is slight.

The winged sea-snails (Pteropods) are beautiful creatures found floating on the high seas. With their large, ciliated velum and rudimentary foot they represent the Veliger or larval condition of the Gastropods. There is scarcely a more strikingly beautiful and strange object in nature than the Spirialis with its large heavily ciliated velum, which may be caught in our harbors with the towing net and compared with the young veligerous gastropods often captured in the same net.

The egg of Cavolinia undergoes total segmentation, and before the large yolk-spheres are absorbed, the spherical embryo swims about like a larval infusorian with a crown of cilia. It may now be called a Trochosphere. Soon the larva assumes a conical form

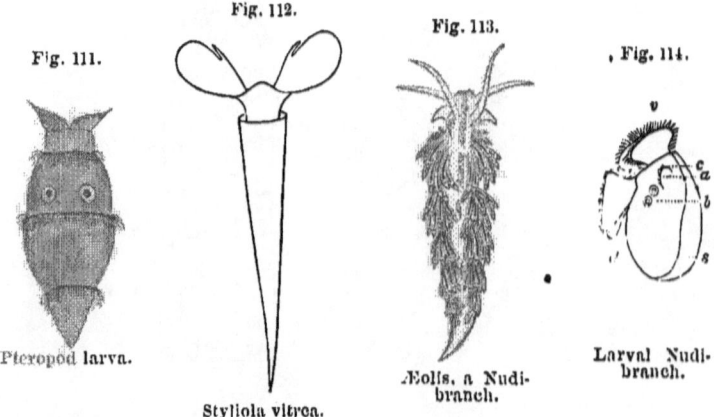

Fig. 111.

Fig. 112.

Fig. 113.

Fig. 114.

Pteropod larva.

Styliola vitrea.

Æolis, a Nudibranch.

Larval Nudibranch.

and subsequently the velum greatly expands. Afterwards the Cavolina, with its projecting foot, assumes a form much like the veliger of Trochus (Fig. 121, B). Fig. 111 (after Gegenbaur) represents a singular Pteropod veliger after the velum has disappeared, consisting of three distinct ciliated segments, like a worm. Fig. 112, after Verrill, represents an adult Pteropod, *Styliola vitrea*, enlarged three times, with the wings of the velum.

Bulla, Æolis and Doris, represent the Opisthobranchiate or naked mollusks, which either, as in the two latter genera, have no shell, with the gills arranged singly or in tufts on the back, or possess a white shell, as in Bulla, the bubble shell. Fig. 113 (from Verrill's Report), represents *Æolis*. Fig. 114[20] (after Schultze)

[20] Fig. 114, *d*, foot; *s*, nautilus-like deciduous shell; *v*, velum.

represents the young Tergipes, a naked sea-slug allied to Doris, with its large ciliated velum and foot, the animal being partly surrounded by a large shell (s). This shell is finally dropped with the other deciduous larval organs, the gills grow out from the back and the soft elongated body of the adult nudibranch, (as this animal is called,) is finally attained. It is a singular fact, discovered by Sars, that in the egg-capsules of Dendronotus as many as six embryos develop side by side.

We will now more carefully study the course of development of a Bulla (*Acera bullata*) as given by Langerhans.

In this animal the yolk of the egg subdivides into two spheres of segmentation, one being much smaller than the other and differing in color. Each of these two cells subdivides into similar halves. The two larger cells then remain passive, while the smaller form a mass of nucleated cells which in two or three days form a layer surrounding the central, inactive yolk cells. On the fifth day arises the first indication of the shell, and on the same day is developed a furrow, the primitive mouth, which separates the cephalic end from the postoral extremity. On the seventh day appear the rudiments of the organ of hearing, and on the day after, the operculum. On the ninth day the pharynx, stomach and intestine begin to develop. On the fifteenth day the otolites are seen in the ear. The liver is next formed, and a few days after the eyes and nerve ganglia, when the larva hatches.

Fig. 115.

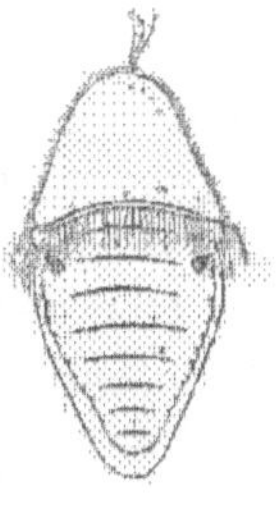

With the mode of development of Chiton, a cyclo-branchiate Gastropod, Lovén has made us acquainted. The larva leaves the egg oval in form, with a ciliated ring in the middle of the body and a long tuft of large cilia on the head. Afterwards it becomes annulated, as in Fig. 115 (after Lovén) and two eye specks appear. Its resemblance to a worm larva is now remarkable. It soon settles down into a quiet life as a Chiton (Fig. 116, *C. ruber*, represents a species found on our shores, from Verrill's Report, after Morse), and the limestone plates correspond to the primitive larval rings.

Fig. 116.

Chiton.

Veliger of Chiton.

Of the mode of development of the other marine univalve shells (Prosobranchiate Gastropoda), I cannot do better than avail myself of the recent papers of Dr. Salensky. His studies were made on shells living in the Black Sea, but we have species of Calyptræa and Trochus on our own coast.

Calyptræa sinensis lays its eggs in pear-shaped capsules attached to the same mussel or stone on which it lives. The young of the same brood develop at the same time. Development begins with the total segmentation of the yolk. After it divides into eight cells the blastoderm forms, which consists of a single layer of cells, the result of the subdivision of the first four spheres of segmentation, which grow over and envelop the yolk spheres, thus forming the two germinal layers (ectoderm and endoderm). The cells of the outer layer multiply and form the blastoderm, from which the skin, mantle and external organs, as well as the walls of the mouth arise, while, as in the articulates, the alimentary canal with its dependencies, the liver, etc., arise from the periphery of the yolk cells, the central mass being absorbed.

As soon as the blastoderm is formed, a heap of cells arise and the ectoderm pushes in at a spot which becomes the ventral side of the body. This is the primitive mouth. The anterior part of this cellular heap is the first indication of the "head-vesicle," which becomes a provisional organ well developed in the larva, and is also seen in the embryo fresh-water snails (Pulmonata). The sides of the primitive mouth form the two "sails" of the velum or swimming organ, so characteristic of the larval mollusks, and which was first noticed by Forskal, who wrote on animals just a century ago. Finally, the posterior edge of the infolding, which is also at first a little mass of cells, is the first indication of the foot. The whole surface of the embryo is now covered with cilia, and by their movement the embryo with its fellows, rotates in its capsule.

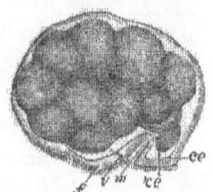

Fig. 117.

Veliger of Calyptræa.

The next change consists in the growth and differentiation of the parts already sketched out. The germ of the foot extends backwards, the mouth-opening deepens and becomes tube-like, the first indication of the pharynx (Vorderdarm). The next most important change is the presence of a layer of cells between the outer and inner germinal layers, which is called the middle germ layer, with cells very unlike the outer layer, from which are developed the muscles of the foot and head as well as the heart

itself. Salensky thinks that this middle layer arises from the
outer. It appears first on the ventral side of the embryo. The
germ is now of the form indicated by Fig. 117 (*ce*, ectoderm;
'*ce*, middle layer, the yolk spheres representing the inner layer,
or endoderm ; *m*, mouth ; *v*, velum ; *f*, foot. After Salensky).

The next important chapter in the life history of the Calyptræa,
is the appearance of the mantle, which arises as a disk-like thickening of the outer germ-layer on the back of the embryo. In the
middle of the disk the shell grows out as a cup-like cavity which
is connected only around the edge with the mantle, but is free in
the centre. The ears or auditory vesicles next appear, which, like
the eyes, begin as an infolding of the outer germ-layer.

Up to this time the entire body has been symmetrical. Along
the longitudinal axis of the body are the foot, the head-vesicle,
the germ of the alimentary canal, and on each side a lobe of the
velum. The alimentary canal, now further developed, begins to
curve to the left, and as the shell grows, the visceral sack, or postoral portion of the body, hangs over on one side. Not until the
organs of sense appeared, the ears with their otolites, and the eyes
with their pigment cells, did Salensky discover any trace of a
nervous system, and then it was not the cephalic, but the ganglion

Fig. 118.

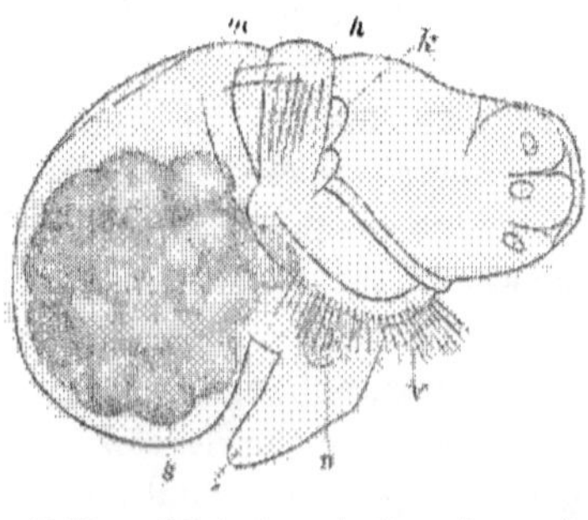

Veliger of Calyptræa farther advanced.

of the foot which first arises as
a mass of nerve cells from the
ectoderm.

Fig. 118 (after Salensky) represents the asymmetrical larva
with the shell enveloping a large
part of the body, and the velum
(*v*) and foot (*f*) well developed.
The larval head forms a third
of the whole body and is still
finely ciliated. The temporary
larval heart (*h*), a large oval
vesicle, is situated on the right side of the back of the embryo,
between the head and anterior edge of the mantle, in quite a different position from that of the adult heart, which afterwards arises
as a new organ. The larval heart contracts rhythmically sixty
times a minute. This is an entirely different organ, says Salensky,
from the pulsating vesicle or "heart" seen by Duben and Koren
in Purpura (Fig. 119, *P. lapillus* and egg capsules, from Verrill's

Report) and Buccinum, or the contractile vesicle found by Semper in Ampullaria, Cypræa, Murex and Ovulum, or the dorsal vesicle of the Pulmonates (snails). There is, however, a similar larval heart in Nassa.

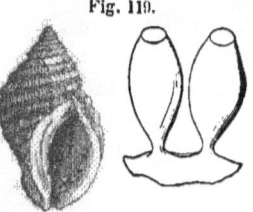

Fig. 119.

At this stage also appears the primitive kidney (Fig. 118, *k*), also a deciduous organ, the permanent, adult kidney arising in another part of the body far behind the larval heart. It resembles the primitive kidneys of the snails (Pulmonates), and appears first as a sort of necklace consisting of four yellowish cells, situated next to the larval heart.

Purpura and Egg Capsules.

Meanwhile the more the posterior part of the body grows, the larger and more spiral becomes the shell, until the helmet shape of the adult is approached. At this stage also the gill-cavity appears, but there is as yet no trace of the gill itself.

In a succeeding stage the foot has increased in length, the spire of the shell has begun to topple over as it were and fall on one side like a skull cap, and now the adult heart (the pericardium being formed first), and permanent kidney and gills grow out. The gills originate from the ectoderm. It is not until this period that the end of the intestine and anal outlet is formed. The provisional larval organs now begin to disappear, the cephalic vesicle (larval head) grows smaller, the primitive kidneys disappear. Of the larval visceral organs only the heart remains which, though smaller, still pulsates. It now rests under the mantle in the branchial cavity. There are now two gill-leaves, and finally the permanent heart is formed. The further changes consist in the perfection of all these organs and the development of the shell into the helmet shape of the adult. Fig. 120 (after Morse) represents the common *Calyptræa striata* of our own coast. We have seen that the usual five stages have been undergone, *i.e.* the egg, morula, gastrula (not so well marked as in the pond snail, Fig. 122), veliger and adult.

Fig. 120.

Calyptræa striata.

The metamorphoses of Trochus represent another type of development in the Gastropods, which illustrate points less clearly wrought out in the Calyptræa.

The eggs of *Trochus varius* are very small, spherical, and laid

in masses of jelly on sea weeds. The morula, or mulberry mass,
forms as usual. The blastoderm arises from a few small
clear spheres of segmentation situated at one pole of four primitive dark morula cells. The four vitelline or primitive cells,
instead of remaining passive as in Calyptræa, subdivide, as well
as the blastodermic cells. The egg now becomes flattened at
one pole and slightly pointed at the other, the latter being the
anterior end.

In six hours after development begins, the outer layer begins
to form, and the first organ to arise is the velum, which at first
consists of a swollen ciliated ring on the anterior end of the embryo. This stage (Fig. 121, A, v, velum, after Salensky) is equivalent to the trochosphere (Lankester) of the pond snail. It will
thus be seen that the development of Trochus is now very different from that of the Calyptræa, where the velum, head-vesicle
and foot arise simultaneously. A little later the mouth and œsophagus arise. Salensky remarks that the Prosobranchiate Gastropods
as a rule develop like Trochus. In Vermetus, however, according
to the observations of Lacaze-Duthiers, the velum does not arise
in the form of a ciliated crown, but as a paired organ. Salensky
adds, however, that in other respects there is a strong analogy
in Calyptræa to Vermetus and Buccinum and Purpura, which
develop like the former mollusk, having a similar larval heart and
primitive kidneys, though the mode of development of the external organs is almost wholly unknown. There are thus five genera of Prosobranchiate Gastropods which develop as in Calyptræa,
all belonging to the suborder Ctenobranchiata.

On the other hand, *Paludina vivipara, Neritina fluviatilis*, and
certain Pteropods (*Tiedemannia neapolitana, Carolinia gibbosa*)
and a Heteropod (Pterotrachea) are provided, as in Trochus, with
a ciliated crown, the first organ lying behind the primitive mouth.

"A good starting point," adds Salensky (whom we have in reality
been quoting all along), "for the comparison of the development of
Trochus and allied forms, with that of other animals, consists in
this stage (Fig. 121, A). A cursory glance at the illustration will
convince one that this condition of the Trochus embryo is similar to the larva of some Annelides. Examples of such Annelid
larvæ may be seen in some Sabellidæ (*e. g., Dasychone lucullana*) or
Spio (*S. fuliginosus*). The latter in escaping from the egg have
a more or less oval body consisting of two layers, its only organ

a ciliated crown on the anterior part of the body. The idea of an analogy between the Mollusca and Annelid larva has already been suggested by Gegenbaur. Still more strongly does it follow from these facts, that in the Annelides, as surely as in the Mollusks, the mouth-opening, with the pharynx, arises immediately after the formation of the ciliated crown and somewhat behind the same. Immediately after the formation of the rudimentary pharynx arise the characteristic organs of the two types: in the Annelides the body segments with their appendages; in the Mollusks the foot, shell and two velar lobes."

Salensky then compares the development of Trochus with the Rotifer, Brachionus, and finds some striking analogies. His facts we shall present hereafter in describing from his memoir the life-history of a rotifer.

In the second period of development of Trochus, the true Veliger state is entered upon. The mantle and shell are formed much as in Calyptræa. The body is now flattened, and the ciliated crown projects very slightly. The shell (*s*) has grown considerably.

Fig. 121, B, after Salensky, represents this stage. The pharynx (*d*) arises through a tube-like invagination of the outer germ-layer, behind the ciliated crown (*v*). At the same time behind the mouth arises

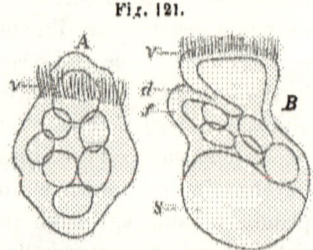

Fig. 121.

Larval Trochus.

a projection, which indicates the beginning of a foot (*f*). Within the foot, as well as in the anterior part of the body, may be noticed the middle germ-layer, which arises as a layer of cells between the outer and inner germ-layer.

In the following stage the form of the larva is somewhat changed. The shell begins to unroll spirally on the under side of the body. The velum grows more than the middle portion of the head, and the lateral lobes become larger. The operculum also arises on the posterior portion of the foot.

Coming now to the mode of development of the Pulmonate mollusks (fresh-water and land-snails), we find that the aquatic forms undergo a complete metamorphosis, while in the land-snails there is no metamorphosis, and they are hatched in nearly the same form as the adult.

The life history, particularly the earlier stages, of the common pond snail (*Limnæus stagnalis*) of Europe has been worked out with much care by Prof. Ray Lankester, his observations confirming those of Lereboullet, Pouchet and other's so far as they extended.

The eggs of Limnæus are deposited in June on the under side of water-plants, in capsules enclosing one, rarely two eggs, and

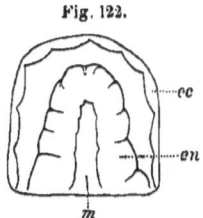

Fig. 122.

Gastrula of the Pond Snail.

surrounded by a mass of jelly. After segmentation the Gastrula (Fig. 122, *m*, mouth ; *ec*, ectoderm ; *en*, endoderm) is formed, the primitive digestive cavity or mouth resulting probably from an infolding of the ectoderm. Lankester believes that this orifice or mouth is temporary, the mouth of the adult being a later production. The primitive mouth closes as the embryo enters on the Veliger state, in the earliest stages of which the embryo is oval and surrounded by a ciliated ring, much as in the larval Trochus (Fig. 121, A). This state is called by Lankester the "Trochosphere." A definite Veliger stage is finally attained ; the foot is large and bilobed, the mantle and shell then arise and the larva soon passes into the definite molluscan condition, with a shell, creeping foot, mantle-flap and eye-tentacles. The young snail hatches in about twenty days after life begins.

Professor Lankester confirms the suggestions already made by Gegenbaur, Morse and Salensky regarding the resemblance of the larval mollusks to young worms. He remarks also that both the Trochosphere and Veliger forms are "well known and characteristic of various groups of Worms and Echinoderms, and the latter is seen in its full development in the adult Rotifera, and in the larval Gasteropoda and Pteropoda. The identity of the velum of larval Gasteropods, with the ciliated disks of Rotifera, seems to admit of little doubt, and it would be well to have one term, *e. g.*, velum, by which to describe both. The Trochosphere is the earlier, more or less spherical form in which the velum is represented by an annular ciliated ridge, and which is sometimes (*e. g.*, *Chiton*) provided with a polar tuft of long cilia.

"The cell, polyblast (morula), gastrula, trochosphere, and veliger phases of molluscan development are not distinctive of the molluscan pedigree ; they belong to its præ-molluscan history. The foot, shell-gland, and the odontophore are organs which are distinctively molluscan — the last characteristic of the higher Mollusca only — the other two of the whole group, and their appearance must be traced to ancestors within the proper stem of the molluscan family tree. The foot is essentially a greatly developed lower lip."

We would add that the Molluscan as well as Annelid Trochosphere may be directly compared (morphologically, not histologically) with the embryo Infusoria (see Fig. 28, E, p. 38) and the ancestry of the Mollusca as well as the Vermes should, as Haeckel declares, be traced back to the Infusoria, perhaps the parentforms of the entire animal world above the Protozoa.

The usually hermaphroditic Cephalophora, as a rule, to sum up the different phases of their metamorphosis, pass through the following stages :

1. Egg.

2. Morula.

3. Gastrula. (sometimes suppressed?).

4. Veliger (the earliest substage being the Trochosphere, which passes into the generalized Cephalula form ; or, restricted to the mollusks, the Veliger stage).

5. Adult mollusk, with foot, shell and often lingual ribbon (odontophore).

LITERATURE.

Sars. Development of Nudibranchs. (Wiegmann's Archiv. 1837, 1840, 1845).

Pouchet. Théorie positive de l'Ovulation spontanée, etc. Paris, 1847.

Leydig. Ueber Paludina vivipara (Siebold and Kölliker's Zeitschrift, 1850).

Koren and *Danielssen.* Bidrag til Pectinibranchiernes Udviklingshistorie. Bergen, 1851, 1856. (Wiegmann's Archiv, 1853).

Kölliker and *Gegenbaur.* Entwickelung von Pneumodermon. (Siebold and Kölliker's Zeitschrift, 1853).

Gegenbaur. Untersuchungen neber Pteropoden und Heteropoden. Leipzig, 1855.

Claparède. Anatomie und Entwickelungsgeschichte der Neritina fluviatilis. (Müller's Archiv, 1857).

Lacaze-Duthiers. Histoire de l'Organization, du Dévelopment, etc., du Dentales. (Annales des Sciences Nat. 1858).

Lereboullet. Recherches d'Embryologie comparée sur le Dévelopment de la Truite, du Lézard et du Limnée. (Annales des Sciences Nat., 1862).

Salensky. Beitrage zur Entwicklungsgeschichte der Prosobranchien. (Siebold and Kölliker's Zeitschrift, 1872.)

Langerhans. Zur Entwickelung der Gastropoda Opisthobranchiata. (Siebold and Kölliker's Zeitschrift. 1873).

Lankester. Observations on the Development of the Pond Snail. (Quart. Journ. Microscopical Science, 1874.)

Fol. Études sur le Développment des Mollusques (Pteropods). (Archiv. Zool. 1875.)

Consult also Keferstein, the author of vol. 3 of Bronn's Classen und Ordnungen der Thierreichs; 1862-66; and papers in different journals of Alder and Hancock, Carus, Krohn, Lacaze-Duthiers, Lovén, Müller, Reid, Schmarda and Semper.

XVI. THE CEPHALOPODA.

Development of the Cephalopods. Though the homologies of the Cephalopods with the Cephalophora, particularly the Pteropods, are quite direct, yet the cuttlefishes differ greatly in their mode of growth, particularly in the embryological stages. While the work of Kölliker on the development of the Cephalopods is a classic, yet I shall here avail myself in part of Ussow's more recent work. His observations, made at Naples, are based on two species of Sepia, Sepiola, Loligo and *Argonauta argo*, and they agree so well in their embryology, that the following description answers for all. In the partial segmentation of the yolk, Ussow, as Kölliker before him, was reminded of the same process in the eggs of birds and the turtle. It begins on one side of the yolk; a primitive furrow arising, which is intersected at right angles by a second furrow forming four divisions, afterwards eight, until finally a one-layered germinative disk (blastoderm) is formed on a portion of the surface of the egg, on the second day after development begins. The inner germ-layer then arises, which farther splits into two sub-layers (the outer of which is the dermo-muscular, and the inner the intestino-fibrous).

In the second period of development, that of the production of organs, the blastoderm covers the entire yolk. The mantle begins to form, next the rudiments of the eyes arise from the ectoderm, and the mouth appears. The embryo is now like a convex disk, or rather a hollow hemisphere.

On the 10th day the gills, funnel, arms and anal tubercle make their appearance, the germ of the gills arising from the dermomuscular sub-layer of the middle germ-lamella.

On the 11th day the rudiments of the auditory organs, the pharynx and salivary glands arise, as well as the anal orifice, and on the succeeding day the auricles of the heart, the pericardium arising afterwards. The walls of the aorta and of the larger arteries and veins, with the offshoots of the latter (the so-called kidneys), are developed from the cells of the middle lamella, which become elongated and arrange themselves in rows. On the 13th day the ink-sac develops, and the liver. The intestinal tract originates from the primitive invagination of the outer germ-layer (ectoderm) as in Amphioxus, Ascidia, some Cœlenterates, the Brachiopoda, Vermes, etc. As to the mode of origin of the nervous system, Ussow says "I have been compelled to

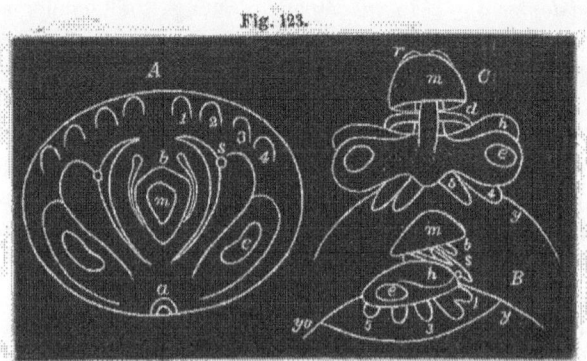

Fig. 123.

Development of the Cuttle Fish.

give up forever the hope of finding any resemblance to its development in the Vertebrata, Tunicata, Annulosa and Mollusca." All the ganglia of the Cephalopoda originate from more or less compact thickenings of the middle germ-lamella (dermo-muscular sub-layer), as in the peripheral ganglia of the vertebrates.

Ussow was unable to trace the origin of the genital glands, as they do not arise until after the animal is three days old, and he could not keep his specimens alive beyond this period.

Now returning to Kölliker's memoir for our information regarding the later stages, Fig. 123, A (m, mantle; b, branchial processes; s, siphonal processes; a, mouth; e, eyes; 1–5 rudimentary arms, after Kölliker) represents the disk-like embryo resting on the surface of the yolk; B, a side view of the embryo when farther advanced (y, yolk sack; h, head), and C the same still older, the yolk sac still smaller, the contents having been partially absorbed. Soon after this the body and arms grow longer, and the animal moves about in its shell.

Fig. 124.

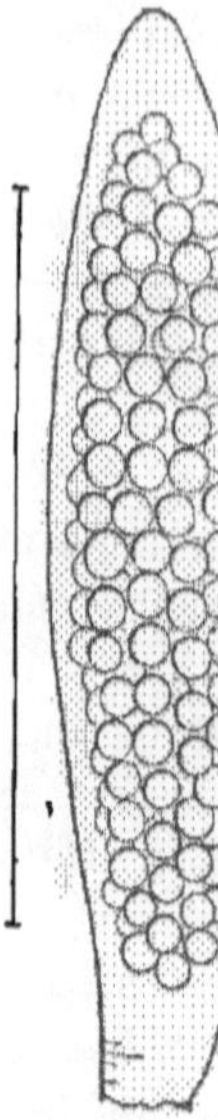

Egg Capsule of Loligo Pealii.

For our information regarding the still later history of our native cuttle fishes we are indebted to the observations of Prof. Verrill, from whose report on the Invertebrates of

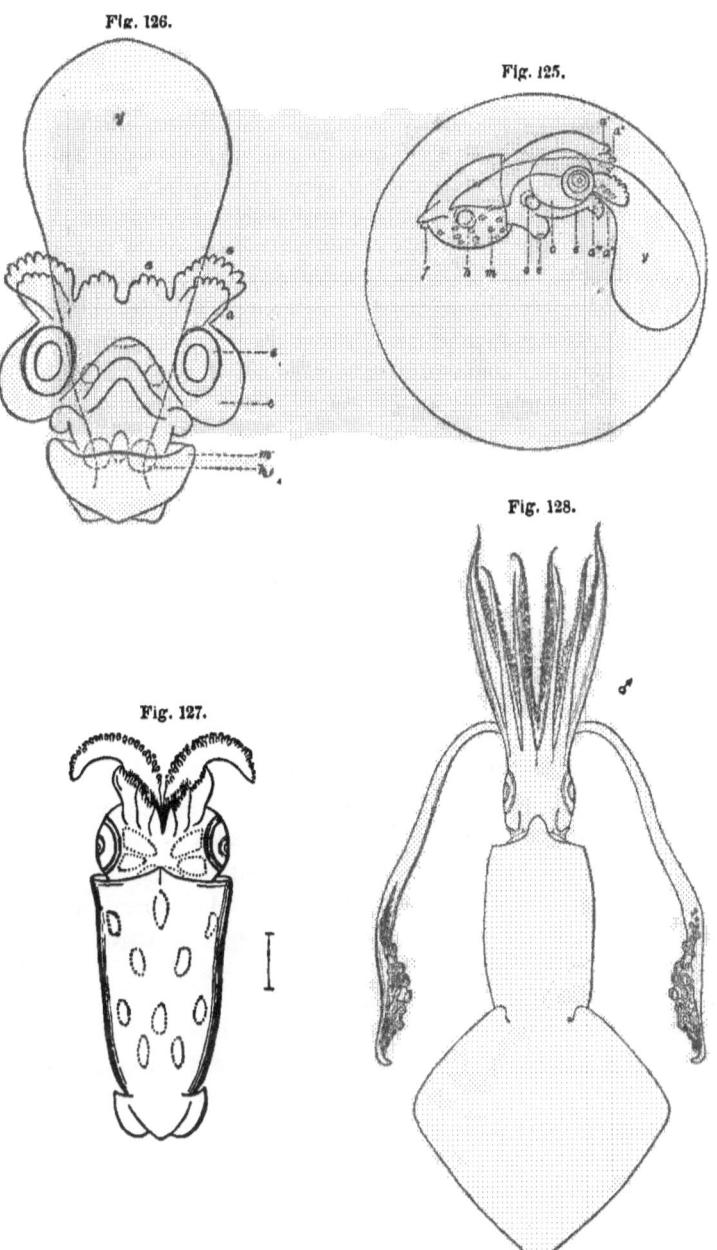

Fig. 126.

Fig. 125.

Fig. 128.

Fig. 127.

Development of a Cuttlefish. After Verrill.

Vineyard Sound, in Prof. Baird's U. S. Fish Commission report, these cuts are taken. Fig. 124 represents the egg-capsule of *Loligo Pealii*. Fig. 125[1] represents the young of the same cuttle fish, with the yolk sac (*y*). Fig. 126 represents the same farther advanced, while Fig. 127 gives an idea of the same after hatching, the yolk having been completely absorbed. Another species of cuttle fish (*Loligo pallida*) is represented by Fig. 128.

Such is the usual mode of development of the cuttle fishes. But in an unknown form probably over three feet in length, as its mass of eggs was thirty inches long, the mode of development is entirely different. The growth of the embryo is greatly accelerated, and immediately after segmentation it assumes a state analogous to the Trochosphere of other mollusca. To Grenacher's beautiful

Fig. 129.　　　　　　　Fig. 130.

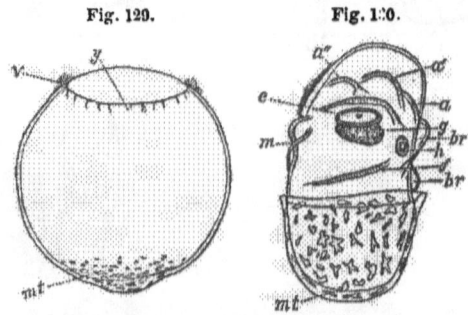

Development of an unknown Cuttlefish.

memoir we are indebted for the fol owing facts regarding the life-history of this cuttle fish, whose adult form is unknown; he studied the eggs found floating in the Atlantic ocean, and was unable to raise it to maturity. After partial segmentation, the process being indicated by from five to eight radiating streaks, on the surface of the yolk, the embryo assumed the form indicated by Fig. 129, which represents the blastoderm growing around the under pole of the yolk mass and approaching the anterior end, where there is a swollen, ciliated band (*v*) apparently identical with the velum of the Trochosphere of the lower mollusca. This is an interesting point, as Grenacher adopts Lovén's opinion that the arms of the Cephalopods represent and

---

[1] Fig. 125 *a*, *a''*, *a'''*, *a''''*, the right arms belonging to four pairs; *c*, the side of the head; *e*, the eye; *f*, the caudal fins; *h*, the heart; *m*, the mantle in which the color-vesicles are already developed and capable of changing their colors; *o*, the interna-cavity of the same; *s*, siphon. The letters in Fig. 126 are the same (after Verrill).

are homologous with the velum of the lower mollusks, particularly the Pteropods, and not with the foot as commonly urged.

This spherical stage is also remarkable for the early appearance of the mantle, with the contractile pigment cells (chromatophores). It will be seen that the entire egg is, as in the lower mollusks, converted directly into the embryo. The embryo soon elongates, the mantle grows, the eyes and arms bud out, and the form of the adult is rapidly sketched out as in Fig. 130 (*m*, mouth; *a, a', a''*, arms; *f*, inner and outer funnel-layer; *mt*, mantle, the dotted line ending in a chromatophore; *h*, ear; *g*, optic ganglion; *e*, eye.

We thus have in the embryology of this form, which seems not very different from Loligo (as may be seen in a more advanced stage figured by Grenacher not reproduced here), a mode of development much more like the lower mollusks than was before suspected.

Of the embryology of the fossil Tetrabranchiate Cephalopods (the Ammonites, etc.) we know from the beautiful researches of Professor Hyatt that the shell in Ammonites as well as Goniatites begins as a minute globular sac; in Nautilus this sac "is not retained, but traces of its former existence are apparent on the apex of the first whorl, in the form of a scar or cicatrix."

Summarizing the known facts regarding the living, dibranchiate Cephalopods, we have eggs and spermatic particles developed in separate sexes, the egg passing through the following phases.

1.   Partial segmentation, analogous to that of Vertebrates.

2, *a*. Trochosphere (?) or germ developing on the surface of the yolk and gradually absorbing it, the Gastrula state suppressed; or, as is more usually the case (*b*), the adult form is directly attained without passing through a morula or gastrula state.

LITERATURE.

Kölliker. Entwickelungsgeschichte der Cephalopoden. Zürich. 1844.

Hyatt. Embryology of the Tetrabranchiates. (Bulletin. Mus. Comp. Zool. 1872).

Lankester. Development of the Cephalopoda. (Annals and Mag. Nat. Hist. 1873, and Quart. Journ. Micr. Sc. 1875).

Grenacher. Zur Entwickelungsgeschichte der Cephalopoden. (Siebold and Kölliker's Zeitschrift, 1874).

Ussow. Zoologico-Embryological Investigations. (Annals and Mag. Nat. Hist. 1875).

Consult also the writings of Van Beneden, Metschnikoff, D'Orbigny, G. & F. Sauberger, Barrande and Verrill.

XVII. THE PLATYELMINTHES.

RETURNING from our journey through the subkingdom of the Mollusca, we will follow the path leading from the Worms up to the Insects. The lowest worms are far more simple in structure than the lowest mollusks. Indeed in organisms like the Vortex, for example, we have forms which serve as a point of departure, ancestral forms, from which the entire animal world above the Infusoria may have been originally derived.

The division of worms is now so vast and unwieldy that it seems impossible to give a general definition of it, and in the present state of science it may be unnecessary. The group embraces all grades of development from simple ciliated forms like the Vortex, Prostomum and Macrostomum, which are scarcely more complicated than the ciliated infusoria, differing chiefly in having genuine cells composing the tissues, up to animals like the earth worms and nereids which are in some respects as high if not higher than the Crustacea and insects.

Claparède in his "Beobachtungen," etc., says that "the Rhabdocœla have interested me on account of their undeniable passage to the ciliated Infusoria. I am truly of Agassiz's opinion that many so-called Infusoria may be simply Turbellarian larvæ; although at first opposed to this opinion I afterwards expressed my views as to the near relationship of the Infusoria as well with the Rhabdocœla as the Dendrocœla. Thus as *Trachelius ovum* forms an evident connecting link between the Infusoria and Dendrocœla, so are the early stages of the Rhabdocœla often scarcely to be distinguished from the Infusoria. In many cases one is in doubt whether he is dealing with a young Turbellarian worm or a ciliate Infusorian." He then describes an Infusorian-like worm in which the mouth opens by a pharynx into a broad body and digestive cavity, with no anal opening. There is thus no digestive cavity separated from the body cavity. There are no other organs except an otolite. This is evidently an immature form, but none the less closely allied structurally to Paramecium and Trachelius.

It should also be remembered that among the worms are many synthetic types which, as regards some organs, remind us of other groups of animals. For example the Rotifers recall the lower

Crustacea, and are by some naturalists regarded as such; the Planarians have been considered by Girard as mollusks, the Polyzoa and Brachiopods are still regarded as mollusks by eminent naturalists, and there are very few who do not place the Tunicates among the latter. On the other hand the Echinoderms are regarded as worms by some, and Amphioxus has been called a worm. Indeed if any one has any prejudices regarding fixed types in nature, and would learn how regardless of preconceived zoological systems the actual state of our knowledge of the lower animals must lead one to become, let him study the animals now placed among the "Worms."

Leaving out of consideration the lowest forms, almost without organs, and many parasitic forms, as a general rule the worms are bilateral, segmented animals with the nervous cords either separate or united by commissures, and resting on the floor of the body under the alimentary canal, which usually (when present) passes directly through the middle of the body. There is in the Annelides a dorsal and ventral blood-vessel, the circulatory apparatus being closed and more highly developed than in the Crustacea and Insects, Limulus excepted. In the lower worms (Platyelminths, Nematelminths, Acanthocephali and Rotatoria) there is a complicated system of excretory tubes, thought by some anatomists to be analogous with the water-vascular system of Radiates.

The organs of locomotion are, when present, simple bristles as in the earth-worm; or there are besides lateral prolongations of the walls of the body forming paddle-like flaps, as seen in the higher Annelides, such as Nereis, etc.

We are now concerned with tracing the mode of development of some of the typical forms belonging to the different subdivisions, the general relations of which may be seen in the following tabular view, which is taken from Gegenbaur's "Principles of Comparative Anatomy," with the addition of the Brachiopoda, which he still retains among the Mollusca. The Onychophora, represented by Peripatus, are also omitted, as since the publication of Gegenbaur's work, Peripatus has been proved by the researches of Mr. Moseley to be a tracheate insect, for in the young genuine tracheæ exist, though they disappear in the adult, or at least have not been discovered.

VERMES.

I.　PLATYELMINTHES.
　　Turbellaria (Vortex, Prostomum, Planaria).
　　Trematoda (Distoma, Monostomum).
　　Cestoda (Tænia, Bothriocephalus).
　　Nemertina (Nemertes).
II.　NEMATELMINTHES.
　　Nematodes (Strongylus, Ascaris).
　　Gordiacea (Gordius, Mermis).
III.　CHÆTOGNATHI (Sagitta).
IV.　ACANTHOCEPHALI (Echinorhynchus).
V.　ROTATORIA (Brachionus, Rotifer).
VI.　POLYZOA (Alcyonella, Flustra, Lepralia).
VII.　BRACHIOPODA (Lingula, Terebratulina).
VIII.　TUNICATA (Appendicularia, Ascidia, Pyrosoma, Doliolum, Salpa).
IX.　GEPHYREA (Sipunculus).
X.　ANNULATA (Hirudo, Balanoglossus, Lumbricus, Serpula, Nereis).

To the Platyelminthes belong the Flat Worms, Flukes and Tape Worms. These are flat-bodied ciliated worms without lateral appendages, usually with hooks or suckers. They are usually hermaphroditic.

Development of the Turbellaria. These lowest of worms, in which there is no true stomach and intestines, but a simple short blind digestive sac leading from the mouth and pharynx, are known to multiply by fission, the body dividing into two. They also possess ovaries and male glands, and reproduce from eggs. We are not acquainted with the life-history of the Rhabdocœlous forms, such as Vortex, Prostomum, etc., except that we know that they produce eggs and spermatic particles. In Prostomum, an orbicular form, the yolk cells are formed in a gland (vitellogene) distinct from the true ovary or germ-forming gland (germogene). As an example of reproduction by fission may be cited the singular *Catena quaterna* Schmarda, which occurs in fresh water at the Cape of Good Hope. Fig. 131 represents two individuals in partial division, and a chain of four individuals, natural size. This form reminds us of the tape worm, in which the joints remain permanently attached. We know nothing

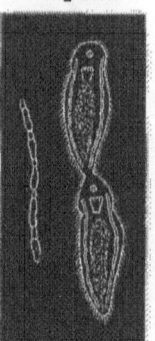

Fig. 131.

Catena quaterna.

further regarding the history of Catena except that it has been found as indicated in the figure here reproduced from Schmarda.

Among the Dendrocœla, or Planarians, and in fact in the flat worms generally, fission takes place. If we cut the common fresh water Planarians into several pieces, each piece will become a perfect worm.

All the fresh water flat worms are born as infusorian-like ciliated bodies which attain maturity without any metamorphosis. As an example of the mode of development of a Planarian worm, may be given the history of *Planocera elliptica* discovered by Girard in Boston and Beverly harbors. The spawning time lasts from the middle of May until the middle of June, the eggs being deposited in a thin viscid band on stones and sea weeds. The egg undergoes total segmentation in four or five days after. A ciliated blastoderm begins to form around the yolk mass, and before the embryo leaves the egg it assumes the larval shape, being an infusorian-like form, with a caudal flagellum. There are no internal organs except two eye-specks.

In eight or ten days after the larva begins to revolve in the egg, and after it has hatched, it stops swimming about and becomes a "mummy-like body" which Girard calls a "chrysalis." In this condition, which apparently corresponds to the encysted state of the flukes, it floats about in the water. Here Girard's observations came to an end. Whether in this resting stage it is swallowed by some other animal, and becomes a parasite before resuming its active life, remains to be seen.

The later history of *Planaria angulata* has been traced by Mr. A. Agassiz. "On examining," he says, "a string of eggs, mistaken at first for those of some naked mollusk, I was surprised to find young Planariæ in different stages of growth with a ramifying digestive cavity, somewhat similar to that of adult specimens, but showing besides, one distinct articulation for each spur of the digestive cavity. The eyes were well developed, and when the young became free, the articulations were still distinct." In the youngest specimen (Fig. 132) observed, the body was almost cylindrical, while as seen in Fig. 133, the body has become considerably flattened. The fact that before attaining maturity the Planarian is articulated is very significant, showing that these low worms, non-segmented in maturity, should not be excluded

from the class of worms, and that the terms "bilateral, articulate"
applies as well to the lowest division (though with many exceptions) of worms as to the true

Fig. 133.

Annelides.

The Turbellaria then, so far as
our limited knowledge extends, develop (*a*) by fission, (*b*) from eggs
fertilized by sperm cells, and pass
through the following stages, not,
however, all observed in a single
species.

Fig. 132.

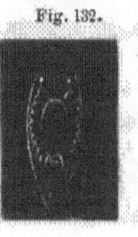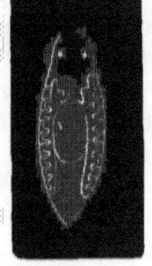

1. Morula.

2. Infusorian-like stage.

Young Planaria.

3. A quiet, encysted (?) stage (Girard's Planocera).

4. Articulated stage observed in one species (Agassiz's *Planaria angulata*).

5. Adult, ciliated, not segmented.

Development of the Trematodes. The flukes are parasitic
worms, with a sucking disk in the centre of the body by which
they attach themselves on or within the body of their host. The
fluke or "liver worm" (*Distoma hepaticum*) lives in the liver of
the sheep and of man. The fishes and snails are much infested
by them, nearly each species having its distinct kind of fluke.
The adult flukes are not ciliated, the alimentary canal ends in a
blind sac, and the sexes are united in the same individual.

For the mode of formation of the egg of the Trematodes, and
the embryonic history of certain forms, the student is referred to
Leuckart's "Menschlichen Parasiten" and E. Van Beneden's
beautiful "Researches." E. Van Beneden has shown that the
development of the Trematodes begins by subdivision of the
germinative cellule or nucleus. The nucleus and nucleolus then
divide and subsequently the "protoplasmic body." The yolk,
however, remains entirely independent of this division, and serves
as nourishment for the other cells forming the body of the
embryo.

From Van Beneden's observations, it appears that the eggs of
the lower flukes as a rule undergo total segmentation, and the
young are hatched either oval, ciliated, Infusorian-like, without
any organs, not even eye-specks, as in Distoma and Amphistoma;
or as in the higher Trematodes, as shown by the elder Van

Beneden, the development is direct, the embryo passing directly into a form like the adult.

For the further history of the fluke we will turn to Steenstrup's famous work "On the Alternation of Generations," wherein is first related the strange history of these animals. While the flukes were well known, as well as the tadpole-like Cercaria, it was not known before the publication of Steenstrup's work in 1842, that the Cercariæ were the free larval forms of the Distomæ. The *Cercaria echinata*, first described by Siebold, is like a Distoma except that the body is prolonged into a long extensible tail. This tail, says Steenstrup, is formed of several membranes or tubes placed one within the other, of which the outermost is a very transparent epidermis, under which is a tolerably thick membrane furnished with transverse muscular fibres or *striæ*, and between each pair of these transverse fibres is placed a globular vesicle which appears to be a mucous follicle or gland; the innermost tube is opaque and of firmer consistence, it contains the longitudinal muscular fibres, and is usually reticulated on the surface. Through the centre of these tubes there passes a slightly narrower canal, which becomes very small towards the extremity of the tail. The existence of the same layers in the body itself of the Cercaria, can easily be demonstrated; but the transversely striated layer is here not so much developed. This description of the Cercaria will remind one of the tadpole-like larva of the Ascidians. The apparent homology in structure of the tail of the Cercaria with that of the Ascidian larva as figured by Kupffer, is striking. This similarity may be seen if the reader will compare fig. 7, Tab. ii, in De la Valette St. George's "Symbolæ," representing a stage in the development of *Cercaria flava* into *Monostomum flavum*. The author figures a row of cells on each side of a central cavity through which passes what is regarded as possibly a nerve. Whether this is not as much a *chorda dorsalis* and spinal nerve as those parts regarded as such in the Ascidian larva, is a subject for future investigation. But in other respects the position of the mouth, the sense-organs, as well as the form of the body strikingly recall the Ascidian larva, so much so that it gives strong confirmation to the opinion that the Ascidians are worms, and that they and the Trematodes have possibly originated from allied forms. In another species, *Cercaria ocellata*, the tail has a lateral fin; and in still another species figured by J. Müller on the same plate (*Cercaria setifera*) unaccompanied by any description, the tail contains an axial row of large cells, with a row on each side reminding one of the embryo of the Ascidian, with its axial row of cells (the germ of the *chorda dorsalis*) and the

Fig. 134.

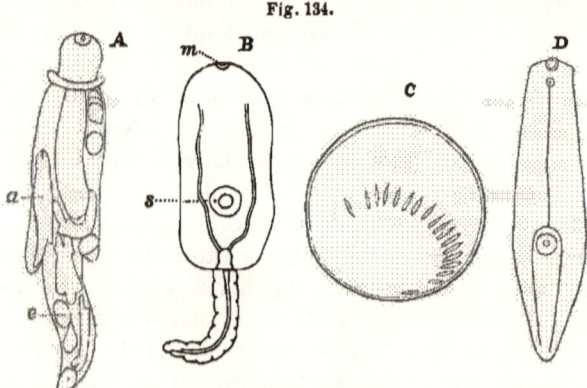

Development of Distoma.

cells on each side; moreover the tail is provided with nineteen pencils of long hairs, each pair arising from a distinct segment, so that in one larval Trematode at least, the annulated structure of the body exists, as well as in the larval Planaria.

Returning now to Steenstrup's narrative, he tells us that these "Echinate Cercariæ (Fig. 134, A, parent nurse; *e*, germs; *a*, nurse; B, larva), are found by thousands, and frequently by millions in the water, in which two of our largest fresh-water snails, *Planorbis cornea* and *Limnæus stagnalis*, have been kept." After swimming about in the water some time they

Fig. 135.

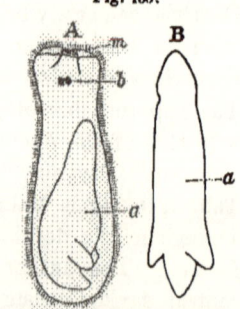

Development of Monastomum.

fix themselves by means of their suckers (B, *s*) to the slimy skin of the snails, in such numbers that the latter look as if covered with bits of wool.

The Cercaria by contracting its body and violent lashing of the tail forces its way into the body of its host, loses its tail, and then resembles a mature Distoma. By turning about in its place and secreting a mucus, a cyst is gradually formed, with a spherical shell. This constitutes the "pupa" state of the Cercaria, first observed by Nitzsch and afterwards by Siebold. Steenstrup thinks that the Cercaria casts a thin skin. In this state the body can be seen through the shell of the cyst, as in Fig. 134, C, where the circle of spines embedded around the mouth is seen.[1] The encysted Cercariæ remain in this state from July and August until the following spring ; and during the winter months in snails kept in warm rooms, they change into Distonias (Fig. 134, D) the mature fluke differing, however, in some important respects from the tailless larvæ. In nature they remain from two to nine months in the encysted state.

"Now," asks Steenstrup, "Whence come the Cercariæ?" Bojanus states that he saw this species swarming out from the "king's yellow worms," which are about two lines long and occur in great numbers in the interior of snails. From these are developed the larval Distomas, and Steenstrup calls them the "nurses" of the Cercariæ and Distomata. They exactly resemble the "parent nurses" (Fig. 134, A) and like them the cavity of the body is filled with young, which develop from egg-like balls of cells. Steenstrup was forced to conclude that these nurses originated from the first nurses (Fig. 134) which he therefore calls "parent-nurses." Here the direct observations of Steenstrup on the *Cercaria echinata* came to an end, but he believed that the parent-nurses came from eggs. The link in the cycle of generations he supplied from the observations of Siebold, who saw a Cercaria-like young (Fig. 135, B) expelled from the body of the ciliated larva of *Monostomum mutabile* (Fig. 135, A, a, nurse developing from ciliated larva ; m, mouth ; b, eye specks). Steenstrup remarks that "the first form of this embryo is not unlike that of the common ciliated progeny of the Trematoda, as they have been known to us in many species for a long time, from the observations of Mehlis, Nordmann and Siebold, and it might at first sight be taken for one of the polygastric infusoria of Ehrenberg, which also move by cilia ; whilst in the next form which it assumes the young Monostomum bears an undeniable resemblance to those animals which I have termed 'nurses' and 'parent nurses' in that species of the Trematoda which is developed from the *Cercaria echinata*."

Thus the cycle is completed and the following summary of

---

[1] Other figures by Steenstrup and other authors show the form of the encysted Cercaria very distinctly, but in the figure given above only the spines are distinctly represented in the plate from which this is copied.

changes undergone by the lower Distomas present as clear a case of an alternation of generations as seen in the jelly fishes.

1. Egg.
2. Morula.
3. Ciliated larva.
4. Cercaria (parent nurse, Proscolex) producing
5. Cercaria (nurse, scolex).
6. Encysted Cercaria (Proglottis).
7. Distoma (Proglottis).

The *Cercaria echinata*, living in snails which are eaten by ducks, have been shown by St. George to develop into the adult Distoma in the body of that bird. It is generally the case that those Distomas which pass through an alternation of generations live in the larval state in animals which serve as food for higher orders. Thus the Bucephalus of the European oyster passes in the encysted state into a fish (Gasterostomum), which serves as food for a larger fish, *Belone vulgaris*, where the cysts of the same worm occur.

Distoma hepaticum, the liver fluke, sometimes occurring in man, is thought by Dr. Willemoes-Suhm to begin its existence as *Cercaria cystophora*, parasitic on a species of Planorbis.

LITERATURE.

Steenstrup. On the Alternation of Generations. 1842. Translated by G. Busk, 1845.
De la Valette St. George. Symbolæ ad Trematodum Evolutionis Historiam. Berlin, 1855.
Leuckart. Die Menschlichen Parasiten. Leipzig. 1868, incomplete.
E. Van Beneden. Recherches sur la Composition et la Signification de l'Oeuf. Bruxelles, 1870.

Development of the Cestodes. In the tape worm there is no alimentary canal, the liquid food being absorbed from the juices of its host through the walls of the body. The head is armed with suckers, hooks or leaf-like soft appendages, while the body is subdivided usually into a great number of segments, each containing an ovary and male gland. While the Turbellaria possess a pair of nerve-ganglia, the Cestodes are not known positively to possess any trace of a nervous system.

E. Van Beneden shows that the egg is formed by two glands, one of which (the germogene) forms the nucleus and nucleolus, while the other (vitellogene) forms the yolk. Development begins very probably as in the Trematodes, by multiplication by division of the nucleus (germinative cell). In the eggs of *Tænia bacil-*

laris E. Van Beneden saw the nucleus subdivide; afterwards the cells are arranged in two layers, and the outer layer is thrown off (this probably corresponding to the amnion of insects and crustacea); the central mass

Fig. 136.

Embryo of Tænia.

forms the embryo, and soon the three pairs of hooks arise as in Fig. 136. Three structureless membranes are secreted around the embryo, which then hatches. The embryo of Bothriocephalus is provided with a ciliated membrane, which corresponds to the first blastodermic moult of the embryo Tænia, which is not ciliated.

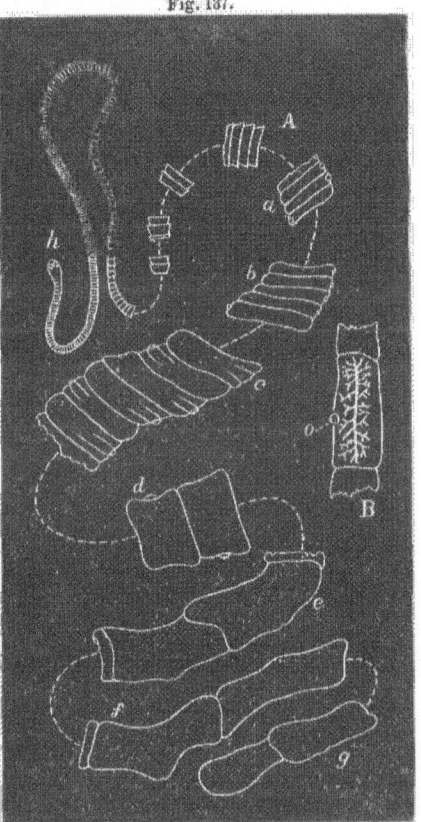

Fig. 137.

Common Human Tape worm.

Now taking up the history of the human tape worm, *Tænia solium* (Fig. 137[1]), the eggs eaten by the hog are developed in its body into the larval tape worm (scolex) called in this species, *Cysticercus cellulosæ*, (Fig. 138; Fig. 139, head enlarged). The head with its suckers is formed, the body becomes flask-shaped (Fig. 138, Cysticercus); the Cysticerci then bury themselves in the liver or the flesh of pork, and are transferred living in uncooked pork to the alimentary canal of man. The body now elongates,

---

[1] *Tænia solium.* A, the worm natural size; *h*, head; *a*, 309th joint; *b*, 448th; *c*, 569th; *d*, 680th; *e*, 768th; *f*, 840th; *g*, 855th joint and last but one. This worm was 10 feet 9 inches long. B, a separate joint (Proglottis) showing the ovary with its outlet *o*; the same joint contains a testis, too minute to show in the figure. Fig. 168. *Cysticercus cellulosæ,* the larval tape worm, *a*, circle of hooks; *b*, suckers; *c*, wrinkled neck; *d*, sac filled with fluid. This and Fig. 166 and 169 from Weinland.

and new joints arise behind the head until the form of the tape worm is attained, as in Fig. 137 (after Weinland).

Now we shall see how the eggs are distribute. The hinderd joints become filled with eggs and then break off, becoming independent animals comparable with the "parent-nurses" of the Cercarias, except that they are not contained in the body of the Tænia (as in the Cercaria), but are set free. The independent joint (Fig. 137, g,) is called a "proglottis." It escapes from the alimentary tract, and the eggs set free are swallowed by that un-

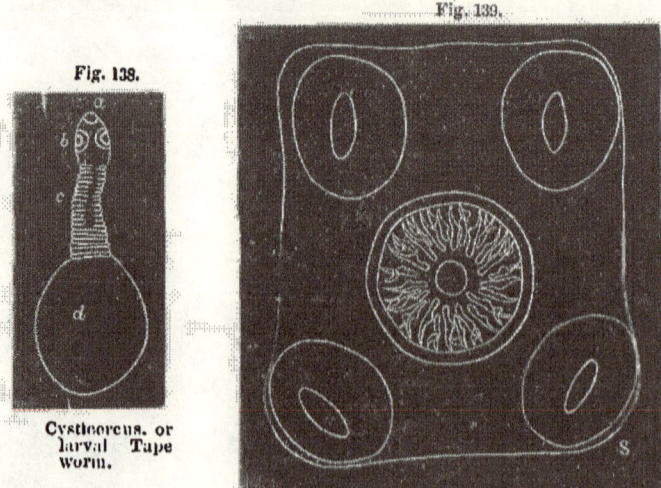

Fig. 139.

Fig. 138.

Cysticercus. or larval Tape worm.

Head of Cysticercus enlarged, showing the suckers (S) and circle of hooks.

clean animal, the pig, and the cycle of generations begins anew. We thus have the following series of changes which may be compared with the homologous series in the flukes :

   1. Egg.

   2. Morula.

   3. Double-walled sac (Planula?).

   4. Proscolex, free embryo with hooks, surrounded by a blastodermic skin.

   5. Scolex (Cysticercus, larva). Body few-jointed.

   6. Scolex (Tænia). Body many-jointed.

   7. Proglottis (adult).

LITERATURE.

P. J. Van Beneden. Les Vers Cestoïdes. Brussels. 1850.
—— —— ——. Memoire sur les Vers Intestinaux. Paris. 1858.

Siebold. Ueber die Band- und Blasenwürmer. Leipzig. 1854.
Weinland. An Essay on the Tapeworms of Man. 1858.
Compare also the works of Leuckart, Küchenmeister, E. Van Beneden and Cobbold.

Development of the Nemerteans. In the development of some of these worms we are reminded of the mode of growth of the Echinoderms, while in others the larvæ attain the adult condition by gradual development. In no order of animals, perhaps, is there a greater range of variation in the mode of development than in these curious worms.

The simplest mode of growth is that described by Dieck in Cephalothrix, where the ciliated larva, after passing through a morula and planula[1] stage (being a two-layered sac, but not a gastrula) leaves the egg and undergoes no metamorphosis, the young worm having no body cavity. In the Nemertes larva of Desor there is a body cavity, but the larva is still an infusorian-like being, and attains maturity by direct growth. Another Nemertean (*N. communis*) has been found by Barrois to have a somewhat more complicated mode of growth than in the larva of Desor. The first

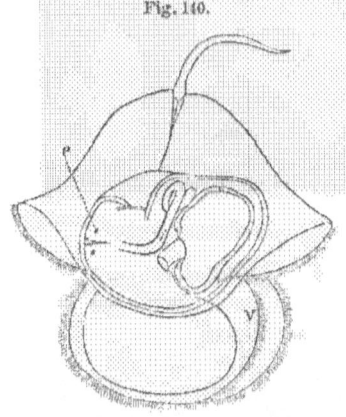

Fig. 140.

stages of development are like those of the larva of Desor, the morula passing, as he claims, into a ciliated "gastrula" state in the egg, the body cavity being formed by invagination of the outer layer of cells, but the animal after shedding an amnion leaves the egg in the Nemertes form, and there is no free swimming stage.

Now we come to those Nemerteans in which there is a very complicated metamorphosis. J. Müller had described an animal caught with the towing net which he called "Pilidium." Busch had suspected that a Nemertes came from the Pilidium, and Leuc-

Pilidium with the Nemertes growing in it.

---

[1] The inner lining of the planula arises before the body cavity is formed, by a differentiation of a second inner cell-layer, as occurs in other worms, zoophytes, etc. Dieck evidently limits the term gastrula to a two-layered sac, with a body cavity formed by the invagination of the ectoderm. Lankester's "gastrula" includes any embryo with a two-layered sac and a primitive cavity. Dieck's planula is like Haeckel's planula of the sponge, the cavity being formed during the segmentation of the egg.

kart and Pagensteeker proved it. Our figure, taken from the
drawings of these two last named authors, shows the singular Pilidium, and the planarian-like Nemertes with the eye-specks (Fig.
140, e), growing in it. How the worm originates in the body of
the Pilidium, and how the latter arises, have lately been fully shown
by Metschnikoff, and to his memoir we are indebted for the
strange history of the mode of development of these worms.

He followed the development of the Pilidium from the egg,
which undergoes total segmentation, leaving a segmentation-cavity. The next occurrence is the separation of a one-layered ciliated blastoderm, the ectoderm, which invaginates, forming the
primitive digestive cavity, from which the stomach and œsophagus
are formed. The larva is now helmet-shaped, ciliated, with a long
lash (flagellum) attached to the posterior end of the body.

After swimming about on the surface of the sea awhile, the
Nemertes begins to grow out from near the œsophagus of the
Pilidium. On each side of the base of the velum (v) of the Pilidium appear two thickenings of the skin, one pair in front, the other
behind ; these thickenings push inwards, and are the germs of the
anterior and posterior end of the future worm. The anterior pair
become larger than the posterior ; the part of the disk next to the
œsophagus thickens ; at the same time the alimentary canal of
the Pilidium grows smaller and only a narrow slit remains. The
disks now divide into two layers, the outer much thicker than
the inner. A new structure now arises, a pair of vesicles near the
hinder pair of disks ; these are the "lateral organs" of the future
worm. Soon the anterior pair of disks unite and the head of the
worm is soon formed, when the elliptical outline of the flat worm
is indicated, and appears somewhat as in Fig. 140 (i, intestine
of the worm). The yolk mass, with the alimentary canal of the
Pilidium, is taken bodily into the interior of the Nemertes, the
Pilidium skin falls off, and the worm seeks the bottom.

Metschnikoff discovered five other species of Pilidium, and
thinks this mode of development is not an uncommon occurrence.
This manner of development is directly comparable with that of
the echinoderm from the Pluteus.

To show the wide range of metamorphosis existing in the Ne-
mertcans, we may cite the case of a Nareda studied by Mr. A.
Agassiz, and whose early stages are like those of the higher
Annelides ; in fact so much so that Milne-Edwards and Claparède

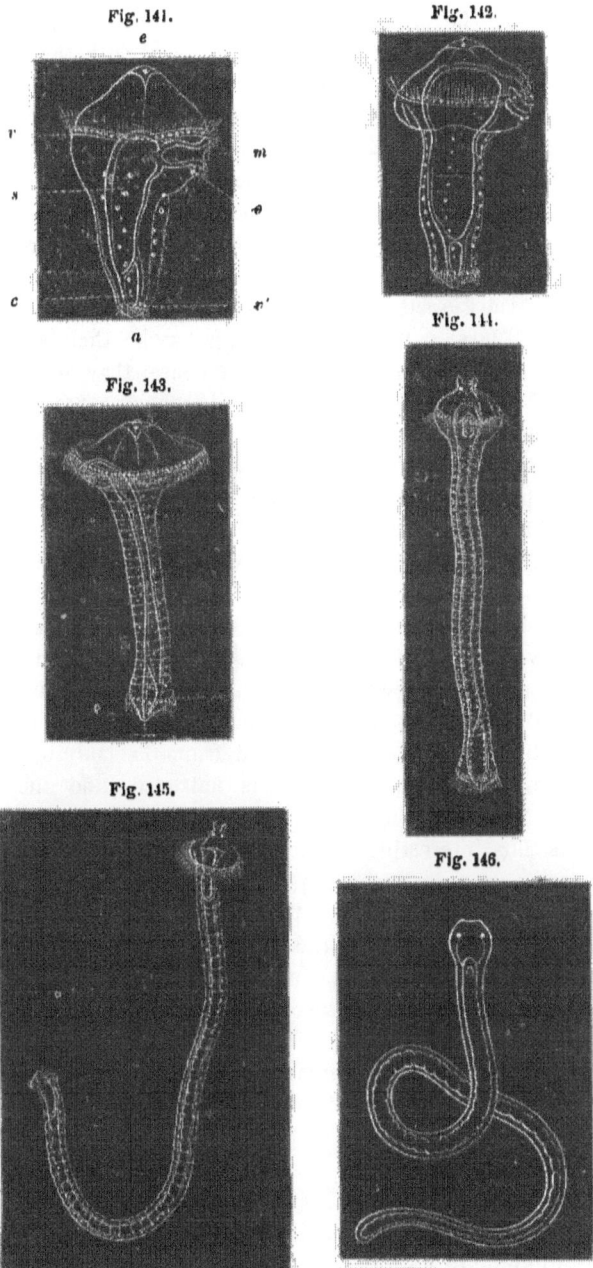

Development of a Nemertean worm. After A. Agassiz.

associated "the larva of Lovén" (which Mr. Agassiz has traced
without any doubt to the Nemertean worm) with that of Polynoë,
a representative of the highest family of Chætopod worms. In
the first stage (Fig. 141, *a*, anus; *c*, intestine; *m*, mouth; *o*,
œsophagus; *s*, stomach; *e*, eye-speck; *v*, ciliated ring) the larva
is not ringed; this figure may be compared with figure 85 on p.
88 to show how much alike the worm and Echinoderm larvæ
appear. The new rings are formed between the anal rings and the
older anterior rings, as in annelid larvæ, and in fact in the embryos of the Insects and Crustacea. Figs. 142 and 143 represent
the ringed larva. "A number of rings make their appearance at
once, and are the more distinct the nearer they are placed to the
mouth." The worm now greatly elongates, more segments are
added and it appears as in Figs. 144 and 145, with the ciliated
crown, the small short tentacles and eyes. The worm now swims
about slowly and creeps over the bottom, and is nearly a quarter
of an inch long. It will be observed that the larva differs from
those of other Annelides, as Mr. Agassiz states, in the absence of
"feet, bristles or appendages of any sort, except the two tentacles
of the head; and, were it not for these, it would seem as if the
young worm were the larva of some Nemertes-like animal." Fig.
146 represents the worm over four months after the stage represented by Fig. 145; the articulations have disappeared and a
month later the head is separated from the body by a neck, the
tentacles disappear, the body is flattened, and the Nemertes
(Polia) form is attained.

It is thus interesting to know that the young Echinoderm (Fig.
85), the young mollusk (Fig. 121 B), and the young Nemertean
worm pass through a similar free-swimming Cephalula stage. We
shall see farther on that the young Balanoglossus and the true
Annelides pass through a similar phase. The changes through
which the Nemertean worms pass are the following, though it
should be borne in mind that different species pass through different cycles of growth, some exhibiting no metamorphosis, the
stages being more or less condensed in the embryo state

1. Egg.
2. Morula.
3. Planula (or Gastrula?), hatching as a
4. Ciliated Infusorian-like larva, or a
5. Pilidium or a Cephalula.

6. Nemertes (*a*) budding out from the Pilidium, or (*b*) arising by direct growth from the Cephalula.

LITERATURE.

Lorén. Jakttagelse ofver Metamorfos hos en Annelid. (K. Vet. Akad. Handlingar. Stockholm, 1840. Translated in Archiv fuer Naturgeschichte, 1842, and Annales des Sc. Nat. 1842.)

Desor. Embryologie von Nemertes. (Muller's Archiv, 1848.)

Leuckart and Pagenstecher. Untersuchungen ueber niedere Seethiere. (Muller's Archiv. 1858.)

A. Agassiz. On the young stages of a few Annelides. (Annals Lyceum of Natural History. New York, 1866.)

Metschnikoff. Entwickelung der Echinodermen und Nemertinen. (Mémoires Acad. Imp. Sciences. St. Petersbourg, 1869.)

Dieck. Beiträge zur Entwickelungsgeschichte der Nemertinen. (Jenaische Zeitschrift für Naturwissenschaft. 1874.)

XVIII. NEMATELMINTHES (Round worms, Thread worms, Hair worms.)

There is little of interest in the development of the ordinary round worms, which whether free or parasitic are of the usual form, as shown in the Eustrongylus.

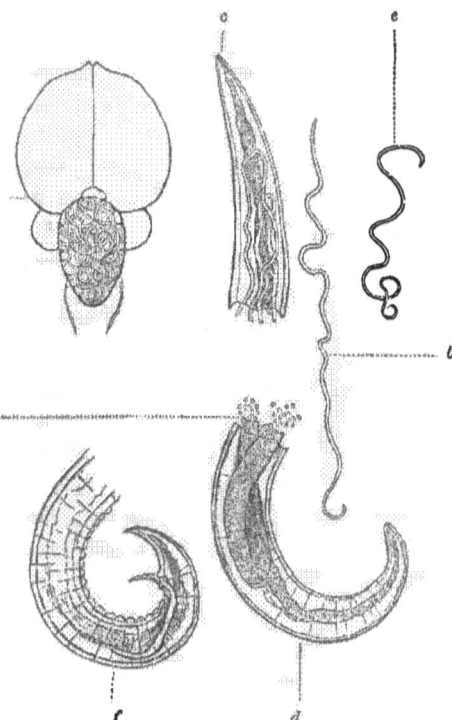

Fig. 147.

The mode of development of all these worms so far as known is very uniform. Development begins in three ways: (1) usually the egg undergoes total segmentation; others (2), as in *Ascaris dentata* and *Oxyuris ambigua*, do not show any trace of segmentation, and (3) in *Cucullanus elegans* there is no yolk, the nucleus absorbing all the vitelline matter which is limpid and transparent (E. Van Beneden). The germ consists of a single row of cells bent on itself somewhat as in Fig 149, which represents a little more advanced state in Sagitta, and there are a few cells representing the entoderm. The Nematode may be said therefore to pass through an incomplete gastrula condition. The adult form is rapidly assumed in the egg. Fig. 148, after J. Wyman, represents the young of *Eustrongylus papillosus* in the egg, and the worm just after hatching. Fig. 147, *a*, several mature worms coiled up in the brain of the snake

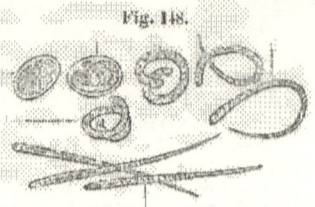

Fig. 148.

Development of a Round worm.

bird; *b*, female; *c*, head much enlarged; *d*, end of the body; *e*, male; *f*, the end of its body, after Wyman.)

The *Trichina spiralis* is the author of the terrible disease called trichiniasis or trichinosis. The young worms exist in the flesh of the hog, where they become encysted, and if swallowed by man, the cysts are dissolved during digestion, and the young worms are set free in the intestinal canal. From here the young bore in all directions in the body, and becoming encysted cause the flesh to look as if sprinkled with white sand.

The development of the hair-worm (Gordius and Mermis) is quite complicated, as the young are parasitic, tadpole-shaped, living in the bodies of insects, especially grasshoppers, in whose bodies the mature worms are found coiled up. M. Villot is now publishing an account of the mode of development of these worms in a monograph appearing in Lacaze-Duthiers "Archives," but not yet completed. These worms are oviparous, laying exceedingly numerous, minute eggs agglutinated together, forming long white strings. The young of one genus live in the aquatic larvæ of flies and were afterwards found by Villot in the mucous layer of the intestines of fishes.

The diœcious round worms pass without metamorphosis through a morula, and a condensed gastrula state (not so well marked as in Sagitta) in the egg, assuming the adult form before hatching. In the hair-worms there is a well marked metamorphosis.

LITERATURE.

Claparède. De la Formation et de la fécondation des Œufs chez les Vers Nématodes. Genève, 1859. Compare also papers by Bagge, Reichert, Siebold, Nelson, Schneider, Perez, E. Van Beneden, Bütschli and Villot.

XIX. CHÆTOGNATHA (Sagitta).

This singular worm had been referred to the crustacea by some, to the mollusca by Forbes, and even to the vertebrates by Meissner. Its development and structure, however, show that it is nearly related to the Nematodes. The mouth is, however, armed with six pairs of bristles; and a double-fin-like expansion of the sides and ends of the body gives it a slightly fish-like shape. This fin-like expansion is seen in the Cercaria, and the young ascidian, and is of little morphological importance. It swims on the surface of the water, not seeking the bottom or living parasitically.

Development of Sagitta. This animal is a hermaphrodite, and the eggs may be found in August well developed. Its develop-

Fig. 149.

Gastrula of Sagitta.

ment has been studied by Gegenbaur and Kowalevsky, by the latter in great detail. The egg undergoes total segmentation, a segmentation cavity being formed and the blastoderm invaginating exactly as in the Nematodes. This results in the formation of a gastrula-condition (Fig. 149) in which the infolding of the blastoderm leaves a well marked primitive body-cavity. Soon at the opposite end of the body another cavity (the permanent mouth) forms, which deepens and connects with the primitive body-cavity (*a*); this closes up at the posterior end, and the true digestive canal is formed. The embryo is oval, but soon elongates, and the adult Sagitta form is attained before the animal leaves the egg.

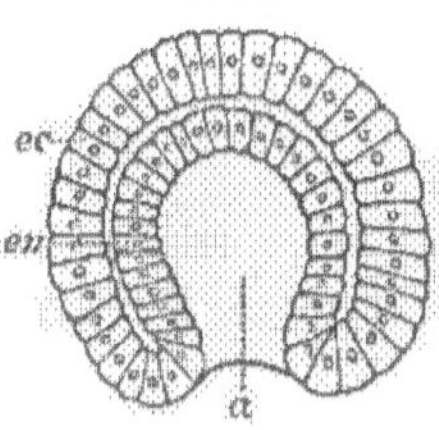

The phases of development are, then, as follows:

1. Morula.
2. Gastrula (well marked, but not ciliated and free).
3. Adult Sagitta.

LITERATURE.

Gegenbaur. Ueber die Entwickelung der Sagitta. Halle, 1857.
Kowalevsky. Embryologische Studien an Würmen und Arthropoden. (Memoirs Acad. Imp. Sciences. St. Petersburg, 1871.)

XX. ACANTHOCEPHALI.

The Echinorhynchus (Fig. 150, head, after Owen); 151, the same, with the proboscis retracted (*a*, oral pore; *bb*, protractile muscles; *cc*, retractile muscles; from Owen), a singular worm,

without a mouth or alimentary canal, but with a large proboscis
armed with hooks, evidently lives by imbibition
of the fluids of its host. It is a not uncommon
parasite of fishes. Fig. 152 represents an al-
lied(?) form (*Koleops anguilla*) described by Dr.
Lockwood, who found it in the eel (American
Naturalist, vi, 1872).

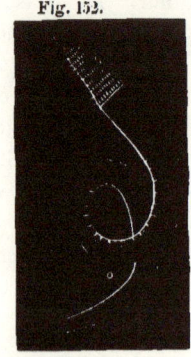

Fig. 152.

Koleops.

Development of Echinorhynchus gigas. Schneider has given the only account we have of the
early stages of this worm. "The ova of this
worm are scattered upon the ground by the pigs.
Here they are eaten by the larvæ of *Melolontha
vulgaris* (a beetle allied to our June beetle), and
thus arrive at their further development. The
ova burst in the stomach of the larva, and the embryos contained

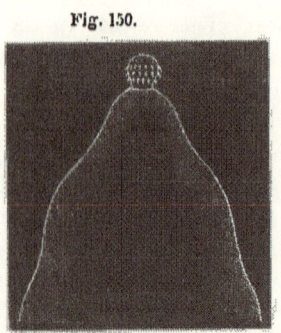

Fig. 150.

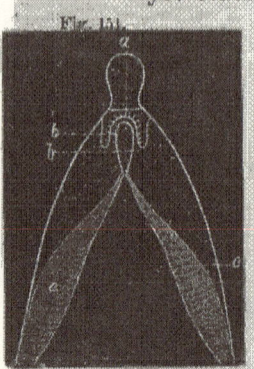

Fig. 151.

Head of Echinorhynchus.

in them can then penetrate, by means of their spines, through the
intestine into the body cavity of the larva; here they become developed, and again reach the intestine of the pig by the agency of
the larva.

"The larvæ infested with Echinorhynchi live on until their metamorphosis into cockchafers. . . . . When the embryos have
arrived at the body cavity of the larvæ of Melolontha, they remain for some days unaltered and capable of motion; they then
become rigid, acquire an oval form, and envelope themselves in a
finely cellular cyst, which is formed of the connective tissue of
the larva. The skin of the embryo, with its circlet of spines at
the anterior extremity. continues at first to be the skin of the
growing larva; and it is only at a later period, when the forma-

tion of the hooks commences, that it is thrown off, when it forms a second cystic envelope. The embryo, or rather the larva, proceeding from it, divides very soon into two layers, a thick dermal layer and an inner cell-mass, from which the other organs originate." The ovaries and testes are produced at a very early stage.

LITERATURE.

Schneider. On the development of *Echinorhynchus gigas.* (Sitzungsbericht der Oberhessischen Gesellschaft für Natur und Heilkunde. 1871. Translated in Annals and Mag. Nat. Hist., 1871.) See also a paper by Leuckart, 1873.

XXI. ROTATORIA.

The Rotifers, by some eminent naturalists regarded as crustacea, are shelled worms, related to the flat-worms in many respects. The body consists of several segments, and the sexes are very unlike, the small males having the organs more or less rudimental, with no alimentary canal. Like the lower worms they have a set of tubes excretory in their nature and perhaps respiratory, corresponding to the water vascular tubes of the Radiates, but with fine ciliated infundibuliform orifices comparable with the segmental organs of the Brachiopods and higher worms; also a pair of teeth in the pharynx, as in many worms. The anus is situated on the back at the base of the tail. Sometimes the digestive canal ends in a blind sac. The distinctive organ is the retractile, ciliated, paired organ which may be called the velum. Fig. 153[1] from H. J. Clark, represents *Squa-*

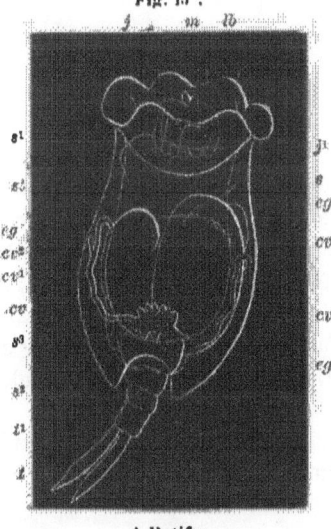

Fig. 15 .

A Rotifer.

[1] *Squamella oblonga,* magnified 200 diameters. From fresh water. A view from below; shell or carapace (*s, s*[1], *s*[2]); *s,* the anterior transverse edge of the carapace; *s*[1], the anterior, and *s*[2], the posterior corners of the carapace; *s*[3], the border of the oval, flat area which occupies the lower face of the carapace; *ib.* the eil a bearing velum of the head; *t,* the fork of the tail (*t*[1]); *m,* the mouth; *j,* jaws; *j*[1], muscles which move *j; st.* stomach; *co,* the contractile vesicle, or heart of the aquiferous circulatory system; *cv*[1], *cv*[2], the right, and *.cr*[3], *cv*[4], the left aquiferous circulatory vessels; *eg, eg*[1], *eg*[2], two largely developed young. — Clark's "Mind in Nature."

mella oblonga of Ehrenberg, found in this country. It is closely allied to Brachionus.

Development of the Rotifers. The sexes are distinct. The females lay both summer and winter eggs, the former being unfertilized, like the summer eggs of the Cladocera (Daphnia). The Rotifers live in damp places in water and revive after being nearly dried up for a long time. Dr. Salensky has been the first to give a complete sketch of the life-history of a Rotifer, *Brachionus urceolaris.*

The eggs of Brachionus are attached by a stalk to the hinder part of the body of the female. The following remarks apply to the female eggs, which are quite distinguishable from the masculine ones. The eggs undergo total segmentation, and the outer layer of cells resulting from subdivision form the blastoderm, when the formation of the organs begins. The first occurrence is an infolding of the blastoderm (ectoderm) forming the primitive mouth, which remains permanently open, the mouth not opening at the opposite end as in Sagitta, but the entire development of the germ is as in Calyptræa, as Salensky often compares the earliest phases of development of the Rotifer with those of that mollusk. The "trochal disk," or velum, as we may call the ciliated disk of the Brachionus, arises as in certain mollusks, as a swelling on each side of the primitive infolding. Behind the primitive hole appears another swelling, which becomes the "foot" or tail.

There is soon formed at the bottom of the primitive infolding a new hole or infolding, which is the true mouth and pharynx, while a swelling just behind the mouth becomes the under lip.

Soon after, the two wings of the velum become well marked, and their relation to the head is as constant as in Calyptræa. The foot becomes conical, larger, and the termination of the intestine and anal opening is formed at the base.

Fig. 154.

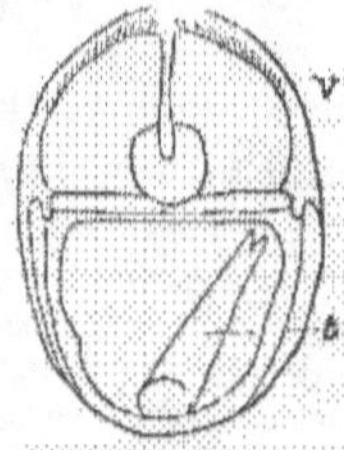

Brachionus nearly ready to hatch.

The internal organs are then elaborated; first the nervous system, consisting of but a single pair of ganglia arising from the outer germ-layer (ectoderm). Soon after the sensitive hairs arise on the wings of the velum.

Fig. 154 shows the advanced embryo, with the body divided into segments, the pair of ciliated wings of the velum (*v*), and the long tail (*t*). At this time the shell begins to form, and afterwards covers the whole trunk, but not the head.

The inner organs are developed from the inner germ-layer (endoderm), which divides into three leaves, one forming the middle part of the intestine, and the two others the glands and ovaries. The pharyngeal jaws arise as two small projections on the sides of the primitive cavity.

The male develops in the same mode as the female. The Rotifers, so far as can be judged from one species, seem to develop in a manner quite unlike other worms, and in the earliest phases much as in some Gastropods, the mode of their embryology not throwing much light on the affinities of the group, which is of doubtful position, though with more of the characters of worms than crustacea.

The young pass through a morula state, and the embryo directly attains the mature form in the egg.

LITERATURE.

Salensky. Beiträge zur Entwicklungsgeschichte der *Brachionus urceolaris.* (Siebold and Kölliker's Zeitschrift, 1872). Compare also the papers of Huxley, Leydig, Cohn, Gosse and Nägeli.

XXII. THE POLYZOA.

The Polyzoa or moss animals derive their common name from their resemblance to aquatic mosses. For example, the fresh water *Fredericella Walcottii* (Fig. 155, after Hyatt) would easily be mis-

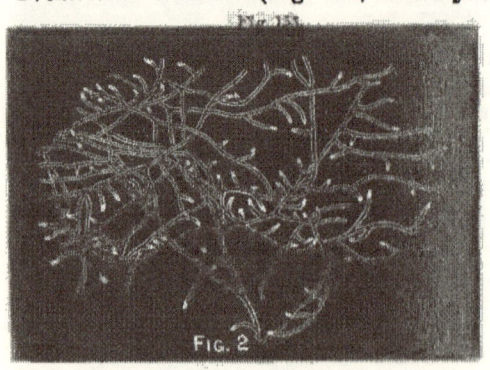

Fig. 156.

Sea mat.

Fresh water Polyzoon.

taken for moss growing on a submerged stick. The marine species have smaller cells and form mat-like encrustations, as in Membranipora (Fig. 156, cells enlarged); or as in *Myriozoum subgracile*

Fig. 157.

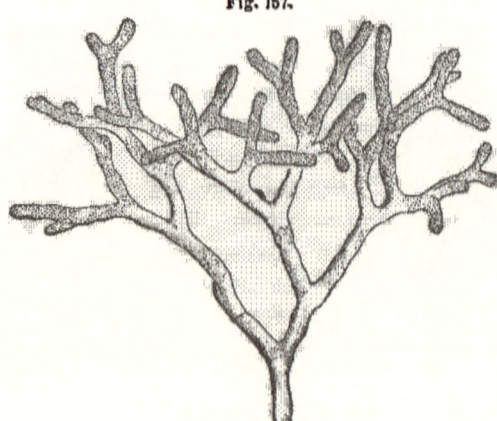

Branching Marine Polyzoon.

(Fig. 157), they form a coral-like branching mass. On magnifying these cells when the animal is alive and extended from its cell, each polypide, as it is called, appears with its crown of tentacles somewhat like a Sabellid worm. This crown of tentacles surrounds the mouth, which leads by an œsophagus into the throat and a stomach, the latter bent so that the intestine beyond ends very near the mouth ; the polypide is thus bent on itself within the cell (cystid) and its body is drawn in and out by muscles. Attached to the end of the fold of the stomach is a cord (funiculus) holding the ovary in place ; this cord extending back to the end of the cystid, as we may call the cell.

Allman regards the polypide and cystid as separate individuals. Now in confirmation of this view we have the singular genus Loxosoma, which is like the polypide of an ordinary Polyzoan, but does not live in a cell. On the other hand, we know of no cystids which are without a polypide (Nitsche).

The affinities of the Polyzoa to the worms are quite decided. In the Phoronis worm, which is allied to Sipunculus, we have the alimentary canal flexed, and the anus situated near the mouth. The Polyzoa have but a single pair of nerve ganglia, and in some cases a tubular heart. The fresh-water species are the higher, and are called Phylactolæmata ; the marine species are termed Gymnolæmata. All the Polyzoa are hermaphrodite, the ovaries and male glands residing in the same cystid, the testes being situated near the bottom, while the ovary is attached to the walls of the upper part of the cell (Rolleston's Forms of Animal Life). Reproduction is both sexual and asexual (or by budding).

Development of the Polyzoa.—Remembering that the cystids stand in the same relation to the polypides as the hydroids to the medusæ, as Nitsche insists, we may regard the polypides as secondary individuals, produced by budding from the cystids. The large masses of cells forming the moss animal, which is thus a compound animal, like a coral stock, arises by budding out from a primary cell. The budding process begins in the endocyst, or inner of the double walls of the body of the cystid, according to Nitsche, but according to an earlier Swedish observer, F. A. Smitt, from certain fat bodies floating in the cystid.

Nitsche has observed the life-history of *Flustra membranacea.* He has traced the budding of one cell or zoœcium (representing the cystid individual) from another. During this process the polypide within decays, leaving as a remnant the so-called "brown body," regarded by Smitt as a secretion of the endocyst and germ of a new polypide. After the loss of its first polypide, it can produce a new one by budding from the endocyst on the side of the stomach. In Loxosoma, young resembling the adult bud out like polyps.

Nitsche does not regard this budding process as an alternation of generations, but states that in Polyzoa of the family Vesiculariidæ, this may occur, as in them some cystids form the stem, and others (the zoœcia) produce the eggs.

The Polyzoa produce winter and summer eggs, the winter eggs, called *statoblasts*, being protected by a hard shell. Fig. 158, after

Fig. 158.

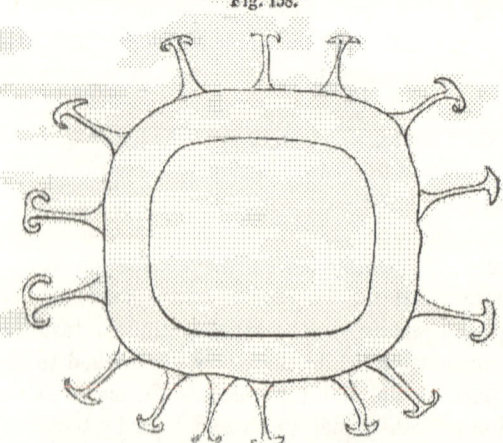

Egg of Pectinatella magnifica.

Hyatt, represents the winter egg of *Pectinatella magnifica*, with spines. These winter eggs crowd the zoœcia, and may be found in them after the polypides have decayed.

Grant first described the ciliated young of the Polyzoa. The Swedish naturalists, Lovén and Smitt, have described the development of the young *Lepralia pallasiana*, which, after passing through a true morula condition, issues from the egg as a flattened ciliated sphere with a single band of larger cilia surrounding one end.

Our figure (159) is copied from Claparède's memoir, and represents the larva of *Bugula avicularia* immediately after escaping from the egg. After swimming about for a while as a spherical ciliated larva, with a bunch of larger cilia (flagellum) at one end, it elongates, looses its cilia and

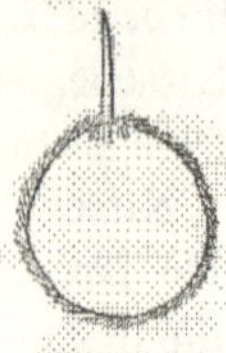

Fig. 159.

Polyzoon larva.

flagellum, and soon the polypide grows inside, the stomach and tentacles arise, and finally the polypide is formed.

In conclusion, the **Polyzoa** increase (a) by budding, (b) by normal eggs and winter eggs. In reproducing from eggs the young passes through :

1. Morula state.

2. Trochosphere, much as in certain worms and mollusks, attaining the

3. Adult condition (zooecium).

LITERATURE.

Smitt. Bidrag till Kännedomen om Hafs-Bryozoernas utveckling.

——— Om Hafs-bryozoernas utveckling och Fettkroppar. (Ofversigt af K. Vet. Aknd. Förh. 1865.)

Nitsche. Beiträge zur Anatomie und Entwickelungsgeschichte der phylactolämen Süsswasserbryozoen. (Archiv für Anat. u. Phys. 1868.)

——— Beiträge zur Kenntniss der Bryozoen. (Siebold und Kölliker's Zeitschrift, 1871.)

Claparède. Beiträge zur Anatomie und Entwicklungsgeschichte der Seebryozoen. (Siebold und Kölliker's Zeitschrift, 1870.)

Consult also papers by Grant, Lovén, Huxley, Hyatt and Hincks.

XXIII. THE BRACHIOPODA.

While the Brachiopods have been regarded by many as closely related to the Polyzoa, there are many features, as insisted on by Prof. Morse, which closely ally them to the Chætopod worms. In his treatise "On the systematic Position of the Brachiopoda,"[1] Morse has given conclusive reasons for removing them from the mollusks and placing them among the worms, and even, in his opinion, among the Chætopods, the highest division of worms. He thus, after giving the anatomical facts in his view sustaining his position, concludes that ancient Chætopod worms culminated in two parallel lines, on the one hand, in the Brachiopods, and on the other, in the fixed and highly cephalized Chætopods.

On the other hand Mr. A. Agassiz, swayed by their relationship to the Polyzoa, remarks that "the close relationship between Brachiopods and Bryozoa cannot be more fully demonstrated than by the beautiful drawings on Pl. v., of Kowalevsky's history of Thecidium. We shall now have at least a rational explanation of the homologies of Brachiopods, and the transition between such types as Pedicellina to Membranipora and other incrusting Bryozoa, is readily explained from the embryology of Thecidium. In

---

[1] Proceedings of the Boston Society of Natural History, xv, 1873.

fact, all incrusting Bryozoa are only communities of Brachiopods, the valves of which are continuous and soldered together, the flat valve forming a united floor, while the convex valve does not cover the ventral valve, but leaves an opening more or less ornamented for the extension of the lophophore."[1]

In his first paper on the "Earlier Stages of the Terebratulina" Morse had shown the same relationship between the young Brachiopod and the Pedicellina.

The two commonest forms on our coast are the *Terebratulina septentrionalis*, found attached to stems or shells in the seas of New England, while the *Lingula pyrimidata* (Fig. 160, A, with the peduncle perfect, retaining a portion of the sand tube ; B, showing the valves in motion, the peduncle broken and a new sand case be-

Fig. 160.

C   B   A

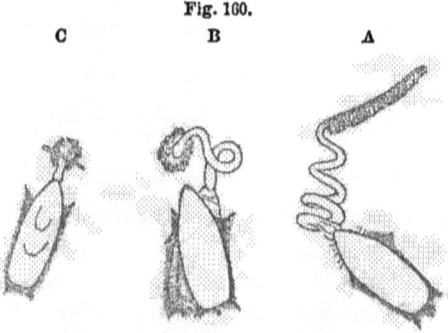

Lingula pyrimidata. After Morse.

ing formed ; C, the same with the peduncle broken close to the body, after Morse) is common in sand between tide marks, from North Carolina to Florida. It is usually free, but sometimes attached.

Development of the Brachiopods. The life-history, from the time that it leaves the egg until it attains maturity, of our common lampshell, *Terebratulina septentrionalis*, has been told by Prof. Morse. Before his account appeared our knowledge was extremely fragmentary. Morse believes that in all the Brachiopods the sexes are separate. The eggs (Fig. 162, A), he says, as in the Annelida, when arrived at maturity, escape from the ovaries into the general cavity of the body, and are thence gathered up by the segmental organs, or oviducts, and discharged into the surrounding water. Whether they are fertilized after they leave the

---

[1] Amer. Journ. Sc. and Arts, Dec., 1871.

parent or before, is not settled. In a few hours after they are discharged the embryos hatch and become clothed with cilia. The earliest stages of the egg of Brachiopods before the larva hatches, were studied by Kowalevsky after the publication of Morse's researches. The Russian zoologist observed in the egg of Thecidium the total segmentation of the yolk (also observed in Terebratulina by Morse), until a blastoderm (ectoderm) is formed around the central segmentation cavity, which contains a few cells. The similar formation of the blastoderm was seen in Argiope, but not the morula stage. After this the ectoderm invaginates and a cavity is formed, opening externally by a primitive mouth. The walls of this cavity now consist of an inner and outer layer (the endoderm and ectoderm). This cavity eventually becomes the digestive cavity of the mature animal. After this the development goes on as previously described by Morse, Kowalevsky's discoveries confirming those of the former observer.

In Terebratulina Morse observed that the oval ciliated germ became segmented, dividing into two and then three rings, with a

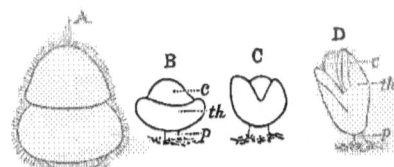

Fig. 161.

Larval stages of Terebratulina.

tuft of long cilia on the anterior end (Fig. 161, A). In this stage the larva is quite active, swimming rapidly about in every direction.

Soon after, the germ looses its cilia and becomes attached at one end as in Fig. 161, B (c, cephalic segment; th, thoracic segment; p, peduncular or caudal segment). The thoracic ring now increases much in size so as to partially enclose the cephalic segment, as at Fig. 161, C. The form of the Brachiopod is then soon attained, as seen in Fig. 161, D, in which the head (c) is seen projecting from the two valves of the shell (th), the larger being the ventral plate.

The hinge margin is broad and slightly rounded when looked at from above; a side view however, presents a wide and flattened area, " as is shown in some species of Spirifer, and the embryo for a long time assumes the position that the Spirifer must have assumed." Before the folds have closed over the head, four bundles of bristles appear; these bristles are delicately barbed like those of larval worms. The arms, or cirri, now bud out as two prominences, one on each side of the mouth. Then as the embryo advances in growth the outlines remind one of a Leptæna, an ancient genus of Brachiopods, and in a later stage the form becomes "quite unlike any adult Brachiopod known."

The deciduous bristles are then discarded, and the permanent ones make their appearance, two pairs of arms arise, and now the shell in "its general contour recalls Siphonotreta, placed in the family Discinidæ by Davidson, a genus not occurring above the Silurian." No eye spots could be seen in Terebratulina, though in the young Theeidium they were observed by Lacaze-Duthiers. The young Terebratulina differs from Discina of the same age in being sedentary, while, as observed by Fritz Müller, the latter "swims freely in the water some time after the dorsal and ventral plates, cirri, mouth, œsophagus and stomach have made their appearance." Discina also differs from Terebratulina in having a long and extensible œsophagus and head bearing a crown of eight cirri or tentacles. Regarding the relations of the Brachiopods with the Polyzoa, Morse suggests that there is some likeness between the embryo Brachiopod, and the free embryo of Pedicellina. Fig. 162, B, represents the Terebratulina when in its form it recalls Megerlia or Argiope. C represents a later Lingula-like stage. "It also suggests," says Morse, "in its movements the nervously acting Pedicellina. In this and the several succeeding stages, the mouth points directly backward (forward of authors), or away

Fig. 162.

G F E D C B A

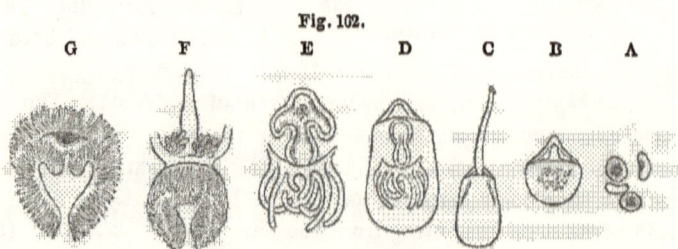

Later stages of Terebratulina.

from the perpendicular end (D) and is surrounded by a few ciliated cirri, which forcibly recall certain Polyzoa. The stomach and intestine form a simple chamber, alternating in their contractions and forcing the particles of food from one portion to the other." Figure 162, E, shows a more advanced stage, in which a fold is seen on each side of the stomach; from the fold is developed the complicated liver of the adult, as seen in E, which represents the animal about an eighth of an inch long. The arms (lophophore) begin "to assume the horse-shoe-shaped form of Pectinatella and other high Polyzoa. The mouth at this stage begins to turn towards the dorsal valve (ventral of authors), and as the central lobes of the lophophore begin to develop, the lateral arms are deflected as in F. In these stages (G) an epistome[1] is very marked, and it was noticed that the end of the intestine was held to the mantle by an attachment, as in the adult, reminding one of the *funiculus* in the Phylactolæmata" (Polyzoa). Turning now to Kowalevsky's memoir, he shows, according to Mr. A. Agassiz, that the larvæ of Brachiopods are strikingly like those of the Annelides. "The homology between the early embryonic stages of Argiope with well known Annelid larvæ is most remarkable, and the resemblance between some of the stages of Argiope figured by Kowalevsky and the corresponding stages of growth of the so-called Lovén type of development among Annelides is complete. The number of segments is less, but otherwise the main structural features show a closeness of agreement which will make it difficult for conchologists hereafter to claim Brachiopods as their special property. The identity in the ulterior mode of growth between the embryo of Argiope and of Balanoglossus, in the Tornaria stage, is still more striking. We can follow the changes undergone by Argiope while it passes through its Tornaria stage, if we may so call it, and becomes gradually, by a mere modification of the topography of its organs, transformed into a minute pedunculated Brachiopod, differing as far from the Tornaria stage of Argiope as the young Balanoglossus differs from the free swimming Tornaria. In fact, the whole development of Argiope is a remarkable combination of the Lovén and of the Tornaria types of development among worms."

At the close of his first memoir Morse again insists on the close relationship of the Brachiopods and Polyzoa; these views, taken with his later views as to the close relationship of Lingula with the Chætopod worms, show how intimately the Polyzoa and Brachiopods are bound together with the Annelides.

---

[1] The free lip seemed to perform all the functions pertaining to the epistome in the higher Polyzoa, and we find it on the inner bend of the arms, as in the Polyzoa, though not occupying the same homological position in regard to the flexure of the intestine." Early Stages of Terebratulina, p. 34.

It will be seen that neither in the Polyzoa nor Brachiopods are there any true molluscan characters, nothing homologous with the foot, the shell gland or odontophore. The Brachiopods should in our opinion be, perhaps, united with the Polyzoa and form a group lower but sub-parallel with the Annelides. The Brachiopods, from the facts afforded by Morse and others, have neither such a nervous system or respiratory or circulating organs, or an annulated body, as would warrant their union with the Chætopods. Morse has fully proved that they are a synthetic type, combining the features of different groups of worms, and this fact apparently forbids their being regarded as a group of Chætopods. Looking at the subject from an evolutional point of view, we should be inclined to regard the Brachiopods and Polyzoa as derived from common low vermian ancestors, while the Chætopod worms probably sprang independently from a higher ancestry.

To sum up, the Brachiopods pass through :—

1. A morula state.

2. A free swimming, ciliated Gastrula condition, formed by invagination of the ectoderm.

3. Free swimming larval annulate Cephalula stage, combining the characters of the larva of Nareda, and of Tornaria the larva of Balanoglossus.

LITERATURE.

Morse. On the Early Stages of *Terebratulina septentrionalis.* (Memoirs Boston Soc. Nat. Hist., 1869.)

———. Embryology of Terebratulina. (Memoirs Bost. Soc. Nat. Hist., 1873).

Kowalevsky. Investigations upon the Development of Brachiopoda, Moscow, 1874. With papers by Oscar Schmidt, Lacaze-Duthiers, F. Müller and McCrady.

XXIV. THE TUNICATA.

LIKE the Polyzoa and Brachiopods, the Ascidians may be said to be worms in disguise. The singular test easily confounded with the mantle of mollusks, the excurrent and incurrent orifices like those of the clam, led naturalists to regard them as low shell-less mollusks, but the structure of more important organs, and the mode of development of these animals, so unlike that of mollusks, has led some of our leading naturalists (Gegenbaur, Hæckel and Ussow) to decide that they should be placed among the worms; while so high an authority in zoölogy as Prof. Oscar Schmidt regards them as not only not mollusks, but as the immediate vermian ancestors of the vertebrates, and as forming a distinct group of animals which he terms *Pro-vertebrata*.

One of the most important characters indicating the true affinities of the ascidians, is the sieve-like pharynx, a prolongation of the digestive canal, resembling that of Balanoglossus. The nervous system, like that of many low worms consists of a single ganglion, and not a chain of them surrounding the œsophagus as in the mollusks. In the tad-pole like Appendicularia, which resembles the larval ascidians, there is a chain of caudal ganglia from ten to eighteen in number, united by means of a nerve sent out from the ganglion in the head. Moreover the heart is a simple tube like that of some articulates. Besides the vermian characters there are some remarkable larval organs which suggest an affinity with Amphioxus and the lower vertebrates. It would thus seem that except in the more secondary external, superficial char-

Fig. 163.

Molgula.

acters there is no good reason for the prevalent opinion that ascidians are mollusks.

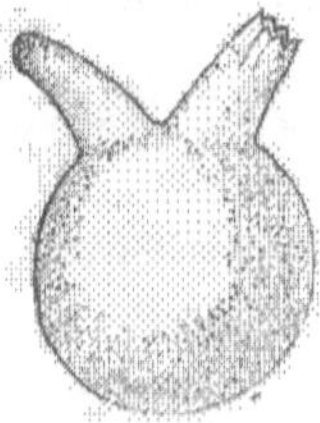

At first sight the typical ascidians look like anything but worms. Fig. 163 (from Verrill's Report) represents *Molgula Manhattensis*, of the natural size. It looks like a double-necked bottle when the two orifices are thrust out. The viscera are enclosed by a thick test or tunic, whence the name of the class, *Tunicata*. This test is rendered tough and dense by the presence of cellulose, a substance secreted usually by vegetable cells, and very rarely found in animals. There are two orifices, the most anterior corresponding to the mouth, and the posterior leading into the anus. The alimentary canal is much bent on itself. The opening of the pharynx is surrounded by a fringe of tentacles, arising from the peritoneum or lining membrane next to the outer test. The capacious pharynx is perforated with slits, and serves as a respiratory cavity comparable with that of the worm, Balanoglossus. At the bottom of this respiratory sac opens the true mouth, which communicates by an œsophagus with the stomach, while the intestine is twisted so that the anus opens near but posterior to the mouth. There is a nervous ganglion on the dorsal side of the body situated at a point between the two external orifices, sending threads to the two openings in the test and the pharynx. The heart is a short tube open at both ends. Its action may be beautifully seen in the transparent Perophora of our coast. The current of blood is momentarily reversed, so that each end becomes, as Huxley remarks, "alternately arterial and venous."

Such in general terms is the structure of a typical simple ascidian as well as the compound ascidians, and the Pyrosoma and Salpa. The aberrant Appendicularia is, as has been observed, provided with a tail, and resembles the tailed young of the higher ascidians.

The ascidians are, for the most part, hermaphrodites, the ovary and testis being lodged in the same individual.

Development. While Milne-Edwards discovered that the larvæ of certain ascidians were tad-pole like, Kowalevsky, in 1866, studied the development of the ascidians and threw a flood of light on their history. The following account is an abstract of his classic memoir. The early stages of most ascidians is typified by the mode of growth of *Phallusia mamillata* Cuv., while the mode of growth from the free swimming larval period to the adult was traced in *Ascidia intestinalis.* Kowalevsky's discoveries were confirmed by Kupffer and others, while exceptional modes of development were pointed out by Lacaze-Duthiers and also Kupffer, who found that the larvæ of Molgula have no tail.

While some ascidians, such as Perophora, increase by budding, creeping by stolons along the fronds of sea-weeds, the common method of reproduction is by eggs and sperm cells. The eggs of Phallusia and the ascidians consist of a yolk, not protected by a yolk-skin, but surrounded by a layer of jelly containing yellow cells.

After fertilization by the sperm cells, which enter the substance
of the egg tail-foremost, the yolk undergoes total segmentation.
The next step is the invagination of the ectoderm, a true Gastrula
state resulting. Fig. 164, A (after Kowalevsky), represents the
Gastrula ; *h*, the primitive digestive cavity ; *a*, the primitive opening, which soon closes ; and *c*, the segmentation-cavity or primitive
body-cavity. After this primitive opening (*a*) is lost to view,
sometime before the embryo has reached the stage B, another
cavity (*n*) appears with an external opening. This cavity is

Fig. 164.

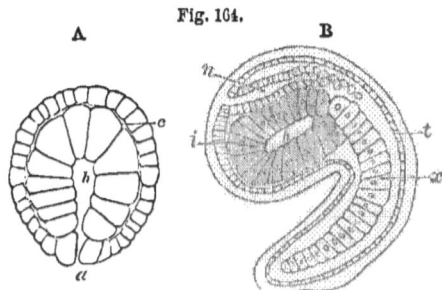

Embryo Ascidian.

formed by a union of two ridges which grow out from the upper
part of the germ. This is the central nervous system, and in the
cavity are subsequently developed the sense-organs. We thus
see, says Kowalevsky, a complete analogy in the mode of origin
of the nervous system of the ascidians to that of the vertebrates,
the nervous cavity, where the embryo is seen in section, being
situated above the digestive cavity in both types of animals.

The next important stage is the formation of the tail. The pear-
shaped germ elongates and contracts posteriorly until of the form indicated at Fig. 164, B (*i*, pharynx ; *t*, epithelium forming the body-
wall). At this period appears the axial string of nucleated cells,
called the *chorda dorsalis*, as it is homologous with that organ in
Amphioxus and the embryo of higher vertebrates. The nervous
system consists of a mass of cells extending halfway into the
tail and directly overlying the *chorda*, but extending far beyond
the end of the latter as seen in the figure. The nerve-cavity (B, *n*)
after closing up forms the nerve-vesicle, a large cavity (Fig. 165, *a*)
in which the supposed auditory organ (*e*) and the supposed eye (*a*)
arise ; this cavity finally closes, and the sense-organs are indicated

by certain small masses of pigment cells in the fully grown ascidian larva.

As the embryo matures, the first change observed in the cord is the appearance of small, highly refractive bodies between the cells. Between the neighboring cells soon appear in the middle minute highly refractive corpuscles which increase in size, and press the cell-contents out of the middle of the cord. After each reproductive corpuscle grows so that the central substance of the cell is forced out, it unites with the others, and then arises in the middle of the simple cellular cord a string of bodies of a firm gelatinous substance which forms the support of the tail. After this coalescence the substance develops farther and presses out the protoplasm of the cells entirely to the periphery. The cord when complete consists of a firm gelatinous substance surrounded by a cellular sheath which is formed of the remains of the cells originally comprising the rudimentary cord. The cells lying under the epithelial layer form a muscular sheath of which the cord (Fig. 165, c) is the support or skeleton.

Fig. 165.

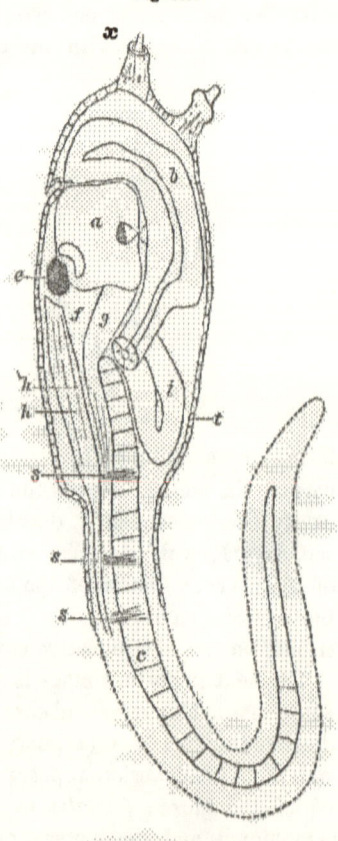

Larval Ascidian.

The alimentary cavity arises from the primitive cavity (Fig. 164, A, h); whether the primitive opening (Fig. 164, A, a) is closed or not, Kowalevsky says is an interesting question. According to analogy with many other animals it probably closes. In Sagitta, Phoronis, Limnæus, Echinus and others, we know that the opening which remains after the first invagination becomes the anus.

The larva hatches in from forty-eight to sixty hours after the beginning of segmentation, and is then of the form indicated by Fig. 165 (copied with some additions and omissions from Kupffer's figure, being partly diagrammatic). This anatomist discovered in the larva of *Ascidia canina*, which is more transparent than Kowalevsky's Phallusia larva, not only a central nervous cord overlying the *chorda dorsalis* and extending well into the tail, while in the body of the larva it becomes broader, club-shaped and surrounds the sensitive cavity (*a*), but he also detected three pairs of spinal nerves (*s*) arising at regular intervals from the spinal cord (*h*, *h'*) and distributed to the muscles (not represented in the figure) of the tail; Kupffer calls *f* the middle and *g* the lower brain-ganglion. The pharynx (*b*), or respiratory sac, is now very large; it opens posteriorly into the stomach and intestine (*i*); *x* represents one of the three appendages by which the larva fastens itself to some object when about to change into the adult, sessile condition; *t* indicates the body-wall, consisting of epithelial cells.

We will now, from the facts afforded us by Kowalevsky, trace the changes from the larval, free-swimming state to the sessile adult Ascidia, which may be observed on the New England coast in August. After the larva fastens itself by the three processes to some object, the *chorda dorsalis* breaks and bends, the cells forming the sheath surrounding the broken axial cord. The muscular fibres degenerate into round cells and fill the space between the chorda and the tegument, the jelly-like substance forming a series of wrinkles. With the contraction and disappearance of the tail begins that of the nerve-vesicle, and soon no cavity is left. The three processes disappear; the pharynx becomes quadrangular; and the stomach and intestine are developed, being bent under the intestine. A mass of cells arises on the anterior end beneath the digestive tract, from which originate the heart and pericardium. In a more advanced stage two gill-holes appear in the pharynx, and subsequently two more slits, and at about this time the ovary and testis appear at the bottom, beyond the bend of the alimentary canal. The free cells in the body-cavity are transformed into blood cells, and indeed the greater part of those which composed the nervous system of the larva are transformed into blood corpuscles. Of the embryonal nervous system there remains a very small ganglion, no new one being formed. The adult ascidian form meanwhile has been attained and the very small individuals differ for the most part only in size from those which are full-sized and mature.

It will be seen that some highly important features, recalling vertebrate characteristics, have occurred at different periods in the life of the embryo ascidian. Kowalevsky remarks that "the first indication of the germ, the direct passage of the segmentation cells into the cells of the embryo, the formation of the segmentation cavity, the conversion of this cavity into the body cavity, and the formation of the digestive cavity through invagination—these are all occurrences which are common to many animals and have been observed in Amphioxus, Sagitta, Phoronis, Echinus, etc. The first point of difference from other animals in the development of all vertebrates is seen in the formation of the dorsal ridges and their closing to form a nerve-canal. This mode of formation of the nervous system is characteristic of the vertebrates alone, except the Ascidians. Another primary character allying the Ascidians to the vertebrates, is the presence of a *chorda dorsalis*, first seen in the adult Appendicularia by J. Müller. This organ is regarded by Kowalevsky to be functionally, as well as genetically, identical with that of Amphioxus. This was a startling conclusion, and stimulated Professor Kupffer of Kiel to study the embryology of the ascidians anew. He did so, and the results this careful observer obtained, led him to fully endorse the conclusions reached by Kowalevsky, particularly those regarding the unexpected relations of the ascidians to the vertebrates, and it would appear from the facts set forth by these eminent observers, as well as Metschnikoff, Ganin, Ussow and others, that the vertebrates have probably descended from some type of worm resembling larval ascidians more perhaps than any other vernian type, though it is to be remembered that certain tailed larval Distomæ appear to possess an organ resembling a *chorda dorsalis*, and farther investigation on other types of worms may lead to discoveries throwing more light on this intricate subject of the ancestry of the vertebrates. At any rate, it is among the lower worms, if anywhere, that we are to look for the ancestors of the vertebrates, as the Cœlenterates, Echinoderms, the Mollusks, Crustacea and Insects, are too circumscribed and specialized groups to afford any but characters of analogy rather than affinity.

For example, the cuttle fish, with its "bone" and highly developed eye, is far more remote from the lowest fish, Amphioxus, than the Appendicularia or larval Ascidia.

Not all Ascidians have tailed larvæ; three species of Molgula have been found to have no tailed young and to attain maturity by direct growth. The young have five temporary, long, slender processes. Now as in other types of animals, as we have already seen, some forms have a metamorphosis and others attain the adult condition by direct growth. Professor Kupffer tells us that in *Ascidia ampulloides*, as observed by Van Beneden, the young has a tail, a *chorda dorsalis* and pigment spots, which are wanting in the young of several species of Molgula, but it has the

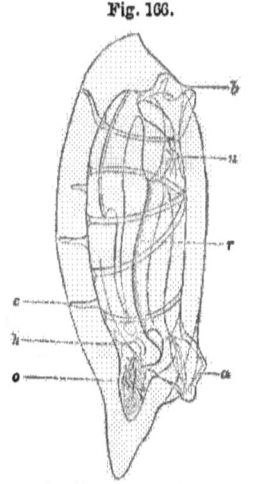

Fig. 106.

five long, deciduous appendages observed in young Molgulæ. Among the compound Ascidians, Botryllus and Botrylloides have tailed young, while in other forms there is no metamorphosis.

Besides the normal mode of reproduction, from eggs, it was discovered by Chamisso, in 1819, that the singular Salpa reproduced by budding; that in other words there was an alternation of generations, there being a sexual, solitary individual which gives rise by budding to chains, or aggregations of simple individuals, which reproduce by eggs. The startling announcement of the poet-naturalist, "that a Salpa mother is not like its daughter or its own mother, but resembles its sister, its granddaughter and its grandmother," was combated at first, but stated to be true by Sars, Krohn and others. Mr. W. K. Brooks, however, claims that the solitary females produce chains of males by budding, and discharge an egg into each male before the birth of the latter, the eggs being impregnated while the males are undeveloped. After the embryos have been discharged from the bodies of the males, the latter grow

---

¹ Fig. 219. *Salp Cabotii*, an individual from a mature chain, three-quarters view enlarged; *a* posterior or anal opening; *b*, anterior or branchial opening; *c*, processes by which the individuals of the chain were united; *h*, heart; *n*, nervous ganglion; *o*, nucleus; *r*, gill. After A. Agassiz, from Verrill's Report.

up, become sexually mature and discharge their spermatic particles into the water, by which they are carried to the eggs within the bodies of the males composing the younger chains.

The Tunicates undergo, then, the following changes :

1. Morula state, or total segmentation of the yolk.
2. Gastrula.
3. Free-swimming tailed larva (or as in Molgula, no metamorphosis).
4. Adult, reproducing sometimes by budding (Parthenogenesis).

LITERATURE.

Chamisso. De Animalibus quibusdam e classe Vermium, etc. Berlin, 1819.

Milne-Edwards. Observations sur les Ascidiea composées des Côtes de la Manche. Paris, 1841.

Kowalevsky. Entwickelungsgeschichte der einfachen Ascidien. (Mem. Acad. St. Petersburg. X. No. 15. 1866).

Kupffer. Die Stammverwandtschaft zwischen Ascidien und Wirbelthieren. (Schultze's Archiv für micr. Anat., vi, 1870).

———. Zur Entwickelung der einfachen Ascidien. (Schultze's Archiv. viii, 1872).

Consult also papers by Sars, Krohn, Huxley, Leuckart, Vogt, Lacaze-Duthiers, Ussow and W. K. Brooks. (Proceedings Bost. Soc. Nat. Hist., 1876.)

XXV. GEPHYREA (Sipunculus).

There are two points of interest connected with these singular worms, *i. e.*, the fact that they were formerly associated with the Holothurians, and that their free-swimming Actinotrocha larva so closely resembles the young Echinoderms. The Sipunculus usually lives in broken shells, building out the mouth with a tube of sand ; the anus is situated near the mouth, while in Priapulus it is situated at the end of the body. In none of these worms are there bristles, or indications of segments, and they in their general appearance with their tentaculated mouth, resemble certain Holothurians, as Synapta. Most of these worms are bisexual, Sipunculus however, or at least certain species of the genus, being hermaphroditic.

Development. The free-swimming larva of Sipunculus was first discovered and named "Actinotrocha" by J. Müller. It is related closely in form to Echinoderm larvæ, as well as to the Pilidium and other larvæ of the Nemertian worms. The fully grown larva is much like the larval Nemertian noticed on p. 132, fig. 141, the disposition of the digestive canal being the same, while on the head is a large umbrella-like expansion, and behind the mouth and on the end of the body is a ciliated band and twelve arm-like projections, like those in certain Echinoderm larvæ. In all respects the Actinotrocha is a true *Cephalula*.

We will now, with Metschnikoff, follow the life-history of the Actinotrocha. The earliest stage he observed was when the larva had a transparent, ciliated body, with an umbrella-like expansion on the head, covering the mouth region, while the end of the body was truncated. The young at this stage was much like a Phoronis larva. Soon four projections arise at the end of the body, and twelve long, arm-like projections grow out by the time the larva becomes mature.

When the larva is about to transform into the Sipunculus, the end of the intestine bends up, opening outwards near the mouth. The umbrella is gradually withdrawn into the mouth, so that finally only a crown of short tooth-like projections surrounds the mouth. Finally the whole umbrella disappears in the œsophagus, is actually swallowed, while the arms on the end of the body are absorbed and disappear, and the end of the intestine projects far out from the body behind the mouth. By this time the Sipunculus form is clearly indicated, the body being long and slender and the mouth surrounded by a crown of short tentacles, and the anal opening is withdrawn within the head. The change from the free-swimming larva to the sedentary worm is effected in a very short time.

The Sipunculus, then, so far as its history is known, passes through a Cephalula stage before transforming into the adult worm.

LITERATURE.

Müller. Archiv für Anatomie, p. 103, 1846.

Metschnikoff. Ueber die Metamorphose einiger Seethiere. (Siebold und Kölliker's Zeitschrift, p. 244, 1871.)

Consult also papers by Wagener, Krohn, **Schneider, Kowalevsky** and Claparède.

XXVI. ANNULATA.

The life-history of Balanoglossus, a peculiar worm found in fine sand along our whole coast from Cape Ann to Beaufort, North Carolina, is one of singular interest. Its free swimming larva was regarded by Müller, who discovered and called it *Tornaria*, as the young of some starfish. Later studies by eminent naturalists only seemed to confirm this opinion, until in 1869 Metschnikoff suggested that it might be the larva of the worm, first described under the name of Balanoglossus, or whale's tongue, by Delle

Chiaji, and Mr. A. Agassiz fully confirmed the suggestion, giving an account of the intermediate stages between the larval and adult condition.

The *Tornaria* (Fig. 167[1] after A. Agassiz) seems in many respects like some echinoderm larvæ, differing from any yet known, however, in having an organ, the so-called heart (*h*) situated at the base of the canal leading from the water system to the dorsal pore. The water system is very fully developed. Mr. Agassiz says that the natural position of Tornaria in the water while moving, is usually with the eye-specks uppermost. "They revolve quite rapidly upon their longitudinal axis, and at the same time,

Fig. 167.

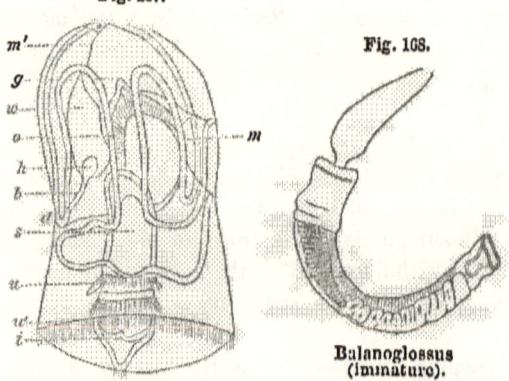

Fig. 168.

Tornaria, or young Balanoglossus.

Balanoglossus (immature).

inclining this axis, advance by a motion of translation, or revolve upon either of the extremities as a fulcrum. Previous to the transformation of Tornaria it is quite transparent; the brilliant carmine, violet or yellow pigment-spots are closely crowded along the broad belt of anal vibratile cilia, as well as smaller spots on the longitudinal bands of smaller cilia. The eye-specks are black and extremely prominent. The large and powerful cilia of the broad anal belt move comparatively slowly, more like the cilia of the embryo of mollusks, as has already been observed by Müller."

The Tornaria soon throws off its disguise of a young Echinoderm, and now begins its strange transformations. Previous to

[1] *a*, anus; *b*, branch of water system leading to dorsal pore, *d*; *e*, eyespeck; *g*, gills; *h*, heart; *i*, intestine; *m*, mouth, *m'*, muscular band from eye to water tube; *o*, œsophagus; *s*, stomach or alimentary canal; *u*, lappet of stomach; *u'*, anal band of cilia; *w*, water system.

any other change two gills develop from the round bag-shaped diverticula of the œsophagus, and afterwards three more pairs of gill-slits arise, somewhat as in the young Ascidian. Agassiz then remarks that the "passage of Tornaria with the young Balanoglossus is very sudden, taking place in a few hours; but unlike the transition from the Pluteus into the Echinoderm, there is no resorbition of any portion of the larva." The body lengthens, the proboscis is indicated and assumes much of the form of the adult, the four pairs of gills are well developed, the cilia drop off first, the longitudinal bands and finally the transverse ones, and then the collar becomes well marked. The young worm, for it rapidly assumes the adult Balanoglossus likeness, though much shorter proportionally, now instead of swimming "creeps rapidly over the bottom by means of its proboscis, which acts as a sort of propeller taking in water at the minute opening of the anterior extremity of the proboscis, and expelling it through an opening on its ventral side immediately in front of the mouth."

Fig. 168, after Agassiz, represents the youngest stage found in the sand, but it differs from the adult simply in the shorter body and less distinct development of the collar, with fewer gills and other unimportant points of difference.

There is considerable difference of opinion regarding the affinities of this worm. On first digging it out of the sand at Beaufort, N. C., it seemed to us a most anomalous form, the large soft proboscis, the singular gills, and the absence of setiform feet, apparently forbidding its relationship to the true Annelides. Yet its true position appears to be between the leeches and setiferous Annelides, with some Nemertian analogies. The reader can choose between the opinion of Gegenbaur that this worm is the type of an order equivalent to the Annelides, or a true Annelid allied to the Terebrellidæ, Clymenidæ and allied Annelides, as suggested by Metschnikoff and Kowalevsky; or that of A. Agassiz who regards it as the type of a family intermediate between tubicolous Annelides and Nemertians."

Turning now to the lowest Annulata, the leeches, in which there are no bristles or gills, while each end of the body terminates in a sucker, it has been found by Rathke and Kowalevsky that their embryology is nearly identical with that of the earthworm, in which there are bristles. In the leeches the sexes are united in the same individual, except in the genus Malacobdella. The eggs after fertilization undergo total segmentation. There is a primitive band much as in insects, and the adult form is attained before the animal is hatched. There is no metamorphosis. So with the earthworms. Kowalevsky studied the mode of development of two species. As nothing has heretofore been known of the life-history of so common a creature we will delay a moment to learn the results of the Russian naturalist's observation. The eggs of the European *Lumbricus agricola* were laid while the worm was in confinement in January and February. They were laid in numerous capsules, sometimes as many as fifty eggs in a capsule, though usually only three or four embryos were to be found in a capsule. The egg-capsules of *Lumbricus crubellus* were found in dung. They were much smaller and contained but one egg.

Segmentation is total, and after the embryo-cells are arranged in two layers, the innermost layer (endoderm), invaginates and forms a primitive cavity. The embryo at this time seems, then, not to correspond to the gastrula condition of other worms, although as in other worms, the Ascidians, Insects and Vertebrates, there are two primitive germ-lamellæ. Later in embryonic life, a primitive band like that of insects (which will be described farther on), rests on the outside of the yolk, as in the leach (*Hirudo medicinalis*). Finally, the form of the earthworm is attained before it breaks through the egg-shell, and it hatches without undergoing a metamorphosis, in a condition differing but slightly from that of the adult worm, so familiar to us, the body being proportionately shorter and thicker near the middle.

We now come to the sea worms, or Annelides, in which there are external gills and often a complicated locomotive apparatus, consisting of fleshy oar-like projections from the body, and strong bristles. They have free-swimming larvæ, which by a complicated metamorphosis, comparable with that of the Nemertian worms, attain the adult worm-condition.

A singular type is Phoronis, which lives in a membranous tube attached to rocks, and recalls strikingly the appearance of a Polyzoan, as it has a true lophophore and the intestine opens externally near the mouth. It is in fact a connecting link between the Annelides and the Polyzoa. Its life-history as told by Metschnikoff is nearly identical with that of Sipunculus.

We will now in a fragmentary way study the mode of development of certain typical Annelides, beginning with the lower forms.

The common *Spirorbis spirillum* (Gould) whose·minute nautilus-like shells cluster on the common Fucus of our coast, lays its eggs

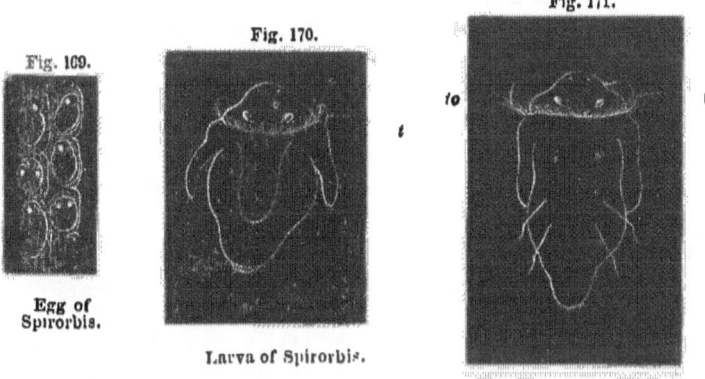

Fig. 169.

Egg of
Spirorbis.

Fig. 170.

Larva of Spirorbis.

Fig. 171.

Older larva of Spirorbis.

in strings formed of two rows (Fig. 169, after A. Agassiz), and laid on the sides of the body within the shell. The young ciliated embryos may be seen in the eggs, the eye-spots being very distinct. Fig. 170 (this and Figs. 171, 172, after A. Agassiz) represents the embryo just after ·hatching. It will be seen that it is already far advanced before leaving the egg, and Agassiz thinks that the free-swimming life of the larva does not last more than from eight to ten hours, as "it frequently happens during a night that the smooth sides of the vessel are completely covered with small limestone tubes, formed by the young Spirorbis hatched the evening before." Fig. 170 represents the young Spirorbis soon after its escape from the egg,

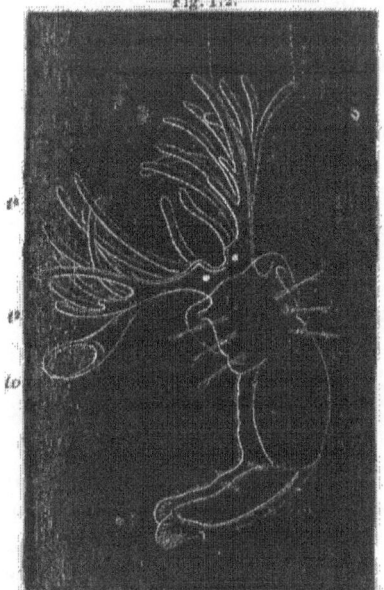

Fig. 172.

Young Spirorbis.

having only one tentacle (*t*) developed on the right side. In a succeeding stage (Fig. 171) the opercular tentacle (*to*) which is destined to act as a door to the hole of the cell, begins to grow out, and there are two pairs of bristles. Shortly after this the young Spirorbis hatches, and before building its limestone tube assumes the form indicated by Fig. 172, in which there "are nine rings," with tentacles nearly as branching as those of the adult, and a well formed operculum which with advancing age loses all trace of its former tentacular nature." The subsequent changes are very slight.

The metamorphoses of the other sea worms are well marked, and the larval forms present a great variety of shapes. As a rule, perhaps, the eggs undergo total segmentation, and the embryo leaves the egg in the Cephalula condition, the head-end being large and full, with the alimentary canal more or less flexed. In some cases, as in *Terebrellides Stroemii* Sars, observed by Willemoes-Suhm, the young leaves the egg as a Trochosphere, ("Atrocha" of Claparède and Metschnikoff, who observed the same stage in Lumbriconereis?) like that of certain mollusks and the Poly-zoa, being spherical, with a long, ce-phalic tuft of cilia, two eye-spots, and a zone of cilia, but without any bristles. Others, as in Leucodora, are similar, but provided with a few long setæ, which act as oars.

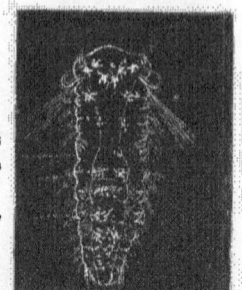

Fig. 173.

Young Polydora.

The early stages of the embryo have not yet been studied, so that we are not in possession of any certain knowledge regarding the development of the embryonal membranes and the presence or absence of a gastrula condition.

Soon after the larva leaves the egg, branches of bristles appear and the body is divided into segments. Fig. 173 (this and Figs. 174, 175, 176, 177, 178, after A. Agassiz) represents an advanced larva of Polydora. Fig. 174 and 175, illustrate the early stages of Nerine.

The early stages of *Phyllodoce maculata* are indicated by figures 176, 177, 178. The subsequent changes are not important, con-sisting chiefly of the addition of a great number of segments and the growth of smaller bristles. How the adult forms appear may be known by a glance at the accompanying figures of certain sea worms of our coast described and figured by Prof. Verrill, from

Fig. 175.

Fig. 174.

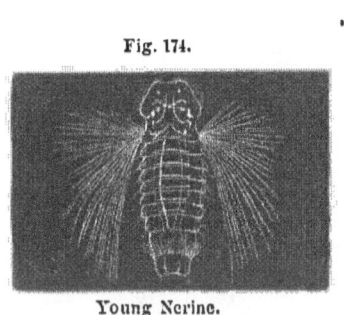

Young Nerine.

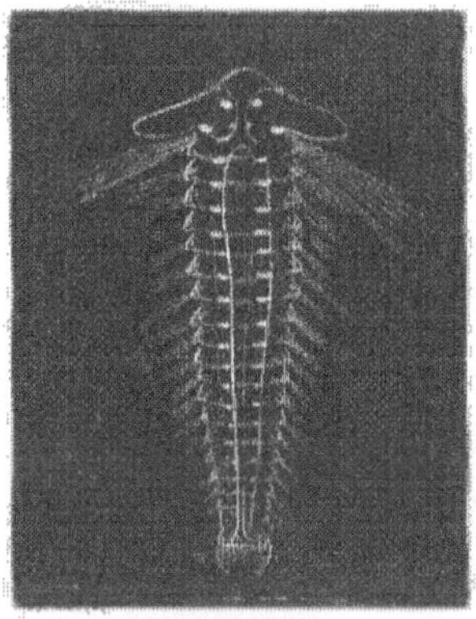

Older Nerine.

whose reports the figures are taken. Fig. 179, represents *Clymenella torquata*, 180, *Euchone elegans*, and fig. 181, a not uncommon and very elegant worm, *Cirratulus grandis*.

Besides the normal mode of reproduction by eggs, certain

Fig. 178.

Fig. 176.

Fig. 177.

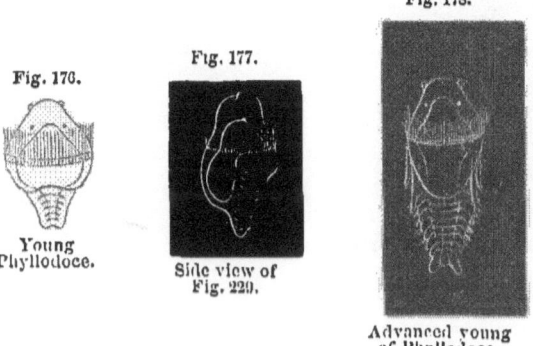

Young
Phyllodoce.

Side view of
Fig. 229.

Advanced young
of Phyllodoce.

worms reproduce by self-division or budding; such are Nais, Sabella, Filograna, Protula, Syllis, Autolytus, and others. In the latter worm as well as in Syllis there is, according to A. Agassiz, an alternation of generations, an asexual form giving rise to male and females, while these sexual and asexual forms are so unlike each other as to pass for different species and even genera.

The Annulata, then, to sum up what is known of their life-

Fig. 179.   Fig. 180.

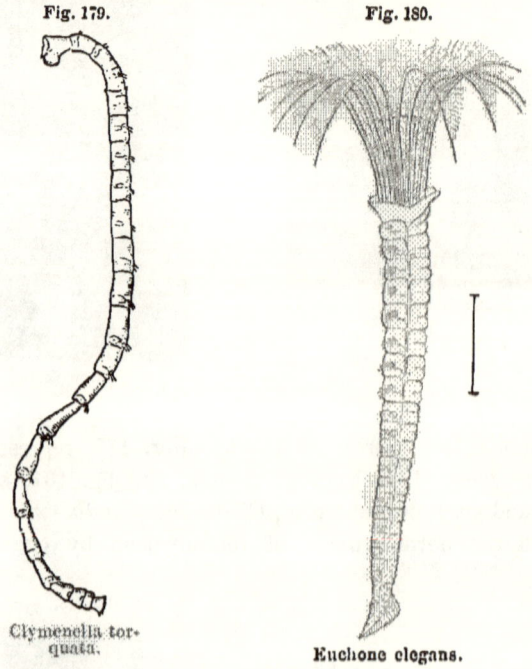

Clymenella torquata.   Euchone elegans.

history, besides reproducing by budding and parthenogenetically, usually lay eggs, and pass through the following stages :

1. Morula state.
2. ? Gastrula (not observed).
3. Atrocha or Trochosphere.
4. Cephalula
5. Adult.

LITERATURE.

Milne-Edwards. Observations sur le Développment des Annélides. (Ann. Sc. Nat. III. 145, 1845).

Sars. Zur Entwickelung der Anneliden (Archiv für Naturg. T. I, II, 1845).

Busch. Beobachtungen ueber Anat. und Entwickelung einiger Wirbelloser Thiere. Berlin, 1851.

Rathke. Beiträge zur Entwicklungsgeschichte der Hirudineen. Leipzig, 1802.

A. Agassiz. On alternate Generations in Annelides. (Jour. Bost. Soc., N. II. vii, 1862.)

Claparède. Beobachtungen ueber Anat. und Entwicklungsgeschichte Wirbelloser Thiere, etc. Leipzig. 1863.

————— *and Metschnikoff.* Beiträge zur Keuntniss der Entwickelungsgeschichte der Chætopoden. (Siebold und Kölliker's Zeitschrift, 1868).

Compare also the writings of Lovén, A. Agassiz and Kowalevsky, already cited, and papers by Krohn, Leuckart and Pagenstecher, Frey and Leuckart, Schultze, J. and Max. Müller, Busch and Willemoes-Suhm.

Fig. 181.

Cirratulus grandis.

XXVII. THE CRUSTACEA.

HAVING left the worms, we come now to a more circumscribed group of articulated animals, in which the jointed body is protected by a more or less dense tegument. Moreover there are attached to the body jointed appendages, serving as feelers, jaws or legs. The barnacles, water fleas, shrimps and crabs are tolerably familiar forms, and therefore we will not pause to discuss the anatomy and classification of these animals, merely premising our account of their development with the following tabular view of the main divisions of the group:

CRUSTACEA.

SUBCLASS I.	SUBCLASS II.
DECAPODA (Lobsters and Crabs).	TRILOBITA.
TETRADECAPODA (Sow Bugs, Beach Fleas).	MEROSTOMATA (King Crab).
NEBALIADÆ (Shrimp-like forms).	
PHYLLOPODA (Leaf-footed Shrimps).	
CLADOCERA (Water-fleas).	
OSTRACODA (Bivalved Water-fleas).	
COPEPODA, including SIPHONOSTOMA.	
CIRRIPEDIA including RHIZOCEPHALA (Barnacles).	

Development of the Barnacles. Before we turn to the life-history of the barnacles, let us look for a moment at the mode of development of those strange parasites, the Rhizocephala, whose larval feet become by a retrograde process of development converted into long irregular root-like extensions which ramify in the body of their host. The animal itself, as it adheres by means of its root-like feet to the under side of the abdomen of the crab on which it lives, would be readily mistaken for a large wart or sausage-like bunch. This shapeless mass is the mature Rhizocephalon, apparently the last term in the series of degradational forms so numerous among the lower Crustacea. This sac-like body is filled with eggs.

After total segmentation the embryo rapidly grows and hatches in an oval form with no distinct head, but with an oval shield-like disk covering the insertion of the three pairs of jointed swimming feet, ending in long bristles which aid in locomotion. This larval Rhizocephalon is comparable with the young of the water-fleas or copepods, called "Nauplius' (see also Fig. 203), but differs from them in the shield-like expansion of the body, and in the presence of a distinct abdomen ending in a movable caudal fork. But however well developed is the body generally, the young root-barnacles, as we may term them, have no mouth, or so far as known, stomach or intestine, so that after swimming about freely for a few days, they change into the "pupa" state, in which they bear a remote resemblance to the bivalved Ostracodes.

The broad shield of the larva has now become folded together like the covers of a pamphlet, enclosing the body of the pupal root-barnacle. The foremost limbs (to avail ourselves of Fritz Müller's description in his "Facts for Darwin") have become transformed into very peculiar adherent feet (prehensile antennæ of Darwin). From the ends of these feet grow out two filaments which are possibly, as Müller suggests, the "commencements of the future roots." The two following pairs of feet are rejected, six pairs of forked swimming feet have meanwhile grown out on the abdomen, while the tail ends in two short appendages. These pupæ are also mouthless and soon attach themselves by means of their adherent feet to the abdomens of crabs and hermit crabs. The other feet drop off, the filaments grow down into the body of their host, entwining around the intestine or ramifying through the liver. "The only manifestations of life which persist in these non plus ultras in the series of retrogressively metamorphosed Crustacea, are powerful contractions of the roots, and an alternate expansion and contraction of the body, in consequence of which water flows into the brood-cavity and is again expelled, through a wide orifice" (Müller).

Such is the ordinary history of a Peltogaster or Sacculina, but Mr. Darwin tells us of another form (Cryptophialus minutus) which undergoes the larval state in the egg, hatching in the pupa condition, while another form (a species of Peltogaster?) also leaves the egg in the pupa form.

The barnacle has a somewhat similar life-history. It passes through a stage of total segmentation of the yolk and hatches as a Nauplius-like free-swimming larva, but differs from the Rhizo-cephalus larva in having a mouth, stomach and intestine, while the body is covered by a triangular shield, the anterior corners of which are prolonged into horns, while the posterior angle extends beyond the tail, the forked abdomen hanging down below this long spine. The anterior feet (corresponding to the anterior antennæ) are simple, while the two pairs of posterior feet are forked, ending in long bristles.

These well armed creatures swim vigorously about on the surface of the water for a season, moulting several times before assuming the bivalve, pupal condition.

The pupa is almost identical in appearance with the bivalved Sacculina, having no mouth, and with a similar arrangement of limbs, except that no filaments are developed on the anterior pair of limbs, and they possess a pair of compound eyes.

The pupal condition is so much alike in the two groups, as stated by Fritz Müller, that we scarcely see why they should be separated as different groups, as Müller is disposed to regard them, but prefer to consider them as subordinate groups of Cirripedia.

The shield of the bivalved " pupal " barnacle becomes converted into the multivalved barnacle, the solid shell of the latter, as in the true sessile barnacles; becoming so unlike the thin valves of the pupa, that, as is well known, even Cuvier supposed them to be mollusks, though there were the jointed feelers and the articulate plan of the nervous cord as witnesses of their crustacean affinities. The swimming feet of the larval barnacle become the long slender " cirri," which serve to draw in the food, creating currents setting in towards the mouth. Strange as is this retrograde development, we shall see it paralleled among the fish lice.

To sum up, the barnacles and root-barnacles, which are hermaphrodites, except in one family (Abdominales) pass through the following stages of development:

1. Morula.
2. Nauplius or larva.
3. A bivalved " pupal " stage.
4. Adult retrograde condition.

LITERATURE.

Thompson. Zoological Researches and Illustrations. I. i. 1828–29.
Burmeister. Beiträge zur Naturgeschichte der Rankenfüsser. Berlin, 1834.
Darwin. A monograph of the subclass Cirripedia. 2 vols. London, 1851–54.
Müller, Fritz. Die Rhizocephalen. (Archiv für Naturgeschichte, 1862.)
Van Beneden, E. Recherches sur l' Embryogénie des Crustacés. III. (Bulletin de l'Acad. Roy. Belgique, 1870.)

Development of the Copepods. As the true Copepods and their allies, the fish-lice or Siphonostomatous Copepods, travel the same developmental road until the larval stage is completed, the early stages here described apply to the species of both groups. The embryonic development, however, is very simple. The sexes are distinct, and the females (Fig. 182, *Cyclops quadricornis*, after Clark) in many cases swim about as seen in the figure, with a sac of eggs attached to each side of the body.

Fig. 182.

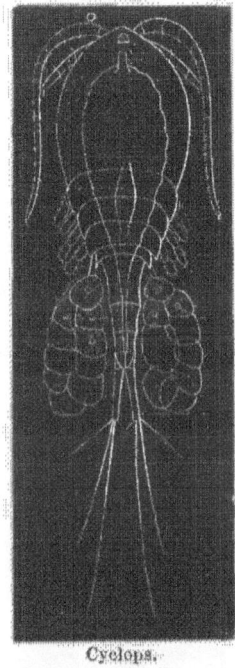

Cyclops.

The embryo in those species of Copepods which have been examined, is formed in the following manner, as observed by E. Van Beneden.

The egg undergoes total segmentation, resulting in a layer of blastodermic cells surrounding the yolk. These cells increase in length on one side, forming the blastodermic disk, or "primitive streak." On the ventral surface of this disk, viz., the side pointing outwards, the three pairs of limbs arise simultaneously, and the Nauplius (or larva) directly hatches, its body being more or less oval and rounded.

In this simple condition, with no separation of the body into a head-thorax or abdomen, and with a simple unpaired eye and a labrum, it swims about. Its farther transformations can be traced by any one who will take the pains to keep these water-fleas in aquaria.

Before the larval Copepod leaves the egg it moults twice; the first is the "blastodermic skin" secreted by the blastodermic cells, and exuviated before the limbs bud out. This blastodermic moult, comparable to the serous membrane of Arachnides and the true insects, has been observed by Van Beneden to be the larval membrane of Gammarus, and he has recognized it as surrounding the embryo of Sacculina, Leptomera, Caprella, Nebalia and Crangon.

The second or Nauplian moult takes place after the larval form is attained, but before the embryo hatches. The skin peels off when the appendages are of a certain length and before they are jointed.

At the moment of birth, says Van Beneden, the appendages

are distinctly jointed and provided with simple or branched bristles. The alimentary canal is distinct, so is the eye; and the nerve-ganglion is recognizable while the blood circulates in the body-cavity.

Fig. 183.

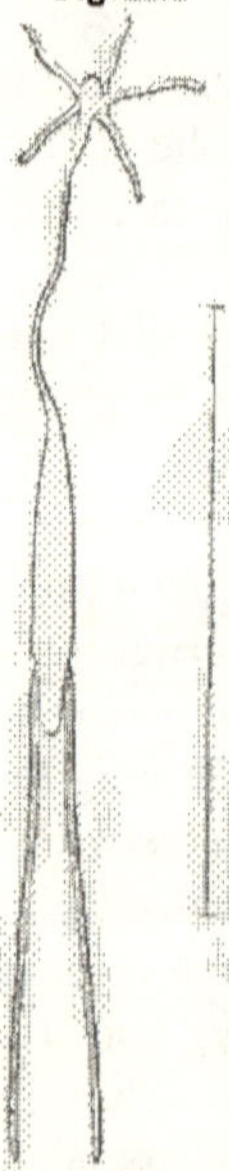

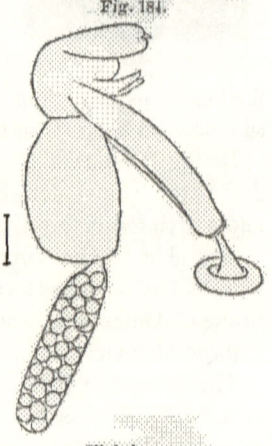

While most Copepods leave the egg in this perfected, Nauplius condition, the embryo Anchorella and Hessia, according to the researches of Van Beneden, pass through a Nauplius state in the egg; then three pairs of abdominal feet grow out, and an abdomen, consisting of five well marked segments, is differentiated from the cephalothorax. This stage is called the cyclopian stage by Van Beneden. Now this embryonic stage of the Lernæans, or fish lice, corresponds to the stages undergone by the free swimming young of Cyclops and other Copepods.

The Nauplius of Cyclops in growing to maturity elongates, while mouth-appendages, abdominal segments and appendages arise after successive moults, until the adult form is attained.

In the parasitic genera, the larva is either a Nauplius, as in Achtheres and Chondracanthus (in Actheres the young has but two pair of appendages) or, as in Anchorella and others, a cyclops-like being, which

Fish Louse.

after swimming around for awhile fastens itself by its appendages to the gills of some fish. Then begins the race between the organs of vegetative and animal life, the former far outstripping the latter. As in the Lernæa of the cod the appendages grow deep into the flesh of its host like twisted and gnarled roots, while the shapeless sac-like body is, as in the Sacculina, a simple sac filled with eggs. Or the body is still without segments, as in *Lerneonema radiata* (Fig. 183, from Verrill's Report) and ends in two attenuated ovaries; or as in *Actheres Carpenteri*, Fig. 184 (from Hayden's Report), which lives on trout, the deformation is less, and the body is divided into a head and abdomen, the latter in the female bearing two egg-sacs.

Fig. 184.

Fish louse.

To recapitulate the changes undergone by the Copepods in attaining maturity, they pass through the following phases of development:

1. Morula.
2. Nauplius.
3. Cyclopian (in certain genera embryonic) stage.
4. Adult Copepod, in some forms being a degraded more or less amorphous parasitic condition.

LITERATURE.

Nordmann. Mikrographische Beiträge zur Naturgeschichte der Wirbellosen Thiere. Berlin, 1832.

Claus. Ueber den Bau und die Entwicklung einiger parasitischer Crustaceen. Cassel, 1858.

Van Beneden, E. Recherches, IV. (Bull. Acad. Bruxelles, 1870.) See also Fritz Müller's Facts for Darwin. Translation. London, 1869.

Development of the Ostracodes and Cladocera. Of the life-history of the bivalved Ostracodes we only know from Claus' studies

Fig. 185.

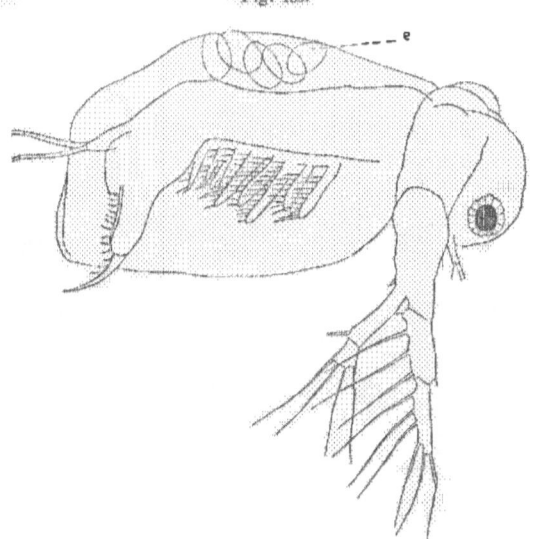

Sida.

that "the youngest stages are shell-bearing Nauplius forms." It seems evident that these creatures undergo no metamorphosis.

Of the development of the Cladocera, such as the fresh-water Daphnia and Sida (Fig. 185, from Hayden's Survey) we have more certain knowledge. The eggs are borne by the females in so-called brood-cavities on the back under the shell. The females bring forth two sorts of eggs, *i.e.*, the "summer eggs," which are laid by asexual females, the males not appearing until the autumn, when the females lay the fertilized "winter eggs," which are surrounded by a very tough shell.

Dohrn observed the development of the embryo in the summer eggs. At first the embryo has but three pairs of appendages, representing the antennæ and two pairs of jaws. It is thus comparable with the Nauplius of the Copepods, and thus the Cladocera may be said to pass through a Nauplius stage in the egg.

Afterwards more limbs grow out, until finally the embryo is provided with the full number of adult limbs, and hatches in the form of the mature animal, undergoing no farther change of form.

LITERATURE.

Dohrn. Untersuchungen ueber Bau und Entwicklung der Arthropoden. Leipzig, 1870.

Development of the King Crab (Limulus). Here we must turn aside from the true Crustacea to study the development of the king crab, so unlike in its organization to the normal Crustacea, and remarkable for being an ally of the trilobites.

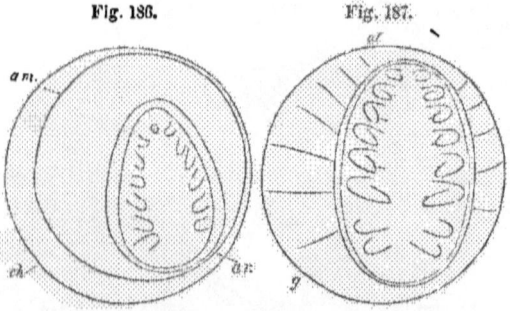

Fig. 186.   Fig. 187.

Embryo of King Crab.

Unlike most Crustacea the female king crab buries her eggs in the sand between tide marks, and there leaves them at the mercy of the waves, until the young hatch. The eggs are laid between the end of May and early in July, and the young are from a month to six weeks in hatching.

After fertilization the yolk undergoes partial segmentation, much as in the insects. When the primitive disk is formed (much as in the spiders and certain crabs) the outer layer of blastodermic cells peels off soon after the limbs begin to appear, and this constitutes the serous membrane (Fig. 186, *am*) which is like that of insects.

Then the limbs bud out, the six pairs of cephalic limbs appear at once as in Fig. 186. Soon after the two basal pairs of abdominal leaf-like feet arise, the abdomen becomes separated from the front region of the body, and the segments are indicated as in Fig. 187. A later stage is signalized by the more highly developed dorsal portion of the embryo, an increase in size of the abdomen, and the appearance of nine distinct abdominal segments. The segments of the cephalothorax are now very clearly defined, as also the division between the cephalothorax and abdomen, the

Fig. 188.   Fig. 189.

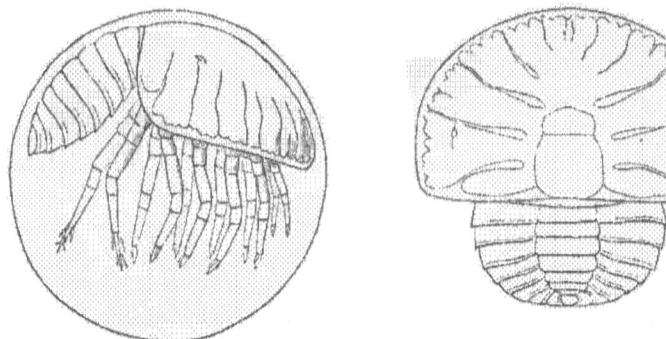

King Crab shortly before hatching; trilobitic stage.

latter being now nearly as broad as the cephalothorax, the sides of which are not spread out as in a later stage.

At this stage the egg-shell has split asunder and dropped off, while the serous membrane has increased in size to an unusual extent, several times exceeding its original dimensions and is filled with sea water in which the embryo revolves.

At a little later period the embryo throws off an embryonal skin, the thin pellicle floating about in the egg. Still later in the life of the embryo the claws are developed, an additional rudimentary gill appears, and the abdomen grows broader and larger, with the segments more distinct; the heart also appears, being a pale streak along the middle of the back extending from the front edge of the head to the base of the abdomen.

Just before hatching the head-region spreads out, the abdomen being a little more than half as wide as the cephalothorax. The two compound eyes and the pair of ocelli on the front edge of the head are quite distinct; the appendages to the gills appear on the two anterior pairs, and the legs are longer.

The resemblance to a Trilobite is most remarkable, as seen in Figs. 188 and 189. It now also closely resembles the fossil king crabs of the Carboniferous formation (Fig. 190, *Prestwichia ro-*

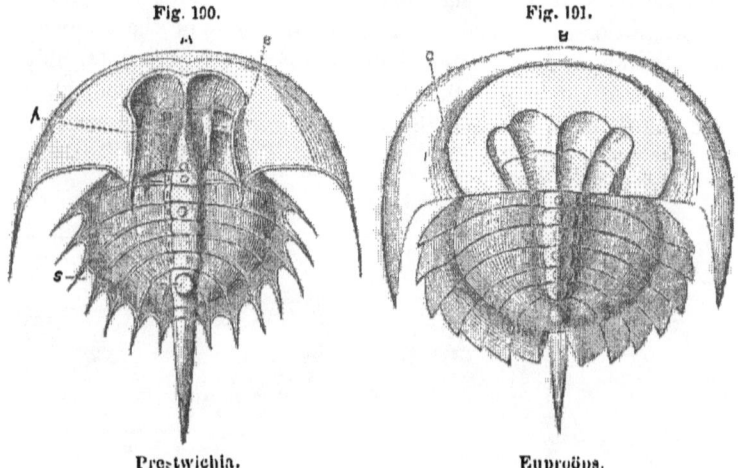

Fig. 190.   Fig. 191.

Prestwichia.   Euproöps.

tundatus, 191, *Euproöps Danæ*, from Worthen's Paleontology of Illinois).

In about six weeks from the time the eggs are laid the embryo hatches. It now differs chiefly from the previous stage in the abdomen being much larger, scarcely less in size than the cephalothorax; in the obliteration of the segments, except where they are faintly indicated on the cardiac region of the abdomen, while the gills are much larger than before. The abdominal spine is very rudimentary; it forms the ninth abdominal segment.

The reader may now compare with our figures of the recently hatched Limulus, that of Barrande's larva of *Trinucleus ornatus* (Fig. 193, natural size and enlarged). One will see at a glance that the young Trilobite, born without any true thoracic segments, and with the head articulated with the abdomen, closely resembles the young Limulus. In Limulus no new segments are added after birth; in the Trilobites the numerous thoracic segments are added during successive moults. The Trilobites thus pass through a well marked metamorphosis, though by no means so remarkable as that of the Decapods and the Phyllopods.

The young swim briskly up and down in the jar, skimming about on their backs, by flapping their gills, not bending their bodies. In a succeeding moult, which occurs between three and four weeks after hatching, the abdomen becomes smaller in proportion to the head, and the abdominal spine is about three times as long as broad. At this and also in the second, or succeeding moult, which occurs about four weeks after the first moult, the

Fig. 192.

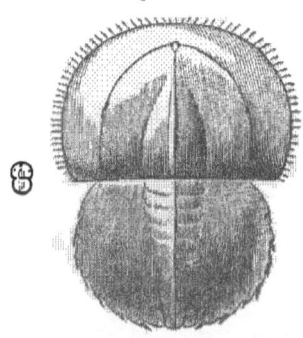

Fig. 193.

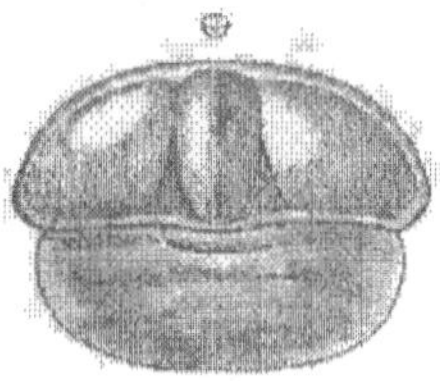

Larva of a Trilobite.

Larva of the King Crab.

young king crab doubles in size. It is probable that specimens an inch long are about a year old, and it must require several years for them to attain a length of one foot.

The stages of growth, to recapitulate, are as follows: —

1. Peripheral or partial segmentation of the yolk.

2. No true Nauplius stage, but the six legs appear simultaneously.

3. Trilobitic stage.

4. Adult Limulus form attained before hatching.

LITERATURE.

Packard. The Development of Limulus Polyphemus. (Memoirs Boston Society of Natural History. 1872.)

Consult also papers by Lockwood, Dohrn, and E. Van Beneden.

Development of the Phyllopods. We will now return to the true Crustacea, and trace the mode of growth of the leaf-footed forms, beginning with Limnadia (Fig. 548, *L. Agassizii* Packard, in Hayden's Report), a form with whose development we are acquainted.

These shelled crustaceans live in pools which often dry up in summer. The eggs after leaving the oviduct are arranged above the back under the carapace, where they remain for one or two days in midsummer, or for several days during September. The eggs of the European *L. Hermanni* are irregular in form and enclosed in a solid calcareous shell composed of two valves. So thick is the shell that Lereboullet was unable to study the development of the embryo.

The young are hatched in from five to ten days after the expulsion of the eggs from under the carapace. The freshly hatched larva is a nauplius, with the body rather long and with two pairs of appendages bearing bristles, the anterior pair being forked; there is a single eye in the middle of the head and an enormous labrum. Lereboullet states that the larvæ "have a great resem-

Fig. 104.

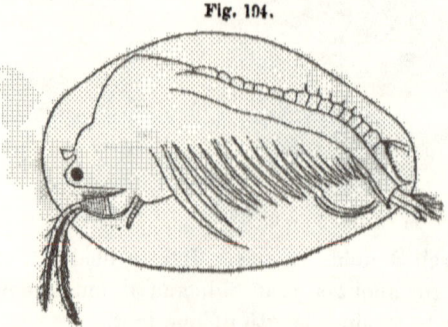

Limnadia Agassizii.

blance with the larvæ of other branchiopod crustacea, among others with those of Branchipus and Artemia. But the larvæ of these two genera have antennæ, which are wanting in the larvæ of Limnadia, while also the larvæ of Artemia have no labrum." About the beginning of the second or third day, the two halves of the carapace begin to grow out from the sides of the base of the abdomen. They finally unite over the back forming a sort of a hinge, and at length enclose the body, with the exception of the head and extremity of the abdomen. When the creature is fully grown, the head and tail are entirely covered by the shells of the carapace. I have found the young of *L. Agassizii* about half a line in length in a pool on Penikese Island early in August. The pool a few days after dried up, and the young met the fate so common to these Phyllopods, but the eggs, protected by their solid calcareous covering, undoubtedly withstand the desiccation for over one year, and thus the species is preserved.

The larval development of *Apus* (Fig. 195, *A. æqualis* Packard, in Hayden's Report) has been studied by Zaddach. We know nothing of the embryology of this animal. I have, however, been able to discover that the blastodermic skin, like that of Limulus, consists of a single layer of moulted cells. Zaddach represents the chorion, or egg-shell, as splitting apart just as in Limulus, and

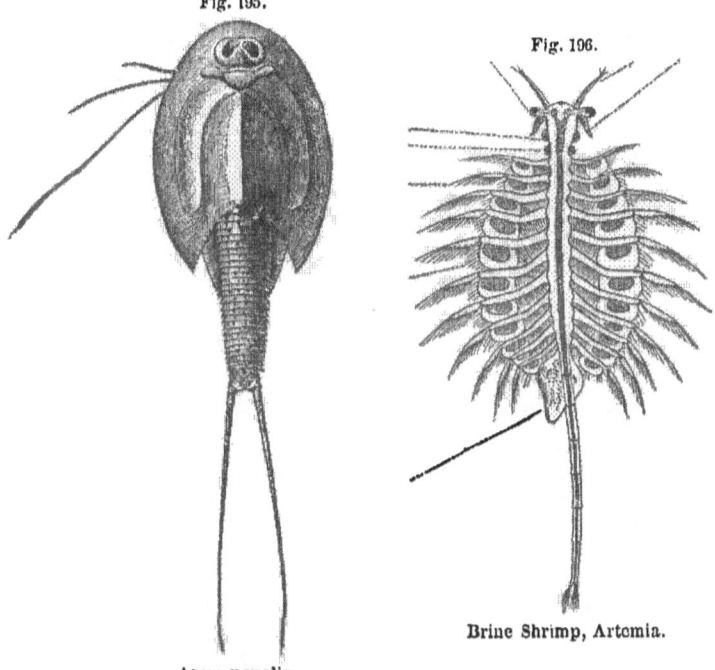

Fig. 195.

Fig. 196.

Brine Shrimp, Artemia.

Apus æqualis.

the embryo surrounded by an inner membrane, which is the blastodermic skin.

The young breaks out of its blastodermic skin in the nauplius form, with two pairs of appendages. After a moult a third pair is added and the larva appears as in Fig. 197, *b*. The numerous foliaceous feet, to the number of sixty, are added during subsequent moults.

Of the embryological development of Branchipus and Artemia (Fig. 196, *A. gracilis*, after Verrill) we also know nothing. The young is hatched in a nauplius condition (Fig. 197, *a*) but with three pairs of limbs. I have observed a similar nauplius-brood in the *Artemia fertilis* of Great Salt Lake.

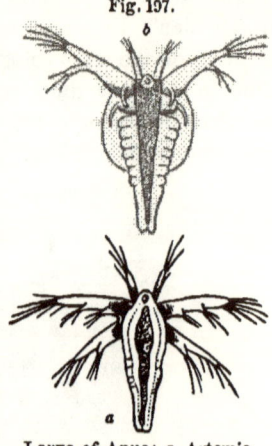

As in Apus, new pairs are added at subsequent moults until the adult form is attained. Siebold has shown that the summer broods of females reproduce by budding, as is probably the case in Limnadia and also Branchipus and Artemia, the males not appearing until towards autumn, though I have found males of *Artemia fertilis* in great abundance in Great Salt Lake late in July. Fig. 198 represents *Branchipus* (Branchinectes) *Coloradensis* (Packard, in Hayden's Report), the female being distinguished by the short clasping antennæ, and the long egg-sac at the base of the abdomen.

Larva of Apus; *a*, Artemia.

The Phyllopods, then, with whose embryological development we are not acquainted, after hatching pass through a nauplius stage, and the adult condition is attained after a number of moults.

LITERATURE.

Joly. Histoire d'un petit Crustacé (Artemia salina), etc. (Annales des Sc. Nat., 1840.)
Zaddach. De Apodis cancriformis Anatome et Historia Evolutionis. Bonn. 1841.
Lereboullet. Observations sur la Génération et le Développement de la Limnadia Hermanni. (Annales des Sc. Nat., 1866.)

Development of Nebalia. A great degree of interest attaches to the life-history of this animal, which is not uncommon in deep water off our coast. It is a relict of a group still older than the king crab, being represented in the primordial rocks by Hymenocaris, and in lower Silurian strata by Discinocaris and Peltocaris, and in the upper Silurian by Ceratiocaris and other forms, gigantic in size (some of them being about seven inches long) compared with the recent Nebalia, which is about half an inch in length. Nebalia is regarded by Metschnikoff as a Decapod; it may be regarded at least as a connecting link between the Phyllopods and Decapods, and as a prophetic type preceding, in paleozoic time, the introduction of the mesozoic Decapods.

Judging by the plates of Metschnikoff's memoir, for the text is written in Russian (a sealed language to us), the early development of Nebalia is apparently identical with that of Oniscus, as studied by Bobretzky, and probably all the Tetradecapods, and also with that of perhaps the majority of the Decapods. As in Oniscus the segmentation is partial, the blastodermic cells arising from the subdivision of a polar cell, finally forming a blastodermic disk consisting of a few large cells. At first but three pairs of appendages arise; these corresponding to the two pairs of antennæ, and the third to the mandibles. At this period the abdo-

Fig. 198.

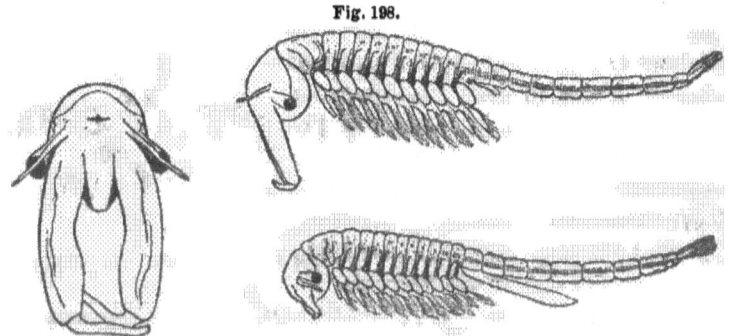

Branchinectes Coloradensis, and front view of head of the male.

men is distinct from the cephalothorax, but on the whole the embryo may be said to pass through a nauplius stage.

Then the two pairs of maxillæ and two pairs of feet arise simultaneously, the abdomen increases considerably in length, when the ten other pairs of foliaceous feet spring forth. Meanwhile the bivalved carapace grows out from behind the eyes, covering the cephalothorax and base of the abdomen. The young hatches soon after the shield is developed and the further changes are but slight.

The Nebalia, then, in brief, passes through the following stages:
1. Partial segmentation of the yolk.
2. Nauplius stage (in the egg).
3. Larval form like the adult; with no metamorphosis.

LITERATURE.

Metschnikoff. The History of the Development of Nebalia. (In Russian.) St. Petersburg, 1868.

Development of the Tetradecapods. Much good work has been done since the days of Rathke, on the mode of growth of the fresh and salt water sow-bugs, etc. (Isopods), and the beach fleas (Amphipods). The development of the *Asellus aquaticus* of Europe has been studied by E. Van Beneden. He found that the segmentation of the yolk is partial; that after a blastodermic moult the two pairs of antennæ are formed before the mandibles and maxillæ, the embryo passing through a Nauplius phase. At this time the embryo moults again. Like all Tetradecapods the young hatch in the form of the adult, there being no metamorphosis. Perhaps the most careful study of the embryology of the higher crustacea, with the improved means of examination instituted mainly by Kowalevsky, is that of *Oniscus murarius*, a sow-bug, by Dr. N. Bobretzky, a student of the eminent Russian zoologist. The following is an abstract of his paper. The egg is provided with a chorion and yolk skin. The first change after fertilization is the origin of the formative or original blastodermic cells, which arise at one pole of the egg. As a result of the self-division of the single primitive blastodermic cell, there arises a disk corresponding to the primitive streak of other articulates, consisting of a single layer of large spheres of segmentation. It thus appears that the segmentation is partial.

Before one-half of the surface of the egg is covered, the middle and inner germ-layers are indicated by a mass of cells in the concavity of the outer layer, resulting from the division of certain cells of the outer layer. This primitive mass is the first indication of the innermost (third) and middle layers. The third or inner layer consists of large cells mingled with the yolk cells, among which they press. (He finds this to be the case also in Crangon and Palæmon.) There are, then, three germ-layers as in the vertebrates.

The primitive disk, or streak, then forms by the cells of the outer layer assuming a cylindrical form. The first indication of the intestine is an invagination of the hinder end of the primitive band. A larval skin, like that of Asellus and other crustacea, arises when the first traces of the appendages appear. Bobretzky finds that, contrary to Kowalevsky's opinion, the inner germ-layer in the crustacea agrees with that of vertebrates. Soon after the limbs grow out, a cross-section shows that it is due to a bulging out of the outer germ-layer, the cavity being filled with cells of the middle layer. Now appear the first indications of the liver, a layer of large cells forming the liver sac. After the appendages appear, the nervous cord arises as a thickening of the outer layer on the ventral side of the primitive band, and consists of three or four layers of roundish cells. Fig. 199 (this and Fig. 200, after

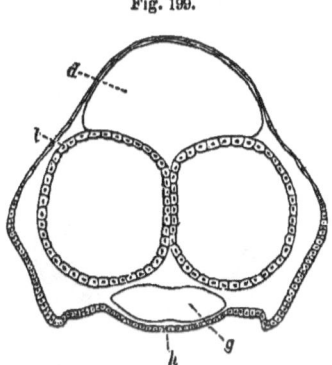

Fig. 199.

Section of Embryo Sow-bug.

Bobretzky) is a transverse section of an embryo in nearly the same stage as the embryo Amphipod (Fig. 201) ; *d*, indicates the intestine, and *l*, the two lobes of the liver ; *g*, a transverse section of the nervous cord, and *h*, the walls of the body (hypodermal layer). The opening of the liver into the intestine is shown in another section made and drawn by Bobretzky.

One of the most difficult problems to solve in the embryology of the Arthropods is the origin of the large intestine. It is known that it arises out of the yolk sac, but how and where it takes its origin remained without an answer. "After I had ascertained," says Bobretzky, "in the Astacus and Palæmon the peculiar relation of the intestino-glandular cells to the yolk, I could, in these Crustacea, follow step by step the origin of the epithelium constituting the walls of the large intestine. This epithelium first appears in the liver sac." He found the same mode of origin in Oniscus. The next step is the disappearance of the yolk, while the large intestine is fully formed, but there is as yet no communication with the stomach, there being a double wall of cells shutting off the large intestine.

The heart is the last to be formed ; it arises from the middle layer, though Bobretzky was unable to study its early development. Fig. 200 is a transverse section of the body showing the viscera ; *h*, indicates the heart ; *hp*, hypodermal layer, or body wall ; *m*, muscular wall of the intestine ; *e*, epithelial lining of the

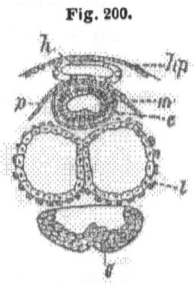

Fig. 200.

Section of advanced embryo Sow-bug.

intestine ; *p*, the dividing wall between the heart and the intestine ; *l*, the two lobes of the liver ; *g*, ganglion, the clear space being filled with the fine granular substance of the ganglion. Nothing has been said of the development of the external parts. The two antennæ in Oniscus and Asellus are the first to bud out (Nauplius stage) and then the remaining appendages of the head and thorax appear together, and subsequently the abdominal feet are formed. The abdomen is curved up and backwards, while in the Amphipods it is bent beneath the body, as in Fig. 201, and this is really, as Fritz Müller observes, the only important difference between the embryos, at an early stage, of the two groups. The embryo Isopod at the time of hatching closely resembles the adult, there being no metamorphosis.

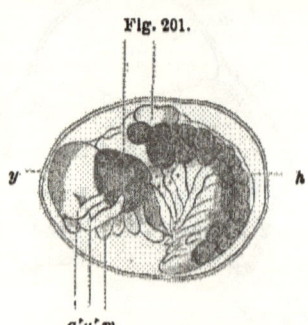

Fig. 201.

Embryo of an Amphipod.
h, head; *a′a′*, antennæ; *y*, yolk; *m*, mouth-parts.

The development of the Amphipods or beach fleas, is nearly identical with that of the Isopods. The eggs of certain species undergo total segmentation, while those of other species of the same genus (Gammarus) partially segment, as in the spiders, and in a less degree the insects, showing the slight importance to be attached to this matter, and that Hæckel's term *Morula* when used for the total segmentation of Crustacea is of little significance, how much it may be in the lower animals. It should be borne in mind that it has been used in the present work mainly as a convenient term to avoid circumlocution.

Fig. 201, after Müller, represents the embryo of a Corophium, magnified ninety diameters, in which all the limbs are developed.

Summary of changes:—

1. Segmentation of the yolk partial, or total (Morula).

2. Nauplius state in the egg.

3. Larva hatching in the form of the adult with the full number of feet; no metamorphosis.

LITERATURE.

Van Beneden, E. L' Oeuf. Brussels, 1870.

———. Recherches sur l'Embryologie des Crustacés, I. (Bull. Acad. Bruxelles, 1869.)

Dohrn. Die embryonale Entwickelung des Asellus aquaticus. (Siebold and Kölliker's Zeitschrift, 1867.)

———. Zur Morphologie, Reisebemerkungen aus Taurien. Leipzig. 1837.

Rathke. Untersuchungen ueber die Bildung und Entwickelung der Wasser-Assel (Asellus aquaticus). Leipzig, 1832.

Bobretzky. Zur Embryologie des Oniscus murarius. (Siebold and Kölliker's Zeitschrift. 1874.)

Development of the Decapods. When we come to the stalk-eyed
Crustacea, such as the shrimps and crabs, we are introduced to
a group of animals in which there is a most striking metamorphosis, as first shown by Thompson. The life-history of a Decapod is full of interest and significance, as the phases which some
present from the larval stage up are as varied and astonishing as
the biography of any animal known. In the group as a whole,
we have species in which the metamorphoses are attended by
great detail and complexity of form, the animal shifting its garb
as if an actor with many parts to perform in the drama of life,
while in its co-species these phases may be mostly suppressed, and
the few it does undergo, rapidly assumed and discarded within
the narrow compass of the egg-shell.

One Decapod, the shrimp Penæus, studied by Fritz Müller, on
the coast of Brazil, is an exception to all other stalk-eyed Crustacea in hatching as a true nauplius, and then by a complicated
series of metamorphoses assuming the zoëal and finally adult life.
On the other hand, there is the common lobster, or fresh water
craw fish, in which the free nauplius and zoëa stages are suppressed, being undergone in the egg, and which hatches in nearly
or quite a similar form to the fully grown animal. Between these
stages there are all grades in other Crustacea.

As regards the development of the embryo, there is in those
species which undergo a metamorphosis, a quite similar mode.
The yolk so far as known (Scyllarus, Astacus, etc.) undergoes
partial segmentation : no case of a total division is as yet known.
After the formation of a short round primitive streak, or band,
the limbs arise. In several cases observed by Dohrn, the three
anterior pairs of limbs, namely, the two antennæ and the mandibles were developed simultaneously and before the others appear.
The embryo may with truth, then, as Dohrn states, be said to pass
through a nauplius condition in the egg, as much as a mammal
passes through a fish-like stage. He observed this nauplius-stage
in the embryo of Scyllarus, Pandalus and Galathea. I have observed it in *Lupa hastata* at Charleston, S. C., and in *Libinia ca-
naliculata*. It is not improbable that most crabs pass through a
nauplius state in the egg. As if in proof of the supposition that
this is a true nauplius *in embryo*, we have the fortunate discovery,
by Fritz Müller, of the fact that a Brazilian shrimp (Penæus, allied
to *P. setiferus* of Florida) leaves the egg "with an unsegmented
ovate body, a median frontal eye, and three pairs of natatory feet,

of which the anterior are simple, and the other two biramose; in fact, in the larval form, so common among the lower Crustacea, to which O. F. Müller gave the name of *Nauplius*. No trace of a carapace! No trace of the paired eyes! No trace of masticating organs near the mouth which is overarched by a helmet-like hood!" Let us, with Müller, follow the subsequent history of this young shrimp. After passing through the nauplius condition (Fig. 202) it acquires several pairs of appendages (maxillæ and maxillipedes), but as yet no true legs. It is now a typical zoëa (Fig. 203) having two compound eyes, a carapace and a jointed body. The next

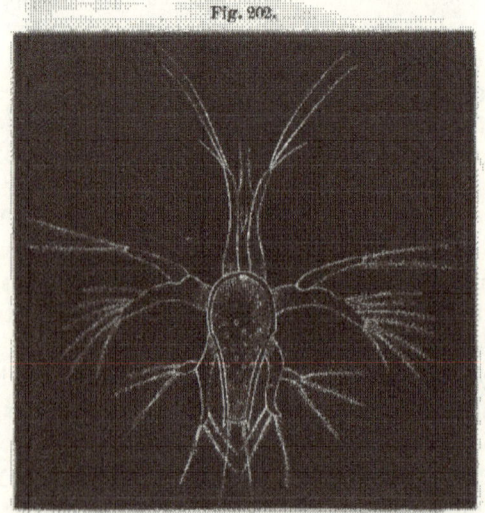

Fig. 202.

Nauplius, or larva, of a Shrimp.

important step is the appearance of the five pairs of thoracic feet, and soon the mature form of the prawn is attained.

Most true Decapods, namely, the shrimps and crabs, are hatched as zoëæ (Fig. 204, after Thompson, represents the zoëa of *Carcinus mœnas*), and swim about awhile in this state, the swimming feet being the antennæ and jaws and foot jaws, which afterwards acquire their special functions.

Now one species of the genus Alpheus, observed by the writer at Key West, is hatched in a more advanced condition; in what may be called a super-zoëal state, namely, it possesses not only five pairs of thoracic feet, but also five pairs of swimming, biramose abdominal feet, with the characteristic large claw! Here we have a sup-

pression of a true zoëal free swimming condition, just as we have
seen to be the case in all the other groups of the animal kingdom,
where one species may be born in an extremely imperfect condition, and another, even of the same genus, in a very perfect state,
the intermediate phases being rapidly assumed and as rapidly
discarded in the embryo.

A less extreme case is that of the lobster, which hatches without
abdominal feet, but still with well developed thoracic legs.   The

Fig. 203.

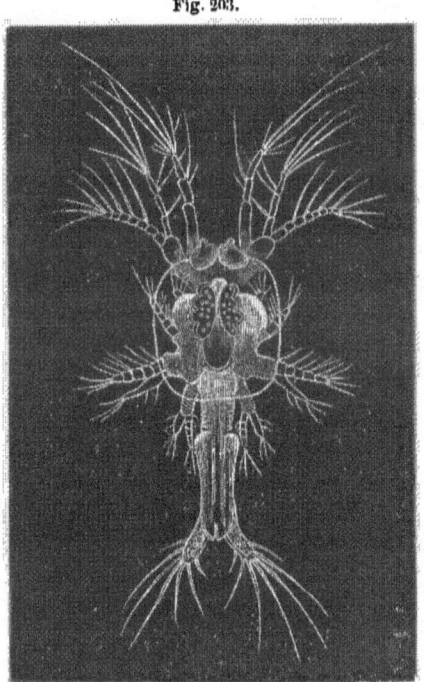

Zoëa of the same Shrimp.

larva is super-zoëal.   The most extreme case, namely of an entire
absence of a metamorphosis, is the cray-fish (Astacus and Cam-
barus), which hatches exactly in the form of the parent.

These facts are paralleled by the metamorphoses of the insects,
where the terms "larva" and "pupa" are exceedingly arbitrary,
the larval bee or fly attaining maturity only after a series of surprising changes, while the larval grasshopper simply differs from
the adult in having no wings.

Crabs breed all through the spring and summer. At Charleston, S. C., on the 12th of April, I found the eggs of the edible crab, *Lupa hastata*, containing embryos in all stages of development from the nauplius to the zoëa. The fiddler crabs (*Gelasimus pugnax*) at Fort Macon, N. C., during the middle of May, carried eggs in which the polar cells, or formative cells of the blastoderm, were present, while others contained zoëæ, with the two claws alike, and it is probable that the strange inequality in size of the claws in these animals does not show itself until after one or more moults.

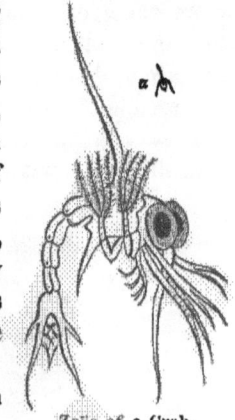

Fig. 204.

Zoëa of a Crab.

The development of the lobster has been studied with much care by Prof. S. I. Smith. The lobster breeds between April and November. Fig. 205 [1] represents the embryo just before hatching. After hatching it swims

Fig. 205.

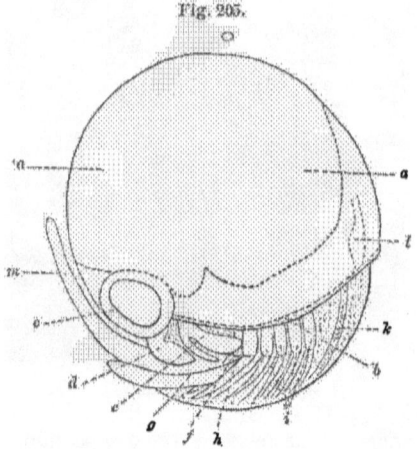

Embryo of the Lobster.

around with only the thoracic feet. After moulting, the abdominal

[1] Fig. 258. Embryo some time before hatching, removed from the external envelope and shown in a side view, enlarged 20 diameters. *aa*, dark green yolk mass still unabsorbed; *b*, lateral margin of the carapax marked with many dendritic spots of red pigment; *c*, eye; *d*, antennula; *e*, antenna; *f*, external maxilliped; *g*, great cheliped which forms the big claw of the adult; *h*, outer swimming branch of the same; *i*, the four ambulatory legs with their exopodal branches; *k*, intestine; *l*, heart; *m*, bilobed tail seen edgewise. After Smith.

feet arise.   After a second moult it is half an inch long and loses

Fig. 206.

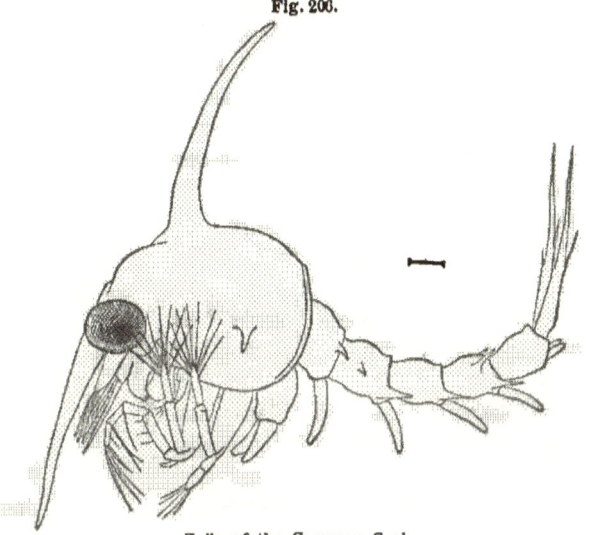

Zoëa of the Common Crab.

Fig. 207.

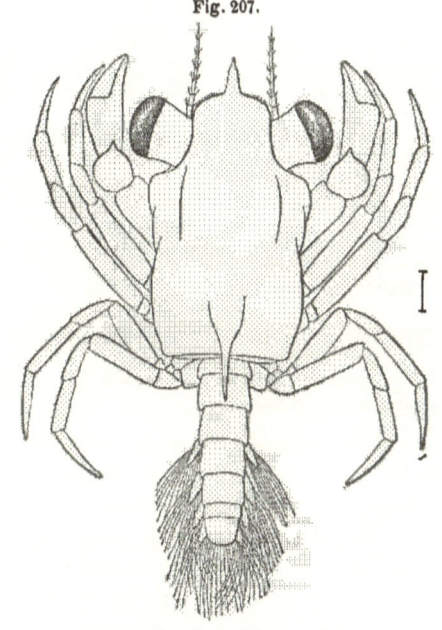

Megalops of the Common Crab.

its formerly Mysis-like appearance and closely resembles the adult.

Soon after this it leaves the surface of the water and seeks the bottom. Specimens three inches long are quite like the adult.

Besides the zoëa stage, many crabs pass through a stage intermediate between the zoëa and adult. This is called the *Megalops* stage, as it was supposed to be an adult animal and described under this term, just as early observers mistook the Nauplius and Zoëa for adult Crustacea. Fig. 206 (this and 207 after Smith) represents the zoëa of the common Crab (*Cancer irroratus*) in the last stage just before it changes to the megalops condition, and Fig. 207 the megalops of the same, magnified thirteen diameters. In two cases, *Eriphia spinifrons*, and a species of Gecarcinus, or the land crab of the West Indies, there is no metamorphosis, the young being like the adult.

Summary of the life-history of the Decapods:

1. Partial segmentation of the yolk.

2. Nauplius stage; either free swimming or undergone in the egg.

3. Zoëa stage; sometimes suppressed.

4. Megalops stage; in many crabs; in a few cases no metamorphosis.

5. Adult.

LITERATURE.

Rathke. Untersuchungen ueber die Bildung und Entwickelung des Flusskrebses. Leipzig, 1829.

Thompson, J. V. On the double Metamorphosis in the Decapodous Crustacea. (Phil. Trans. London, 1835.)

Müller. Facts for Darwin. 1863.

Dohrn. Untersuchungen ueber Bau und Entwicklung der Arthropoden. (Siebold and Kölliker's Zeitschrift. 1870. Jenaischer Zeitschrift. V. 1871.)

Smith. The Metamorphoses of the Lobster and other Crustacea (in Baird's Report on Fish and Fisheries, U. S. 1873).

With papers by Thompson, Rathke and Claus.

XXVIII. THE INSECTA. (Tracheata.)

Under the term Insecta may be included the three groups of Myriopods, Arachnids and true six-footed insects, or Hexapoda. All differ from the Crustacea in having, as a rule, for there are exceptions among the mites, a distinct head, separate from the thorax, and in breathing by internal air-tubes (tracheæ) instead of external gills. Without spending any time in describing the metamorphoses of the winged insects, accounts of which may be found in any entomological work, we will briefly describe their embryological development, from sources less generally accessible.

Development of the Myriopods. Though Newport's classical memoir on the development of Julus will be found useful for the post-embryonic stages, the indefatigable Metschnikoff has recently cleared up the embryological development of these animals, so that we are now in possession of a life-history of these creatures, the early phases of whose existence had thus far eluded the scrutiny of embryologists.

We will now follow Metschnikoff in his studies, beginning with the history of a Polydesmus-like form, *Strongylosoma Guerinii,* an inhabitant of the island of Madeira. The eggs were laid during a period extending from February to the end of May. Before ovipositing the female buries herself in the earth one or more inches below the surface, then depositing one or two hundred eggs in the manner of several other Myriopods. The eggs are spherical, yellowish-white, and from 1–3 mm. in diameter.

The egg undergoes total segmentation, the process beginning in six or eight hours after it is laid, and ending on the fourth or fifth day. By this time the primitive band rests on the outside of one-half of the egg. A furrow next arises (compare Fig. 218 *a* of the Podurid, Isotoma) on each side of which the primitive ridges afterwards swell up. The two germ-layers now arise, the inner originating in a small mass of cells on each side of the furrow. The antennæ bud out, and subsequently three additional pairs, namely, the mandibles, the second maxillæ (the first pair wanting in the Chilognaths as in the Poduridæ) and the first pair of legs; and now the two ends of the body meet over the yolk as in the Podurids, the head touching the tail.

The brain is now formed from the outer germ-layer (ectoderm), the mouth and anal opening also being formed by an invagination of the same outer layer, the inner layer constituting ultimately the muscular walls of the digestive tract, while the epithelial lining of the large intestine also arises from the inner germ-layer.

By the fifteenth, or early on the sixteenth, day the "boring apparatus," a chitinous point by which the embryo cuts open the shell, appears on the head. The legs now assume their form, the fourth and fifth pair belonging to a single segment. The embryo now moults, the skin forming a cuticle enveloping the embryo after the shell splits asunder. The nervous cord arises from the middle portion of the upper germ-layer, though the division of the layer into an epidermal and nerve-layer has not yet taken place.

By the sixteenth, the chorion is cut through by the point of the egg-shell breaker, when it splits apart, and the embryo thus remains covered by this membrane until the larva is ready to creep about, a curious fact first observed in Julus by Newport.

By the seventeenth day nine or ten true segments are formed, and the appendages begin to show articulations, while beneath the skin, the fourth, fifth and sixth pairs of feet arise as little sacs, opening in the middle line of the body. The two stigmata arise as a fine tube with a small opening on the basal end of the third pair of feet, the walls of the tube (trachea) being due to an in-pushing of the outer germ-layer. The epidermis is now well defined and the nervous cord is isolated from the skin, while on the nineteenth, or last day of embryonal life, the hairs arise over the body. The embryo would now easily be mistaken for a Podurid, so remarkable is the resemblance, owing to the similar number of body-segments, and the large head, wanting in both animals the true maxillæ.

On the twentieth day the larva breaks through the membrane, and the head is clearly separated from the body. The larva closely resembles the young Julus, being as yet cylindrical, and having but nine rings besides the head.

In *Polydesmus complanatus* of the Madeira Islands, the egg also undergoes total segmentation, but the embryo develops more rapidly, being by the fifth day covered with a membrane. Meanwhile the antennæ have appeared, and on the sixth day five additional pairs of limbs bud out, namely, the mandibles, second maxillæ (labium) and three pairs of legs. There is no shell breaker, the shell bursting, however, on the tenth day. The mandibles arc very large, almost covering the labium. The larva is cylindrical, the body (the head excepted) consisting of seven segments.

Fig. 208.

Polydesmus.

The development of the singular *Polyxenus lagurus*, a little short creature with the body covered with fascicles of hairs, was observed by the Russian embryologist in Switzerland.

The egg undergoes total segmentation, but the blastoderm is restricted to one pole of the egg, being disk-like. The antennæ and mouth-parts arise as in the foregoing genera, but the three pairs of legs appear simultaneously. Metschnikoff found amœboid bodies, like those in the mites, moving about in the egg, having previously separated from the blastoderm.

We now come to the development of the Thousand-legs (Fig. 209) which was first studied by Newport. Our skilful Russian embryol-

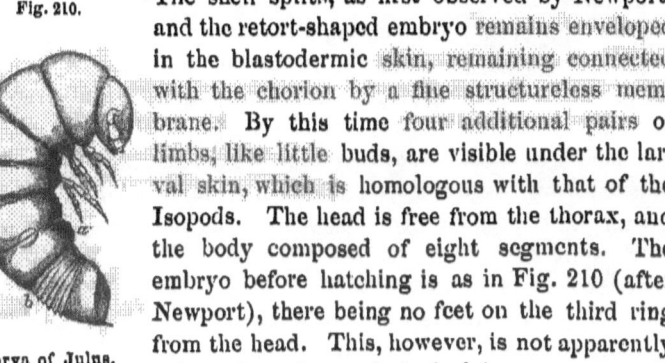

Fig. 209.

ogist, with all the advantage of modern means of investigation, and possibly by observing more transparent eggs than those studied by the famous English zoologist, has thrown a flood of light on the embryonic stages of a species (*Julus Morelettii*) observed by him in Madeira. The eggs were laid in November, rarely in the spring, and not at all in the summer, being deposited in rounded masses under the surface of the earth, as in the other Chilognathic myriopods. They are oval, dirty greenish white, with the shell unfortunately more opake than in the other genera mentioned. Here, also, as in the others, the segmentation was total, a thing not known to occur in the Hexapods (the Podurids excepted), and rarely in the Arachnids, chiefly in the mites. The primitive band arises on one side.

Julus.

There is a blastodermic moult, like that of many Crustacea, and corresponding to the "deutovum" of certain Acari. The two germ-layers were observed to arise as in the other genera, while the three cephalic appendages (antennæ, mandibles and second maxillæ) appear as in the other Myriopods.

Fig. 210.

The shell splits, as first observed by Newport, and the retort-shaped embryo remains enveloped in the blastodermic skin, remaining connected with the chorion by a fine structureless membrane. By this time four additional pairs of limbs, like little buds, are visible under the larval skin, which is homologous with that of the Isopods. The head is free from the thorax, and the body composed of eight segments. The embryo before hatching is as in Fig. 210 (after Newport), there being no feet on the third ring from the head. This, however, is not apparently a fact of much morphological importance, as in

Larva of Julus.

Geophilus the embryo has a pair of feet on each body segment. In the figure, *a* indicates the rudiments of the new limbs, and *b*, the six new rings growing out from between the penultimate and last ring of the body.

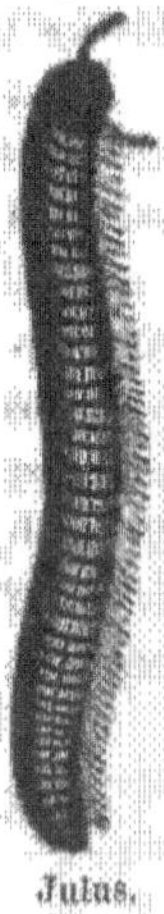

Metschnikoff discovered in all the embryo Myriopods studied by him certain paired bodies which he names "primitive-vertebræ-like bodies." He has also noticed them in the scorpion, the Phalangids, Araneids, Mysis and some other Crustacea, Termes and several Oligochete worms.

When we turn to the embryology of the Poduridæ we shall see how much alike those insects and the Chilognaths are in the mode of development of the embryo, and should also bear in mind the fact that the Poduras also have but a single pair of maxillæ, while Scolopendrella is half insect and half Myriopod. The conclusion that the Myriopods are a subclass of the class of insects is thus based on morphological and embryological grounds.

A later paper of Metschnikoff's gives us, for the first time, the **life-history of Geophilus**, one of the centipedes or Chilopod Myriopods. He found that the yolk undergoes a total segmentation, and the primitive band surrounds one-half of the yolk. In the next stage observed the antennæ and three pairs of jaws were developed (for there are besides the mandibles, two pairs of maxillæ, like those of insects, in the centipedes) besides twenty-three segments. The anal opening was situated in the unsegmented end of the body. In the next stage the primitive band is much longer than before, and the head and tail approach nearer to each other, while there are now from forty-four to forty-six body segments, most of them bearing rudimentary appendages, though there are none as yet on the end of the body. In a succeeding stage the head is much larger, the body longer and curved over the yolk, while the egg-shell breaker is situated on the second maxilla. In a following stage the body is still more elongated and the joints of the antennæ appear. The embryo now slips out of the split shell, the body being very long and cylindrical, not yet flattened as in maturity (Fig. 211 represents an American Geophilus), while the feet are not jointed, and resemble the ventral cirri of annelides.

Fig. 211.

Geophilus.

We see, then, that the centipedes (Chilopoda) differ from the thousand-legs (Chilognaths) in the mouth-parts being of the same number as in insects, and that the young are born with a pair of feet on each of the three segments behind the head, while the larva is provided with nearly the full number of feet on the rest of the body, there being no metamorphosis. The body, at first cylindrical, afterwards becomes flattened. Thus the centipedes may be said in some degree to pass through a Julus condition, and at all events, both morphologically and embryologically, the centipede is a more highly developed creature than the thousand-legs, a view we have always taken, but felt was rather based on *a priori* conceptions than on a sure basis of facts, now happily afforded by the beautiful researches of Metschnikoff. To sum up the phases of development of the Myriopods we have, then: —

1. Morula stage.

2. A hexapod larva (Leptus form) as in the Thousand-legs; or, as in the Centipedes, there is no metamorphosis, the young being like the parent.

3. Adult.

LITERATURE.

Newport. On the Organs of Reproduction, and the Development of the Myriopoda. (Phil. Trans. 1841.)

Metschnikoff. Embryologie der doppelt-füssigen Myriapoden (Chilognatha). (Siebold and Kölliker's Zeitschrift. 1874.)

———. Embryologisches ueber Geophilus. (Siebold and Kölliker's Zeitschrift. 1875.)

Development of the Mites. Coming now to the mites and spiders, we find some peculiar features in the life-history of the former which deserve attention, though space compels us to be brief at the risk of being obscure. Most mites pass through a metamorphosis, some undergoing striking changes within the egg. For example, the *Atax Bonzi*, which is a parasite on the gills of fresh water muscles, first hatches in an oval form enveloped in a membrane (deutovum). From this "deutovum" is developed a six-footed larva. In this second larva state it is free, moving over the gills of the mussels, finally boring into the flesh of its host to undergo its next transformation. Here the young mite increases in size and becomes round. The tissues soften, the limbs are short and much larger than before, the animal assuming an embryo-like appearance, and moving about like a rounded mass in its enclosure. After a moult it assumes the so-called "pupa-state." During this process the limbs grow much shorter and are folded beneath the body, the animal being immovable, while the whole body assumes a broadly ovate form, and looks like an embryo just before hatching, but still lying within the egg.

In the genus Myobia, a parasite of the European field-mouse, there is not only a " dentovum," but also what Claparède calls a " tritovum-stage," there being two stages with distinct embryonal membranes before the six-legged free larval state is assumed, the larva when hatching having thrown off two membranes, as well as the egg-shell. Certain bird-mites pass through four stages to reach the male condition, while the females pass through as many as five before attaining sexual maturity. Fig. 212 illustrates the six-legged larva of the tick, which is simply a large mite. The eggs of the mites either undergo total segmentation or a partial one, as in the spiders.

The water-bears or Tardigrades are born with four pairs of legs, not undergoing any metamorphosis. Not so, however, with certain worm-like mites, which by their parasitic life lose all resemblance to other mites and are

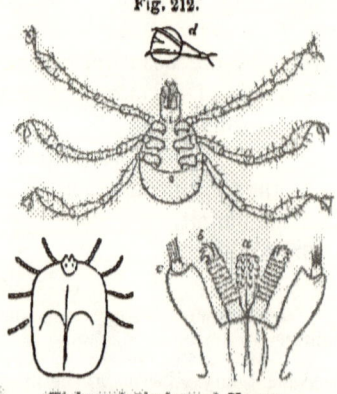

Fig. 212.

Tick and Six-legged Young.

often mistaken for intestinal worms. I refer to the Pentastoma and Linguatula. Here the metamorphosis is backwards, the young after passing through a morula condition, being born as short, plump, oval mites, provided with boring horny jaws, but with only two short rudimentary legs.

Finally, we come to those problematical forms, the sea-spiders, or Pycnogonidæ, which are often referred to the Crustacea, whose development has been so faithfully studied by Dr. Dohrn. The yolk undergoes total segmentation, and the young are hatched with three pairs of legs, which after moulting attain in some species an extraordinary length.

To sum up, then, certain mites pass through either : —

1. A Morula state, or the yolk only partially divides.

2. Sometimes one or two embryonal stages (dentovum and tritovum).

3. A six-legged larval state.

4. Eight-legged " pupal " state.

5. Adult.

LITERATURE.

Claparède. Studien an Acariden. (Siebold and Kölliker's Zeitschrift. 1858.)
Leuckart. Bau und Entwickelungsgeschichte der Pentastomen. Leipzig und Heidelburg. 1860.

Dohrn. Untersuchungen neber Bau und Entwicklung der Arthropoden. Heft. I. 1870.

Consult also papers by Dugès, Doyère, Miller, Van Beneden, Robin and others.

Development of the False-scorpions (Fig. 213). Some most un-expected features occur in the life-history of these little tailless

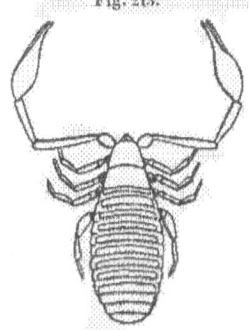

Fig. 213.

scorpion-like creatures, which are found living under the bark of trees, and under stones, etc. The female runs about in early summer pressing the eggs to the under side of its body by means of its claws or nippers.

Here, as in most mites, the segmenta-tion of the yolk is total. The blastoderm forms, and then a singular feature ensues, namely, the collection of an albuminous substance between the egg-shell and the

False-scorpion.

blastoderm, increasing the size of the egg very materially and containing small bodies; suggesting an em-bryonal membrane, though Metschnikoff does not regard it as truly such. Soon the blastoderm becomes two-layered.

Next arise the rudiments of the two large claws, before any other limbs appear; at the same time a huge projection forms on the head, with indications of muscular bands. This strange appear-ance is merely a sort of temporary upper lip. At this time the end of the body is conical and curved beneath the abdomen. In this imperfect stage the embryo sheds a skin and then breaks through the delicate egg-membrane, becoming free, though the larva, kan-garoo-like, is still attached to the under side of the mother Cheli-fer, where it remains until it has completed its metamorphoses, though of course it derives no nourishment from its mother.

Now the embryo-larva is nearly as long as broad, with the sin-gular hood-like upper lip, and the rudiments of the first pair of feet directly behind the enormous rudimentary nippers. Within are no signs of a digestive sac or any other organs, simply a mass of yolk cells.

In the second larva-state the body is broader than long, the "upper lip" diminutive in size, and the mandibles and four pairs of legs are present. Here also, as in the scorpions and the spi-ders, four pairs of deciduous abdominal feet appear (such as our author has also seen in Phalangium and Forficula). There are now seven segments in the abdomen.

The larval skin is after a while ruptured, and the insect deserts its parent, in a form like that of the mature animal.

It will thus be seen that the first larva of Chelifer is comparable with that of certain low mites, but very different from the Scorpion, its nearest ally, the segmentation of the yolk being total, as in most mites, the sea spiders, Pentastoma and the Tardigrades, while the larval condition is on a still lower plane of existence than the Nauplius of the lower Crustacea. The false-scorpion differs in its mode of growth much more from the spiders, the scorpion and other Pedipalps, than the harvest-man (Phalangium), Phrynus or the Acarina.

The harvest-men, or daddy-long-legs, as the researches of Metschnikoff and Balbiani show, develop as in the spiders, differing from them only in the want of a provisional post-abdomen and the relatively smaller abdomen.

The false-scorpions pass through, then :—

1. A Morula stage.

2. Hatching in the first larval state, with but one pair of appendages (maxillæ).

3. Second larval state, with all the limbs present, but enveloped in a larval skin.

4. Throwing off the larval skin, becoming free and with the form of the adult animal.

LITERATURE.

Metschnikoff. Entwicklungsgeschichte des Chelifer. (Siebold and Kölliker's Zeitschrift für wissens. Zoologie. Leipzig, 1871.)

Development of the Scorpions, etc. (Pedipalps). In a beautiful memoir by Metschnikoff on the embryology of the scorpion we have full details regarding the embryonic life of this animal, which brings forth its young alive early in summer; being one of the very few viviparous insects known. His studies were made on three species of Scorpio found in southern Europe. The females are big with young at the end of spring or early in summer. I have observed this to be the case with the scorpion of the Florida Keys.

The earliest phases of development take place in the follicles of the ovary. The blastoderm is formed out of a few polar cells just as in the higher crustacea (Isopods and Decapods). It is at first a round disc, which eventually splits into two germ-layers. Soon it becomes oval, the larger end being the head-end. The next step is the formation of a primitive longitudinal furrow, and afterwards of two transverse creases dividing the germ into three portions, the anterior the head, the middle portion the thorax and abdomen, and the third, the so-called post-abdomen.

The egg now leaves the follicle and descends into the oviduct. The head grows broader, and by this time the germ is subdivided into twelve segments, from which the appendages next bud out. The mouth may be discerned, the claws are indicated, the post-abdomen is folded on the body and the nerve-ganglia may be detected arising from the outer germ-layer. The embryo is now surrounded by a membrane composed of two layers of quite dissimilar cells.

A singular feature, also noticeable in other Insecta, is the presence of six pairs of deciduous abdominal feet, which directly assume the form of horizontal plates, each with a terminal button, which finally disappear, the four pairs of stigmata taking their place; the second pair, however, become converted into the comb-like tracheal gills, so that it is evident that the latter are exvaginate stigmata. The germ (primitive band) is now broader, and the limbs have a more definite outline and are jointed, while the head is narrower than before, assuming the shape of that of the adult.

Metschnikoff claims that there are three germ-layers in the Scorpion, homologous with those of the vertebrates.

A summary of the chief events in the development of the scorpion is as follows:

1. Partial segmentation of the yolk, the embryo developing within the oviduct.

2. The young is brought forth by the mother, in a form exactly like the adult, and about half an inch long, about a dozen being produced in a season.

LITERATURE.

Rathke. Zur Morphologie. Reisebemerkungen aus Taurien. 1837.
Metschnikoff. Embryologie des Scorpions. (Siebold and Külliker's Zeitschrift. 1870.)

Development of the Spiders. From the life-history of one spider we may learn that of all, as there is much uniformity in the mode of development of all those species whose growth has been yet observed. The eggs are laid usually in silken cocoons. All undergo partial segmentation of the yolk, which is surrounded by

a blastoderm, which thickens on one side forming the primitive
band, eventually becoming marked off into rings or zones, as in

Fig. 214.   Fig. 215.   Fig. 216.

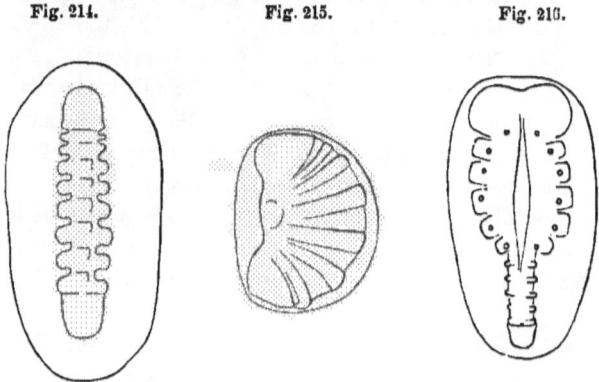

Development of the Spider. After Claparède.

Fig. 214. The primitive band elongates, new segments appear
(Fig. 215), until finally the germ appears, when drawn as if spread
out, as in Fig. 216. Besides the rudi-
ments of the two pairs of head-appen-
dages (*i.e.*, the mandibles and maxillæ)
and the four pairs of legs, there are at
first four, as in figure 216, and subsequently six pairs of deciduous abdominal feet, as in the Scorpion and two
other species of tracheate insects.

Fig. 217.

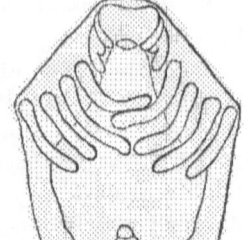

Advanced embryo of the Spider.

Soon the mouth-parts and legs grow
longer, and the embryo spider lies on
the surface of the yolk as seen in Fig.
217. Finally, the head, originally distinct from the thorax, becomes soldered
to the thorax; the eyes appear and the
animal is rapidly perfected, the spider being hatched in a form
like the adult, differing only in size and its paleness of color; the
changes in after life being almost imperceptible. All spiders,
then, so far as known:—

1. Undergo in the egg state a partial segmentation of the yolk,
and

2. Are hatched in the adult form, having no metamorphosis.

LITERATURE.

Herold. De Generatione Aranearum in Ovo. Marburg, 1824.
Claparède. Recherches sur l'Evolution des Araignées. Utrecht, 1862.

Development of the true Insects. While the history of the winged insects before hatching is much the same in the different orders, there are some exceptional modes of development possessing a high degree of interest on account of the resemblance to the mode of embryonic growth of still lower animals. First I will give an epitome of the changes observed by myself within the egg of a

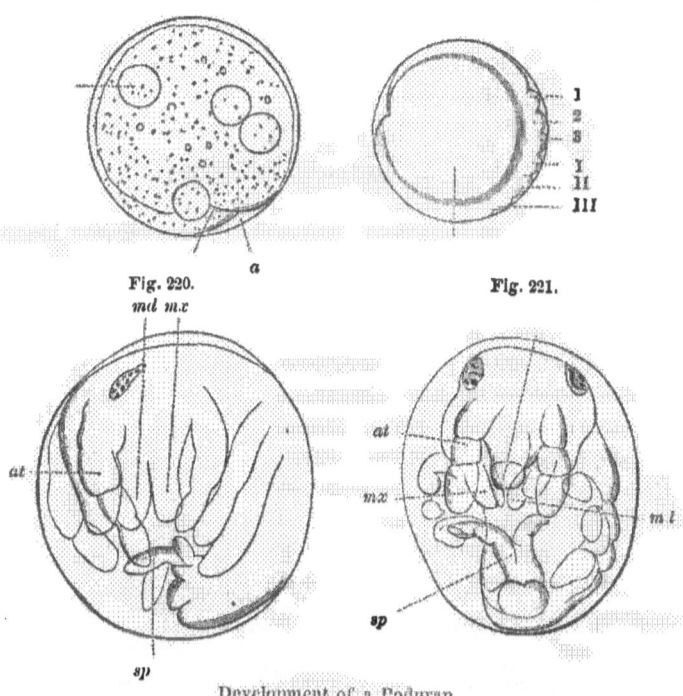

Fig. 218.　　　　　Fig. 219.

Fig. 220.　　　　　Fig. 221.
md m.x

at

at

mx

m.l

sp

sp

Development of a Poduran.

Poduran. The eggs were not studied until after the formation of the blastoderm, but Ulianin of Moscow has ascertained that the eggs of certain Podurids undergo total segmentation, in this feature, as indeed in some of the other phases of embryonic life, closely resembling the Myriopods. Fig. 218 shows the primitive band infolded at *a*, as in the Myriopod germ. A more advanced stage (Fig. 219) shows the rudimentary appendages (1-3, I-III) the second maxillæ or labium, not being present. (It will be remembered that a pair of maxillæ are also wanting in the Thousand-legs.) The next change is the clos-ure of the body-walls over the yolk, and the appearance of the rudiments of the "spring." By this time the serous membrane is formed, being a tough membrane enveloping the germ. In a succeeding stage the intestine is formed and the rudiments of the antennæ and legs have greatly increased in size. Still later, the appendages begin to show traces of joints. In a later period (Fig. 220, 221 *a*) the head is quite

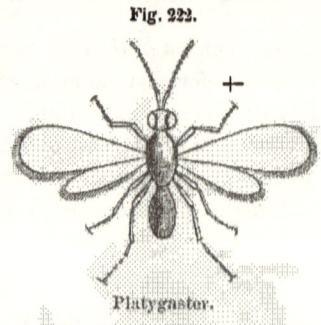

Fig. 222.

Platygaster.

Fig. 223.

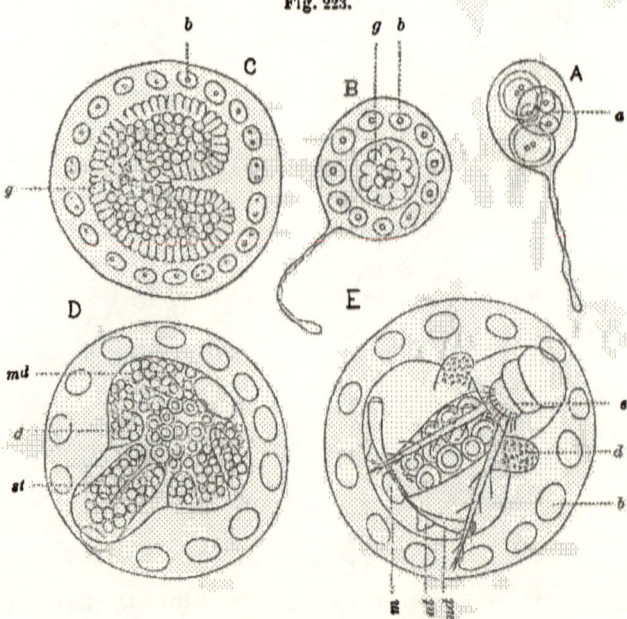

Development of Platygaster.

separate from the rest of the body, the antennæ (*at*) are of much the same shape as in the larva, while the upper lip (labrum) and clypeus are clearly indicated, and the spring (*sp*) is fully formed. Soon after, the "finishing touches" are, as it were, put on, and the mandibles and maxillæ (*md* and *mx*) are withdrawn within the head, when the embryo throws off the chorion and serous membrane and runs about in a lively way.

Coming now to the true winged insects, we are met with a very exceptionable mode of development, observed by Ganin in certain species of minute ichneumon flies, some of them egg-parasites. The ovary of Platygaster (Fig. 222) differs from that of most other insects in that it is a closed tube or sac. Hence it follows that at

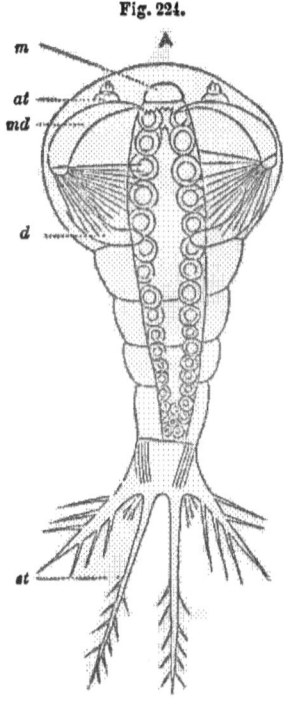

Fig. 224.

every time an egg is laid, the egg-tube is ruptured. The egg is a single cell. Out of this cell (Fig. 223 *A*, *a*, arise two other cells, but the central cell (*a*) gives rise to the embryo, which as seen at *B*, *g*, originates from the nucleus of *A*, *a*, while the circle of cells, *b*, form an equivalent to the serous membrane or blastodermic skin of other insects and crustacea. The germ farther advanced, as in *C*, *g*, reminds us of the embryo of certain low worms. *D* and *E* are successive stages in the growth of the provisional larva (Fig. 224, *m*, mouth; *at*, antennæ; *md*, mandibles; *d*, deciduous organs). In this condition it clings to the inside of its host by means of its temporary hook-like jaws (*md*) moving about like a Cestodes embryo. The nerves, blood vessels and air tubes are wanting, while the alimentary canal is simply a blind sac, remaining in an unorganized state.

First larva of Platygaster.

It then passes into the second larval state (Fig. 225) like that of the ichneumon flies, and the remaining changes into the pupal and winged state are as usual.

In Polynema, the larva in its first stage is very small and motionless, and with scarcely a trace of organization, being a mere flask-shaped sac of cells. After five or six days it passes into a worm-like stage, and subsequently into a third stage (Fig. 226, *tg*, three pairs of abdominal tubercles destined to form the ovipositor; *l*, rudiments of the legs; *fk*, portion of the fatty body; *at*, rudiments of the antennæ; *fl*, imaginal disks or rudiments of the wings).

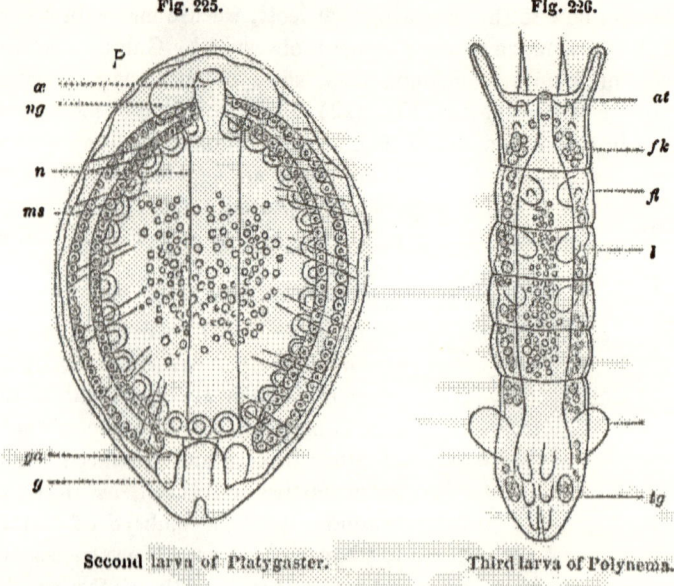

Fig. 225.

Second larva of Platygaster.

Fig. 226.

Third larva of Polynema.

Fig. 227.

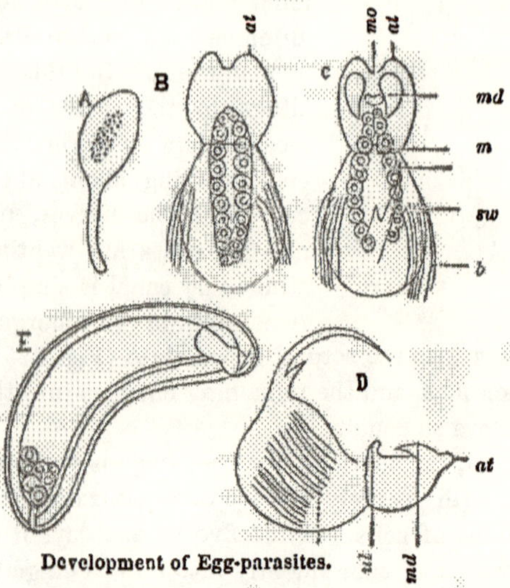

Development of Egg-parasites.

The larva of Ophioneurus is at first of the form indicated by Fig 227, *E*. It differs from the genera already mentioned, in remaining within its egg-membrane, and not assuming their strange forms. From the non-segmented, sac-like larva it passes directly into the pupa state.

The development of Teleas is like that of Platygaster. Fig. 227, *A*, represents the egg; *B*, *C* and *D*, the first stage of the larva, the abdomen being furnished with a series of bristles on each side. *B* represents a ventral, *C* a dorsal, and *D* a profile view; *at*, antennæ; *md*, mandibles; *mo*, mouth; *b*, bristles; *m*, intestine; *sw* the tail, and *ul* the under lip or labium. Not until the beginning of the second larval stage is the primitive band formed.

In all the other insects whose early stages have been studied, there is a remarkable uniformity, all travelling nearly the same developmental road until just before hatching, when they assume the characteristics belonging to the larval forms of their respective orders. For example not until very late in embryonic life do the germs of a bee, a bug, a beetle or a fly, or even a dragon fly, differ in any essential point.

We will, then, give a general and brief account of the mode of growth of the germ, not dwelling on the metamorphoses of insects. The egg after fertilization shows the first sign of the new life thus originated by the appearance of a few polar cells; these multiply and surround the egg with a single layer, thus forming the blastoderm. The segmentation of the yolk is thus peripheral and partial. On one side of the egg the blastodermic cells elongate, forming a thickening, called the primitive streak or band, which in some insects sinks into the yolk. By this time the serous membrane (*s*) has moulted and envelopes the germ and yolk. The germ soon splits into an outer (ectoderm) and inner layer

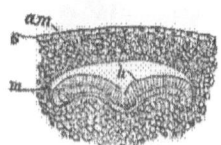

Fig. 228.

(endoderm) and then sheds the true amnion, which as in vertebrates, peals off from the primitive band or germ, and acts as a protective membrane.

In Fig. 228 (after Kowalevsky), representing a transverse section of the embryo of a Sphinx, we see the relation of parts.

Section of Sphinx embryo.

The primitive band has sunk into the yolk which is surrounded by the serous membrane (*s*) or blastodermic skin (formerly, but erroneously termed the amnion). The primitive band is seen to be formed of two layers, *h*, the outer, and *m*, the inner. In the outer is subsequently formed the nervous cord and air vessels, while from the inner arise the digestive canal and its glands and

Fig. 229.

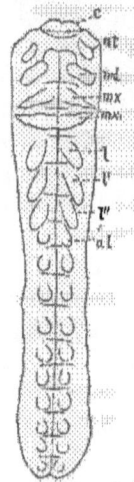

the organs of circulation. The amnion (*am*) envelopes the germ. From the ventral side of the primitive band bud forth the appendages of the head, the thorax, and as in the embryo caterpillar, the ten pairs of abdominal legs, *i.e.*, one to each ring, a portion of which disappear before it hatches, no caterpillar having more than five pairs of prop-legs. Fig. 229 (after Kowalevsky) represents the primitive band of the Sphinx, with the four pairs of head appendages (*c*, upper lip; *at*, antennæ; *md*, mandibles; *mx, mx'* first and second maxillæ), and the three pairs of thoracic legs (*l, l' l''*) succeeded by the ten pairs of abdominal legs. The observer will notice that all the appendages, whether of the head or thorax or hind-body, are alike at first, being simple outgrowths of the outer germ-layer.

Sphinx embryo.

When in a more advanced stage, as seen in the accompanying figure (230, *am*, serous membrane; *db*, amnion; *vk*, forehead) of the embryo louse, the antennæ are longer than the mouth-parts, and the legs are still larger. Afterwards those features characterizing the different orders of insects appear, and shortly before hatching we can ascertain to what group the embryo belongs.

As regards the development of the internal organs, the nervous system is the first to show itself, the alimentary canal is next formed, and the stigmata and air-tubes arise as invaginations of the outer germ-layer. The development of the salivary glands precedes that of the urinary tubes, which, with the genital glands are offshoots of the primitive digestive tract. Finally the dorsal vessel is formed. Fig. 231 (after Kowalevsky) is a transverse section of the embryo bee; *g*, is a nerve ganglion; *i*, the alimentary canal; *m*, muscular bands running to the heart (*h*);

Fig. 230.

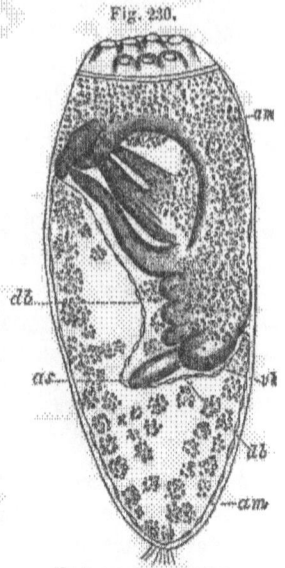

Embryo of the Louse.

d is a gland, and *t*, indicates the trachea, its mode of origin being illustrated on the left side of the figure where it is seen in communication with a stigma or air-hole (*s*).

So far as we know (the Thysanura and certain minute ichneumous excepted) there is in the winged insects a remarkable uniformity in their mode of development, and it is difficult to determine what embryological characters may be set down as distinguishing even the different orders, but they will probably be found, if anywhere, in the form of the advanced embryos.

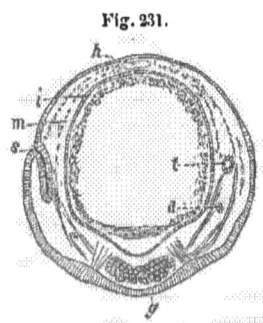

Fig. 231.

Section of advanced Sphinx embryo.

A summary of the most important events in the life-history of insects is as follows :—

1. Peripheral (partial) segmentation of the yolk (in the Podurœ a true Morula condition).

2. Larva hatched in the form of the adult (in Aphis and Miastor producing young alive), but wingless, and undergoing an incomplete or complete metamorphosis.

3. Pupa (in a species of Chironomus producing young).

4. Adult, usually winged, sometimes propagating asexually.

LITERATURE.

Herold. Disquisitiones de **Animalium vertebris carentium in Ovo Formatione.** Frankfurt a Maine. 1835-38.

Kölliker. Observationes de prima **Insectorum Genesi.** Turici, 1842.

Zaddach. Untersuchung ueber die Entwickelung und den Bau der Gliederthiere. Berlin. 1854.

Leuckart. Die Fortpflanzung und Entwickelung der Pupiparen nach Beobachtungen an Melophagus ovinus, Halle, 1858.

Huxley. On the Agamic Reproduction and Morphology of **Aphis.** (Phil. Trans. London, 1859.)

Weismann. Die Entwickelung **der Dipteren im Ei.** (Siebold and Kölliker's Zeitschrift, xiii, 1864.)

Metschnikoff. Embryologische Studien an Insecten. (Siebold and Kölliker's Zeitschrift, 1866.)

Melnikow. Beitrage zur Embryonalentwicklung der Insekten. (Archiv für Naturgeschichte, 1869.

Brandt. Beitrage zur Entwicklungsgeschichte der Libelluliden und Hemipteren, etc. (Mémoires Acad. Imp. St. Petersburg, 1869.)

Ganin. Ueber die Embryonalhülle der Hymenopteren und Lepidopteren Embryonen. (Mémoires Acad. Imp. St. Petersburg. 1869.)

———. Beitrage zur Erkenntniss der Entwickelungsgeschichte bei dem Insekten. (Siebold and Kölliker's Zeitschrift, 1869.)

Consult, also, papers by J. Müller, **S. Wagner,** Van Grimm, Balbiani, Dohrn and **Packard.**

XXIX. THE LEPTOCARDII (Amphioxus).

In the adult Amphioxus, we behold a vertebrate without a true back bone, but a dorsal cord like that of certain larval Ascidians; with no brain, no true heart, but with a vascular system resembling that of worms; with primitive kidneys like the segmental organs of worms, and with the front end of the alimentary canal perforated with gill-slits, like those of Ascidians and the Balanoglossus worm rather than vertebrates. Viewing the body externally, it has no true head as in fishes, nor appendages supported by bony axes, like the fins and arms or legs of vertebrates. Yet on making a section of the body, the relation of the chief anatomical organs is on the vertebrate plan, a nerve-cavity being situated above the digestive cavity, the vicarious back bone, or *chorda dorsalis*, separating the two cavities.

It will thus be seen that the line separating the vertebrates from the rest of the animal kingdom is in a degree artificial, and that the beings most like the ancestors of the present vertebrates are to be looked for in some lower branch.

Development of Amphioxus. Again when we study the development of Amphioxus, we shall find, that while there are important points in which the embryology of this animal differs much from that of the higher vertebrates, still, as observed by Balfour, "all the modes of development found in the higher vertebrates are to be looked upon as modifications of that of Amphioxus."

For the life-history of the lancelet, we turn to Kowalevsky's classical memoir. He found the eggs issuing in May from the mouth of the female, and fertilized by spermatic particles likewise pouring out from the mouth of the male. The eggs are very small, 0.105 millimetres in diameter. The eggs undergo total segmentation, exactly as in the sponge, the ascidian, the mammal, and even as in man, and leaving a segmentation cavity which becomes the body-cavity.

The blastoderm now invaginates and the embryo swims about as a ciliated gastrula, comparable with that of the sponge, or Sagitta (Fig. 149). The body is now oval, and the germ does not differ much in appearance from a worm, starfish, snail or ascidian in the same stage of growth. No vertebrate features are yet developed.

Soon the lively ciliated gastrula elongates, the alimentary tube arises from the primitive gastrula-cavity, while the edges of the flattened side of the body grow up as ridges which afterwards, as in all vertebrate embryos, grow over and enclose the spinal cord. By this time the transverse muscular bands appear.

By the time the embryo is twenty-four hours old it assumes the form of a ciliated flattened cylinder, with both ends much alike. It is now somewhat like the Ascidian embryo (Fig. 164, *B, n*), there being a nerve-cavity, the nerve-tube, with an external opening, which afterwards closes.

The vertebrate character, namely, the embryonic back bone (*chorda dorsalis*) has now appeared, and extends to the front end, beyond the end of the brain, instead of being confined to the posterior portion of the body as in the Ascidians (Fig. 164, *B, x*).

In the next stage observed by the Russian embryologist, the Amphioxus-form was attained, the body being compressed and deeper in the region of the mouth, though there is no true head. The first gill-opening now appears, the mouth having previously been formed, and afterwards twelve such openings appear; the pharynx is thus provided with ciliated slits, as in the Ascidians, the Balanoglossus; and, on the other hand, all embryo vertebrates. The embryo lancelet is still ciliated, but these swimming-hairs disappear eventually and the young animal seeks the bottom and burrows finally in the sand. When the larval Amphioxus is still very small, the body is not symmetrical, the mouth is far on one side, and on the lower edge is a circle of external filaments surrounding the mouth, comparable with the fringe of filaments of the Ascidians, the clam or certain worms.

It seems to result from these and other facts, not here presented, that while the Amphioxus is a low, embryonic vertebrate, which graduates into the fishes through the lamprey and Myxine, the early history of Amphioxus unmistakably points back to wormlike parents; and on the other hand that of the vertebrates indicates their descent from an Amphioxus-like ancestor.

Briefly recapitulating the chief events in the life of the lancelet, we find the following well marked stages:

1. Morula.
2. Gastrula (ciliated).
3. Ascidian-like larva.
4. Adult.   LITERATURE.

Kowalevsky. Entwickelungsgeschichte des Amphioxus lanceolatus. (Memoires de l'Acad. Imp. des Sciences de St. Petersbourg, 1867).

XXX. THE PISCES.

Development of the Sharks and Skates (Selachians). These fishes are either oviparous or viviparous. The dog-fish brings forth her young alive, while the skates and many sharks lay square eggs with a tough horny shell (Fig. 232, after Wyman). The yolk is not enclosed in any membrane like the vitelline membrane of birds, but lies freely in a viscid albumen filling the egg-capsule.

We will now, in order to make out a tolerably complete life-history of a Selachian, condense Balfour's account of the early stages of the dog-fish (Mustelus), and close with the latter stages of the skate, as given by the late Professor Wyman. The blastoderm or germinal disk is a large round spot darker than the rest of the yolk and marked off from the rest of the egg by a dark line (really a shallow groove). Segmentation occurs much as described in the bony fishes, reptiles and birds. The upper germ-layer (epiblast) arises much as in the bony fishes, the Batrachians and birds, while the two inner germ-layers are not clearly indicated until a considerably later stage. The segmentation-cavity is formed much as in the bony fishes. There is no invagination of the outer germ-layer to form the primitive digestive cavity and anus of Rusconi, as in Amphioxus, the lamprey, sturgeon and Batrachians, but the Selachians agree with the bony fishes, the reptiles and birds, in having the alimentary canal formed by an infolding of the innermost germ-layer, and with no anus of Rusconi, the digestive tract remaining

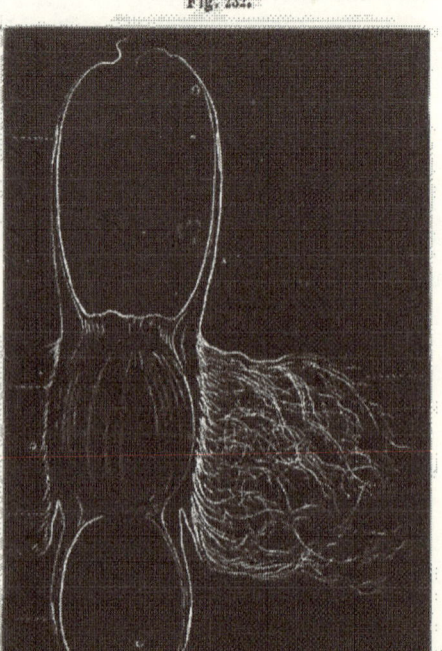

Fig. 232.

Egg of the Skate.

in communication with the yolk for the greater part of embryonic

Fig. 233.

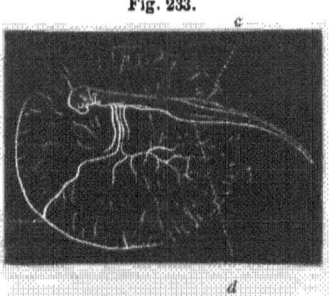

Embryo Skate.

life by an umbilical canal. This mode of origin of the digestive cavity, Balfour regards as secondary and adaptive, no "gastrula" (Hæckel) being formed as in Amphioxus, etc. The embryo now rises up as a distinct body from the blastoderm, just as in other vertebrates, and there is a medullary groove along the middle line, and by the time this has appeared the middle and inner germ-layers are clearly indicated. After this development goes on much as in the chick.

At this time the embryo dog-fish externally resembles the young trout; the chief difference is an internal one, the outer germ-layer not being divided into a nervous and epidermal sub-layer as in the bony fishes.

The next external change is the division of the tail-end into two caudal lobes. The notochord arises as a rod-like thickening of the third germ-layer, from which it afterwards entirely separates, so that the germ, if cut transversely, would appear somewhat as in the embryo bird (Fig. 251).

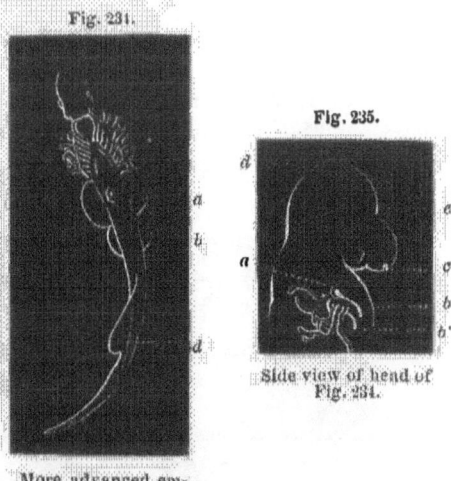

Fig. 234.

Fig. 235.

More advanced embryo Skate.

Side view of head of Fig. 234.

Now the protovertebræ arise, and about this time the throat becomes a closed tube. The head is now formed by a singular flattening-out of the germ, like a spatula, while the medullary groove is at first entirely absent. The brain then forms, with its three divisions into a fore, middle and hind brain. Soon about twenty primitive vertebræ arise, and by this time the embryo is very similar, in external form, to any other vertebrate embryo, and finally hatches in the form of the adult.

Not so, however, with the skate (*Raia batis*) as it presents an additional chapter in its life-history, discovered by Professor Wyman. Fig. 233 (this and those following after Wyman) shows the young skate resting on the large yolk-sac. It is eel-shaped, the dorsal (*c*) and (*d*) anal fins extending to the end of the tail as in the eel. Fig. 234 represents a more advanced embryo, showing at *a* and *b* the pectoral and ventral fins, and at *d*, the temporary anal. Fig. 235 is a side view of the same enlarged (*a*, first branchial fissure, largest at its outer end;

Fig. 236.

Shark-shaped embryo Skate.

this enlarged portion corresponds with the future spiracle; *b*, the inner end; the first arch is in front of the fissure; *b'*, the second fissure, in front of which is the second arch, bearing a fringe; *c*, nasal fossa; *d*, projection of the optic lobes; *e*, cerebral lobes.)

Soon after, the embryo skate becomes shark-shaped, as in Fig. 236, while Figs. 237 and 238, represent a lateral and dorsal view of the embryo (*b*, facial disk; *a*, pectoral; *c*, ventral fin; *e*, gill-

Fig. 237.

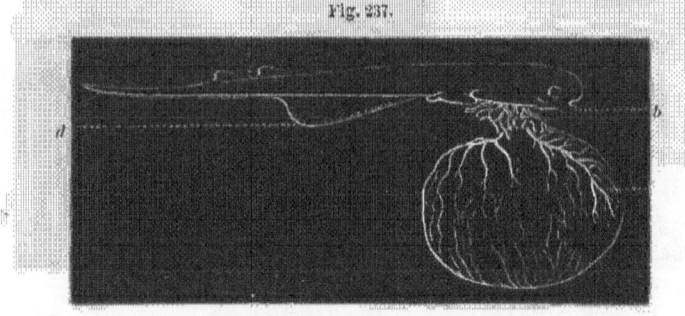

More advanced embryo of Skate.

fringes). There are at first seven branchial fissures, the most anterior of which is converted into the spiracle, which is the homologue of the Eustachian tube and the outer ear-canal; the seventh is wholly closed up, no trace remaining, while the five others remain permanently open.

Fig. 239 represents the newly hatched skate, when the form of the adult is closely approached (*a*, yolk-sac in the cavity of the abdomen, connecting with the intestine, *b; c,* embryonic portion of the tail, which disappears in the adult (Wyman).

A condensed summary of the chief events in the life of a Selachian, is as follows :—

1. Partial segmentation of the germinal disk.

2. The embryo arises as a distinct body from the germinal disk (the "gastrula" condition being suppressed).

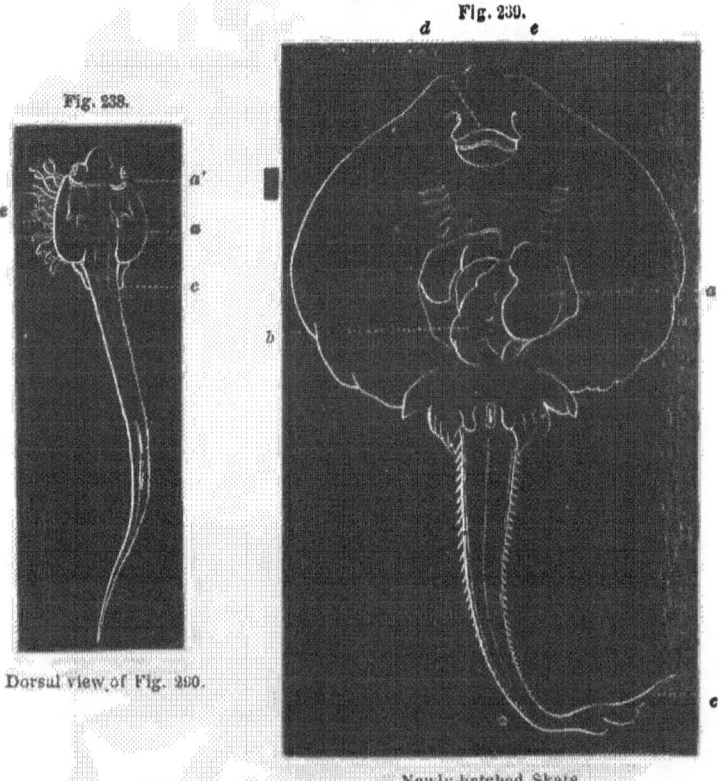

Fig. 239.

Fig. 238.

Dorsal view of Fig. 239.

Newly-hatched Skate.

3. The embryo appears like that of any other vertebrate, until finally

4. The shark or skate form is assumed just before birth, or hatching from the egg.

5. The skates pass through a shark-like form, before attaining the adult shape.

LITERATURE.

Wyman. Observations on the Development of *Raia batis.* (Memoirs Amer. Acad. Sc., 1864).

Bambeke. Recherches sur le Développpment du *Pelobates fuscus* (Mémoires couron-nés Acad. Belgique, 34, 1870.)

Balfour. A preliminary Account of the Development of the Elasmobranch Fishes. (Quart. Jour. Micr. Science, 1874.)

Development of the bony Fishes. During their reproductive season, the bony fishes, such as the stickleback, salmon and pike, are more highly colored than at other times, the males being especially brilliant in their hues, while other secondary sexual characters are developed. The female deposits her eggs either in masses at the surface of the water, as in the cod and goose fish, or at the bottom on gravel or sand as in most other fishes, the male passing over them and depositing his "milt" or spermatic

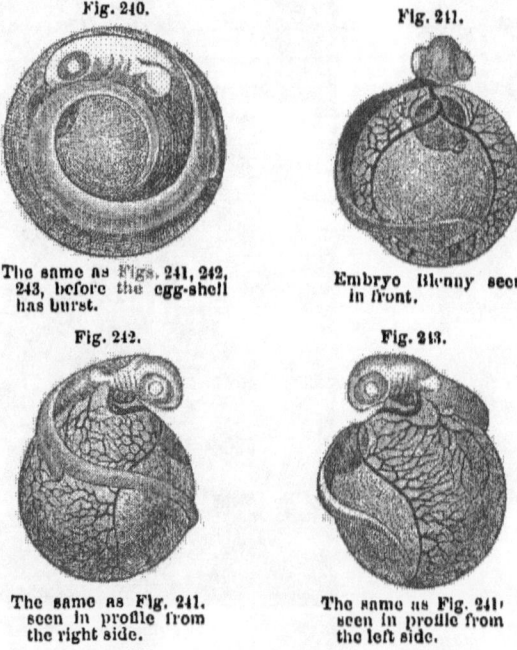

Fig. 240.

The same as Figs. 241, 242, 243, before the egg-shell has burst.

Fig. 241.

Embryo Blenny seen in front.

Fig. 242.

The same as Fig. 241, seen in profile from the right side.

Fig. 243.

The same as Fig. 241, seen in profile from the left side.

particles. The egg has a thin transparent shell, and the yolk is small, covered with a thick layer of the "white."

The eggs after fertilization undergo partial segmentation, the primitive streak, notochord, nervous cord and brain developing much as described in the section on the embryology of birds. That the embryo before us is a fish is soon determined by the absence of an amnion and allantois, and by the fact that the germ lies free over the yolk like a band. Figs. 240, 241, 242, 243 (copied by Agassiz [1] from Rathke), represent an advanced stage of the embryo Blenny (*Zoarces viviparus*) in various positions, with the eyes, gill-arches, fins and vitelline network of blood vessels on the outer surface of the yolk sac.

In the pike the heart begins to beat about the seventh day, and by this time the alimentary canal is marked out. The primitive kidneys are developed above the liver. The air-bladder (probably the homologue of the lungs of higher vertebrates) arises as an offshoot opposite the liver from the alimentary canal, and the gall-bladder is also originally a diverticulum of the intestine. The urinary bladder in the fish is supposed to be the homologue of the allantois of the higher vertebrates. The principal external change is the appearance of the usually large pectoral fins.

The embryo pike hatches in about twelve days after development begins and swims about with the large yolk bag attached, and it is some seven or eight days before the young fish takes food, living meanwhile on the yolk mass. The perch hatches in twelve days after the egg is fertilized, and swims about for eight or ten days before the yolk is absorbed. The vent opens in the pike four days, and in the perch six days, after hatching. The gills gradually develop as the yolk is absorbed.

The tail in most bony fishes (the Gadidæ excepted, according to Owen), is heterocercal as in the maturer sharks, but subsequently after the fish has swam about for a while and increased in size it becomes homocercal or symmetrical. The scales are the last to be developed.

In the large size of the pectoral fins, the position of the mouth, which is situated far back under the head, the heterocercal tail, the cartilaginous skeleton and uncovered gill-slits, the embryo salmon, pike, perch, etc., as Owen observes, manifest transitory characters which are permanent in sharks (*Selachii*).

A summary of the changes undergone in the bony fishes is as follows :

1. Segmentation partial.

2. A gastrula-condition in the lamprey and sturgeon, but not in the bony fishes (trout, etc).

3. The embryo arises as in any other vertebrate.

[1] The Structure and Growth of Domesticated Animals," 20th Ann. Report of the Secretary of the Massachusetts Board of Agriculture. Boston, 1873. These and Figs. 253-263, 266, were kindly loaned by Mr. C. L. Flint, the Secretary.

4. Adult form attained at the time of hatching or birth, in the viviparous species; certain forms undergoing slight metamorphosis.

LITERATURE.

Vogt. Embryologie des Salmones (in Agassiz, Hist. Nat. des Poissons d'l'eau douce de l'Europe Centrale.) Neuchatel, 1842.

Lereboullet. Recherches d'Embryologie Comparée sur le Développement des Brochét, de la Perche, etc. (Annales des Sc. Nat. Paris, 1855)

Œllacher, Beiträge zur Entwicklung der Knochenfische, etc. (Siebold and Kölliker's Zeitschrift, 1873, 74.)

Kowalevsky, Owsjannikoff, und Wagner. Entwickelung der Störe (Sturgeon. Bulletin Imp. Acad. St. Petersburg, xiv. 1873.)

With the writings of Kupffer, Götte, Ray Lankester and Owsjannikoff.

XXXI. THE AMPHIBIA.

Development of the Amphibia. Passing by the Dipnoa (Ceratodus, Protopterus and Lepidosiren) of whose development we as yet are totally ignorant, and the Simosauria, Plesiosauria and Ichthyosauria, we come to the salamanders and toads and frogs, or Amphibia. The early history of the extinct Archegosaurus, Dendrerpeton and Labyrinthodonts died with them, and we can only predicate from the imperfectly known structure of the adult forms that their young possibly developed in a manner like that of the living batrachians.

As in the fishes the batrachians are most highly colored during the breeding season. The males of certain newts acquire the dorsal crest and a broader tail-fin, aiding in the process of fecundation (Owen), and other secondary sexual features are added, especially to the male during the reproductive season. After an imperfect sexual union the salamanders deposit their eggs on the leaves of aquatic plants. The eggs of the toad are laid in long strings, those of the frog in masses. In these creatures each egg is fertilized as it is extruded, and the egg then swells greatly, the yolk appearing as a dot in the large jelly-like mass surrounding it.

Until we have a detailed embryology of the Amphibians, studied in the light of the newer school of embryology, the reader must be content with the following summary of Owen's account.

The segmentation of the egg in the Amphibia is total, the process beginning usually about three hours after impregnation in the frog, and lasting twenty-four hours. The primitive streak, the notochord and nervous system then arise as in other craniated Vertebrates. After the appearance of the branchial arches, the gills begin to bud out from them, finally forming the larger gills of the tadpole. The embryo now rests on the large yolk sac, much as in the embryo fish, but this is entirely absorbed before the embryo leaves the egg. Before the yolk-sac is absorbed a communication opens between the alimentary canal and the branchial cavity in the head (bucco-branchial cavity of Owen), "and this opens externally on the lower part of the head by a vertical fissure, on each side of which a small protuberance buds out, forming a special organ of adhesion — a pair of temporary cephalic limbs." (Owen.) Now the gills having got their growth, the remnant of the yolk enclosed by the abdominal walls, and the tail well developed, the tadpole bursts its egg membrane and swims about freely. In Italy, Rusconi found that the tadpoles hatched in four days, in England they hatch in five days, and the period may be prolonged to four weeks by cold weather. It is a common sight in Maine to see frogs' eggs laid in ponds still containing ice and snow.

The tadpole is much less developed than the larval fish or any other vertebrate; the intestine is not yet formed, and in other important characters it is lower in organization than the freshly hatched fish. It is also a vegetarian, eating decaying leaves; the mouth is small and round, the alimentary canal is remarkably long, the intestine coiled up in a spiral, the mouth is small, destitute of a tongue and the beak unarmed with teeth. "About the middle period of aquatic life the true or permanent kidneys begin to be formed from and upon the primordial ones; and the basis of the óvaria, or testes, may now be discerned. The oviduct is soon distinct from the ureter; but the testes retain the same excretory duct as the kidneys; their *vasa deferentia* communicate with retained cæca of the primordial kidneys before penetrating the later glands; the upper or anterior ends of the first remain for some time behind the heart." (Owen.)

"Soon after the external gills have reached their full development they begin to shrink, and finally disappear; but the branchial circulation is maintained some time longer upon the internal gills; these consist of numerous short tuft-like processes from the membrane covering the cartilaginous branchial arches; they are protected by the growth of a membranous gill-cover, which, as the external branchiæ are absorbed, leaves only one small external orifice, by which the branchial streams, admitted by the mouth, continue to be expelled. The chief distinction between the fully

developed branchial circulation in the Batrachian larva and that of
the fish consists in the presence of small anastomosing channels,
between the branchial artery and vein of each gill, proximad of the
gill itself. The tongue makes its appearance when the fore limbs
are developed."

The vertebræ of the tadpole are biconcave, but in the change to
the adult are converted into cup-and-ball joints, by ossification of
the substance of the cavities, and its coalescence either with the
fore (Pipa) or back (Rana) part of the centrum. The remarkable
changes in the hyo-branchial apparatus and the skull are described
by Owen.

The accompanying figures (from Tenney's Zoology) represent
the external changes of the toad from the time it is hatched until
the form of the adult is attained. The tadpoles of our American
toad, as observed in the European toad by Owen, are smaller and
blacker in all stages of growth than those of the frog. The tadpole
is at first without any limbs (Fig. 244) ; soon the hinder pair bud out.
After this stage (Fig. 245) is reached the body begins to diminish
in size. The next important change is the growth of the front

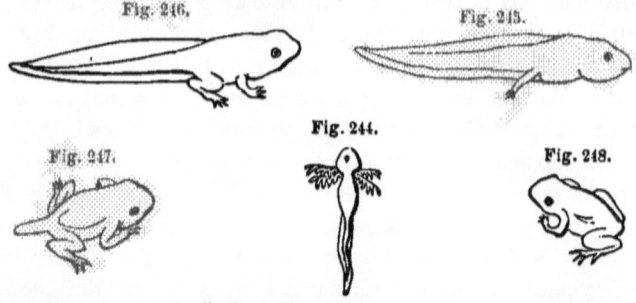

Metamorphosis of the Toad.

legs and the partial disappearance of the tail (Fig. 246), while
very small toads (Figs. 247 and 248), during midsummer, may be
found on the edges of the pools in which some of the nearly tailless tadpoles may be seen swimming about. When the tadpoles
are hatched late, the gills are often retained through the winter,
as large tadpoles of frogs are often found in pools by breaking
through the ice. It is three years, according to Owen, before the
Amphibia are capable of breeding.

"In the newts (Triton) the gills are in three pairs, larger and
more complex than in the frog ; the fore limbs are the first to

emerge, and the gills persist long after the hind limbs are developed." (Owen). While as a rule the eggs of newts or salamanders are laid in the water, the red-backed salamander lays its eggs

Fig. 249.

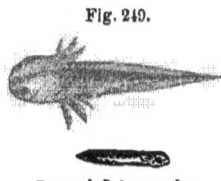

Larval Salamander.

in damp places on land, though the young are provided with gills. Fig. 249 (after Hoy) represents the young of *Amblystoma lurida* on the tenth day after hatching, the lower figure the natural size of the freshly hatched young. In the Surinam toad and Hyla of the island of Mauritius there is no metamorphosis, the young hatching with the form of the adult. The Siredon or Axolotl of Mexico, according to Dumeril, lays eggs, though a larva, while, as in the Axolotl, the larva of *Amblystoma mavortium*, originally described as an adult animal under the name of *Siredon lichenoides* (Fig. 250, from Tenney's Zoology) has been found by Professor Marsh

Fig. 250.

Siredon or larval Salamander.

to drop its gills and assume its adult form when brought to the sea level, its original habitat being the lakes situated in the Rocky Mountains at an altitude of 4500 – 7000 feet.

Professor Owen has well summed up the wonderful changes undergone in these metamorphoses, which are nearly paralleled by those of the vegetarian larval gnat with biting jaws and gills into the blood-sucking volant, air-breathing fly; entirely new organs replacing the deciduous ones of the larva, and the body in attaining maturity being made over anew. "In the metamorphoses of the Batrachia," says the distinguished comparative anatomist, "we seem to have such process carried on before our eyes to its extremest extent. Not merely is one specific form changed to another of the same genus; not merely is one generic modification of an order substituted for another, the transmutation is not even limited by passing from one order (Urodela) to another (Anoura); it affects a transition from class to class. The Fish becomes the Frog; the aquatic animal changes to the terrestrial one; the water-breather becomes the air-breather; an insect diet is substituted for a vegetable one. And these changes, moreover, proceed gradually, continuously, and without any interruption of active life. The larva having started into independent existence as a fish, does not relapse into the passive torpor of the ovum to leave the organizing energies to complete their work untroubled by the play of the parts they are to transmute, but step by step each organ is modified, and the behavior of the animal and its life-sphere are the consequence, not the cause, of the changes."

"The external gills are not dried and shrivelled by exposure to the air, nor does the larva gain its lungs by efforts to change its element and inhale a new respiratory medium. The beak is shed, the jaws and tongue are developed, and the gut shortened, before the young Frog is in a condition to catch a single fly. The embryo acquires the breathing and locomotive organs—gills and compressed tail—while imprisoned in the ovum; and the tadpole obtains its lungs and land-limbs while a denizen of the pool; action and reaction between the germ and the gelatinous atmosphere of the yolk, or between the larva and its aqueous atmosphere, have no part in these transmutations. The Batrachian is compelled to a new sphere of life by antecedent obliterations, absorptions and developments, in which external influences and internal efforts have no share."

While the passage we have quoted is an attack against Lamarckianism, we do not see but that in a long course of generations of the ancestors of the present species of amphibians, the metamorphoses may have become gradually established, finally becoming the normal history of each individual; the changes of the individual epitomizing the successive steps in the collective life-history of the entire group of Amphibians. That changes in the physical surroundings induce important modifications of structure is seen in the exceptional mode of metamorphosis of the Surinam Pipa, or the Hyla of Mauritius, and on the other hand, in the prematurity of the axolotl, which near the level of the sea drops its gills, while from four to six thousand feet above the sea it retains its gills and even produces young.

To recapitulate, we have the following stages of development in the Amphibia:

1. Morula (segmentation total).
2. The embryo develops as in the bony fishes.
3. Young with external gills hatching with a fish-like form, but

much less advanced in internal organization; or, rarely, hatching in the adult form, the metamorphosis being suppressed.

4. Larval forms retained as in the Menobranchus, Siren, Meno-pona and salamanders; or dropped, as in the toad and frog.

LITERATURE.

Swammerdam. Biblia Naturæ. 1737.
Reichert. Vergleich. Entwickelungsgeschichte der nackten Amphibien. 1838.
Rusconi et Configliachi. Histoire Nat. Développement et Metamorphose de la Sala-mandre terrestre. Pavia, 1854.
Schultze. Observaticnes nonnullæ de Ovorum Ranarum Segmentatione, 1863. With papers by Prévost and Dumas, Newport, Horne, Dumeril and Marsh.

XXXII. THE REPTILIA.

Development of the Reptiles. We now come to study the embryology of those vertebrates in which there is an important embryonal membrane, the *amnion*, developed, besides an *allantois.* The early stages of the reptilian embryo are so much like those of the bird that the reader is referred to the account of the development of the chick for a more complete history of the early phases of embryonic life in the reptiles.

As with birds, the eggs are enormous in size, and like those of the ostrich they are laid in the sand, where they are left by the parent to be hatched by the warmth of the sun.

Professor H. J. Clark, in his "Mind in Nature," tells us that of all eggs those of turtles are by far the most easily preserved in a healthy state during the time of incubation. "All that is required to obtain them is to collect a number of turtles in early spring, before May, and keep them enclosed in some shady spot where they can have easy access to water and soft earth, and to feed them well with fresh herbage, such as plantain-leaves, lettuce, beet-leaves, etc., etc., and in the course of time, usually in May and June, they may be caught, at early dawn, digging holes in the earth with their hind legs, and depositing therein their brood of eggs, and then covering them up."

The lizards, snakes, and crocodiles, lay their eggs in sand or light soil, the iguana in the hollows of trees, while certain lizards and snakes are viviparous. Agassiz has discovered the extraordinary fact that in turtles fecundation does not appear to be an instantaneous act, resulting from one successful connection of the sexes, as it is with most animals, but "a repetition of the act, thrice every year, for four successive years, is necessary to determine the final development of a new individual, which may be accomplished in other animals by a single copulation." From the same source we learn that *Chrysemys* (Emys) *picta* does not lay its eggs before the eleventh year. Our other turtles probably lay their eggs from the eleventh to the fourteenth year, according to the species. The operation takes place in the month of June, both at the north and south, climatic differences not seeming to have any effect upon this particular function.

Before segmentation of the yolk, the nucleus, or germinal vesicle, undergoes self-division. According to Agassiz and Clark " this takes place, at least to a certain extent, without the influence of fecundation within a year, but at the same time has been seen only in those eggs which have been expelled from the ovary. Finally they become the original cells, " the primitive embryonic cells " engaged in the composition of the different organs of the body. In the bony fishes, according to Œllacher, the germinal vesicle is ejected bodily from the germinal disk, and Foster and Balfour think this fate awaits that of the birds. In insects the germinal vesicle is supposed to undergo self-division and form the nuclei of the cells of the blastoderm.

The segmentation of the yolk has been fully observed in *Glyptemys* (Emys) *insculpta*. "The process of segmentation is not so regular, and there does not seem to be always, in the beginning, a symmetrical halving of the embryonic area, as has been observed among birds; but in other respects it resembles what takes place within the eggs of the latter animals, and finally results in shaping out the embryonic disk." Agassiz and Clark, from whom we have quoted, think, however, that, from certain phenomena observed by them, the whole mass of the yolk becomes segmented.

The formation of the primitive streak, the amnion, allantois, and *chorda dorsalis*, are much as observed in the chick, and for an account of the early stages of the embryo reptiles, the reader is referred to the chapter on the embryology of birds. The lungs arise as hollow sacs projecting from the sides of the throat; the liver is a thickening of the same membrane from which the stomach is formed, while the reproductive glands "arise in intimate connection with the posterior end of the intestine."

By the time that the heart has become three-chambered, the vertebræ have reached the root of the tail, the eyes have become entirely enclosed in complete orbits, and the allantois begins to grow. Soon after, the embryo turns upon its axis, and always rests on its left side. The nostrils may now be recognized as two simple indentations at the end of the head, and at first are not in communication with the mouth, but soon a shallow furrow leads to it.

The shield begins to develop by a budding out laterally of the musculo-cutaneous layer along the sides of the body, and the growth of narrow ribs extending to the edge of the shield. "The feet, or rather paddles, of the lower forms of turtles, the Chelonioidæ, do not remain in a partially undeveloped state, as might be expected from what is observed among other vertebrates, but undergo what may be called an excess of development; the bones of the toes becoming very much elongated, and the web—which remains soft among some turtles with moderately elongated toes, — is hardened by the development of densely packed scales, so that the whole foot is almost as rigid as the blade of an oar. At this time the embryo of *Chelydra serpentina* snaps at everything which touches it."

Of the development of the Saurians, or lizards, we have no complete account. The advanced embryo of the lizard, as figured by Owen (448), is like that of the turtle without its shell.

As regards the development of snakes, Owen, deriving his information from Rathke's work, tells us that in the oviparous snakes (*Natrix torquata*) the embryo partially develops before the egg is laid, while the young hatches in two months after the egg is deposited. By this time the amnion is perfected, "the head is distinct, and shows the eye-ball and ear-sac; also the maxillary and mandibular processes. The allantois is about as large as the head." The long trunk of the serpent grows in a series of decreasing spirals, and when five or six are formed, the rudiments of the liver and the primordial kidneys are discernible." At the latter third of embryonic life the right lung appears as a mere appendage to the beginning of the left.

A summary of the changes in the egg undergone by the reptiles is as follows:

1. Segmentation partial, possibly total (morula?).

2. The embryo develops much as in the bony fishes until the embryonal membranes appear.

3. Formation of an amnion.

4. After the alimentary canal is sketched out, the allantois buds out from it.

5. The shield of the turtle develops and the reptilian features are assumed.

6. The embryo hatches in the form of the adult.

LITERATURE.

Rathke. Entwickelungsgeschichte der Natter. Königsberg, 1837.
——. Entwickelung der Schildkröten. Braunschwieg, 1848.
——. Ueber die Entwickelung und den Körperbau der Krokodile. 1866.
Agassiz and Clark. Embryology of the Turtles in Agassiz's Contributions to the Natural History of the United States, II, part iii. Boston, 1857.

XXXIII. THE AVES.

Development of Birds. So much alike are all the living species of birds that the embryology of a single kind is in all probability a type of that of the others. The development of the domestic fowl has been studied in more detail than any other vertebrate, since it is easy to hatch the eggs artificially, and from their large size they can be examined more readily than the eggs of fishes. Our account of the embryology of birds will be taken from the admirable history by Foster and Balfour in their "Elements of Embryology," and we shall freely use their work, often quoting them, word for word, where it is not possible to farther condense their language.

The eggs of the hen are fertilized in the upper extremity of the oviduct, whether before or after the "white" of the egg is deposited is unknown, but at any rate before the shell is deposited around the "white."

First day. As the first result of impregnation the germinal vesicle disappears, probably being, judging from the analogy of the bony fishes, bodily ejected from the germinal disk. Then begins the process of segmentation of the yolk, which goes on at about the time the shell is formed. Segmentation is partial, being restricted to the germinal disk of the ovarian egg; the result is the formation of the blastodermic disk, which is the beginning of the embryo, resting on the upper surface of the yolk and appearing as a pale round spot seen in the freshly laid egg. This blastoderm at first consists of two layers of cells, the upper made up of nucleated cells, and the lower of irregular rounded massss called "formative cells."

Now begins the marking out of the embryo, which develops in the "*area pellucida*" a transparent rim (encompassed by the "*area opaca*") surrounding the blastoderm. The first step is the origin of an inner germ-layer, the two others having previously arisen, so that we now have the three germ-layers found in all vertebrates and in some invertebrates. From the outer layer (epiblast) arises the tegument and walls of the body, with the nervous cord; while from the second (mesoblast) are formed the heart and the vascular system or blood-vessels, and the stomach and intestines. The third and innermost layer is called the "hypoblast." By the sixth or eighth hour these three membranes become definitely established. The middle layer now thickens and thus causes the appearance known as the "primitive streak," along the middle of which runs the depression known as the "primitive groove." In front of the primitive groove appears the "medullary groove," and below it the notochord or "*chorda dorsalis*" originates from the cells of the middle layer. This notochord (Fig. 251, *ch*) lies directly beneath the medullary tube

Fig. 251.

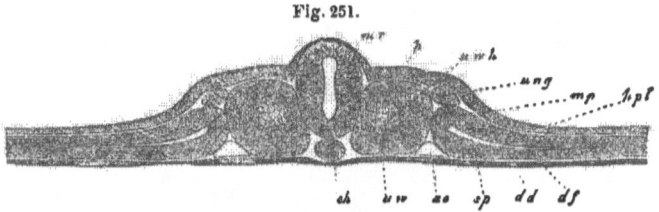

Section of an embryo Hen.

(*mr*) and between the outer and third germ-layer in the form of a flattened circular rod. The blastoderm is now folded anteriorly like the letter S; this is called the "head-fold," and soon after the "tail-fold" is formed in a similar way. These two folds meet in the middle, thus forming the body of the embryo.

Next the primitive groove and streak disappear as the sides of the medullary groove rise up, when they finally meet, forming the neural tube, or hollow in which the nervous cord is developed.

About this period the first pair of protovertebræ make their appearance. They arise from the mesoblast as two cubical masses (Fig. 251[1], *u w*) lying one on each side of the notochord. Two more pairs appear behind the first pair before the first day is

---

[1] Fig. 251; *dd*, third or inner germ-layer (darmdrüsenblatt or hypoblast); *ch*, *chorda dorsalis* or notochord; *uw*, primitive vertebræ, or protovertebræ; *uwh*, cavity in the protovertebræ; *ao*, primitive aorta; *ung*, Wolffian duct; *sp*, split in the middle-germ layer, the beginning of the pleuro-peritoneal cavity (mesoblast) by which it is divided into two layers, the lower layer (*df*) the splanchnopleure (or darmfaserblatt), the upper layer (*hpl*) being the somatopleure (hautplatt), the two layers unite at *mp* (Kölliker's mittelplatt); *mr*, medullary tube (rückenmark); *h*, outer germ-layer (hornblatt or epiblast).

ended. "Out of the protovertebræ are formed not only the permanent vertebræ, but also the superficial dorsal as well as certain

Fig. 252.

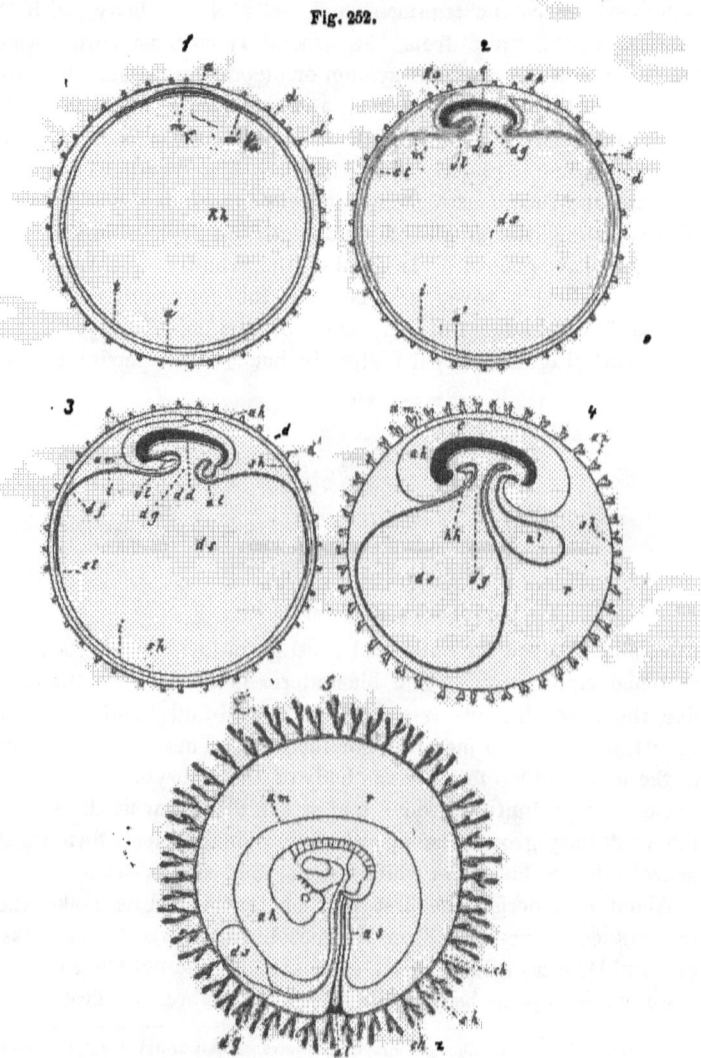

Early stage of a Vertebrate (Fowl).

other muscles and the spinal nerves. The pair of protovertebræ first formed corresponds not with the first cervical vertebra of the adult chick, but rather with the third or even fourth; for though the majority of the protovertebræ are formed regularly behind the first pair, two or even three pair may make their appearance in front of it" (Foster and Balfour).

Fig. 251 (from Kölliker) is a cross section through an embryo chick of the second day magnified 90–100 times, showing the relations of the medullary tube, *chorda dorsalis* and protovertebræ.

Meanwhile the middle layer has split into two layers ; the upper (or outer) leaf is called the " somatopleure," so-called from its giving rise to the body walls, while the lower (or inner) leaf is called the " splanchnopleure," as it is destined to form the alimentary canal, and the liver and other glands originating from the digestive cavity.

The amnion next arises from certain folds of the somatopleure. As the embryo thickens and sinks into the yolk two folds grow out of the head and tail end respectively (Fig. 252, 2, *ks* and *ss*). These finally meet and coalesce on the fourth day over the back of the embryo, forming the amniotic cavity (Fig. 252, 3, *ah*) in which the embryo lies. The fluid which fills this cavity is called the amniotic fluid.

The allantois arises as an appendage of the alimentary canal, budding out at the hinder end of the embryo. It finally grows (as in Fig. 252, 4, *al*) so large as to curve over the embryo, serving as a fœtal respiratory organ.[1]

Second Day. By the time the embryo is thirty hours old the outlines are bolder, more distinct and the tissues firmer, so that

---

[1] Fig. 252. Five schematic figures showing the development of the fœtal egg-membranes, where in all except the last the embryo is represented as if seen in longitudinal section. 1. Diagram of egg with *zona pellucida*, blastoderm (*a, t*) germinal disk and embryo. 2. Egg with the first traces of the yolk sac (*d*) and amnion (*ks, ss* and *am*). 3. Egg with the amnion uniting and forming a sac; the allantois (*al*) budding out. 4. Egg with the villi of the serous membrane (*sz*); the allantois larger; embryo with mouth and anal opening. 5. Egg in which the vascular layer of the allantois lies close to the serous layer and has grown into the villi of the same, constituting the true chorion (*ch*). Yolk sac much smaller, about to be drawn into the cavity of the amnion.

d, yolk-skin; *d′*, villi of the yolk-skin; *sh*, serous membrane: *sz*, villi of the serous membrane; *ch*, chorion (vascular layer of the allantois) *chz*, true villi of the chorion (arising from the projections of the chorion and the sac of the serous membrane); *am*, amnion; *ks*, head-fold of the amnion; *ss*, tail-fold of the amnion; *ah*, cavity of the amnion; *as*, sheath of the amnion for the navel string; *a*, the first beginning of the embryo arising from a thickening of the outer layer of the blastoderm *a′*; *m*, thickening forming the germ in the middle layer of the blastoderm (*m′*), which at first only reached as far as the germinal disk, and afterwards forms the vascular layer of the yolk-sac (*df*) which connects with the intestino-muscular layer (darmfaserblätte); *st, sinus terminalis; dd.* intestino-glandular layer (darmdrusenblatt) arising out of a part of *t*, the inner layer of the blastoderm (afterwards the epithelium of the yolk-sac; *kh,* cavity of the whole blastoderm can be removed from the egg with much greater ease than before. The head-fold has now become more prominent than before. The nerve-tube, at first of uniform thickness dilates anteriorly forming the first cerebral vesicle, and the second and third cerebral vesicles successively form; the protovertebræ increase rapidly, and soon the embryonic chick presents the appearance of the embryo rabbit of nearly the same age.

The alimentary canal commences as a *cul de sac*, closed in front but widely open behind, situated below the anterior end of the medullary tube. The heart originates also in the head-fold at about the time the protovertebræ are formed, and the rudiment is situated below the fore gut or rudiment of the alimentary canal; by the end of the first half of the second day it is flask-shaped, with a slight bend to the right. "Soon after its formation the heart begins to beat, its at first slow and rare pulsations beginning at the venous and passing on to the arterial end." Its movements begin before the cells of which it is composed are differentiated into muscle or nerve-cells. To provide channels for the fluid pressed out by the contractions of the heart, the heart divides into the two primitive aortæ, and connects with other embryonic temporary arteries and veins. Meanwhile in the vascular area and *area pellucida*, the arteries, capillaries and veins rapidly develop, and blood disks arise as amœba-like cells separating from the adjacent cell-mass of the mesoblast (middle germ-layer), while the vessels are contemporaneously forming; the red blood corpuscles not being true cells, but nuclei. The first half of the second day ends with the rise of the rudiment of the Wolffian duct. "It is important to remember that the embryo of which we are now speaking is simply a part of the whole germinal membrane, which is gradually spreading over the surface of the yolk. It is important also to bear in mind that all that part of the embryo which is in front of the most anterior protovertebræ corresponds to the future head, and the rest to the neck, body and tail. At this

the blastoderm, which afterwards becomes *ds*, the cavity of the yolk-sac; *dg*, passage way of the yolk; *al*, allantois; *e*, embryo; *r*, original space between the amnion and chorion, filled with albuminous fluid; *el*, anterior body-wall in the region of the heart; *hh*, cavity of the heart without the heart itself.

In Figs. 2 and 3, the amnion is for the sake of clearness represented as situated too far away from the embryo; so also the cavity of the heart is drawn too small and the embryo too large, since except in Fig. 5, they are only drawn diagrammatically. These and Figs. 251, 264, 265, 267 and 268 are from Kölliker's Entwickelungsgeschichte des Menschen und der höheren Thiere.

period the head occupies nearly a third of the whole length of the embryo" (Foster and Balfour).

In the second half of the second day, among the most important changes are the appearance of the second and third cerebral vesicles, the optic vesicles, while the "first rudiment of the ear is formed as an involution of the epiblast on the side of the hind brain or third cerebral vesicle."

Third day. This day is one of the most eventful, as the rudiments of so many important organs now first appear. First, the embryo, now almost completely enveloped by the amnion, turns around so as to lie on its left side. The heart, originally formed under where the brain is destined to lie, moves backward into the trunk, and by this time (the third day) the neck has been formed, in which appears the four branchial fissures, the most anterior being formed first. It is these temporary fissures which correspond to the branchial fissures of Amphioxus. "On account of this resemblance—in fact by some assumed as an identity both in form and function—the fissures have been called by embryologists the *branchial fissures* (compare Fig. 235) and the vessels [passing between them] the branchial aortæ, the former corresponding with the passages between the gills of fishes, and the latter with the vessels which supply the gills with blood" (Clark's Mind in Nature, p. 311).

In fact the embryo bird in some respects is now as far advanced in organization as the Lancelet, and may be rudely compared with that animal, though the incipient neck, head and brain are features which the Lancelet lacks.

The eye commences as a lateral outgrowth of the fore brain, in the form of a stalked vesicle subsequently converted into the optic nerve, while the lens is formed by an involution of the skin of the body (outer germ-layer) over the front end of the optic vesicle. The ear is also at first simply an involution of the outer germ-layer (epiblast) forming a pit, or "otic vesicle," which is destined to form the internal ear, containing the bones and other parts of the inner ear. The nose begins as two shallow pits formed by the sinking in of the outer germ-layer. Each of these pits is situated next to the olfactory vesicles (afterwards nerves), but at first there is no connection between the pits and the nerves as between the pits and the mouth, the latter not being yet formed, since it arises afterwards as an extension inward of the cleft between the first branchial folds and its branch, as the jaws or maxillæ arise from the first fold, the upper jaws being two branches of the fold, the fold itself being the under jaw, while a lozenge-shaped cavity between the fold and its branches becomes the mouth.

Meanwhile, for all the changes in the different organs are going on contemporaneously, the vesicles or lateral expansions of the nerve-tube appear, the vesicles of the cerebral hemispheres developing, whilst the separation of the hind-brain into the cerebrellum and *medulla oblongata* takes place. The digestive cavity is during the third day also, differentiated into the fore-gut and hind-gut, the former further subdividing into the œsophagus, stomach and duodenum, and the hind-gut into the large intestine and cloaca. The lungs arise as two pocket-like appendages of the alimentary canal immediately in front of the stomach; while the liver is originally two diverticula, and the pancreas a single offshoot, from the duodenum.

Fourth day. With a decided increase in size by this day, the amnion becomes more distinct, and the allantois is visible. The wings and legs now appear as flattened conical buds arising from the "Wolffian ridge," a low ridge running from the neck to the tail, those forming the wings being scarcely distinguishable from the rudimentary legs.

The olfactory grooves appear at this time and the partition heretofore existing between the mouth and throat is absorbed and disappears.

The protovertebræ have, by this time, increased in number from thirty to forty. The upper portion (muscle-plate) having previously separated to form the muscles inserted in the skeleton (episketal muscles of Huxley), has left the remainder of each protovertebra as a somewhat triangular mass, the upper angle of which grows up and meets its fellow in the median line above, thus enclosing the nerve-canal. On the lower side each protovertebra sends out a similar growth enclosing the notochord. " While the inner portion of each protovertebra is thus extending inwards around both notochord and neural canal, the remaining outer portion is undergoing a remarkable change. It becomes divided into an anterior or præaxial, and a posterior or postaxial segment. The anterior, which is the larger and more transparent of the two, is the rudiment of the spinal ganglion and nerve, while the posterior, which remains more particularly connected with the extensions round the neural canal and notochord, goes to form part of the permanent vertebra. In this way each protovertebra, having given rise to a muscle-plate, is farther subdivided into a ganglionic rudiment, and into a mass which we may speak of as a 'primary' vertebra, consisting as it does of a body or mass investing the notochord, from which springs an arch covering in the neural canal." (Foster and Balfour.)　The conversion of the primary vertebræ or membranous vertebral column into the permanent vertebræ is "complicated by a remarkable new or secondary segmentation of the whole vertebral column," so that "each permanent vertebra is formed out of portions of two consecutive protovertebræ. Thus, for instance, the tenth permanent vertebra is formed out of the hind portion of the tenth protovertebra, and the front portion of the eleventh protovertebra, while its arch, now attached to its front part, was attached to the hind part of the tenth protovertebra." (Foster and Balfour).

By the sixth day the notochord begins to diminish, and disappears by the time the bird is hatched, while by the twelfth day the ossification of the bodies of the vertebræ commences, the process beginning in the second or third cervical, and thence extending backwards. The ribs begin as a downward growth from the exterior of the vertebræ, becoming by the sixth day separate from the bodies of the vertebræ.

Between the eightieth and one hundredth hour of incubation the permanent kidneys arise, and previous to this the sexual glands have arisen out of the middle germ-layer, from the germinal epithelium lying at the upper end of the pleuroperitoneal cavity. In this epithelium may be seen certain large cells, the primordial ova, which are at first seen in male as well as female embryos, so that in early stages it is impossible to distinguish the sexes. Between the eightieth and one hundredth hour, however, the primordial ova disappear in those embryos destined to be males, while they enlarge and multiply in the female. "The large nucleus of the primordial ovum becomes the germinal vesicle, while the ovum itself remains as the true "ovum." The testes begin to arise on the sixth day.

Fifth day. This period is signalized by the further growth of the allantois, and by the appearance of the knee and elbow, and of the cartilages which precede the formation of the bones of the digits and limbs; as well as by the formation of the primitive skull, with the development of the parts of the face, and the formation of the anus.

The cranium, from the researches of Rathke, Parker and others, is formed from the middle germ-layer, and in the fourth day is simply membranous; after that time the tissue composing it becomes cartilage. After the fourth day the primitive skull consists of two portions, *i.e.*, a sheet of cartilage ensheathing the notochord from its anterior end to the first vertebra. "This sheet of cartilage forms an *unsegmented* continuation of the vertebral bodies. It is to be considered as the most anterior portion of the axial skeleton, in which the segmentation has become obliterated; and as such is equivalent not to one, but to a (hitherto not certainly determined) number of vertebræ." (Foster and Balfour. For the farther changes in the development of the skull the reader is referred to Parker's memoir on the Development of the Skull of the Common Fowl, or the excellent, illustrated abstract in Foster and Balfour's "Elements.")

Not until the sixth day are distinct bird-characters developed. Hitherto it would be almost impossible to distinguish the embryo from a reptile or mammal. During the sixth and seventh day the wing and foot assume a bird form, the crop and intestinal cœca make their appearance, "the stomach takes the form of a gizzard, and the nose begins to develop into a beak, while the incipient bones of the skull arrange themselves after the avian type. . . . From the eleventh day onwards the embryo successively puts on characters which are not only avian, but even distinctive of the genus, species and variety." By the ninth or tenth day the feathers originate in sacs in the skin, these sacs by the eleventh day appearing to the naked eye as feathers, the sacs however remaining closed as late as the nineteenth day, though many are an inch in length.

The nails and scales begin to appear on the thirteenth day. "By the thirteenth day the cartilaginous skeleton is completed, and the various muscles of the body can be made out with tolerable clearness. Ossification begins, according to Von Baer, on the eighth or ninth day by small deposits in the tibia, in the metacarpal bones of the hind-limb, and in the scapula. On the eleventh or twelfth day a multitude of points of ossification make their appearance in the limbs, in the scapular and pelvic arches, in the ribs, in the bodies of the cervical and dorsal vertebræ, and in the bones of the head, the centres of ossification of the vertebral arches not being formed till the thirteenth day."

While the blood is at first aerated by the allantois, and there is a partial double circulation of the blood; as soon as respiration begins a completely double circulation is formed.

After the sixth day muscular movements of the embryo probably begin, but they are slight, until the fourteenth day, when the embryo chick changes its position, lying lengthways in the egg, with its beak touching the chorion and shell membrane, where they form the inner wall of the rapidly increasing air chamber at the broad end. On the twentieth day or thereabouts, the beak is thrust through these membranes, and the bird begins to breathe the air contained in the chamber. Thereupon the pulmonary circulation becomes functionally active, and at the same time blood ceases to flow through the umbilical arteries. The allantois shrivels up, the umbilicus becomes completely closed, and the chick, piercing the shell at the broad end of the egg with repeated blows of its beak, casts off the dried remains of allantois, amnion and chorion, and steps out into the world." (Foster and Balfour).

A brief summary of the changes undergone by the developing chick will be seen to be nearly identical with that of reptiles :

1. Partial segmentation of the yolk.

2. The embryo develops much as in the bony fishes until the embryonal membranes appear.

3. Formation of an amnion.

4. After the alimentary canal is sketched out, the allantois buds out from it.

5. The avian features appear from the sixth to the tenth day.

6. The embryo leaves the egg in the form of the adult, and like the reptile, is at once active, feeding itself.

LITERATURE.

Harvey. Exercitationes anatomicæ de Generatione Animalium. London, 1651.

Malpighi. De Formatione Pulli in Ovo. London, 1672.

Haller. Sur la Formation du Cœur dans le Poulet. London, 1758.

———. Elementa Physiologiæ, Liber xxix. 1766.

Wolff. Theoria Generationis. Halle, 1759.

Pander. Dissertatio inauguralis sistens Historiam Metamorphoseos quam Ovum incubatum prioribus quinque diebus subit. Würzburg, 1817.

———. Beiträge zur Entwickelungsgeschichte des Hühnchens im Eie. Würzburg, 1817.

Purkinje. Symbolæ ad Ovi Avium Historiam. Vratislav, 1825.

Von Baer. Ueber Entwicklungsgeschichte der Thiere. Königsberg, 1828.

Reichert. Das Entwicklungsleben im Wirbelthierreich. Berlin, 1840.

Erdl. Die Entwicklung des Menschen und des Hühnchens im Ei. Theil 1. Leipzig, 1845.

Remak. Untersuchungen über die Entwicklung der Wirbelthiere. Berlin, 1855.

Parker. On the Development of the Skull of the Common Fowl (Phil. Trans. CLVI, I. London, 1866.)

Foster and Balfour. The Elements of Embryology, Vol. i. London, 1874.

With the works of Coste, Allen Thompson and others.

XXXIV. THE MAMMALIA.

That fishes, amphibious reptiles and birds should lay eggs, seems quite in the course of nature, but that a mammal should grow from an egg appeared incredible to Haller, who in 1778 publicly disputed Degraef's discovery, six years previous, of the egg of the rabbit. That all mammals grow from eggs was fully proved by Von Baer in 1827, while Coste, Valentin and Jones in 1834 and 1835, showed that the mammalian egg is homologous with the eggs of the lower vertebrates.

The ovarian egg of a mammal, such as the rabbit, is shown at Figs. 253, 254 and 255. It is exceedingly minute, from the small

Fig. 253.   Fig. 254.   Fig. 255.

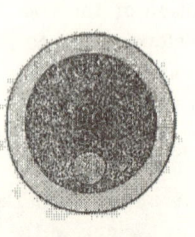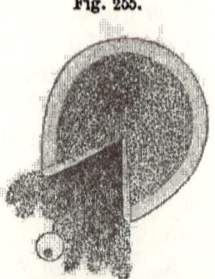

Ovarian egg of rabbit. Magnified 125 diameters.

Ovarian egg of rabbit, freed of the cells which surround the zona pellucida in Fig. 253. Magnified 125 times. The germinative vesicle shines through the yolk as a light spot.

The same ovarian egg of the rabbit as in Fig. 254, opened with a needle. The yolk with the germinative vesicle and dot are flowing out. Magnified 125 times.

quantity of yolk-substance in it; but in the duck bill (Monotremes) the egg is quite large, with more yolk-matter, being from two-and-a-half to three lines in diameter; while in the kangaroo, the egg is a tenth of a line in diameter.

Development of the Mammals. As in the Amphioxus and the

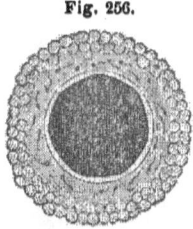

Fig. 256.

Amphibians, the egg undergoes total segmentation. Fig. 256 represents the egg of the dog surrounded by the cells which partly conceal the *zona pellucida*, with the spermatic particles swimming just within. Fertilization (a process apparently identical with that seen in the egg of the sponge, Fig. 42,) having been effected, the yolk subdivides as seen in Figs. 257–263, and the mulberry state (Morula) is soon assumed.

Egg of Dog fertilized by the spermatic particles seen in the zona pellucida.

To relate how the blastoderm divides into two germinal layers and afterwards into three, how the primitive

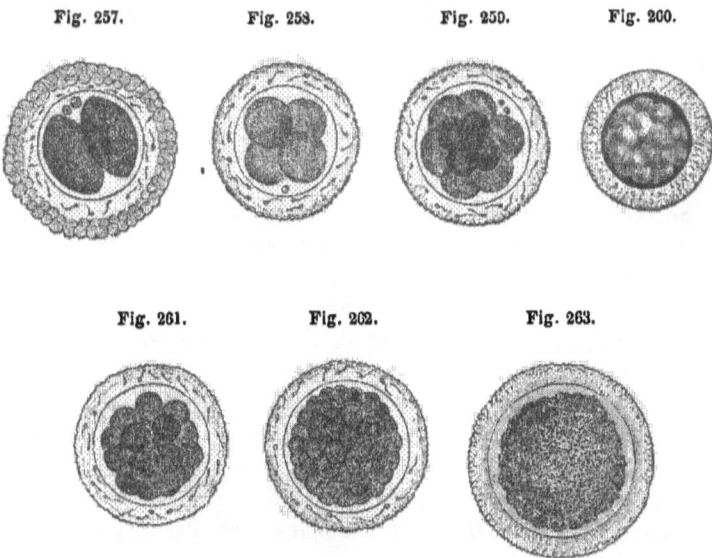

Fig. 257.   Fig. 258.   Fig. 259.   Fig. 260.

Fig. 261.   Fig. 262.   Fig. 263.

Different Stages of segmentation of the yolk in the Egg of the Dog.

streak, the notochord, and the sides of the medullary groove which rise up and enclose the spinal cord, and the protovertebræ appear, would be but a repetition of the account of the mode of development of the chick. About the end of the first day, the germ appears as in Fig. 264,[1] which represents the embryo rabbit when slightly over a line in length. At this time the amnion surrounds the head-end of the primitive band as if with a hood ; the three primary divisions of the brain, into fore, middle and hind brain, are now well marked, and immediately after this stage the blood vessels arise, forming the vascular network permeating the germinal disk, on which the embryo rests, the heart being at·first a simple tube,

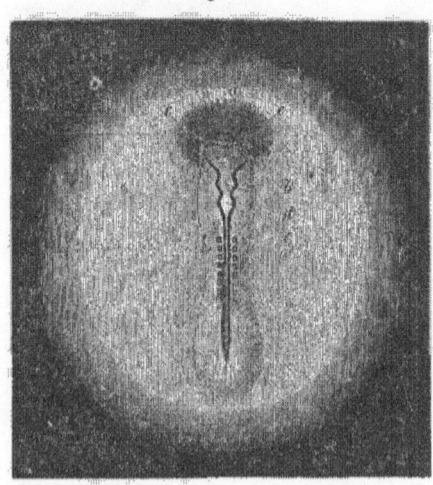

Fig. 264.

Embryo rabbit, about one day old.

afterwards twisted and finally dividing into the two auricles and ventricles.

Succeeding changes, including the formation of the gill-slits, limbs and tail are exactly as those represented by Fig. 267 and 268 of the human embryo, and correspond to similar phases of the fishes, amphibians, reptiles and birds. By the twenty-fifth day the embryo dog appears as in Fig. 265, and soon after this period the distinctive mammalian features are brought out, when finally the characters peculiar to dogs appear. At the time of its birth the young mammal is usually of large size, as compared with its parent, as in the cat, dog and monkey ; but in the duck-bill (Ornithorhynchus), the young is only one inch and two lines in length, naked, and in nearly as helpless a condition as the young marsupial.

The young marsupials are very small and embryonic in form when born. The opossum, whose period of gestation is from twenty to twenty-six days, brings forth helpless young which are

---

[1] Fig. 264. Germinal disk and germ of a rabbit about one day old, seen from the back. *a*, edge of the head-end of the amnion; *b*, fore-brain; *c*, lateral expansion of the same, or primitive eye-vesicle; *d*, middle, *e*, hind-brain. There are eight protovertebræ, between which is situated the spinal cord. Enlarged ten times. Copied from Bischoff, by Kölliker.

naked, and only eight-tenths of an inch in length from the mouth to the end of the tail. The kangaroo (*Macropus major*), an animal as large as a calf, and whose period of gestation is thirty-six days, produces young which measure only an inch from the mouth to the root of the tail. On the other hand the whales at birth are

Fig. 265.[1]

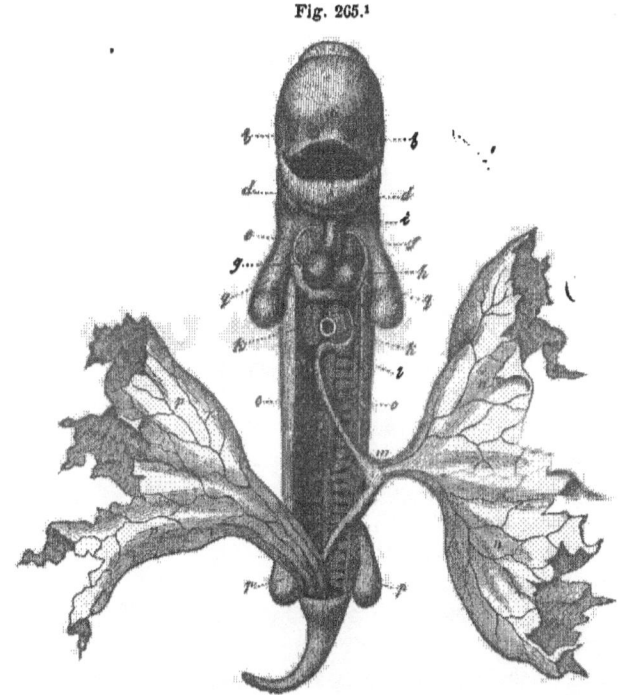

Embryo dog, twenty-five days old.

remarkably large and mature in form. The remaining mammals (Didelphia), besides the chorion and amnion, which are discarded at birth, are, in the embryo condition, provided with an important

[1] Fig. 265, front view of the embryo of a dog at the end of the twenty-fifth day, magnified twice. The embryo seen sideways would appear as in Fig. 208, but has been straightened out and enlarged, with the anterior ventral wall removed, so that the ventral cavity appears more capacious than in nature, and the heart seems to lie exposed. *a*, nasal cavities; *b*, eyes; *c*, lower maxillæ (first gill-arches); *d*, second gill-arches; *e*, right, *f*, left auricle; *g*, right, *h*, left ventricle; *i*, aorta; *k*, liver-lobes with the cavity of the *vena omphalo-mesenterica* between them; *l*, stomach; *m*, intestine, united by a short narrow yolk-canal with the yolk-sac *n*; *o*, Wolffian body; *pp*, allantois; *q*, anterior, *r*, hinder extremities. Copied by Kölliker from Bischoff.

organ, the placenta, or after-birth, a development of the allantois, serving as an organ of respiration as well as to nourish the fœtus, and carry off its effete products by means of the maternal circulation.

The Mammals, then, as a rule, pass through the following stages :—

1. Morula.

2. Remaining stages as in the birds, until the mammalian characteristics appear.

8. Adult form at birth ; or subembryonic, as in the duck bill and marsupials.

LITERATURE.

Barry. Researches on Embryology. (London Phil. Trans., 1838–40.)

Bischoff. Entwicklungsgeschichte des Kaninchencles, Hundecles, Meerschweinchens, und Rehes. 1842–54. (Four separate works.)

Owen. Comparative Anatomy and Physiology of Vertebrates. Vol. ili, London, 1868.

XXXV. THE BIMANA (Man).

Absolutely identical in his mode of embryonic growth with the placental mammals, man's developmental history until shortly before birth, is probably but a repetition of that of the rabbit or dog. Like his blood relations, the lower mammals, he derives his origin from a minute sac of protoplasm, which is at first, as in the eggs of all animals, like a Moner, having no nucleus. It then becomes nucleated and nucleolated like any egg, and is $\frac{1}{120}$ of an inch in diameter (Fig. 266[1]).

This egg, on contact with several sperm cells, likewise simple sacs of protoplasm, immediately undergoes segmentation, probably (though this point has not yet been proved) exactly as in the dog and even in the sponge, and indeed in animals of all grades. A blastodermic disk, from which originates the primitive streak, which subdivides into the two primitive germ-layers, comparable with the two-layered sac of the free swimming embryonic Amphioxus, next arises, and from it are formed the nervous cord and notochord (Ascidian stage) and protovertebræ.

Fig. 266.

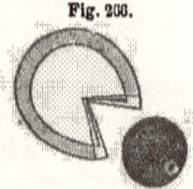

Human Egg.

He next attains a stage of development that may be compared

with that of the adult Amphioxus.   After the brain appears he is
like a young shark or fish.   He next reaches the stage (Fig. 267 [1])
characterizing the embryos of
all amphibians, reptiles, birds
and beasts, when the rudiments of the four limbs appear.   The amphibian character, the want of an allantois,
is now dropped, and development advancing, he rises to a
level with the reptiles, birds
and mammals, the allantois
now having formed (Figure

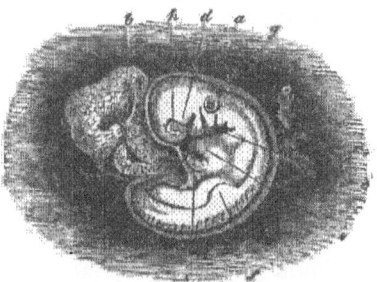
Fig. 267.

Human embryo, third week.

268 [2]).   When five weeks advanced the characters separating man
from the ordinary mammals
begin to appear, and at this
time when compared with the
embryo dog of the twenty-
fifth day, the head is seen to
be higher on the crown, owing
to the greater development of
the brain, and the tail is proportionately shorter.   Immediately after this, the hinder
extremities lengthen, the head
enlarges in the cerebral region
and the human form is clearly
indicated by the seventh week,
the subsequent changes con-

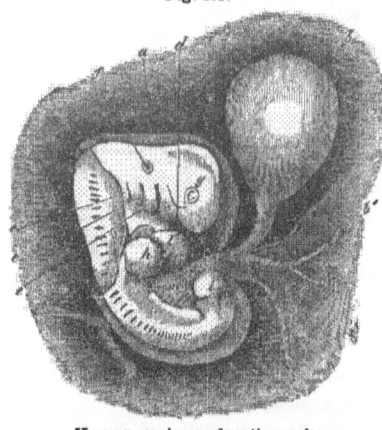
Fig. 268.

Human embryo, fourth week.

sisting in the remodelling of the outlines, in which it passes
through a generalized ape-like figure, until the human form is
shaped out.   At birth he casts off the amnion, chorion and pla-

[1] Fig. 267. Human embryo at the end of the third or beginning of the fourth week,
enlarged. a, amnion; b, yolk-sac; c, first gill-arch, or lower jaw; e, second gill-arch,
behind which are two others with gill-slits between them; f, indications of the arms;
g, primitive ear-vesicle; h, eyes; i, heart. Compare figure of the embryo skate (Fig.
225).

[2] Fig. 268. Human embryo of the fourth week. a, amnion, partly removed on the
back; b, yolk-sac; b', yolk canal; c, under jaw or first gill-arch; c, c', c'', second and fourth gill arches;
f, primitive ear-vesicle; g, eyes; h, fore, i, hinder limbs; k, navel-string with a portion
of the amnion; l, heart; m, liver. This and Fig. 267, from Kölliker.

centa, and enters the world helpless, naked and toothless, not attaining full maturity until from the fifteenth to the twentieth year. During this time he undergoes a partial metamorphosis, discarding temporary organs, such as the first set of teeth, the first set of eye-lashes, and undergoing important changes of the external form of the body as well as of the internal organs.

In giving our summary of the life-history of man, we will enter a little more in detail than in the other vertebrates. It will be seen that the embryonic life of man is almost an epitome of the animal kingdom, beginning with characters common to the moners and the worms, and ending with the vertebrates. The stages which he passes through are, then, as follows :

1. A minute mass of protoplasm, like a moner. (Compare Protomonas, Fig. 3A.)

2. Egg stage. (Compare Fig. 42.)

3. Morula stage. (Compare Fig. 43.)

4. A suppressed gastrula stage ? at least a two-layered·sac, as in Fig. 252, 1. (Compare Fig. 44.)

5. Ascidian stage with a notochord. (Compare Fig. 164, B).

6. Amphioxus stage, having no brain or skull, but with gill-slits.

7. Fish stage, with brain and skull.

8. Reptile stage, having an amnion and allantois.

9. Mammal stage, with a placenta.

10. Quadrumanous stage, like the tailless apes.

11. Man.

LITERATURE.

Kölliker. Entwicklungsgeschichte des Menschen, etc. Leipzig, 1861.
Pouchet. Traité du Developpment de l'Homme et des Mammifaires. Paris, 1843.
Hæckel. Anthropogenie. Entwickelungsgeschichte des Menschen. Leipzig, 1874.

INDEX.

www.ingramcontent.com/pod-product-compliance
Lightning Source LLC
Chambersburg PA
CBHW030806020726
47499CB00006B/1783